The Last Guardian
Of Magic

THE LAST GUARDIAN OF MAGIC

Randall Andrews

iUniverse, Inc.
New York Lincoln Shanghai

The Last Guardian Of Magic

iUniverse books may be ordered through booksellers or by contacting:

iUniverse
2021 Pine Lake Road, Suite 100
Lincoln, NE 68512
www.iuniverse.com
1-800-Authors (1-800-288-4677)

Because of the dynamic nature of the Internet, any Web addresses or links contained in this book may have changed since publication and may no longer be valid.

This is a work of fiction. All of the characters, names, incidents, organizations, and dialogue in this novel are either the products of the author's imagination or are used fictitiously.

ISBN: 978-0-595-47345-8 (pbk)
ISBN: 978-0-595-91624-5 (ebk)

Printed in the United States of America

CONTENTS

WEDNESDAY, SEPTEMBER 6

THURSDAY, SEPTEMBER 7

PROLOGUE

▼

Egypt, 4,000 years ago

A wide expanse of shimmering desert sand stretched between two high dunes several miles east of where Aratek walked. There was a fluid pseudo-motion to the image that suggested the presence of a vast lake of pristine water, fed by some invisible spring hidden deep beneath the ground. It was an attractive thought to conjure, but not a convincing one. Aratek's attention was captured by the sight, but only for the briefest of moments, and then he continued on his way. He had been a creature of the desert his whole life and could not even remember when he was still young enough to be fooled by the tricks that are played by the heat and the sand. It was the same cruel lie that the desert teased with day after day when the temperature climbed so high so early in the morning.

The sun shone down its light with such force that it seemed the sand might flare up into a golden blaze at any moment, transforming the desert's surface into a massive sheet of molten glass. In every direction the blinding glare of reflected beams dominated the view to the end of what could be seen, where the clear, cloudless sky appeared to rest its unfathomable weight down upon the land.

Only in the direction from which Aratek had come was the monotony of the panorama disrupted. There, shrunken with distance, was Memphis, the capital, and beyond it the Nile River, the aorta of living Egypt.

Aratek carried his sandals as he walked, not ignoring the burning in his feet, but accepting it, perhaps even savoring the vibrancy of the sensation. The radiant energy that saturated the sand was transferred up through his soles and into his soul, carrying with it exhilarating waves of gratifying pain. He did not fear pain. He knew that when controlled, pain could be manipulated for one's own uses. He employed this fire in his feet as a beacon, his focal point for achieving perfect singular concentration.

All the background noise in his mind needed to be pinched out before he reached his destination for the day's journey, an outcropping of bedrock that protruded from the sand just ahead. Every flaw and feature of that stone had long ago been committed to memory. It would take a place of honor in his greatest achievement, the pinnacle stone of his masterpiece and the terminus of his grandest vision. Aratek wondered how many eons had passed while the rock had rested there, repeatedly exposed and reburied under the sand, waiting to serve its destined purpose.

Even before placing the headdress of Shu's Plume upon his brow, a familiar tickle of something more than just adrenaline began creeping up Aratek's spine in a hot shiver.

The man had grown old in years by the standards of that age. However, his age was defied by a muscular physique and a long, confident stride, which had lost none of its youthful grace. The streaks of metallic silver that snaked through his once tar-black hair gave a distinguished rather than elderly impression. Everything about his physical appearance was impressive, but the most notable of his features were his eyes. The intensity of his stare never faltered, making it seem that he was constantly aware of every detail of the space and activity around him. Many strong men had flinched under the pressure of that stare. It is said that the eyes are windows to the soul. If so, then the potency of Aratek's gaze might have been the result of an exceptionally bright soul's light being forced to shine out through ordinary windows, like a floodlight's radiance condensed into a penlight's beam.

As his focus tightened, Aratek's mind came to resemble an extensive library. It was just as filled with carefully organized knowledge and recorded memories, and just as quiet as well. Marching across the desert toward his objective, he strode simultaneously through the aisles of his cognitive library on feet that were flying electrons. The knowledge that he wished to recall was stored on one of the front shelves of the library where he kept the volumes most regularly visited. This one told the legend of the Plume of Shu, and finding it was an effortless routine. He always recalled the legend before calling upon his power.

The legend began with the Egyptian's primordial god of air, Shu, who was distressed over the distance that separated his children, the earth god, Geb, and the sky goddess, Nut. Shu devised a plan that might allow closeness between his offspring, and the fulcrum of his plan would be a mortal man. That man was Aratek's ancestor, and like Aratek, he had the power to command magic.

According to the legend, Shu set his plan into motion with the forging of an animal by means of his divine thought. The animal was a vulture, the greatest of all birds. However, it was much more than an ordinary vulture, for when Shu created the bird he wove into its flesh a tiny part of his own immortal strength. The bird would be a vessel of powerful magic, a channel through which that magic could be transferred to its intended master.

Shu came to the first Builder, Aratek's ancestor, in a dream and summoned him to a desolate location in the deep desert. The god told the man that a gift awaited him there that could be used to profoundly magnify the extraordinary talent that had been his from birth. In return for this celestial gift, the man was to use his enhanced power to build a magnificent structure to honor the Pharaoh and to stand as a timeless symbol of the glory of Egypt.

The man left his home immediately upon waking and walked without rest for three days across the harsh desert. Not even once did he pause to rest for fear that he might forget the directions that had been delivered to him in the dream. When he finally reached his destination, the man was completely parched and without enough remaining strength even to stand. Just as he was prepared to admit defeat and give himself over to the next life, a wide shadow enveloped him. Squinting his eyes against the relentless sun, the outline of an unnaturally large vulture circling down through the air appeared overhead. The man was terrified by the size of the creature and at the prospect that it might not wait for him to pass over before sampling his flesh.

Knowing that he was defenseless in his weakened state, the man decided that he would not try to chase the great bird away, and in making that decision his fear was diminished. The desert scavenger landed gracefully before him, staring coldly with its lifeless, black eyes. The man held out his hand as if offering himself to the bird, closed his eyes, and prepared to die.

Suddenly, pain screamed through the man's body, a thousand times more torturous than any animal's maul could ever be. It took all his remaining will to pry open his burning eyes, and what he saw was an impossible image of the vulture completely engulfed in brilliant, blue flame. The fire was consuming the animal right before his eyes. He pleaded with his own body to pull away from the churning flames, but to no avail. The pain was so intense that it seemed he, too, might soon be devoured by the blaze. His every muscle clinched simultaneously, his body arced in a convoluted pose of rigor, and his jaws gaped in a silent scream of agony.

Then, just as suddenly as they had arrived, the fire, the pain, and the vulture were gone. The man, who had only one moment before knelt before the gates of the afterlife, felt more alive than ever. In his hand was the gift that had been promised to him, a long black feather, as light and as hard as anything he had ever felt. Its magic renewed the man's strength and started a tingling at the back of his mind. At that moment, the desert fell utterly silent, as if the whole world was holding its breath, waiting to see what the man would do with his newfound strength.

The legend always concluded with the revelation of Shu's secret intention. It was his hope that with the aid of the gift, the man would be able to erect a monument so massive it could serve as a bridge between the earth and the sky, the realms of his son and daughter.

That man, the first Builder of Egypt, used the Plume of Shu to construct the Sphinx in hopes that it would appease the primordial god who had bestowed the gift upon him. The man lived an exceptionally long life, but eventually he walked again down the path that leads from this world to the next. Before passing over, he trained another who had been born with the talent so that the work of Shu's desire could continue. And so the Plume was passed along through many generations, all of whom contributed to the growing magnificence of the Egyptian landscape, until it came finally to Aratek, and in his hands Shu's gift commanded greater power than ever.

After living more than a full life, Aratek had finally reached his own autumn, and a pupil had been chosen for him to mentor. The boy was fairly gifted in his ability to manipulate the magic, and he was full of ambition, but all the effort of his training was for naught. Aratek had decided long ago that the Plume's cycle of succession would end with him. He would be the last of the great Egyptian Builders, and he would be the last man to harness the power of Shu's gift. Any future contributions that might be added to Egypt's architecture would pale utterly in comparison to his stone legacy.

Any of the great Builders was much more than just a man, and Aratek was much more than just one of the Builders. He was by far the most talented in all the history of the line and the most powerful man alive in his time. Everyone knew this to be true, including the Pharaoh, who resented him for his abilities.

Aratek had spent his entire adult life laboring on architectural creations that could hide any others in existence within their shadows. His magic had wrought works that armies of laborers could not duplicate. Upon completion, his last endeavor would be the champion of all man-made things in the world, and it would be the best effort to date at realizing a primordial god's dream of a stairway to heaven. All of this was Aratek's gift to Egypt, to Shu, and to the Pharaoh. However, instead of being rewarded for his incredible achievement, he would be punished through eternity, as all the Builders were, for accomplishing feats that the Pharaoh never could.

The curse that the Pharaoh cast upon Aratek was anonymity. The three marvels that were his life's work would travel through the ages as unsigned masterpieces, associated only with the names of the Pharaohs that would later use them as their personal tombs.

The resentment that the Pharaoh felt toward Aratek was felt just as deeply in return, but foresight to the afterlife restrained the greatest Builder when thoughts of revolt played in his mind. Aratek, for whom superhuman power was a birthright, had lived his whole life serving rather than being served because of the promises of the life that would come after death. In this life he was much more than just a man, but in the next life the Pharaoh would become a god, and that knowledge kept all mutinous agendas trapped in the realm of fantasy.

Aratek stared down upon the rough mass of native stone with eyes that saw not only what was, but also what could be. He looked with a hallucinatory false clarity beyond the cracked and misshapen surface of the rock to within, to where he was certain a flawlessly shaped block was trapped. He would use his power to set free the perfect form so that it could become the final piece of the design that had lived inside his mind for years. When completed, that design would have been used to erect the most geometrically pure and dimensionally awesome structure that the world had ever seen.

When the soft music of the desert became muted, and the spectacular hues of sunlight on sand dissolved away, leaving only lifeless shades of black and gray, Aratek knew that he was ready.

With the Plume of Shu resting in its headdress upon his brow, he raised his right hand slowly before him and opened his fist. Invisible energy raced between his hand and the rock until it became almost as if he could feel its surface at his fingertips. Making a slow sideways sweep with his extended fingers, Aratek traced a gentle arc through the air, and a thin cloud of dust floated up from the top of the stone. A second, slightly faster wave in the opposite direction drew away larger particles, like tiny grains of sand. Back and forth his muscular arm swept. Each wave was faster than the previous and peeled away more stone until large sections of the rock were exploding away as if from internal detonations.

Sixty seconds later, Aratek's arm dropped to his side. He stood as still as if he were one of the desert's permanent fixtures, a sandstone statue. One by one his muscles relaxed, and the colors and sounds of the world around him crept gradually back to vividness. He stared at the massive cloud of dust that still swirled before him. His sight could not yet penetrate the chaotic haze to where a magnificent display of geometry and art lie silent, a calm eye in the center of a violent storm. He did not need to wait for the millions of particles of airborne debris to settle in order to know that his effort was successful. The block would be perfect, as they all had been for many years. The task had become automatic, effortless.

Aratek closed his eyes and smiled at the image that manifested itself in his mind. His masterpiece was nearly complete, and soon he would make the journey to the afterlife. Once the pyramid was finished, he could finally rest.

The secret tomb that Aratek had constructed for himself lay near the river about twenty miles upstream from the city. The small chamber where his body was to rest forever lay deep within the bedrock at the end of a long tunnel that none but he could have carved. When the time arrived, his small band of loyal servants would seal his body inside the secret tomb and reduce its entrance to an anonymous piece of the desert sandscape.

Across his chest would lay the Plume of Shu, and on the surface of his sarcophagus would be one beautifully written copy of the forbidden story of the Builders and the legend of Shu's gift. Even if no living soul would ever read the tale, it was a comfort to Aratek to know that the truth would be there, right beneath the people of Egypt, and there it would remain with the Plume of Shu and its greatest master until the end of eternity.

That was the plan. In truth, however, its rest would be interrupted after just 4,000 years, a few brief moments compared to eternity.

And so the greatest Builder was laid to rest. The days and the months and the years passed by and eventually there were none left who remembered the name Aratek. Onward time marched, indifferent to any force that might try to hurry or hinder it. Time simply continued as it always does until centuries and then millennia had slipped by, and eventually the wondrous works of the Builders came to be known as the mysteries of ancient Egypt. Aratek's masterpieces became tourist attractions.

Over the course of those thousands of years the world changed in dramatic ways. Prominent civilizations were built and destroyed and rebuilt again, and humankind spread across the globe until nearly every corner of the wild land was conquered and inhabited. New scientific understanding lead to new technology, which in turn lead to the construction of metal towers much taller even than Aratek's great pyramid. The steel behemoths were so tall that the name given to them suggested that they might even scrape the sky. The structures were astounding to all who laid eyes upon them, but no one knew to wonder whether or not the realms of Geb and Nut had finally been bridged.

All this was the epic evolution of human civilization for four thousand years, and yet somehow man himself changed very little. Now and then and here and there all through the passage of that time there were born those like the Egyptian Builders whose minds were extraordinary. Some lived out their entire lives without ever realizing their own abilities. Society could so completely ingrain within a person the commonly accepted beliefs of what was possible and what was not, that they were unable to believe in themselves, in the possibilities of their own potential. There were others though, who did believe and embraced their talent. These people who commanded the magic were often feared and less frequently revered. They were called witches and wizards and sorcerers and spellcasters. In modern times, however, it was science, not magic, that was predominantly responsible for the shaping of civilization.

Yet magic did not disappear. Good and evil forces of those who possessed the gift continuously worked to gain an advantage over each other by increasing their power and their numbers. This cold war of magic carried on under the noses of the world for centuries until one finally came who was powerful and cunning enough to bid for rule over all the peoples of the earth. And in an ironic twist of fate, the time and place of that man's birth coincided very closely with the Plume of Shu finally being unearthed from its age-old desert grave.

Friday, September 1

A Reluctant, New Beginning

Kyle Adams had never been the type to relish in unbridled optimism, but rarely did his mood turn as grim as it was on the morning of the first day of his senior year of high school. However, only the hardest of judges would have called his disposition unjustified. The end of summer vacation and the return to school is an unappealing transition for any teenager, and for Kyle, who was simultaneously struggling to adjust to life in a new town in a new state with a new family, it was the most foreboding "first day back" ever. He was starting out anew among strangers, and so far they did indeed seem fairly strange. Moving from the heart of Illinois' biggest city to a tiny town in Michigan's northern woodlands would require some adjusting, and it would take time. And last, but not least, as the final cherry on top, it was Friday, ordinarily Kyle's favorite day, but spoiled utterly by someone's brilliant idea to begin the school year at the end of a week instead of the beginning.

Kyle eyed the decrepit looking old brick building that was Steel City High School that morning suspiciously, estimating that it was the size of a single wing of his old school in Chicago. Although there weren't any gang tags or other graffiti as he was accustomed to seeing, it appeared that renovation was equally overdue there as it had been in the city. The building's faded red bricks were at least halfway overgrown with sprawling ivy plants, but the impression they left was one of neglect rather than prestige. They looked less like the result of a careful botanical design than they did weeds on steroids. The Ivy League it was not. It seemed to Kyle that nature had caught everybody in a state of lull and was gradually retaking the real estate for itself. Maybe, he thought, in another decade or two the vines would grow heavy enough to start cracking mortar and bringing down some architecture.

The meager size of the building and the number of cars (mostly pick-up trucks actually) in the adjacent parking lot led Kyle to estimate that the entire population of his new school would be significantly less than that of his old class. For better or worse, life in Steel City, Michigan was going to be different, and not just a little bit.

There weren't any metal detectors set up at the doors when Kyle entered the school, and that, too, was different. However, even up there in the sticks there was some security in place. Fifteen feet inside the main school entrance stood a giant mountain-man that would turn out to be the school's principal, a.k.a. Sheriff Tanner to his students.

The green flannel shirt that Tanner wore contained enough material to function as a blanket for anyone living in the normal range of human stature. Kyle gauged the man to be even larger than most of the players he'd seen at the Bear's games that his second foster father had taken him to. Dark brown hair appeared to cover him almost completely, on his face, his neck, and even on the back of his burly paws, which seemed to be permanently attached to his hips. The only clean spot was his head, and it was so clean that it gleamed beneath the fluorescent lighting like a chrome bumper polished to a high shine.

Tanner had positioned himself right in the middle of the hallway, just inside the entrance, and standing among the students he looked like a redwood grown up in the middle of an apple orchard. Kyle reasoned that his intention was to have at least a little corner of his broad shadow fall on every student as they entered for their first day back. Immediate intimidation might save some time and effort on down the road.

The Paul Bunion administrator picked Kyle immediately out the group (not enough to rightly call a crowd), pegging him as a new kid.

"Welcome to Steel City High, Mister …?"

For just a moment, Kyle considered offering a made-up name, but then he remembered where he was. Anonymity wouldn't be an option in a place like this.

"Adams," Kyle finally offered along with his extended hand, "Kyle Adams."

"From Chicago, right? Well, Kyle, I think that you'll find things around here are a little quieter than what you're used to. I'm sure you'll have no trouble settling in, but if you do get snagged anywhere just let me know and I'll do what I can to fix you up. I'm Mr. Tanner. I'm the *principal* here."

Kyle noted an extra bit of emphasis placed on the word "principal." It was subtle, but unmistakable, and he took it to mean that "principal" in this case carried something beyond the usual meaning. Tanner's nickname among the students confirmed that the impression was accurate. He was the sheriff of his little community within a little community.

Kyle's right hand actually disappeared for a few seconds while Tanner gave it a shake that was powerful, but genuine. Likewise, Tanner's voice, though deep and gruff, carried a ring of sincerity. He spoke like he might to one of the teachers, not just a lowly student, demanding respect, but offering it as well. Tanner wasn't going to be one to take any crap, that was clear, but he didn't seem like the type that would go out of his way to hassle you either. Kyle could live with that.

Without another word, Tanner moved on to another student, a tall, tan girl wearing a tight, short skirt. Judging from the principal's reaction, Kyle guessed that she'd be modeling bib-overalls within the hour.

As he glanced over the steady trickle (not enough to rightly call a flow) of students making their way down the main hallway, Kyle was struck once again by how small the place really was. They could call it Steel *City* if they wanted to, but he wasn't fooled. He was from the city, he understood what a city was, and he was sure that Steel *City* wasn't one.

Steel City had been uncreatively named after the big steel mill was built down next to the equally uncreatively named Mill Pond, which wasn't really much more than a swollen section of the Brooke River. The river's name, which required only slightly more thought, was in reference to the Brooke Trout that hid down in many of its deeper holes. Just like basically everything else around the town, and the town itself, the river was pretty small and so were the trout. Consequently, fishing was not a major pastime for the Steel City residents. Weekends for the townsfolk were more frequently spent drinking beer with friends at "The Bar" and playing pool or drinking beer with family at home and playing euchre.

The town had just sort of sprung up after the mill was built back in '62. The mill employed about as many people as everything else in the town combined, and while it was doing well, so was Steel City. A couple of years after the mill opened the school was built, along with the Post Office, The Bar, the Country Kitchen Restaurant, a one-truck firehouse, and a dime store that would later be converted into Tank's Gas Station and Party Store. It had taken a little longer to finally get the blinking light put up at the intersection of Main Street and Riverside Road, but it had been a proud enough moment when it finally happened to warrant everybody wasting an extra big portion of their paycheck at The Bar that night.

Not quite twenty years after that, they must have started making steel a little cheaper somewhere else, because the mill shut down. By then, the town had grown up enough to be self-sustaining, but just barely. A big part of the population headed out right then, and the numbers had continued to dwindle ever since.

Steel City showed up on most of the Michigan state maps, but not all of them. Its people, in general, were hard-working, down to earth, and practical. None of them had the slightest clue as to what an incredibly important event had occurred there a long time ago, right next to the Brooke River. It was a spot between the old mill and town, in the woods that grew behind Kyle's new foster home. Of course the house hadn't been built yet when it happened. Neither had the mill or any part of Steel City for that matter. The whole area had been nothing but unspoiled nature back then when the two most powerful men on earth met and fought to the death.

Kyle was late for his first class. The secretary had given him a hand-written copy of the combination for his locker, and he'd mistaken her 19 for a 14. It was surely the sorriest excuse for a nine he'd ever seen, and it made Mrs. Stewart the first Michigander ever to land on Kyle's shitlist. Not that his list was any sort of a dangerous place to be. He certainly wasn't the sort of kid that went around making trouble.

It was five minutes after the bell when Kyle finally reached room number 11. He found it funny that there didn't need to be a 1 or 2 or 3 in front of the room numbers since the whole place was sitting there on one floor. It wasn't funny enough to make him laugh though, or even crack a smile. It was going to take something better than that to pull him out of such foul spirits as he was in.

The door was shut when he finally reached it, which was one more thing to add to the "make a break for it" side of the scale, and it probably would have tipped the scale right over if Sheriff Tanner hadn't been patrolling at the other end of the hall at that same moment. After one deep, calming breath, Kyle knocked. The door was opened almost immediately by a ridiculously happy looking woman wearing a "smile" pin on her sunflower print dress.

"Well, I just betcha that you're Kyle Adams," she said with a smile so big it made her eyes squint. "You're the first name on my list and the last one to show up for class." She paused as if waiting for someone to laugh. No one did. "Let's see," she continued, "should I mark you as tardy or not? I suppose it is the first day, but …"

The degree of sarcasm in the woman's voice would have been borderline appropriate for kindergarteners in Kyle's opinion, and it sort of made him want to puke. There was another awkward pause as the teacher seemed once again to be waiting for some sort of audience response.

"Could I sit while you decide?" It was the driest voice Kyle could produce, and now the giggles finally came.

"You can sit right up here next to my desk if you want to be a smart guy," she spouted back, never breaking her permagrin. This prompted a couple of muted laughs as well, but not from Kyle.

"No, I don't think that'll be necessary," Kyle responded without enthusiasm.

"Good. In that case you can go take that seat right behind Jimmy over there, after you introduce yourself to the class and share the highlights of your summer vacation."

I'd rather share my toothbrush with a cat that just finished cleaning its own butt. That really would have got the audience rolling, but Kyle held it in. It had been a lousy start to what he was sure was going to be a long, lousy day.

Most of the rest of the day crept by at a snail's pace, every hour feeling like three. The only period that went by more quickly was sixth, Kyle's biology class which was right after lunch. In that period all the students had to take concentration tests for some psychology research project. Kyle had already taken part in a similar study at his last school in Chicago, but he gladly participated again as it was a welcome alternative to science.

The taste that was left in Kyle's mouth after his first day was not a pleasant one. Nothing was familiar, except one thing, but it was that one thing that he'd sort have hoped would be different. He was disappointed, but he wasn't surprised. After all, even if the kids, the teachers, the classes, and everything else were new, Kyle was still the same. It would work out differently than it had in the city, but somehow or other he would end up in the same place that he always ended up, at the threshold of acceptance. There wasn't any good reason for it as far as Kyle could see, but he had always felt like he couldn't quite fall into stride with his classmates, even his friends, and he felt like they knew it.

Kyle was a pretty good athlete and a pretty good student. He'd never been all-state in any sport or gotten a 4.0, but he'd never been cut from a team or failed a class either. He was medium height with a medium build, and he kept his straight brown hair cut at a medium length. He had never been particularly shy or outspoken, not a real go-getter, but definitely not lazy. If there was anything truly remarkable about Kyle it was how completely average he was in so many ways.

Not surprisingly, Kyle had been in a little trouble in his life, but not too much. He certainly wasn't the sort of kid who went around looking for mischief, but occasionally mischief managed to find him nonetheless. But he never let himself get out of hand. Kyle's quiet, inner voice, his instinct, had always told him that he'd be better off mostly avoiding the spotlight. Occasionally, when he felt the sting of loneliness while standing in a crowded hallway at school, it was that same voice that would comfort him with promises of the future, of bigger and brighter days to come. *Just be patient,* it seemed to whisper, but the patience of a teenager can stretch only so far.

Part of Kyle was glad to hear the final bell ring at the end of the school day, but another part was not. Spending another minute in the crumbling, hillbilly training facility that was his new school would have been too long, but heading home to a new house and new foster parents wasn't an appealing prospect either. Kyle found himself surprised at how potently he missed the stink and noise of Chicago.

"Why don't you toughen up a little, Adams?" Kyle suggested to himself under his breath. He'd meant for it to be a private comment, and so it barely even registered when someone responded.

"What's that? Did you ask me something?" inquired the kid standing in front of the next locker over.

Kyle had seen him there several times during the day, but hadn't caught his name. He was short and bordering on fat. Kyle thought that he might not have looked fat at all if it hadn't been for a pair of tiny, circle-lens glasses that were propped up on his wide nose. They were so small that they made him look relatively big.

"No," Kyle replied, "just talking to myself."

"But I thought I heard you say "Adam"," the chubby neighbor pressed. "That's my name. I'm Adam."

The suspicion in the boy's eyes told Kyle that he was accustomed to picking up on not-so-nice comments aimed at him from local conversations. Not too surprising considering the combined effects of being short and borderline fat. The funny little glasses and a sparkling set of rubber band-equipped braces certainly didn't help either.

"My last name's Adams," Kyle explained. "I'm Kyle Adams, and I really was just talking to myself."

"As long as you don't start hearing answers, right?" The chubby kid smiled, which wrinkled his nose slightly, which in turn lifted his tiny specs up a little higher on his round face.

Kyle managed to return the smile, but couldn't quite bring himself to force out a laugh. He was thinking about how it must feel to have those rubber bands always pulling to keep your mouth shut, and hardly even heard the unoriginal joke.

"It was good to meet you, Kyle. Probably see you Monday," Adam said as he turned and started down the hall.

Kyle nodded and slammed his own locker shut. Just as he bent over to pick up his backpack there was a small outbreak of laughter from somewhere down the hallway. When he looked up he saw a pile of books, half open and half closed, spread out at the feet of Adam, his new locker neighbor. Adam was standing in the center of a ring of laughing students, his fleshy cheeks suddenly painted red and his eyes squeezed down to slivers behind his little, circle-lens glasses.

All of the kids around him were laughing, but special enthusiasm was coming from one tall kid who was standing on the other side of the spilled books, opposite Adam. Kyle pegged his type immediately. He was bigger than most of the other kids, sported a scraggly, blondish beard, and right at that moment he looked extraordinarily pleased with himself. It was pretty clear what had just happened.

If Steel City High didn't have anyone worse to offer in the bully department, then Kyle wasn't particularly impressed. Some of the "bullies" at his old schools had doubled as organizers of small time prostitution rings and drug trafficking businesses. Kyle suspected that the oaf he was looking at didn't possess the intelligence or the courage to organize a spelling contest for first graders.

Kyle felt sympathetic for his new locker neighbor's moment of humiliation, but he knew better than to step into the middle of anything. Adam was fine. Laughter could be painful, but only for a while. The last thing he wanted to do on his first day was to get labeled a troublemaker.

It seemed clear that Adam wasn't going to make any bold response, and so after a moment, when the image of flying books and flailing arms grew stale, the small group of spectators started to disperse. Last to turn and go was the scummy-looking bully, whose chest was heaving as he tried to catch his breath after an exhausting roll of laughter. Kyle saw that the back of his varsity jacket said "Dickers."

Suddenly, Adam, who'd been standing there motionless over his books, rushed forward. With surprising quickness, he grabbed the zipper of Dickers' backpack, which was slung over his right shoulder, and jerked it halfway open. The bully spun around so fast that a yellow folder sailed out of his pack and all the papers he'd collected that day scattered.

A second bloom of laughter erupted in the hallway, and this time Kyle laughed along with them. He laughed outloud, and he enjoyed it thoroughly. It was the first good laugh he'd had since moving to Michigan.

Dickers, who was now standing practically in front of Kyle, flashed him a glare that was not discretely a threat, but Kyle didn't care and continued to laugh. He'd never been scared of bullies, not even the genuinely dangerous ones back in the city. His gut told him that Dickers would turn out to be more bark than bite, more show than go.

The reddening bully shifted his laser beam stare back to Adam, and he let his unzipped pack drop to the floor. "Oh, that was cute, fatty. Suppose you're feeling like quite the man now."

"I don't care what you do, Dickers," Adam said evenly, "because now they're all laughing at you. They don't like you either."

Kyle thought that it was probably an astute comment. Dickers looked like the loner sort of bully as opposed to the pack leader type, and his reaction to Adam's words confirmed that it must have been true.

With a hard, two-hand shove, Dickers sent Adam stumbling backward into his own locker next to Kyle. Adam's substantial girth slamming against the hollow metal sounded like a car crash. The buzz in the hall began building again, and everybody packed in close to get a good view. Kyle took this as a good sign for Adam. In Chicago, everyone would have been running away, and that was bad.

Kyle could see jaw muscles clinching through the untrimmed, blondish beard as Dickers strode forward. It was a shame that Adam was going to get pummeled right after his big, shining moment. *Oh well,* Kyle thought. *It happens.*

Then Kyle stepped out between Adam and the pissed-off bully. He didn't mean to, and he didn't want to, but some troublesome part of him that wasn't listening to reason had taken control of his legs.

Just leave it alone. Leave it! But it was too late by then, Dickers was almost on top of him. Kyle didn't feel particularly worried as much as he felt annoyed with himself for getting mixed up in something that he could have avoided. He knew that the excitement would draw Tanner any second, and he didn't care to ruin the good impression he felt he'd made with the principle that morning.

Dickers was mad to the point where he was going to hit someone for sure, and since Kyle was in the way of his original target, it was probably going to be him. The bully swung a big, slow right hook that Kyle sidestepped easily. The punch had been thrown so recklessly that the miss supplied almost enough momentum to send Dickers headfirst into the lockers. Almost enough, but not quite. Kyle supplied the rest. It wasn't much more than a little shove on the way by, a quick pass by a skilled matador, but it resulted in a wicked header against the door of Kyle's locker.

Dickers crumpled to the floor, and for several seconds he just froze, one palm covering each eye. Kyle wondered briefly if he might be crying, but he wasn't. When his hands finally came down, two things were immediately clear. One, the locker dive had given Dickers an instant goose egg on his forehead, but hadn't done any serious damage, and that was good. Two, the impact hadn't been enough to knock the steam out of him, and that was bad.

Dickers got up slowly, shaking noticeably either from the knock to his melon or from his boiling anger, Kyle couldn't tell which. As the big hick pulled himself up from the floor, the crowd of students cheered and rooted, hoping for more excitement. Kyle wasn't really paying much attention to the audience's encouragement, but he correctly gathered the impression that they were pulling for the home team. Apparently they preferred the local jerk to the big-city immigrant.

"Get up, Dickers?" "Come on, teach the city boy some manners!" "Kick his ass!" "Smoke him, Dickers!"

Kyle didn't think that Dickers was going to smoke him. In fact, if his first effort was any indication of how tough a kid he was in a scrap, Dickers would have been better off staying on the floor and faking a KO. It would have been better for Kyle as well, much better. If they really ended up swinging, he'd be done with SCHS before he'd really even gotten started.

"Did you hear them all laughing at you, Dickers?" Adam's voice piped in. "I never heard them laugh so hard at anybody, not even me."

That comment marked the official end of Adam's big, shining moment. Dickers nailed him with a good jab, right square in his wide nose. Blood gushed, Adam squealed, and one round lens from his funny, little glasses flew through the air.

Now Kyle was ticked-off as well. His quiet, inner voice was suddenly not so quiet, and it wasn't telling him to restrain. It was demanding action.

Kyle wasn't worried about getting into trouble with Tanner anymore, or his new foster parents, or anybody else. Someone needed to stand up for Adam, and since it didn't look like there were going to be any other volunteers, it would be him by default. Since etiquette clearly seemed to be out the door at that point, Kyle balled his fist and wound up to take a homerun swing as soon as Dickers turned around.

And then everything froze. All the strain evaporated from Kyle's muscles, and his arms fell limp at his sides. In an instant he had forgotten all about Dickers, but that was okay, because Dickers had forgotten about him as well. Both of the combatants stood there transfixed along with most of the gathering of spectators. All of the tension in the air had disappeared in an instant, and it was quiet except for one hypnotically gentle voice. Although the voice was as soft as a cat's purr, Kyle knew that he couldn't have missed it even with an air horn sounding into each of his temples.

"Don't worry about your glasses," the voice advised gently. "Glasses can get fixed a lot easier than people can. I'll walk down to the office with you, and Mrs. Stewart will know what to do for your nose, and if you want I'll stay with you until you're feeling better."

The girl was softly beautiful, just like her voice. She had straight blonde hair that hung past her shoulders, dark, bronze skin, and a thin frame. Her voice had shocked Kyle because he was sure he'd never heard anything like it, and then her face shocked him again because he was sure he'd seen it before. Of course the odds that he'd really met her were astronomical, but she was so familiar that it gave him the chills. He was awestruck.

"Could someone pick up Adam's glasses, please?" she asked in her delicate voice.

Two boys standing nearby stepped forward immediately like peasants who had just received a command from royalty.

The girl accepted the broken frame and the loose lens and then started down the hallway with her arm over Adam's slumped shoulders.

Kyle could still hear the girl speaking as they departed, doing her best to comfort her whimpering companion. About halfway down the hall the girl glanced back over her shoulder. Her clear, chicory-blue eyes found Kyle and held him for just a moment, almost as if under a spell.

"Lucky dork."

The comment pulled Kyle back into time, but he still wasn't thinking very clearly. It took a second to realize whose comment it had been. Dickers was just standing there stupidly, like a deer frozen in headlight beams. The whole pack of students watched Adam and the girl walk down the hallway for a moment, and then one by one they continued on to wherever they had been headed in the first place. Dickers strolled off eventually as well, never saying anything more. In fact, he'd never even looked back at Kyle again after the girl had shown up. It was as if they'd all been mesmerized. It was like magic.

Kyle picked up his things and headed down the hall as well, not wanting to wait around for Tanner to finally show up asking questions about the bloodied student in his office.

As he passed through the front doors of the school, Kyle was struck without warning by a wave of nausea. His stomach twisted and gurgled, threatening to expel the greasy lunch he'd eaten that day in the cafeteria. The blood seemed to drain from his head, and the ground beneath his feet felt dangerously unstable. The beating of his own heart pounded in his ears, and suddenly he was very afraid.

After stumbling down the concrete steps outside the doors, Kyle headed quickly across the parking lot. He walked as fast as he could, barely able to stop himself from breaking into a run, and he didn't slow down until he was nearly a quarter of a mile down Riverside Road.

"What the hell is your problem?" Kyle asked himself as he struggled to slow his breathing. There was no obvious explanation for the way he had just acted. He was certainly not prone to panic attacks, assuming that's what had happened. He hadn't even broken a sweat during the whole scene with Dickers, but there he was terrified over … over what? He didn't even know.

Pull it together, Adams, this place is Candyland compared to where you grew up. There's nothing dangerous here.

But even as Kyle struggled to assure himself that it was true, his inner voice kept bringing doubt back up to the surface of his thoughts. As ridiculous as it seemed, there was something dangerous. Steel City, Michigan wasn't just any other little hick town, and Kyle hadn't ended up there by chance. The whole place felt off balance, like a ship floating in a rough sea, the kind you get when there's a storm on the way.

A familiar and dreaded feeling of purpose stopped Kyle between strides. Whatever is was that he'd been waiting for all his life, he wouldn't have to wait much longer. Some mysterious, hidden part of the world was about to open up, to reveal wonderful or terrible things.

Kyle listened to his own thinking, and laughed at himself in response. *You walk around thinking crap like that and then wonder why you can't fit in.*

It had turned out to be quite a first day at Steel City High School for Kyle Adams. He couldn't have guessed that it would turn out to be his last as well.

A STRANGE DISCOVERY

A tall man with an awkwardly crooked nose watched curiously as Kyle hurried across the parking lot in front of SCHS. He sat in the back seat of a black Lincoln Towncar behind windows tinted so darkly that he was completely hidden from anyone outside. He deliberately massaged his pointed chin between a thumb and forefinger, wondering about the curious display he'd just witnessed. It had almost appeared that one of the students leaving the school had reacted to him. He was sure that the boy couldn't have seen in through the tinted windows, or at least nearly sure. It had probably just been some stupid redneck kid acting paranoid because of whatever he'd smoked in the boy's bathroom that day, but still he was left with an uncomfortable twinge of doubt.

The tall man dismissed the whole line of thinking after a moment and glanced at his watch, feeling his patience slipping. Dr. Simpson was running late, and Ramius King was not a man who was accustomed to being kept waiting.

Jack Tanner leaned out through the door of the school office, stopping Spencer Simpson between strides as he was headed for the front door.

"Didn't anyone tell you?" Tanner asked in his big, bass voice. "Teachers are supposed to stay here working until there's just enough time to go home and rest up for the next day."

Simpson looked as though he wasn't sure how to take the comment, seriously or in fun.

"I guess I was just, ah, thinking that maybe I could, ah, get more done at home, I guess," the new teacher stuttered.

Tanner tried not to cringe as the timid man stumbled through his words. "How did your classes go today?"

"Oh, ah, fine. The kids were really, ah, enthusiastic."

Tanner knew exactly what he really meant by that. He'd peaked into the biology room a couple of times that day, and the kids looked like they were running right over him. Tanner had to restrain himself from barging in and taking over. That would have made things worse though, undermined Simpson's authority completely.

"I'm glad to hear that," the Sheriff replied. "You're bound to have some snags as a new teacher, everybody does. Ask for help when you need it."

"Oh, of course. I'm sure that I'll be fine, ah, you know, once I get, ah ..."

Just then, to Simpson's relief, Tanner bolted away after a couple of girls who were racing down the hall, leaving the awkward conversation unfinished. Simpson could see the Lincoln parked out in front of the school and knew that he needed to hurry. As he rushed out the door, he inadvertently fell into stride with a couple of greasy-haired junior boys who had terrorized his first period.

"What's up, Mr. Simpson? This pimp-ride picking you up? You must do a little business on the side to afford service like this."

The boys laughed, hustling to keep up with Simpson as he scrambled for the car. He stopped just in front of the back passenger's side door, wishing desperately that the kids would go away.

"Hey, you think maybe we could borrow this some night to go cruising for honeys? We'd take it easy on you in class if you let us. Well, easier anyway."

The kids' flurry of laughter that followed was cut short when the driver's door suddenly swung open. A smallish, bald-headed man of indeterminable age stepped out and slowly made his way around the front end of the Lincoln, his lifeless, gray eyes shifting smoothly from one boy to the next as he approached. He continued around steadily, but unhurriedly, until he stood practically on the toes of the taller of the two students, who suddenly seemed to have forgotten the humor of his comments.

The short man's bald head shined like it was polished marble, and all his exposed skin had a dull smoothness to it like sun-faded, gray plastic. When he finally spoke, it seemed like his lipless mouth hardly moved, like the words just slipped out.

"Perhaps it would be prudent of you boys to put a little distance between yourselves and this automobile," the strange looking man offered threateningly, his voice a cold hiss.

The boys didn't hesitate, spinning on their heels and heading down the sidewalk, instructed by their guts to be afraid of the short man. Spencer Simpson, however, didn't have to rely on instincts, he knew from experience to be afraid. Mason Stone was a dangerous man, a killer.

Inanimate gray eyes tracked the retreating boys for a few seconds and then patiently drifted over to meet Simpson's.

"You're so pathetic, *Doctor*," Mason hissed.

Simpson cringed in spite of himself as he climbed into the back seat of the car next to another man, perhaps the only man, whom he feared even more than Mason Stone.

Adam Horton's tears had finally dried up, but without his glasses things still looked out of focus. However, he could see well enough to know who that had been talking with Mr. Tanner outside the office. It was Mr. Simpson, the new science teacher who taught Adam's third period biology class. That was the class that Adam had expected to be his favorite, but the first day had changed his mind.

The entire period had been horrible. First of all, they had to take part in some really stupid research project that Mr. Simpson was conducting for a friend who was doing graduate work in psychology. They all had to try to do these incredibly ridiculous "mind over matter" kinds of tasks. It had been total nonsense, a foolish waste of time, but that wasn't nearly the worst of it.

The class had been out of control the whole period. Mr. Simpson obviously didn't have the first clue about how to manage a classroom. Some kids love to be in a class with that sort of teacher, but not Adam. Adam liked the really strict teachers who could keep the kids quiet. Quiet kids weren't calling you a dork or flinging spit-wads at you. Nobody was quiet in Mr. Simpson's room, especially Brent Dickers. Dickers had spent the entire period thinking up new "Adam's so fat" jokes and sharing them for the entertainment of the whole class. After what had happened in the hallway, Adam was sure that Monday would be worse.

Adam bit down lightly on his lower lip and tried to think about something else. The first thing that popped into his head was Kyle, his new locker neighbor. Kyle had stepped in between Dickers and himself. It was almost hard to believe even though it had just happened a little while ago, but it was true, and it was encouraging. When Adam had given his version of the story to Sheriff Tanner, he had made sure to make it clear that Kyle deserved a commendation, not an expulsion.

For the moment, his nose wasn't hurting and his eyes were dry. A strange thought occurred to Adam then, and he giggled at how silly it sounded. His glasses were broken, maybe his nose as well, and yet it had quite possibly been the best he'd felt after any first day back to school. His glasses could get fixed, and Mrs. Stewart said that she thought his nose would be fine even if there was a minor break. Much more important than those things was Kyle Adams standing up for him when he needed help, the kind of thing that a friend would do. Sure, he'd still got busted in the nose, but first everyone had seen that someone was there to be on his side. It probably wasn't any big deal to Kyle, but it was a big deal to him.

On top of that, there was Lily Goodshepherd who had come to his aid after he got creamed. *Lily Goodshepherd!* Adam would have been willing to take ten more of Dickers' best roundhouses for another walk down that crowded hallway with Lily's arm over his shoulder. He thought about how jealous all of the guys in the hall must have felt of him, of *him*, and his cheeks pulled up into a stainless steel and rubber band smile, and one red wad of toilet paper fell from his nose.

The buses were away, and the parking lot was clear just like Riverside Road, at least as much of it as Kyle could see. In fact, other than the road itself, Kyle couldn't see a single man-made thing anywhere. There weren't any apartments or office buildings, any fast-food restaurants or gas stations, nothing. And it was quiet. Kyle thought that maybe he could hear frogs calling from the roadside ditch up ahead somewhere, but it might have been crickets instead for all he knew. The road disappeared up over a hill in either direction, and on both sides of it was forest. Kyle knew that over to the right somewhere, still too far off to hear, the Brooke River ran pretty much parallel to the road.

All of a sudden, Kyle was struck with an irresistible urge to go into the forest, to see if he could find a spot where there were no man-made things to see at all, not even the road. For some reason it was an exciting idea to be somewhere with only the things that God had decided to put there. Kyle knew there were places like that all over the world, but there weren't many around Chicago. He'd always thought of "undisturbed nature" as a term for some deep desert or tropical jungle, but there it was, ten feet from the road. What could he say, he was a city kid.

Impulsively, Kyle started off into the woods, and he never thought to check back and see when the road finally fell out of sight. He gradually became aware of a hundred different sounds emanating from all directions. Most of them were faint, but occasionally there were louder ones, a squirrel scurrying away across the fallen leaves or a gust of wind rattling the skeletal branches of a swaying elm overhead. Kyle listened to all the sounds at once and found that it was musiclike. He had heard a jazz concert one time where the players didn't use any sheet music. Instead, they just played whatever sounded right and felt right at the moment. The woods sounded sort of like that, except the sounds were simpler and the rhythm more complex.

All of Kyle's other senses were equally stimulated. Countless smells and tastes floated in the air. He dragged his hands through the low-growing leaves as he walked and was surprised to find that some were sharp and rigid, while others were smooth, but brittle, and yet others were as soft as cloth. He hardly blinked his eyes, not wanting to miss a thing, anxious to see what small wonder might appear next.

With all his senses turned up to maximum sensitivity, Kyle had no spare thought to devote to the path of his journey or to his destination. Eventually he found himself following along some sort of trail through the undergrowth, narrow, but unmistakable. He wondered if it might be a deer trail, but couldn't be sure.

Mellow happiness washed over Kyle just as mysteriously as the fear had back at the high school. He had never felt so totally immersed in the present moment in his whole life. There were no regrets or anxieties bouncing around in the back of his mind, no expectations or concerns of any kind. There was only the woods. He didn't care about the past or the future, one of which was already done and couldn't be changed, and the other would arrive sooner or later and couldn't be avoided.

About twenty minutes walk from the road, Kyle stepped out into a clearing, or at least that's what he thought it was at first. As soon as he'd been able to hear the river his pace had quickened to just short of a trot. Bunches of green leaves had been sailing by as his feet planted one after the other along the dirty, little trail. He hadn't even seen it coming, but one second there was the trail and the forest, and in the next second both were gone.

A clearing, Kyle thought, was a place in the woods where there weren't any trees. As he inspected the area more closely, he realized that there were actually plenty of trees, and big ones, but they were all dead. The place felt empty because where the space in the rest of the forest was nearly saturated with green growth, this space was mostly just space. Only the bones of the forest that had been there long ago remained.

The trunks of the long dead trees were black, almost ashen looking, but Kyle didn't think that fire could have wiped out such a localized area in the middle of the big woods. What branches remained atop the black trunks appeared to bend out toward the direction from which he had come. He supposed at first that their lean could be an indication of which way the predominant winds blew, but as he slowly walked around the perimeter of the circular area, he realized that not all of the trees were leaning in the same direction. In fact, it looked almost as if they were bent outward from the center of the dead zone, as if some giant explosion at the circle's midpoint had pushed them all away, and there they had stuck, frozen at that moment forever.

That didn't sound like a very reasonable explanation for the phenomenon, but Kyle felt drawn toward the center of the area nonetheless. All of the hundreds of sounds that had flooded Kyle's ears along his hike were now gone except for the steady gurgling of the nearby river. And even the river sounded muffled somehow, although it didn't look like it was a section of particularly slow moving water. It just seemed to be flowing a little more carefully as it passed the barren section of the woods, on its tiptoes so to speak. Kyle understood that perfectly because he felt the same way. His instincts were telling him that this was no place to go tromping around haphazardly.

In the middle of the black trees was the strangest thing that Kyle had found yet during the whole extremely strange day. A small tree, not much taller than Kyle himself, grew at what he thought must be the exact center of the pseudo-clearing. Despite its shortness, the tree had a very old shape, and it reminded him in that way of the ancient bonsai trees of Japan. Its single trunk snaked around back and forth to the level of Kyle's eyes and then branched out into four, and then sixteen, and eventually hundreds of tiny braches. The trunk was only about as thick as a baseball bat handle all the way up from the ground to the first fork, and it was just as white as all the surrounding trees were black, and so were all its tiny, fluttering leaves. It wasn't white like the bark of a birch, but like ivory, pure white.

Covering every square inch of the milky surface was what Kyle at first took to be some sort of strange writing, maybe the carved initials of decades worth of teenage sweethearts, but a closer look revealed that it was actually the carving of woodworms. The little grooves that the worms had left as they tunneled along turned and ran and doubled back sporadically, but somehow they seemed to all add up to some sort of complex order, just how the hundreds of random sounds of the woods had added up to music.

Kyle stepped forward with the caution of a tightrope walker. He was completely mesmerized by the unearthly appearance of the tree, and part of him wanted desperately to reach out and touch it, but he couldn't. As his opened palm came to within inches of the thin trunk, his whole body began to shake like he had accidentally found an empty light bulb socket. The rush of energy was exhilarating, not painful, but there was no explanation for it, and Kyle was scared. He withdrew his hand and retreated from the ghostly tree.

As Kyle backed slowly away, his legs felt like they were made of silly putty, and when his back met the trunk of the nearest black tree corpse, his knees gave in altogether. He sat there on the damp ground and struggled to slow down his racing mind. When he opened his eyes for a moment, it seemed like the forest was spinning, but when he closed them for a moment, it seemed like he was spinning.

The previous night, Kyle had hardly slept, consumed with anticipation about his first day at his new school. Leaning his head back against the rough bark of the tree behind him, Kyle thought that after the day he'd had, he'd have enough to think about to keep him awake for a month. Then, just a moment later, with all the day's events racing figure eights through his mind, Kyle fell asleep.

THE DREAM

A cool breeze touched lightly across Kyle's face. Slowly, he opened his eyes, wondering why they'd been closed in the first place. He found himself straddling the yellow line of a dark, deserted city street. A faint blush of pale light, barely visible, hung in the air not far from where he stood. Slowly, Kyle came to realize that the street was not completely deserted after all. As the faint light began to gain strength, he could see that in the center of the illuminated area was a person, a girl judging from the shadowy outline of long, straight hair falling over narrow shoulders.

The light continued to grow and the girl was revealed plainly. She was softly beautiful and strangely familiar. Although his thoughts were fuzzy and moving in slow motion, Kyle felt certain that he had seen the girl in his dreams before.

His mind shuddered at the bizarre realization. He knew that he was dreaming.

As he scanned around at the charcoal brick buildings that lined the street, Kyle recognized that the place was familiar as well. He felt sure that he had met that girl, walked that street, and lived that dream a thousand times. He also knew that in another few seconds he would wake up, and it would all be forgotten again, just like it had been a thousand times before.

The light now shone all the way to the edge of the colorless buildings. It seemed to Kyle that the girl was not merely situated at the center of the light, but was actually its source. Feathery, bluish rays radiated out from her in all directions, an aura that was the only color in the entire setting. Everything else was painted in dismal shades of black and gray. She was a bright star in a dark sky, perfect, but something was wrong.

The girl's eyes cried out to Kyle wordlessly. Her expression wasn't exactly fear, but some emotion that existed between fear and sadness. Kyle thought that it looked like she might somehow sense the grave events of the approaching future, just as he did.

At the edge of what the girl's light revealed, Kyle sensed some quiet movement. He squinted through the darkness, straining to spot another character lurking in the shadowy alleyways of his dreamscape, but the source of the motion was not hiding between the buildings. It was the buildings. Brick after charcoal brick was laid down as if from thin air. The walls were extended right before Kyle's eyes until every door and alleyway was plugged shut, every possible escape route sealed.

Kyle spun on his heels. No monster had snuck up behind him, just men, hundreds of them, all relatively young, and all cloaked in black. Half hidden in the darkness, Kyle couldn't distinguish any one of the men from any other. He could see, however, that they were approaching, marching steadily forward in mechanical synchronization.

Kyle knew instinctively that they were there for the girl, to snuff her light and complete the blackness of the street. He felt shocked to discover that he was not afraid. He knew that he should be paralyzed with fear, but he wasn't. He knew why he was there, and he was ready to do whatever he had to do to protect the light

The power that radiated out from the approaching troop of dark soldiers was palpable. They were more than ordinary men, Kyle knew, but still he was not afraid, for he had power in this place as well. He would do whatever he had to do to protect the girl.

Kyle tensed in anticipation of the eminent confrontation. As every muscle in his body clenched, he felt a hard resistance in his right fist. He looked down and discovered that it was a staff he held, black and twisted and covered with shallow grooves. It was impossibly light, and yet hard as anything he'd ever felt.

Kyle's quiet, inner voice told him hold the staff out, to make sure these shadowy enemies recognized who it was that they faced. At the moment the staff was raised, the dark army froze between strides. Several of the figures in the front row of the formation staggered backward, and one man actually dropped to his knees on the black asphalt.

The staff appeared to rest motionless in Kyle's grip, but he could feel it vibrating microscopically a million times a second. The energy that tingled first in his hand was now diffusing throughout his entire body. He felt almost weightless, but immoveable at the same time. These hundreds of foes, he promised himself, would not be enough.

Clearly, the men were afraid of Kyle and the strange weapon that he wielded. A couple of moments that felt like hours in the dream slipped past without any motion or sound anywhere in the street. Perhaps there wouldn't have to be a battle after all.

That thought was just becoming hope for Kyle when suddenly the stillness was shattered. A wall of sound like a tornado wind charged up the street toward Kyle, and when it reached the ranks of shadowy soldiers, it brushed them aside as if they were made of dandelion fluff. Kyle squeezed the staff with all his strength and braced himself before the coming tidal wave of sound. A last second glance over his shoulder ensured him that the girl was still safe. Her expression hadn't changed, but her light now seemed to flicker intermittently.

The ferocious wind screeched in Kyle's ears. He felt as though every electron orbiting every atom in his body was accelerated to the brink of breaking free from its nuclear bond, reducing him to atomic dust. He forced himself to think of the girl. He had to hold his ground, whatever it took.

When the screeching finally passed, a ringing remained in Kyle's ears, but his other senses began to function again. To his utter amazement, Kyle saw that somehow one of his foes remained standing. No, as his vision cleared he realized that it was not one of the dark soldiers. This figure was clad all in black, but was taller and much older than any among the ranks had been. A high, pale forehead turned into black hair fringed in silver, all slicked back over the top of his head. In the center of his pinched face was a long, awkwardly crooked nose and two cold, black eyes that glared unblinkingly at Kyle with horrifying calmness. This man was not afraid of him, not at all.

What if I can't protect her? Kyle cursed himself for allowing the question to form in his mind, and suddenly the doubt threatened to erupt up through his dry throat. So this was why Kyle had never been afraid of school bullies or dark basements or barking dogs. He'd been saving his fear for the Tall Man, for Ramius King.

Kyle awoke with the taste of blood in his mouth, and his brown hair stuck coldly to his forehead. He probed the inside of his bit cheek with a pinky finger and sighed at the thought of another unconsciously self-inflicted wound. He figured it to be the thousandth time he'd ever woken up with tooth marks in his lip or nail marks in his palms. Maybe it was a blessing that he could never remember his dreams.

It was nearly dark and Kyle knew that his new foster parents would be worried. It would have seemed like a serious issue any other day. He picked up his backpack and started along the bank of the river, which he knew would lead him eventually back to his new home.

As Kyle moved away along the bank of the river, two pairs of carefully hidden eyes intently watched him depart. The first set of eyes were set deep in the leathery face of an old man, whose heavily wrinkled, bronze skin and braided, gray hair accentuated his strong Native American features. The second pair of eyes, hidden some fifty meters from the first, belonged to a black wolf. So dark and still was the animal that he could easily have been mistaken for a burned tree stump by anyone passing by. Only the golden glow of his eyes might have given him away.

As Kyle slipped finally from view, the old man took a deep breath, stretching out stiff muscles that had been frozen in one position for nearly an hour while the boy had napped against the tree. It grew a little harder each day to keep from dwelling on the inevitability of his age. No one commanded any sway over the passage of time and the cycling of life. Not even someone like him.

"I'm getting too old for this shit, Wolf," spoke the old man in a low, hoarse voice, finally breaking the silence that was left in Kyle's absence. He froze again after speaking the complaint, listening carefully for even the slightest stir of motion. He hadn't seen the wolf in hours, but knew that he wouldn't have gone far.

"I'm too old," the man repeated in his raspy voice, more to himself this time than to the wolf. He stood slowly, struggling to straighten his bowed spine, and produced a corncob pipe from an inner pocket of his denim jacket. He doubted that smoking would do much to ease the disappointment that had settled like lead in the bottom of his stomach, but it couldn't hurt. Not much more than an hour ago, it seemed that his age would no longer be of any great concern, that after all his long years of vigilance his release had finally come, but once again fate had intervened. *Why had the boy held back?*

The black wolf suddenly appeared, having never made the slightest sound to announce his approach. The old man started and dropped his smoking pipe. As he stooped to retrieve it, he offered a few choice profanities to the animal between raspy coughs. When his eyes reached the level of the wolf's, he looked up and paused. It seemed that in the animal's gaze he could see concern that mirrored his own. Pretty soon their waiting would be over, one way or another.

That night, Jack Tanner sat up in a log-frame wood bed, listening to his wife mumbling unintelligibly in her sleep. It had been a pretty good first day back, but something was keeping the principal/sheriff awake when he knew he needed to sleep. Actually, he was pretty sure that it was two things, or people to be more specific.

The first one was Spencer Simpson, the new science teacher that had been hired to replace Tom Warbler. It had been a real loss for the district when Tom had passed away a month ago in an accident down at the Mill Pond. It was bizarre enough for a former Navy frogman to die by drowning, and then when Simpson had shown up days later inquiring about science positions … It was silly for a grown man to allow himself to dwell on such fantastic suspicions, but Jack couldn't help it. He'd probably just seen too many Perry Mason reruns, but you never knew. Twenty-four years in the public schools had taught Jack to trust his gut, and every time Spencer Simpson was around he felt queasy.

Jack knew that it wasn't that uncommon for people from various other fields to decide to teach as their second career, but Simpson hardly seemed the type. The Doctor's quiet voice and strained social manners made him an unlikely candidate to lead a classroom. Despite his impressive credentials, Jack had hesitated in hiring Simpson for the position, but there had only been two applicants, and the other had been Jenny Bird, who served drinks down at The Bar. She hadn't even known that you needed to be certified to teach.

The other name that kept popping into Jack's head was Kyle Adams, the new kid from Chicago. Jack considered himself an excellent judge of character, and he'd been given a good first impression of Kyle. The little incident between him and Brent Dickers was probably nothing to worry about. Everybody knew that Brent was a jerk, and to be honest, it was good to have a couple of kids around who wouldn't take his kind of bullshit. Kyle had a strong handshake and an honest voice, but there was something else about him that Jack couldn't quite put his finger on. It was just a little nagging bit of suspicion, but he couldn't shake it. Kyle definitely wasn't just another kid.

Jack Tanner wasn't the only one up late that Friday night in Steel City. Lily Goodshepherd also sat restlessly in the dark, unable to find her way to sleep, and coincidently one of the things keeping Jack awake was also lingering in her thoughts.

It was very rare for a boy to genuinely capture Lily's attention. She'd never had a boyfriend and had trouble imagining how she ever could. Lily wasn't blind or stupid. She recognized how the boys at school looked at her and knew that they thought she was pretty, but she also knew that she'd never been invited to a holiday dance, or been passed a love note in class, or been asked out on a single date. Being pretty wasn't enough. The kids at school had always kept their distance from her, willing to be friendly, but never really friends. They all thought that she was different from them, and they were all right.

She wasn't exactly sure how long it had been, but at some point Lily had started to distance herself from the other kids as much as they distanced themselves from her. This was especially true with the boys, and that's why it was so peculiar that she should find herself thinking almost constantly about the new boy at school. They hadn't even talked, just shared a glance across the hallway, but there had been something in that look that had captured her. The new boy was an outsider like her. She didn't see any good reason that he wouldn't be able to fit in, but she didn't suppose that anyone saw clearly what it was that made her different either. However, unlike Kyle, Lily understood quite clearly what it was that set her apart from the other kids. It was the magic.

She cursed it everyday as the root of her loneliness, but she cherished it also. It didn't just make her different, it made her special, but what difference did that make if no one else could ever know? *No one could ever know.* How could she ever be truly close to anyone while keeping secret the thing that made her who she was?

She wished that there was just one person that she could tell, one person with whom she could share everything. It certainly couldn't be her father. Lily's father was a good man, hard working and decent, but ordinary, and he lived an ordinary life and liked ordinary things. He could never handle the knowledge that his own daughter was so unordinary. No one could ever know.

That's why Lily had been so upset by the tests that had been administered at the school that day. The students had been asked to try and do impossible things like heating up a glass of water and increasing the speed of a swinging pendulum just by thinking about it. The other kids laughed afterward. It was a joke to them, trying to do impossible things, but to Lily it was no joke, because she knew that those things were not as impossible as they seemed. She hadn't tried very hard when it had been her turn. She didn't think that she had made anything happen, but then again, she couldn't be sure.

Lily walked silently over to her bedroom door and put her ear gently against it. Besides the ticking of the grandfather clock that stood in the hallway outside her room, the house was perfectly quiet. Assured that her father was already asleep, Lily snuck back over to her bed. She sat cross-legged on top of the patchwork quilt her grandmother had made for her on her sixteenth birthday, nearly a year and a half ago. The moon that night was round and bright, and its soft, golden beams provided just enough light for Lily to see the snow-globe that sat on the bed before her.

The smooth glass sphere rested atop a darkly stained fruitwood base that looked like it could have been cast iron instead under the dim moonshine. Inside the globe was a tiny porcelain Santa Claus being towed along in his sleigh by eight tiny porcelain reindeer. All across the bottom of the globe there spread a thin layer of sparkling, white flecks, no larger than salt grains, which could become quite convincing snowflakes when the light was low and the imagination was willing.

Lily reached down and cupped her hands around the globe, nearly touching her palms to the glass, but never quite. She took a deep breath, and then slowly reached out with her mind, through the glass, through the water, right down to the sparkling, make-believe snow. She closed her eyes and conjured an image of a December night when the flakes blew sideways in the wind, the kind of night when she really appreciated the warmth of her grandma's quilt. When she opened her eyes again the snow was still flying. Around and around the twinkling, white flecks swirled, so fast that the porcelain Santa and his team were blurred from sight. Lily let herself become lost in the miniature scene and smiled the sweetest smile that no one ever got to see.

SATURDAY, SEPTEMBER 2

THE FORTUNE TELLER

Rosalind Sanchez sat suddenly upright in her bed, awake in a heartbeat. The early morning daylight filtered through her eyelids, tempting her to open them and see the day which had already begun without her, but she resisted, squeezing them closed. Experience had taught Rosa that as soon as her eyes opened the clarity of the dream from which she'd just escaped would begin to degrade. Experience also taught her that it had been no ordinary dream from which she'd just awakened, it had been a premonition. There was never any doubt. The emotions racing through her were too powerful and desperate to have been evoked by a normal dream.

A bead of sweat dangled precariously at the tip of Rosa's small nose, and once again she struggled to concentrate, to block out the distractions. This had been an important vision, and its every detail needed to be replayed in her mind immediately. The premonition had been typical for the sort except for one thing, and it was that one thing that she so desperately sought to memorize before the images began to fade.

Rosa had dreamed herself standing at a street corner on the far side of town. It wasn't an area that she frequented, but it was familiar enough to recognize. As usual, the first person that she saw was the one who would need her help. He was a mostly bald, middle-aged white man, nicely dressed and lacking in even the slightest hint of a tan. Obviously he was a snow bird, a tourist from somewhere up in the northern states. Miami wasn't the tourism Mecca that it once had been, but its extremely southern locale still drew quite a few once the summer months were over, and they were generally easy to pick out of the crowd. This man stood out like a firefly on a dark night, drawing attention like a beacon. He looked like an outsider, an uncertain stranger. A target.

Down the street the man strolled, oblivious to everything but his own private musings and the long evening shadow that matched his steps across the hot asphalt. Rosa, already sensing the impending danger, longed to call out to the man, to warn him that he was headed into trouble, but of course she was only an observer, unable to help or interfere in any way. All she could do was watch. As her sense of foreboding increased, panic set in, just as it always did. It was a panic beyond what another person's worst nightmare could induce, because this was no fantasy, but real life, or soon to be.

Rosa spotted the trio of shadowy young men before the snow bird did, but then he wasn't looking for them and she was. Not that she was expecting to see those three specific individuals, but she knew that someone else would be arriving in the scene, and soon. Her premonitions were never happy dreams. Her gift never allowed her to glimpse a baby's first step, or a couple's first kiss, or a reunion between old friends. Instead, her visions were full of violence and cruelty, the very grimmest of what the future had to offer. So, Rosa knew that the pasty tourist wasn't about to arrive anywhere safe and sound. He was the first on stage in this play in her mind, and that meant he was the victim, which in turn meant that the three street kids just making their entrance had to be the villains. Almost everyone in her visions was one or the other. Almost everyone.

The three young men casually shuffled out into the center of the sidewalk, blocking the path of their approaching prey. Still the man continued on, lost in the unsuspecting naiveté of his hazard-free midwestern life. Only when he veered to slip past the trio and was immediately blocked once again by their corresponding shift, did he finally seem to shake free of his carefree vacation daze. Neither the tourist nor the three young men said a word. All four stood there staring. The looks on the faces of the trio were hungry and anxious, while the older man looked suddenly terrified, recognizing at last the peril into which he'd stumbled.

Just then, when Rosa knew the attack was imminent, another character unexpectedly entered the scene, momentarily delaying the inevitable. Out from a nearby alleyway strolled another man, dressed as shabbily as the three muggers, but significantly older. There was something else that set this man apart as well, he was familiar. In the dim light of the overhead streetlamp, the tuft of hair at the man's chin didn't look red, but it was, she knew. The look on his long face made it clear that he immediately recognized the situation for what it was.

There was a flurry of abrupt motion that Rosa seemed to be able to feel as well as see, and then she was awake. She sat upright in bed, gasping for breath, and fighting the urge to open her eyes and escape back into the safety of the present moment.

Most of Rosa's premonitions were similar in that they showed a misfortune that was soon to befall someone near to where she lived, close enough that she could recognize the setting and intervene if she dared. And the people in the visions were almost always strangers. Once in a while though, it was different. Once in a while she'd glimpse a faraway place that she didn't recognize, and a face that she did. There were only three people who returned repeatedly to her visions, two she didn't know and one she did.

The ragged looking man she'd just seen interrupting the mugging was one of those three, and he'd appeared in her dreams at least a dozen times. She called him Redbeard. He possessed an odd combination of old and young features which made it difficult to judge his age. He was taller than average, fairly thin, and his long face ended with a red flame of a goatee. His pale green eyes always looked tired, and their gaze was always cast to the ground. Rosa had no idea who he was.

Then there was Grandmother, an elderly woman who'd appeared nearly as many times as Redbeard. She was a bent-over, little lady of at least ninety years, but beneath her neatly fixed white hair, she had a serious face, weathered, but willful and confident. Somehow, despite her advanced age and diminutive stature, Rosa thought Grandmother always seemed like someone who needed no taking care of. In fact, she seemed like someone who was in charge. In charge of who or what, Rosa had no idea.

The third person who frequented Rosa's dreams, the only one of the three she'd met, was Ramius King. Every dream that involved him was a nightmare, as was every waking moment that she'd ever spent in his presence.

Only twice had one of these three recurring characters appeared in a vision where Rosa recognized the setting. In the first one, she'd seen Ramius King interrogating a prisoner in an abandoned warehouse not far from where she lived. The next day, King had arrived at her door, drug her forcibly from her own home, made *her* his prisoner, and taken her to that very warehouse. It was there, on that day, when the Tall Man had *used* her for the first time. He'd called her his private fortune teller.

The dream from which she'd just awakened had been the second, and only other, time that one of the three repeaters had appeared close to home. Redbeard was coming to Miami, if he wasn't there already. What that meant for Rosa, she could only guess.

A Charitable Thief

On that same morning in that same city, just a few short miles from Rosa's apartment, Michael Galladin sat on the curb of a street which had become very familiar to him. His thin, plaid shirt was damp with lingering dew from the warm night, and it was just as dirty as his hands and face were. The shock of red hair that sprouted from the tip of his long face was dirty as well and clearly hadn't been trimmed in weeks. He was alone on the street that morning, which is exactly what he'd been hoping for, a few moments of solitude during which he could complete a few last minute preparations. A few moments would be enough. Michael had thought through his plan over and over again, and he felt confident that all his bases were covered.

His disguise, if it could truly still be called that, was certainly a convincing one, except for one small detail that could be added quickly enough. Michael looked down at himself, at the grime that coated his shirt and hands and the army surplus boots and camouflage pants that had become so comfortable. He recognized just how easily he had been able to slip into the character, how quickly he'd become the vagrant he had at first only pretended to be. It was something of a disheartening realization to make, but at this point he didn't have much for spirits left to dampen.

Casually, Michael unscrewed the cap from his plastic one liter bottle of Pepsi and proceeded to spill half of the fizzing beverage down the gutter drain at his feet. Then, from a thigh-high pocket of his camo pants, he retrieved a pint bottle of the cheapest whiskey sold at the corner party store. He emptied half of the bottle's contents into the Pepsi, turning the color of the mixed fluid inside a noticeably too light shade of caramel brown. Then he put the pint to his lips, tossed back a mouthful, and swished it around for a few seconds before spitting it down through the sewer grate. Michael cringed at the taste of the straight alcohol, but managed not to cough. He let a few splashes of the remaining liquor fall over his clothes, and with that, the disguise was finally complete.

The rest of the booze went down through the sewer grate along with the bottle, an act that prompted a very brief smile across Michael's face. It was a last scrap of proof that he had not entirely become the vagabond that he so looked and felt like. No self-disrespecting bum would ever pour good liquor down the drain.

A silver Lexus turned around the corner of the block just then, capturing Michael's attention. The sleek car pulled smoothly into its usual parking place on the opposite side of the street, and the engine died immediately. The man that stepped out of the car was just as polished as it was. His custom-tailored three-piece hung smoothly over his pudgy body. Michael thought to himself that the suit was just as much a disguise as what he was wearing, an attractive wrapping over an ugly man.

The man retrieved a briefcase from the back seat before throwing the door shut and setting the alarm. He started across the street, but paused when he noticed Michael sitting on the curb. The Suit, as Michael called him, didn't even try to hide his disgust, as a familiar sneer spread over his fleshy, red-cheeked face.

"Change, sir?" Michael asked, allowing his voice to slur just a little and intentionally aiming his noxious breath toward the man's face. "Anything you could spare would help."

"I'm sure it would," the Suit agreed, "help buy your next fifth. Listen, dirt bag, I'm getting tired of telling you to drag your grubby self away from here. If you're not gone when I come back out, I'm calling the cops. Got it?"

At that, Michael started to laugh, not simply in keeping with his drunken character, but as a genuine reaction to the Suit's words. Considering the nature of his work, the last thing the Suit was likely to do was ask the police to come and pay him a special visit.

"Go ahead, cheapskate, call the cops," Michael encouraged. "Maybe *they* can spare some change."

The Suit huffed reprovingly, disarmed the alarm at the entrance of Damon's Antiques and Fine Collectibles, and continued on inside.

It had taken a lot of effort and a long time for Michael to track the place down, but he had no other projects into which his effort might be spent, and he was as rich in time as he was poor in basically everything else. Of course that would be changing dramatically in just a few more minutes. In an hour, if every-thing went according to plan, Michael would have more money than he'd know how to spend, but only for a little while. He wasn't going to keep the money for himself, of course. It was justice he was after, not money.

Michael had spent the last few years planning and executing similar heists in a dozen different cities from the east coast to the west and back again. He'd started off small at first, thefts of a few thousand dollars at a time taken from local drug traffickers which he redistributed to the local community. They were acts of des-peration in truth, hopeless efforts to try and satisfy his deep need to do some sort of good, to give any kind of purpose to his life. The targets and the booties had escalated tremendously since then though, as had the risks. If it worked out, the Damon's job would be his biggest score yet. If it didn't work out, then he'd prob-ably end up dead or in jail.

Damon's Antiques and Fine Collectibles didn't attract many customers. Michael knew because he'd been sitting there on that curb in front of the store practically day and night for several weeks. Maybe two or three curious sidewalk shoppers would wander inside each day, but none stayed too long once they saw the limited selection and generally poor quality of the merchandise. To anyone else it would have been a wonder how the store even managed to stay in business, let alone require weekly service from an armored truck. To anyone else, it would have been a mystery how that run-down, half-empty junk store could take in so much cash, but no one else had spent the time and effort that Michael had in searching out the truth.

Actually, Damon's Antiques and Fine Collectibles was just the last stage in what had been a long backtrack for Michael. It had started with Donnie Cash, a punk dope dealer who sold to the local kids just two blocks from one of the city's junior high schools. That two-bit dealer, a junkie himself, eventually led Michael to his supplier, who in turn led to one of the three biggest distributors of illegal narcotics operating in Miami.

Tracing back through the chain of employment had taken Michael a mere matter of days. He'd skulked around with similar slime in similar cities, and he knew the right questions to ask and the right way to ask them. He'd learned all too thoroughly how to become the bum on the corner, the hard-luck loner that no one worried about, or even paid any attention to. Tracking the drug money all the way through its laundering cycle had been more difficult though, and time consuming, but eventually he'd ended up at Damon's. By the time the cash was picked up at the store by the armored car, it was clean as a whistle, completely untraceable and nearly untouchable.

However, that day Michael would touch the money. In fact he would take it, not for himself, but for those who'd suffered at its expense, or others very like them. All he needed to keep for himself was enough to stay fed and take him to his next job, wherever that might turn out to be.

There was just enough time for Michael to think through the steps of his plan one last time before the truck was due to arrive. It was a fairly simple plan, but he had learned through experience that those were the most likely sort to play out successfully. As he considered each of the plan's stages, searching for any possible oversights, Michael did exactly the opposite of what most people in the same situation would have done. He relaxed. His breathing grew deep and slow, and the muscles all through his lean frame loosened themselves one by one from the stiff knots into which the comfortless night's sleep had tied them. It was not a conscious method of preparation, but a habitual one, a conditioning from a very different time in his life intended for a very different purpose.

When the deep, diesel growl of the armored truck first reached his ears, Michael was not afraid, nor even excited. He was calmer than he'd been all morning. He was ready to do what needed to be done, what no one else would do.

Although there was no anxiety in him, no nervous anticipation of the imminent danger that he knew existed, Michael was fully aware of the magnitude of what it was he was about to attempt. Although his plan was a good one, simple and cleverly conceived, there was always the risk of the unexpected, the chance coincidence that could unravel the most tightly woven design. Also, Michael was constantly reminding himself that this scenario was different in one important aspect from any that he'd engineered in the past. This time, there was a bystander. The armored truck officer would serve an integral role in his reacquisition of the people's money. In the past, he had always been able to avoid involving innocents in his schemes, but this time it couldn't be helped. The armored truck pick-up was the best time to move.

The growling voice of the diesel engine diminished to a low grumble once the truck came to a stop in front of Damon's. As he regularly did, the uniformed man in the passenger's seat took a moment after stepping out of the vehicle to inspect the surrounding area, letting his cautious stare fall briefly on each of the few pedestrians that were now strolling up and down the sidewalk. He didn't seem to notice Michael though, despite the fact that the back of the truck was only thirty feet from where he sat. He was just another of the city's helpless homeless, to be pitied from afar at best, but more likely ignored or even despised.

"Change, sir?" Michael asked in his mock-drunken slur. "Anything you could spare would help."

Just like he had every other time, the uniformed man failed to respond. He continued on toward the entrance of the store without acknowledging Michael's presence whatsoever.

But this time, Michael didn't let him go so easily. In a carefully choreographed alcoholic stumble, Michael sprung up from the curb and hurried after the officer, checking his balance repeatedly. He caught up with the man at the store entrance.

"I'm sorry, sir," Michael pressed, "I know you're on the clock, but if you could just spare …"

Just as the door was swinging closed behind him, the armored truck officer looked back over his shoulder, making eye contact with the street beggar behind him for the first time, and what Michael saw in his glance was pity. That was more than what most offered, and once again he felt the reluctance at involving a bystander. Not that there was much of any chance of the officer getting hurt, but this would be a bad day for him at least, a day that might affect his reputation and possibly even his employment status.

It was far from a perfect plan, Michael knew, but plans for such a job were never perfect. All he could do was be careful for the sake of the officer and trust that the good the money could bring to the local needy made the risks worth while.

Michael casually shuffled a few unbalanced steps down the sidewalk until he could see into the cab of the armored truck. The driver of the truck was doing exactly what he always did while he waited for his partner, fiddling with the radio and not paying any attention to what he should have been paying close attention.

When the delivery officer emerged a few minutes later from the shop, he came to a halt several steps outside the door, even before he spotted the muzzle of the black pistol that Michael was holding mostly concealed beneath a folded newspaper.

"This will go better if you stay calm," advised Michael, all of the brashness and intoxication suddenly absent from his voice, replaced with cunning and determination. "Be prompt and precise in following the instructions I'm about to give you and everyone can finish this day as healthy as they started it. Do you understand?"

To the officer's credit, he recognized the situation for what it was immediately upon hearing the shift in Michael's tone. He realized why the alcoholic street bum had chosen this particular section of curb to sit on for the last several weeks, and that in truth, he was no alcoholic street bum at all.

"No matter how fast you run," the officer responded after a moment of consideration, "you'll never get far enough fast enough to get away with this."

"I tend to disagree, sir, but I do appreciate your concern and also the calm that I hear in your voice. I was afraid that you might not be able to maintain your composure so well once this moment arrived."

The officer dropped his head, assuming a posture of defeat, but Michael saw the hidden intent in the act instantly. Out of the corner of the officer's eye, he was glancing over at the truck, hoping beyond hope that for once his partner was being vigilant in his duties. Michael was glad that he had. Seeing his only backup napping in the driver's seat would discourage the officer from trying anything risky.

"Now, here's how this is going to work," Michael explained, drawing the officer's attention back to himself. "You'll set the money bag and your pistol on the sidewalk beside you. Then you'll slowly step back, turn around, and sit down on the ground with your legs crossed. Then I'll pick up the bag, make sure it's filled with lots of money, and call for my ride. I'll be picked up about thirty seconds later, and I'll ride off into the sunset, so to speak. Is any part of that unclear?"

The officer didn't respond. He just continued shifting his stare from Michael to the folded newspaper and back again. For a brief moment, Michael thought he might have seen something new in the man's eyes. It looked like recognition. Could it be that the guard knew Michael from the wanted reports he'd earned in the other cities? That was a dangerous possibility that warranted consideration—later.

"Okay, go ahead and do exactly what I've instructed you to do. And please, sir, for your own sake, do it slowly."

Very deliberately, the officer bent over and set the bag and his pistol gently down onto the sidewalk. The movement brought his face almost directly in front of the newspaper. Michael noted a moment's hesitation as he eyed the peeking muzzle of the hidden weapon.

"Now step back and turn around, sir," Michael directed.

The officer stood upright once again, gave Michael a brief, icy glare, and then turned, took a few steps, and seated himself cross-legged on the sidewalk.

Michael didn't wait thirty seconds to leave. He didn't even wait one. By the time the officer had settled into a sitting position, Michael had already grabbed up the officer's weapon and the money bag and was on the move. He slipped around the corner of the building and into a narrow alley, the first leg of his escape route.

Michael continued to think patiently even as his body exerted to maintain a delicate blend of speed and silence in his flight. As he galloped stealthily through the alley, he listened carefully for signs of pursuit. There were none, but that was hardly proof that the hunt hadn't already begun. If they weren't after him yet, they would be in a matter of seconds, he knew.

Behind Damon's, there was an apartment complex, and living in the ground floor was a family, a couple in their early forties, their teenage son, and an enormous chocolate colored lab name Maverick. As Michael approached the fence that enclosed the apartment's small yard, he tossed aside the Guard's pistol as well as the newspaper he'd been using to hide his own. The time for hiding the gun was past, and the time for using it had nearly arrived.

From up ahead, an eruption of throaty barking shattered the previous silence of the alleyway. The dog's testosterone filled voice was a predator's challenge, and it caused Michael to tense in spite of the fact that he'd been fully expecting to hear it.

In response to the noise of Maverick's alarm call, Michael picked up his pace to a full run, no longer concerned about making noise himself. Now, time was the only consideration. He needed to hurry.

A tight-lipped smile crept over Michael's long face as he ducked around a tall dumpster, hiding him from view from the other end of the alley and finally allowing him to see the giant lab in the nearby yard. Maverick looked like a horror movie wolfman standing erect with his front paws against the fence that surrounded his small, grassy enclosure. As Michael approached, the dog's barking ceased, replaced with a deep and ferocious growl, and his block shaped head quivered as if it took great energy to force the sound out between his tightly clenched teeth.

With absolute fearless calm, Michael raised the pistol and pointed it right into the middle of all those gleaming fangs. He inched a little closer, making sure that his aim was true, bringing the dog's muzzle and the gun's to within a foot from one another. And then he pulled the trigger.

Instantly, Maverick's angry growl fell silent. Without hesitating, Michael pulled the trigger again and again and again. He continued to pull the trigger even as he climbed over the fence and dropped down into the grass beside the dog. He continued pulling the trigger until it felt like the pistol was about a third empty, and then he started walking quickly toward the doghouse at the far side of the yard. Drooling and licking the remains of an errant shot from the top of his nose, Maverick hurried along beside him.

Not wasting any time, Michael popped the fill plug from the back of his black squirt gun, releasing a strong waft of chicken broth which prompted Maverick to whimper feebly with anticipation. Michael placed the gun into Maverick's bowl, allowing the remaining ammunition to leak slowly out, and then scooted it around to the side of his kennel where it would be out of sight from the alley.

"You deserve better than that for your help, buddy," Michael whispered as he climbed up onto the top of the doghouse, "and you'll get better when I come back, I promise. And don't worry, I'll definitely be coming back." From the look of him, the words were wasted on Maverick who seemed wholly occupied with the contents of his bowl.

From the roof of Maverick's house, Michael reached a low hanging branch of the only large tree in the yard, a tall silver maple that held an old treehouse that was invisible through the leaves during the summer months. With the strength and grace of a gymnast, Michael pulled himself up onto the limb and tight-rope-walked its length to the tree house, which he entered immediately.

The little fort in the maple hadn't sheltered anyone in years, not since Maverick's best friend, the teenage son, had moved beyond the tree climbing stage of his life. Some of the floorboards were shaky and the whole thing stank of must inside, but you couldn't see out and you couldn't see in, so it served Michael's purpose just fine.

Just as he'd expected, everything in the treehouse was as he'd left it. On the wall hung a cheap, but clean, collared shirt and a pair of khaki pants, and in a neat pile on the floor was a comb, a bottle of mouthwash, a stick of deodorant, and a brand new container of sanitizing wet wipes.

Michael had already cleaned up for the most part and was just stepping into the khaki pants when a familiar roar of barking sounded from just beneath him. Hushed voices and hurried footsteps came a moment later. At that point, Michael's ingrained sense of constant composure kept him from flinching when most people would have freaked. The urge to peek out the door of the tree house was intense, but logic spoke against such action, and it was logic that ruled the calm man's actions, not desire. No matter how badly he wanted to see his pursuers, he wouldn't, because he knew that if he could see them, then they could see him as well. As long as he stayed quiet and concealed in the treehouse, he was completely hidden. The only way anyone would know he was there was if they actually crawled up into the tree themselves, and judging by the sound of Maverick's continuing verbal assault, no one would be setting foot in the yard anytime soon, let alone climbing the tree. For the time being, patience meant safety.

It was only a matter of seconds before the sounds of the scrambling officers faded away down the street and Maverick's barking fell silent once again. Michael, however, waited another full minute before he continued changing clothes and finished cleaning himself up for the first, and last, day at his new job. Checking his watch one last time, he judged that the timing was right to move along. The money and his dirty clothes were tucked carefully beneath the floorboards of the treehouse, where Maverick would unwittingly guard them until he returned. As long as the apartment owner didn't decide to finally take down the old treehouse that week, everything would be fine.

With balance and care that could never have been achieved by someone stricken with fear, Michael crept away from the treehouse atop one of the big maple's heaviest branches, one that reached past the fence that enclosed the yard and over the adjoining property. That property belonged to one of the city's nicest public libraries. Michael had actually been hired to work at the library nearly a week earlier, but he'd had to tell them that he couldn't start right away so that there would be time enough to complete his surveillance at Damon's. He'd be spending the rest of the day in the basement of the library categorizing a large collection of rare scientific journals that had recently been donated. It would be tedious work, probably dirty as well, but with luck he'd walk out at the end the day with a clean getaway.

By the time the library closed, there wouldn't be many eyes left looking for him, and any that were probably wouldn't recognize him from his description as a filthy street bum anyway. By then Michael would be able to walk away at his leisure. In another week, nobody would be expecting to see him again, and he could return at night for the stowed loot. He felt the hesitation at his decision, the little part of himself that was appalled by the thought of leaving so much money behind, but once again logic was the louder voice, and logic said that carrying it away right then would be risky. In a week, the coast would be clear. Not many men could have been so patient, but then again, not many men could have pilfered so much dough from so many dangerous men as Michael had and never gotten caught.

The head librarian, June Reed, greeted Michael as he entered the library, and once again he was briefly stunned at how familiar she was. Her small frame and wise face, and even the way her white hair tinted bluish beneath the library's fluorescent bulbs, all reminded him so much of Josephine Albright, Grandma Jo.

That was what they'd all called her. Of course she wasn't his real grandmother, but she was one of the most important people in his life. She had opened up a whole new world for him and his brother. She had shaped him into the person he was. The person he was *before*, he amended silently.

He liked the old librarian instantly all over again because of the resemblance and felt his determination stiffen in response. June Reed would be disappointed when Michael never showed up again after his first day of work, but in that one day he'd get as much work done for her as he could.

Later that afternoon, Michael struggled to focus on his work in the downstairs archives of the library. It had been a pretty good day as they went, but he didn't feel happy about the good deed he'd done. He didn't feel any satisfaction from having successfully heisted the drug trafficker's money, and he knew already that even when he gave it away to some deserving homeless shelter or soup kitchen, it still wouldn't be enough to induce any pride. He could call himself a server of justice and think of himself as a modern Robin Hood, but when it came right down to it he was still a thief, and it was not a fulfilling lifestyle.

The more that Michael thought about the reality of the life he was living, the more he was tempted to think about the possibilities of another life he might have lived instead. What if he could have stayed with Grandma Jo? What if he was still a Guardian? What if he still had his brother Sean? What if he hadn't ...

Michael shook his head, trying to chase the last, unfinished question away before it took hold of him. Some memories just couldn't be faced, ever. There was no point in torturing himself with the "what ifs." More and more frequently, it was getting hard for Michael to find a point in much of anything. There was no point in going on with things the way they were though. That much seemed clear.

WHERE PICK-UP TRUCKS
GO TO DIE

Twice during the night Kyle awoke suddenly in his new bed, muscles clenched and sweat beaded on his forehead. Neither time could he manage to recall the nature of the dream that had startled him so, and by morning all memory of his sleep being disturbed at all was wiped clean.

Kyle sat in his bed that morning barely resisting the sputtering sound and delicious aroma of frying bacon that slipped into his room from the kitchen. The gurgling in his stomach was the voice of his famished body pleading with him to get up and go join his new foster parents for breakfast, but he resisted. The house was still a foreign place to him, and the two people in the next room were still barely more than strangers.

Kyle gritted his teeth against the sting of loneliness. He still didn't understand what in the world he was doing in Michigan anyway. In just a couple more months he would be old enough to be on his own. Why he couldn't have stayed with his last foster family in Chicago for at least those couple of months, he couldn't imagine.

"None of this makes sense," Kyle whispered to himself.

The words repeated over and over in his mind, and as they did, their suggestive power increased. Might it be that there truly were some legitimate discrepancies? Was it possible that his suspicions weren't merely the result of his bitterness over the transfer? The more he thought about it, the more confident he became that he wasn't just crying "injustice." The whole situation really didn't make any obvious sense. He had never received a good explanation why he had to leave the family he had been with. Things hadn't been perfect with them, but they weren't that bad either. Things were never perfect with foster families, probably with any families. Even if there was some good reason that they wouldn't tell him, why would they send him from the city where he'd lived his whole life to a very rural part of another state? On top of that, he was now living with a couple who didn't have, and had never had, any other children, foster or otherwise. None of it added up to reason.

Every aspect of this most recent chapter in Kyle's life felt mysterious. As much as he was apprehensive about his new foster home and parents, he was curious. This new place and these new people certainly seemed safe enough, but at the edge of it all, barely perceptible, was a hint of fabrication. He felt certain that not everything was what it appeared.

Kyle tried and tried to piece the clues together, but was never rewarded in the end with any fresh insight. He was tired of thinking, and his concentration suffered increasingly as the bacon smell intensified. It was time to get up.

Kyle opened his bedroom door as quietly as possible and started out toward the kitchen. He could hear his foster parents speaking in low voices, probably thinking that he was still asleep. He couldn't quite make out what they were saying, but it sounded as if they were having trouble finding something, maybe the pancake mix.

He paused for a moment in the living room, noticing something peculiar that hadn't caught his attention earlier. There wasn't a single picture in the room. In fact, Kyle had never seen any pictures of his foster parents, or of their families, their former pets, or their anything else. Was it his imagination getting the better of him, or did the whole house look like it had been filled with spare stuff and hardly lived in?

"Good morning," greeted Kyle's new foster mother from the far side of the kitchen.

"Oh, morning. I was just, um, thinking about, um, breakfast. It smells great." Kyle stumbled through his words, burying away his uncertainties before they could be seen.

Marion Thomas was a stiff-postured woman that Kyle gauged to be in her early forties. She had a deliberate manner and a conservative look that gave her an overall business-like quality. Everything she said, she said with purpose, and everything she did, she did precisely. Her clothes were always ironed, her English always proper, and her hair always pulled up and pinned at each side of her head in a way that reminded Kyle of Princess Leia. She was practicality personified.

"Actually," she replied with some hesitation, "Jerrod and I just decided that this might be a good morning to go out for breakfast. Other than the bacon, we couldn't come up with much to make here. I guess we need to make a grocery run. You need to get out and get to know this town anyway, and this is as good a time as any, right?"

Jerrod Thomas, Kyle's new foster father, was in his early thirties and as unlike Marion in demeanor as he was in age. Jerrod was energetic and spontaneous and allowed basically every thought that formed in his head to spill immediately out of his mouth. He was a little taller than average and had a fit build that matched his energetic personality. How the pair could have ended up married was as much a wonder to Kyle as the rest of the mysterious situation.

About five minutes later, after Kyle had gotten dressed and brushed his teeth, the three of them headed out the door. Kyle was mesmerized once again by the beauty of Jerrod's pride and joy '69 Olds 442, whom he lovingly referred to as Betty. Freshly waxed and shimmering silver in the morning light, the customized muscle car had an eager, aggressive look to it that made Kyle think back to all the wild car chases he'd seen in the movies. He imagined what it would be like to sit behind the wheel of such a powerful machine, listening to the quick, throaty response of the V-8 each time he touched the gas, and feeling the big Hurst shifter lock into position as he worked his way up through the gears. If he was ever in a car chase like those ones in the movies, he'd want to be in a ride like Betty.

Just as they reached the car, Marion let out a scream that drew both Kyle and Jerrod immediately to her side.

"Kill it, Jerrod, Kill it!" she demanded, pointing at the side of the car.

Kyle had never seen Marion show much of any expression at all. Something, he knew, must be very wrong.

"Suck it up, Marion. It's just a spider." Jerrod was wearing a face that showed how thoroughly entertained he was by the fuss his wife was making. "I bet it won't even bite me," he guessed as he reached down, trapping the hairy, brown spider inside a rectangle formed with his thumbs and forefingers, forcing it to crawl up onto the back of his hand. "Help me! Help me!" he shouted in a mockingly fearful voice.

Laughing all the way, Jerrod carried the spider a little ways over into the yard, and with the utmost gentleness, he released it into the grass. As he turned and started back toward the car, he quit laughing. The look on Marion's face left no doubt as to how funny she found her husband's behavior.

"Oh, lighten up, Marion, it was just a spider," Jerrod said lightly.

"I hate spiders, Jerrod, and I almost put my hand right on top of the damn thing."

Jerrod glanced over to Kyle, who was doing his best to seem distracted by something in another direction. Without ever looking away from his new foster son, and with his playtime grin creeping back into place, Jerrod spoke to Marion, "Now, *darling*, we need to be mindful of our language. There are Kyle's tender, young ears to consider."

Kyle couldn't help but smile along with his foster father, although he could see that Marion was still thoroughly perturbed.

"That's true," Kyle chimed in after a moment, "I am only seventeen years old and from Chicago. I'm not used to hearing shit like that."

Marion looked momentarily appalled, but Jerrod roared with laughter. His guffaws were so animated that even Marion's stern demeanor began to give beneath their contagious pressure. Her drill sergeant expression gradually softened, and in another moment all three of them were laughing together. It was good medicine as they say, a shared moment that eased the awkwardness between them.

As they climbed into the car, Marion leaned over nonchalantly and whispered into Jerrod's ear. Kyle was sure that he wasn't supposed to have heard what she said, but he heard it just the same.

"Darling?"

Jerrod's playtime smile was his only response.

"Ever drive a car with positraction, Kyle?" Jerrod asked over his shoulder. "There's nothing like leaving two big, black stripes of rubber on the pavement after a take-off. I'll let you slide in behind Betty's wheel and try it sometime when the boss isn't with us."

As they peeled out from the driveway, spraying gravel across the yard, Kyle couldn't help but smile. It wasn't just Jerrod's recklessness, but also the frustration that was evident in Marion's face, that was so enjoyable. How in the world could they have ended up together?

There wasn't much conversation during the ride into town. Jerrod scanned through the radio stations constantly, complaining about how many "wussy" country songs they played around there and about what he wouldn't give for some real rock and roll. Marion appeared annoyed by his comments and his refusal to let any song play for more than a few seconds, but she remained quiet.

Kyle watched out the window, studying the homes and yards that they passed, looking to discover a little more of the character of Steel City, Michigan. The first things that really grabbed his attention were the pick-up trucks. There was at least one in front of every single home, and some had as many as four. Granted, in the yards where there were several, only one or two looked like they were likely to still be running. The others were settled here and there in varying states of decay. Some were rusted so completely that it was impossible to tell anymore what color they had originally been. One said "for sale" across the windshield in what looked to be finger-painted letters. Not all of the pick-ups were crumbling though. In fact, Kyle saw a few jacked-up 4X4's that he figured must be worth as much as the homes that they were parked in front of.

In one yard, a boy wearing nothing but cut-off blue jean shorts was struggling behind a push lawn mower as his father proudly supervised from the front porch. The boy couldn't have been more than seven years old, and the handle bar of the mower reached to the level of his eyes.

In the next yard, a pair of Golden Retrievers galloped rhythmically back and forth along the length of the clothes line to which they were tethered. That house had a mail box shaped like a giant large mouth bass. Kyle had also seen mailboxes shaped like a beaver, a duck, and a bright green John Deer tractor.

Many of the yards were adorned with decorations that seemed laughable to Kyle, and he wondered if that might actually be the intent behind them. Among his favorites were two small flocks of plastic, pink flamingos, scattered garden gnomes of varying heights and shapes, and a plethora of large tree stumps that had been carved roughly into the shape of mushrooms. There was also a pair of two-dimensional plywood cutouts in one flower garden, one that looked like an exceptionally fat woman bending over in a short dress and the other like a man who was holding a running water hose in a way that suggested he was urinating wildly over the flowers.

At last they reached what Kyle supposed they'd call "downtown" Steel City. It didn't bare even the slightest resemblance to downtown Chicago. Truth be told, downtown Steel City was not much more than a bar, a post office, a gas station attached to a party store, and the Country Kitchen Restaurant.

As they slowed down at the intersection with the flashing light, a young couple walking along the roadside, each holding one hand of the toddler between them, smiled and waved, and all three passengers in the car waved back.

"Who's that?" Kyle asked curiously.

"This isn't Chicago," Jerrod explained with a smile. "People here are just friendly like that."

Kyle wasn't sure if that meant they knew who the people were or not. He assumed that they must know pretty much everybody who lived in Steel City. It was too small a place to ever really be able to keep to yourself, even if you wanted to.

Kyle thought that Jerrod seemed unsure about which driveway was the right one to use for entering the restaurant's parking lot. Maybe, he thought, his foster parents just weren't in the routine of eating out very often. Maybe.

They drove around the small dirt parking lot twice before finding an open spot. Kyle thought that half of the town's population must be in there eating breakfast. Other than a beat-up, old Buick LeSabre whose sheet metal skin had been ravaged by "car-cancer", the 442 was the only car in the lot. They were in truck country.

As they stepped out of Jerrod's Oldsmobile, an elderly man being led by a sad-faced, black hound dog greeted Kyle courteously, and he responded likewise. The man looked as though he might be an older version of the young father they'd passed on the road a minute earlier. Only the color of their hair and plaid work shirts, as well as thirty-some years worth of wrinkles, set them apart. Kyle took note in particular of the hat that the man wore. He'd noticed minor variations on the same basic design resting atop at least half the grown men in Steel City. It was full brimmed, but not big enough to be a cowboy hat. It was creased and dingy looking from everyday wear. It was the sort of hat that had everything to do with functionality and nothing to do with fashion, just like the men who wore them. It was the kind of hat that could shade your eyes and keep the back of your neck from getting sunburned. It was simple and it worked. It was a Steel City sort of a hat.

The white-haired gentleman reached the restaurant's entrance just ahead of Kyle and his foster parents, but paused there to tie up the hound dog, who was apparently accustomed to the routine as he settled himself immediately into a comfortable position. The dog's sloppy lips drooped down to the ground when he rested his chin in the gravel, and his eyes were closed even before the man had the leash tied off on a nearby fencepost.

"This is Black Dog," the man introduced, smiling warmly at Kyle. "Not much of a name I know, but that's just what I started callin' him when he first showed up around my place. I s'pose I'd of picked somethin' better if I'd have known he was plannin' on stayin'."

Kyle paused for a moment, reaching down to scratch Black Dog on his wrinkled forehead. The dog opened his brown eyes to half mast just for a moment and then letting out a small sigh, continued on with his morning doze.

The Country Kitchen Restaurant was hopping, a buzz of activity in every direction. Almost all the tables were full, and the conversations, many reaching between and across several different groups, seemed to be competing in volume, each struggling to be heard over those around it. Three waitresses hustled around in a half-frenzy, taking orders and delivering breakfasts as the cook hollered in a raspy smoker's voice that another table's food was in the window, and a frustrated group of elderly women in the far corner waved their empty coffee cups in the air.

Nearly every square foot of wall space in the Country Kitchen was adorned in one way or another. One wall was almost completely covered in framed newspaper clippings, whose topics ranged from the big snow storm of '84 to the closing of the steel mill to Don Curtin's alleged world record zucchini. Steel City High School sports team jerseys were scattered here and there amongst the collections of old Michigan license plates, Mason jars filled with mysterious looking homemade relishes, and model John Deere tractors. Most of the remaining space was filled with a multitude of wild game mounts of both the fury and scaly varieties. Last, but not least, displayed proudly behind the register, was the first dollar bill taken in after the opening of the restaurant.

Kyle wasn't sure if they were supposed to wait for a hostess or seat themselves, but he wasn't left long to wonder. Jerrod pushed ahead through the crowd without hesitation and slid into a seat at the last empty table in the place. Kyle and Marion followed him over together, but as Kyle sat, Marion remained standing. She shot her husband a look, and instantly he was back on his feet.

"We're going to wash up," Marion explained. "Order us a couple of decaf coffees if the waitress comes before we're back."

"A decaf and a regular," Jerrod corrected.

As his foster parents weaved their way through the crowded dining room, Kyle glanced back toward the entrance just in time to see the old man who owned Black Dog finally making his way inside. Kyle felt a little touch of guilt as he realized that they had taken the last open spot while the man had been tying up his dog. He wondered if Jerrod and Marion would mind if he asked the man to join them. It wasn't something he'd have ordinarily considered doing, but this was the land where people waved whether they knew you or not, after all. What could it hurt? The most dangerous people in Steel City were probably kids who made their own fireworks and old men who made their own booze.

Kyle never had to decide whether to invite him over or not. As soon as the old man was through the door, people from three different groups were calling out his name and beckoning him to join them. Charlie, the old man, paused for a second, scanning over the customers, and then spotting someone that he felt like talking with, he waded into the crowd.

"You mind if I borrow the extra chair from your table, young fella?" the old man asked Kyle politely.

Charlie had dentures that seemed to Kyle to be oversized and way too bright, like a long row of white Chiclets hanging down from his upper lip. Consequently, he was having a tremendous amount of difficulty focusing on the old man's eyes as he spoke.

"Sure, help yourself," Kyle answered. "I was thinking about offering it to you anyway when you first walked in the door. I thought that we might have accidentally snuck ahead of you and taken the last open table."

"No need to worry about that, young fella," Charlie assured. "I could go park at just about any table in here, I think. Where'd you folks move here from anyway?"

Us folks? Kyle wondered to himself. Instantly, Charlie's question had stoked the suspicions that had been smoldering in his stomach all morning. Kyle realized that he was being presented with a golden opportunity to try and find some answers. Charlie was a man who knew about Steel City, but for some reason, didn't seem to know much about Jerrod and Marion Thomas.

"Well, I just moved here from Chicago," Kyle began slowly, considering how best to direct the conversation. "I think that my foster parents have lived here for quite a while though. You don't know them?"

Charlie ran his tongue over his horse-like false teeth, thinking for a moment before responding, seeming to recognize that Kyle was looking for more than just polite conversation.

"No, can't say as I've ever seen those two or yourself before right here this mornin'. But I recognize that fancy lookin' sports car that you folks drove in here. I've been seein' it over at the old Smith place on Riverside Road for must be two weeks or so now. The Smiths just retired to Florida about half way through this summer, so I know that none of you have lived right there for very long. Maybe your foster parents lived somewhere else close by before. Maybe not."

"It seems like they'd at least be familiar to you if they'd been living anywhere right here around Steel City, doesn't it?" Kyle tested further.

"Well, I tell you what, young fella, not so long ago I'd have answered yes to that question without much hesitation, but things here in Steel City are different lately. All of a sudden there're new faces around town that none of us old Steel City lifers recognize. It was about a year ago that the old steel mill opened back up, and I guess that's probably about the same time when things started to feel out of sorts around here."

Kyle glanced over toward the little hallway that led back to the restrooms, surprised that Jerrod and Marion still hadn't returned and wondering if handwashing was really the only reason that they had snuck away.

Charlie turned back toward his own table long enough to ask the waitress for a cup of coffee and tell a silver-topped gentleman who had been tapping him on the shoulder that he'd be with him in just a second.

"Anyway," Charlie continued, "it was a real weird deal when the mill reopened. The people who bought the place didn't hire any locals to work there, not one. They brought in all their own people, and they don't have anythin' more to do with the town as they can. Only sign of them bein' here that we ever see are the fancy black cars that occasionally come into town to pick up a few things at Tank's."

"You mean the employees don't live here in town?" Kyle asked.

"Nope, they got barracks out there for livin' in and eatin' in and everything. Not that anybody really knows how things are out there. The truth is, nobody even knows what it is that they're makin' out there. Can't be steel though, that's for damn sure. They got the wrong sorts of trucks coming in and out for if they was makin' steel."

Just then, Kyle saw Jerrod and Marion emerge from the little hallway on the other side of the restaurant. There was time enough for just one more quick question.

"What do you think they're doing out at the mill, Charlie?"

"Oh, it's hard to say. Could be lots of things I suppose, but I'd guess that it's probably somethin' they ought not be doin'. It figures to me that's why they've been so secretive and all, why they picked an out in the middle of nowhere spot like Steel City in the first place. There's nothin' too special about Steel City. Lots of people call it the place where pick-up trucks go to die, and that's about all it is."

Jerrod and Marion returned a moment later, disappointed that their coffees hadn't arrived yet, but satisfied that the revisions they'd decided to make to their story would be enough to keep Kyle's curiosity in check—at least for a little while longer.

A Peculiar Coincidence

As Kyle sat in the restaurant wondering about what he'd learned of the reopening of Steel City's old mill, Ramius King sat within the walls of that mill wondering about Kyle, and about Lily Goodshepherd.

A faint flavor of incense and Beethoven's Violin Concerto floated gently through the room. The subtle cinnamon odor of the smoke and the meter of the classical music were omnipresent in King's study, bits of refinement that served to mask the uglier sounds and smells of the workrooms just outside the door.

The Tall Man smiled at the familiar creak of his leather office chair as he rose stiffly to his feet, tossing the stack of papers he'd been studying down atop his oak desk. The pale skin of his high forehead wrinkled in an expression of concern and concentration. At this point in time, with the script he'd written playing out so quickly, every coincidence needed to be scrutinized. No detail could be overlooked, no misstep permitted. Ramius King didn't like puzzles, he liked plans, and he expected his plans to unfold without unanticipated complications. The suspicious results of the tests that Spencer Simpson, his captive scientist, had conducted the previous day at the school needed to be thought out carefully, and then appropriate action needed to be taken.

King began to pace back and forth across the room as he often did when deep in thought. His long, graceful strides carried him silently over an extremely expensive Oriental rug that he frequently paused to admire. Around the rug, lining three of the room's four walls, there spread a magnificent display of ancient Egyptian artifacts. Most of the pieces were encased in glass for protection, and all were of museum quality, an absolutely priceless collection.

Pausing for a moment as he caught his own reflection in the front pane of a glass case housing a sheet of decayed papyrus, King scrutinized his own hard features. It occurred to him darkly that the antiquities were not the only things his father had given him. He'd also bestowed a crooked nose, a cold heart, and a childhood's worth of accumulated bitterness and spite. Actually, unlike those other things, the artifacts had never exactly been given, just taken.

With his thoughts still lingering on his father, King pulled himself away from the grim face that stared back at him so pitilessly, and continued his pacing. He wondered absently what his father would have to say about the work he was accomplishing within the walls of the old mill. Immoral, he'd probably have said. Or amoral? The difference between them had never been perfectly clear to King, but he was sure that it was one or the other. His father would certainly have disowned him, even cursed him, for the things that he had done, and continued to do, but his father hadn't lived long enough to get the chance. That was a thought that brought a smile to King's face.

As slow and silent footfalls continued to carry the Tall Man back and forth through his little sanctuary, the incredibility of the coincidence occurred to him anew. What were the odds of two unrelated kids, both with the talent, attending the same tiny, country high school? *Lily and Kyle, Kyle and Lily.* The names repeated over and over again in his mind. He hated the fact that he was spending so much time considering these two children, neither of whom was likely to be deserving of serving his supper, let alone causing him any nuance of anxiety, but the fortune teller's vision couldn't be ignored. He'd watched her visions become reality before, and wasn't about to let this one do the same. Somehow, one of those two kids possessed the potential to threaten him. One of them, as harmless as they appeared, was dangerous. Thus, they couldn't be permitted to live. No chance was worth taking at this point.

King was tempted to bring both of the adolescents to his compound so he could examine them before dispatching them. If it was possible to determine with certainty which of the two was the threat, then the other might still become a useful resource. After all, naturally talented recruits were very rare, a precious commodity. But then again, it was just one more potential soldier, a negligible matter next to the possibility of mistakenly choosing to spare the wrong kid. In fact, he conjectured, that might explain how a child could become dangerous, by means of his own training. Better to eliminate them both to be sure, he decided firmly. The vision had to be avoided at whatever cost. That was the priority.

Once again, his whole train of thought led unavoidably back to the fortune teller. King sneered, the expression of a wild dog just catching the scent of a rival within his territory. He despised the fact that so many of his decisions had been based on the flimsy visions conjured by means of the little seer's mysterious brand of magic. There was no avoiding it though, he knew. To ignore the future that she foresaw was to risk everything, and he couldn't afford to risk anything, not now that his designs were approaching fruition.

Most of one year's work at his Steel City compound was already completed before King had decided that another trip to see the fortune teller was in order. He had utilized her abilities before and knew that now more than ever, he needed to explore every possible outlet of additional security to the success of his agenda. He had learned to treat the fortune teller's premonitions as warning signs, indications of problems that could yet be avoided with some caution. He knew that once someone had glimpsed into the future, they were no longer bound by what they'd seen there. He'd proven it by extracting premonitions from the fortune teller and then preventing them from coming true.

He'd made the trip to Miami, the fortune teller's home, and forced himself into her mind, allowing himself to see through her inner eye. A vision of the future had unfolded before him. He'd seen the products of his work at the Mill completed and poised to fulfill the destiny he'd chosen for them. He'd seen his hunters, led by Mason Stone, ready to show the world the reality of magic's devastating power. And then he'd seen himself. It had been dark, too dark to discern details. There were flashes of light, and then a fiery explosion, so bright that it was blinding. Then, lastly, he'd seen himself die.

"Where was that?" he'd asked her desperately. "Where was that vision taking place?"

"Steel City," she'd answered. "Steel City, Michigan."

It was all terribly difficult to believe, but King had known that the fortune teller was far too afraid to lie. How a threat could be hiding right there in the middle of nowhere in northern Michigan, at the very place that he'd chosen to conduct his experiments, King couldn't imagine. The whole reason that he'd chosen Steel City was because of its remoteness, its isolation from any major metropolitan area where his enemies would be more likely to trace him. He had know that the people of such small towns were unlikely to nose into things bigger than they were, and the old steel mill had been there waiting for him, the perfect structure to transform into the facility he needed to house his work.

Originally, King had considered the possibility that somehow one of his enemies had been able to track him all the way to Steel City. He couldn't think how, but it felt more plausible than the emergence of a brand new threat right there in that same tiny town that he'd made his base of operations. Although, the Tall

Man had learned to accept that in the truly monumental moments of history, bizarre coincidences were commonplace, remote chances that occurred as if guided by some higher power. Apparently, that was the case once again. After all, only such a fantastically unlikely twist of fate could explain the results of Dr. Simpson's tests. Fortunately, this was one inopportune coincidence that could be remedied.

The room in which the Tall Man stood had been one of the first projects that he'd demanded be rushed to completion upon arriving in Steel City. His study had originally been the employee break room for the old steel mill. It had been dank and musty, its decrepit furniture inundated with decades worth of cigarette smoke and mildew. However, the walls were thick, and capable of blocking out most of the noise from the rest of the Mill. He knew that a secluded room where he could be alone with his thoughts would be an absolute necessity if he were to maintain his sanity while living and working in close proximity to such classless and ignorant people. He knew that each day he spent among them would be a risk to his own civility. What if their vulgarity and ignorance became infectious somehow? That was his fear.

He shuffled mentally through the ranks of his people, taking a moment to consider each one, how useful they were and how useful they might prove in the future. Most of the workers were just normal people who possessed some skill that was needed for the lab work being done in the Mill or the general upkeep of the building. King had ordered them to be kidnapped from their workplaces and from their schools and from their homes, from wherever they were available. They had been brought to the Mill by force, lab technicians mostly, but also a plumber, an electrician, a janitor, and of course, most importantly of all, Doctor Spencer Simpson, King's pet scientist. They had all been stolen away from the lives that they had known, brought to the Mill to work as slaves, to each play their little part in the grand scheme of their new master. Most of them were only shells now of the people that they once had been, diminished in spirit by the cruel treatment exacted upon them by the Tall Man and his hunters. They cowered when he passed, and it revolted him. They were pitiful.

His hunters, for the most part, were no better. He had recruited them for years, just as his enemies had their own soldiers, always working to gain an advantage over the other side. Sometimes they were easy to find, spotlighted by fantastic headlines of unbelievable news stories. If one of the gifted was identified this way, then it became a race to see who could retrieve them first. More often though, the recruits were identified by means of tests, similar to the ones that Simpson had conducted at the school under the pretense of psychological research. The Tall Man grabbed up those rare talents who were often unaware of their own potential, and he shaped them, cultivated in them the power and mentality that would serve him best. Often times the magic would eventually consume the person they had been, transforming them spiritually and mentally, even physically in some cases. They were powerful and vicious distortions of men, brutish and simple-minded, but also obedient and anxious for the time to arrive when they could make terrible use of the power and hatred that had been developed within them.

Then there was Mason. Mason Stone was Ramius King's right hand, a superb blend of strength and intelligence. Not that he was any sort of science genius like Simpson, but he had the keenness to pick up on subtle details, the patience to think out his decisions, and the foresight to predict the moves of his allies and enemies alike. Mason also lacked the ability to direct his power offensively as many of the others could, but the highly unusual manner in which the magic had evolved in him had proven equally beneficial.

When Mason had been just another of the hunters, he had demonstrated average ability at best, but his ambition was exceptional. He'd quickly tired of waiting for the opportunity to ascend through the ranks in the normal fashion and began challenging his superiors for the right to be promoted to their position. King, admiring the boldness of the shortish, plain-faced young man, permitted the violence to continue. Despite his apparent lack of natural talent, Mason continually managed to claim victories over his apparently superior opponents by means of cunning and toughness, which impressed King all the more. It was a hard time on the ranks, but already it was becoming clear that Mason Stone was destined for a significant purpose, one that hopefully would make the damage he inflicted worthwhile.

Before finally becoming Ramius King's first general, Mason had done battle with a man who prided himself as the deadliest of the hunters. As the Tall Man watched on, Mason had been impaled with the man's weapon, his talisman, but for whatever reason, he hadn't died. The weapon became lodged in Mason's body, imbedded in his flesh, and there it remained as he killed its former wielder, and there it remained still. Since that time, the weapon's magic had been gradually transforming Mason, converting his human flesh bit by bit with something colder, and stronger.

Not only had Mason Stone become the Tall Man's first general, he'd also become his only true peer, another superior being with whom he could relate, at least to some extent. For a long time, King had considered the distance between common people and himself to be something greater than their separation in power, intelligence, and sophistication. In fact, he considered only two possibilities as to their actual relationship. Either he was human himself, and they were something somewhat less, or else they were human, and he was something somewhat more. He suspected it was the latter.

Lily and Kyle, Kyle and Lily. Once again, the Tall Man marveled at the unlikelihood of the whole situation, two undiscovered talents both attending the same little school in the same little town that he'd just happened to have chosen as his secret work facility. There was a part of King that was so curious, so tempted to bring the two into his compound so that he could see them for himself. Perhaps he would recognize some quality in one of them that might explain how they could possibly threaten him. Perhaps if he could see them ... Or had he already?

A memory intruded upon his contemplation, one that aroused a renewed sense of suspicion. Might he have seen Kyle Adams already? Was it possible that Kyle Adams might just turn out to be the same young man who'd acted so strangely outside the school the previous day? People who possessed the talent could often sense a powerful source of magic, and Ramius King was certainly that, but what were the odds that the very person whom he was searching out would appear right under his nose. It would be another extraordinary coincidence, and there were far too many already.

King wondered if Mason, who'd driven him to the school, had noticed the boy. Or better yet, perhaps Dr. Simpson could remember which student from his first day of classes had been Kyle and what impression, if any, he had made.

Crossing back over to his desk, King hit the intercom button, and in his deep, haunting voice, he summoned his pet scientist.

Solidifying the Chain
of Command

Dr. Spencer Simpson was thinking about his family. Rarely were his wife and son permitted to enter into his thoughts, and for good reason. The pain that inevitably resulted when he conjured their images was difficult to bear. The doctor hardly ever allowed himself to recall his past, and he never dared to consider the future. It had been over a year since he'd last seen his family, over a year since Ramius King had sent his soft-spoken enforcer to steal him away right out of his lab at the university, from his groundbreaking genetics research, from his life.

For the first few months Simpson had hoped, dreamed, that a time might come when he would complete the work that was demanded of him and then be returned to his family. He'd been so wonderfully naïve then. Now, instead of hoping for the work to be finished, he hoped instead that it might continue on indefinitely. The reason being, he was one of a small handful of people in the world who knew of the future that the Tall Man was shaping. When the work was finished, everything was finished. Humankind in its glorious golden age of technology was going to be caught completely off guard. All the peoples on earth would be helpless, then they'd be desperate, and finally they'd kneel at the feet of Ramius King and plead for mercy, just as he had.

Simpson squatted down over a lab table, planting both elbows on its surface in a practiced pose, and carefully lowered the tiny, plastic point of a micropipette through a thin layer of liquid buffer and over one of a series of small, rectangular wells in a shallow dish of agarose gel. He'd used electrophoresis to separate segments of DNA strands so many times that the motions were automatic. He could have done it with his eyes closed—usually. This day, however, was unusual. Even though his method was perfect, his nerves were in ruins and try as he might, Simpson couldn't will the tiny measuring device into stillness. He'd be worthless for the rest of the day if he couldn't find a way to expel the picture of Gregor's face from his thoughts. God, how he missed his boy.

Simpson had been haunted all day by the memory of his son, his greatest achievement, who should just have begun the fourth grade. The doctor had awakened early that morning as he always did and headed straight to work, choosing to forego breakfast and the company that he would have had to share it with. While en route to the lab, he'd been forced to pass by the Monster.

That was how everyone referred to the man, and that was the name that he used when referring to himself, and a fitting name it was. The Monster was one of the Tall Man's most cruel and terrifying hunters. As Simpson understood it, the Monster had been one of the very first of Ramius King's recruits, one of his original followers.

The Monster had once been Landon Lewis, an unnaturally overgrown teenager and an outcast from his peers. He had developed the musculature of a mature man when he was still a child by years, and thanks to the magic that was his from birth, the growing never stopped. When the Tall Man found him, he had quit attending school, no longer capable of coping with the isolation and ridicule handed down by his fearful classmates. Ramius King rescued and enslaved the boy, simultaneously soothing his loneliness and nourishing his resentment of normal people. Under the Tall Man's brutal instruction, the magic and the hatred that were already so strong within the young man grew stronger yet, along with his freakish body.

The young man eventually became so grotesquely disfigured by the cruel hand that nature had dealt him that physically he appeared more monster than human being. And thanks to the tortuous life that Ramius King had delivered him into, his insides became contorted to an equal degree. His spirit continually darkened and his muscles continually grew, but his transformation went further still. Fingernails morphed into claws and teeth into fangs. Green eyes stained red, and so did his skin, from which sprouted a thick coat of coarse, black hair. He truly was a monster.

Spencer Simpson was horrified of the Monster, by his appearance and also by the frequent eruptions of his ferocious temper. He avoided the Monster whenever possible, but that morning they'd been headed in opposite directions down the same hallway. The doctor had watched the misshapen figure lumber toward him, repulsed by what he saw, but unable to look away. He'd been so transfixed that he barely even noticed the other man. The Monster had been leading a new worker toward the main computer room, probably a technician kidnapped from some university or private research facility. Simpson had only caught the briefest glimpse of the young man, but it had been enough.

He was too old, of course, but the face was so close. The young man could have been Simpson's son, Gregor, in another ten years. It was a cruel coincidence, and it had sparked the memories which had been so carefully locked away, drawing them up to the surface where they had stubbornly persisted on through the day.

If only he could have been there to send his son off for the first day of the fourth grade. A fresh wave of heartache stabbed into the doctor, and he set the micropipette down, accepting defeat. He knew that the only one way to fight back the panic that threatened to overwhelm him was to realize that his present circumstances were permanent. The only way to ease the longing he felt for his family was to accept the reality that he would never see them again. Even if he could somehow muster the courage to try and escape ...

He ended the thought there, before it could become a complete treachery. There could never be any attempt at escape, because there was no way to hide, nor protect the ones he loved, from Ramius King. The only way for Simpson to keep his family safe was to live on as a slave, as a man without hope.

The Tall Man's summons came then, his deep, commanding voice booming through the intercom, and without hesitation, Simpson rose and headed for the door. His obedience had been made absolute by a year's worth of fear and suffering.

The questions that the Tall Man asked the doctor were answered immediately and honestly. He described the two students from his first day of classes in as much detail as he could, too afraid to do anything less. For all he knew he might have been helping to send both of the young people to their deaths, and still he was helpless to do anything but blindly obey. He was nothing more than a tool of a wicked man, and he hated himself for it. He hated himself for the way he cowered and stuttered in the face of his evil master, and of course, he hated himself for the sinful experiments that he'd conducted in the old mill.

When King was finally satisfied that he'd heard what he'd wanted from his pet scientist, he sent the doctor away. Mason Stone was called to the study next, and

Simpson knew what that was likely to mean. The Tall Man had come to a decision, and it was time for orders to be given and action to be taken.

The doctor shut the door to the King's study behind him, took three steps away, and then stopped dead in his tracks. There he was again, the young man who looked so cruelly similar to his own precious son. He was stumbling, and occasionally being drug, down the hallway by the Monster, who had one toaster-sized fist full of the young man's curly dark hair. The grotesque creature's snarling voice echoed down between the concrete walls, full of menace and rage, promising the new recruit that he was about to learn a very important lesson.

Simpson just stood there, petrified by his fear, and from the renewed shock of seeing the face that could be a mirror of his own son's in another decade's time. He would take another way back to the lab, he decided, a longer way, but a safer one. But just then, before the doctor could flee, the young man turned back, looked him directly in the eyes, and in a voice full of terror, cried out for help.

The doctor's reaction was not truly a result of anger or sympathy. In fact, it seemed as though there was nothing guiding him at all, as if his whole ability to make decisions had been completely disabled. He saw himself following the sound of the young man's screams down the hallway, but he had no idea why, and no idea of what he might do next.

His pace quickened, and soon the doctor found himself following only a dozen feet behind the Monster and his new plaything. He followed them silently into the next room, the cafeteria, still unable to regain any conscious control over his own actions. About halfway across the room, Simpson paused, reared back, and launched a projectile of some sort at the grotesque form he'd been trailing. It was a glass jar of ketchup that he had no recollection of having picked up. The jar struck the Monster in the back of the head, a shot so accurate that the doctor wondered if it could really have been he who'd thrown it.

The Monster turned back slowly, crimson eyes bulging with rage and inhuman fangs bared beneath a curled, quivering lip. Still holding onto the helpless recruit at his side, the beast reached his other massive hand around to the back of his skull, and when it reappeared it was smeared with red fluid. Simpson couldn't be sure if it was blood or ketchup, but it hardly mattered.

Muscles rippled beneath the shimmering black hair that covered the Monster. The brute stood there in silence for a moment, on the brink of unleashed fury, too angry even to speak. When the words did finally come, they were to the point.

"You're a dead man, little scientist, a dead man!"

At some level the scene struck Spencer Simpson as absurd, even comical, like a talking animal from some bizarre theme park.

And then the Monster had Simpson in his grasp as well, dragging him mercilessly across the cafeteria beside the still hysterical new recruit with the hauntingly familiar face. Simpson still felt the strange sense of detachment, as if he were merely an observer to the traumas being subjected to his own body.

"You're two dead men," the Monster growled beneath his wheezing breath, "dead men!"

Strangely, the doctor realized that he wasn't afraid anymore. After having lived in almost perpetual dread for the last year, he finally found himself become passive. In just another few moments he would be dead, that seemed obvious, and strangely unalarming. He deserved to die for the so-called science that he'd created, and maybe, just maybe, they'd have trouble stealing away another researcher capable of completing the work he'd begun. It was a glimmer of hope.

Smack! The doctor was jarred abruptly back to awareness as his face struck the cold tile of the cafeteria floor. The Monster had dropped him and the new lab tech as well. The massive man-turned-beast stood motionless once again, starring down with hateful eyes at a shortish, bald-headed man who stood blocking his path.

"Landon, you're relieved for the rest of the day," the chalky-skinned man hissed evenly.

In an instant, the Monster forgot all about the two men lying crumpled at his side, the whole of his fury redirected at Mason Stone.

"Nobody calls me that, Stone!" the Monster roared, filling the room with his animal voice. "Nobody calls me that and lives!"

The Monster moved forward one cautious step, and then another, creeping in toward his prey. The red hue of his skin blushed brighter beneath the dark hair that stood on end down the length of his bulging forearms. The bony knuckles of his massive, clenched fists turned white as the muscles beneath the surface flexed and the skin stretched.

Mason backed slowly away, carefully maintaining the distance between himself and the Monster. He was pleased to see that he was successfully drawing the raging fool away from the doctor, but was unsure of what to do next. It seemed unlikely that he would be able to talk the maniac out of his tantrum, but he'd try anyway. With maddening calmness, Ramius King's first general repeated the order, the words slipping slowly from the lipless slit that was his mouth.

"Your commanding officer just gave you an order, Landon. Get to your quarters and stay there until you're called for."

Other hunters as well as a few enslaved workers were gathering into the cafeteria, drawn by the shouting.

"I don't take orders from you, little man!" the Monster roared.

Mason halted his retreat then, allowing the space between his approaching adversary and himself to dwindle. With the crowd looking on there didn't seem to be any alternative left, no way to prevent the confrontation from escalating. All thoughts of diplomacy were shoved aside, and as he stared calmly up at the beast towering over him, a foothill in the shadow of a mountain, Mason proceeded to start the fight that he'd been unable to avoid.

"Landon, I'm sorry this had to happen, but your actions warrant a reprimand and as your commanding officer it's my duty to hand it down."

The Monster attacked then, charging forward with such fantastic speed that Mason never even flinched before the blow struck. One of the toaster-sized fists smashed into the side of the first general's head, and the crushing impact gave off a chilling clap that echoed across the room. The single hit flung the smaller figure to the ground as easily as if he'd been struck by a speeding automobile.

Very slowly, Mason began to pick himself up. He made it to his hands and knees before the second assault arrived, a kick to the ribs that carried so much force that it lifted him several feet into the air. He landed atop one of the cafeteria tables, which nearly buckled under the impact.

Spencer Simpson looked on as if mesmerized. He could see Ramius King's first general sprawled atop the table, motionless. He could see that his plain black dress shirt had been ripped open across the chest by the Monster's kick. He could see that the skin that had been exposed underneath looked like that of a manikin. There were no defined muscles, no rolls of fat, no anything. It looked like the man had been carved from smooth, gray rock.

After a moment, with slowness that suggested patience rather than pain, Mason Stone started to ease himself up, but was immediately crushed back down again. The Monster had picked up another of the cafeteria tables and brought it smashing down from over his head like a sledge hammer, ruining both tables utterly with Mason pinned in between them.

The crowd of onlookers gasped in awe, stunned by the savagery they witnessed.

"Look," cried out one of the assembled, shattering a momentary silence that followed the crash. All eyes followed the point of the man's finger to the wreckage that had just been created in the center of the room. There was a barely noticeable shifting of some of the debris, and then out raised a gray face, caked in dust, but expressionless still.

"I assume this means you'd like to challenge me for my position," came the soft, hissing voice. "I think you're making a mistake, but I accept your challenge nonetheless."

Deliberately, the little man worked his way free of the rubble, regained his footing, and locked stares with his fuming adversary.

An array of expressions, including disbelief and rage, passed over the Monster's inhuman face. Crimson lips curled back to reveal predatory fangs that ground against one another, producing a sickening creaking sound. A scream of fury escaped his throat, like thunder and a train whistle, shrill and deep together, and as everyone in the room looked on in horror he began to swell. The shade of his red skin brightened, his face contorted into a death mask, and he grew. The magic raced through his massive body, fueling him and torturing him.

"What a mess," hissed Mason, sounding mildly annoyed. He surveyed the cluttered room, apparently oblivious to the spectacle taking place before him. "We've been cleaning up after your childish fits for far too long, and it's high time …"

Suddenly, just when it seemed that he might actually burst from the surging energy, the twisted remnant of Landon Lewis hurled himself at Mason Stone. The attack was a blur of red and black, a frenzy of pure primal ferocity that carried the two combatants across the room as if they were riding a gale force wind. Claws raked and jaws snapped. Mason's body, truly dwarfed by the size of the Monster, was raised high into the air and hurled like a child's doll. The sound of the gray-skinned man colliding with the cinder block wall was like a train crash, and the concussion was felt by everyone in the room. Mortar cracked and dust came floating down from the ceiling.

"Landon, Landon, Landon," came a quiet hiss from the first general, who was already starting to right himself again.

The Monster's rage enveloped him. The magic, fed by his wrath, exploded inside, and the last thin fragment of his humanity, and his sanity, crumbled. Over and over again the gentle taunt echoed in his ears.

"Landon, Landon, Landon."

The Monster reared back and charged one more time, expending every last iota of his muscle and magic and malice.

When the resulting cloud of pulverized cement settled somewhat, a giant heap of scattered rubble became visible through a gaping hole in the cafeteria wall. The assembled rushed in for a closer look, anxious to see the gruesome leftovers from this final act of carnage. Pushed unwillingly along with the crowd, Spencer Simpson found himself at the forefront. A buzz of hushed, but excited conversation nearly prevented the doctor from hearing the soft scraping which emanated from somewhere beneath the rubble.

A smooth-skinned gray hand emerged from the pile first, followed by an arm, and the dome of a bald head. The smallish man with the expressionless face pulled himself out of the wreckage and stood over his unconscious foe. The Monster's body seemed to have diminished somewhat in size, and the vividness of his crimson skin had faded.

In his ever-calm, unhurried way, Mason Stone walked stiffly to the ruined wall, grasped a segment of exposed copper pipe that dangled there, and pried it the rest of the way free. The first general raised the simple weapon over his head, and in one smooth motion brought it down again, piercing the chest of the twisted creature that lay at his feet. The Monster's head jerked up, his fang-filled jaws gaping wide, but no sound escaped. Then he fell back and was still.

"Would anyone else care to discuss the chain of command?" The slit-like mouth barely moved as the words slipped quietly out, carrying easily through the silent aftermath of the battle. No one responded.

"Is there a problem?" asked a deep, resonant voice from the far side of the cafeteria. There stood Ramius King, dark and forbidding, an image snatched from Bram Stoker's imagination. Every person in the room knew the voice and turned in unison to face the Tall Man with the strange black feather perched over his brow. King allowed the silence to persist for a moment before speaking again. "If there's not a problem, then why isn't anyone working?"

And at that, everyone scattered, fleeing as if his words had been a poison gas that was now spreading across the room. Spencer Simpson tried to hurry away along with the crowd, but a cold, gray hand reached out just in time to hold him back. Mason's lifeless, unblinking eyes found the doctor's own and restrained him with a stare as surely as any chains could have."

"Dr. Simpson, I understand that your skills are paramount to the completion of Mr. King's agenda," Mason whispered softly enough to ensure that it would be a private comment. "I also understand that you would be difficult to replace. However, you need to understand that difficult does not mean impossible. Watch your step before you get stepped on."

Very slowly, Mason turned away, releasing the cowering doctor who darted away like a caught fish just freed back into the water.

"Mason," came the Tall Man's deep voice again, "I'll see you in my study. And get someone to clean up this mess immediately."

"Yes sir," the first general responded evenly.

Mason remained there for a moment, replaying the engagement in his mind blow by blow. Although it didn't show through his stoic exterior, a flame of exhilaration burned in his belly. The Monster had been a formidable opponent, perhaps the greatest he'd ever faced, and yet he'd never once doubted the outcome of their confrontation.

Secret pride swelled beneath the man's flat, featureless chest, and a series of questions formed in rapid succession in his mind. How far had the magic really taken him? Where did the limits of his strength lie? Was it possible that he had become truly impervious, perhaps even against power as awesome as that wielded by Ramius King?

It was a dangerous thought to have, he knew, but a thrilling one as well.

It's a Date

It was a little before noon when Lily Goodshepherd arrived at the Country Kitchen, just in time to start work before the lunch rush. Other than a sporty looking silver Oldsmobile that seemed very much out of place among all the pick-ups, her decrepit, old Festiva was the only car in the lot. Lily's father had bought the car for her shortly after her sixteenth birthday so that she could go out and start earning a wage somewhere. It wasn't much, but it ran, and it supplied a little bit of freedom that she deeply cherished.

Once, on a Monday morning earlier in the summer, somewhere in June, the Festiva had taken Lily all the way to Lake Michigan and back. It was only an hour drive, but it had seemed much further at the time as she'd listened to the constant sputtering and squeaking of the dilapidated, little car. She had shown up for work that morning, but never started. There had been a problem with the gas grills, and the restaurant had been forced to close until someone could come out to fix it. On an impulse, she'd aimed her little car west instead of going back home and driven until she reached water too wide to see across. She'd sat in the dune sands for hours, letting the chill wind wash over her until the bronze skin of her cheeks became chapped. No one, not even her father, had known where she was right then, and it had been invigorating. She'd stared out over the vast water, and the crisp air brought salty tears streaming down from her clear, blue eyes.

As she sat there, mesmerized by the blue horizon, Lily had imagined how it must have felt for the first European explorers who'd set sail out across the Atlantic Ocean, completely unaware of what they'd find on the other side, if in fact there turned out to be another side at all. They must have been terrified and terribly excited, she'd thought. What an incredible adventure! Lily wished desperately that she could have an adventure of her own someday, get swept up in some dangerous mission like the brave characters in the books that she loved. It didn't seem very likely though. She was hardly brave, and her mundane life in Steel City was hardly dangerous.

After parking the Festiva, Lily gathered up her apron, pens, and hair-tie and headed into work, leaving the doors unlocked. This was hardly the big city, after all, and there wasn't anything worth stealing in there anyway.

Lily smiled as she neared the restaurant's entrance, seeing Black Dog napping on the ground with his graying chin resting atop his front paws. She bent over and gave the tire-eyed hound dog a scratch at the base of his drooping ears. He responded with a grateful whimper and a sloppy lick on the back of her hand. It was more affection than he showed anyone else, save Charlie.

The little bell that hung at the top of the door rang. Lily stood up quickly to get out of the way and found herself standing face to face with the new boy from school.

The two of them stood there stupidly, saying nothing.

"Is this one of your new classmates, Kyle?" Jerrod asked over Kyle's shoulder, prompting him to break free of his momentary stupor.

"No," Kyle blurted, inwardly annoyed for failing to greet the girl properly. "I mean she's not in any of my classes. She goes to my school. Is that what you meant? We're classmates in the same graduating class, but not classmates as far as having any classes together. Actually, we haven't really met." *Smooth, moron. Reeeal smooth.*

"I'm Lily," she said in her delicate voice, offering a slender hand first to Jerrod, then Marion, and finally to Kyle. Kyle shook her hand lightly, but stayed quiet. Jerrod introduced the three of them and then walked Marion over toward the car, telling Kyle to join them when he was done talking.

Another awkward pause followed as the two searched for some new direction in which their conversation might move. It was Lily who finally broke the silence.

"So, did you know Adam before you moved here?" she asked.

As Lily spoke, Kyle was lost in thinking that she might possibly be the prettiest girl he'd ever seen. He was dumbstruck, enchanted by the clear, chicory blue of her eyes, and he didn't hear a single word that she'd said.

"Oh, what?" *Pay attention, moron.*

"You know, Adam Horton," she prompted. "I thought that maybe you two already knew each other because of what happened in the hall."

"Nope. I just met him yesterday. His locker's next to mine. I just got caught in the middle of something between him and that Dickers kid."

"Well, I thought that it was really nice how you stood up for him," Lily said shyly. "I wish more people were willing to do the right thing like that, even when it's not convenient, just because it's right."

Kyle was stunned by the compliment, and his response came automatically, without conscious thought.

"I just got caught in the middle …"

"Well, I thought it was sweet, and I'm sure Adam appreciated it," Lily praised further.

Kyle could feel himself blushing, and lowered his gaze in response, pretending to notice Black Dog for the first time.

"I guess I probably shouldn't keep my foster parents waiting any longer," Kyle offered because he couldn't think of anything else to say. "I'm glad I got to meet you here–this morning–like this–Lily." *Spit it out already, doorknob!*

"Actually," Lily went on hesitantly, "we close at eight on Saturdays."

"Oh," Kyle answered uncomprehendingly.

"I'll be here at eight o'clock, I mean, getting out of work. You know, if you happened to be around."

"*Oh!*" Kyle could have kicked himself for being so thick. "I guess I'm not really sure about where I'll, I mean, I guess … I think that I will be around here at eight."

"I really ought to get to work," Lily said as she started to turn away, "and I'm sure your foster parents are ready to go. I hope I'll see you this evening."

Kyle just smiled in response, fearful of doing any further damage by trying to speak again. When the door closed behind Lily Goodshepherd, ringing the little bell again, Kyle turned and hurried over to the 442, flustered and euphoric, and most of all anxious to get to eight o'clock.

"You dog!" said Jerrod accusingly as Kyle climbed into the back seat of the car. "One day at the new school and you're already working the babes. That's quick work, buddy."

"Thanks for breakfast," Kyle responded, embarrassed and hoping to steer conversation elsewhere.

Surprisingly, Jerrod seemed to take the hint, and let it go at that. All the way home, Kyle's new foster parents argued over the radio station while he mentally rehearsed things he could say to Lily later that evening. Maybe he'd even be able to impress her with a couple of complete sentences.

Lily froze just inside the door of the restaurant. Several coffee drinkers from a nearby table greeted her, but she didn't respond, apparently lost in some far away thought.

What in the world did you just do? she asked herself silently. *Did you just make a date with that boy? With that boy that you just met?*

Lily didn't know any of the boys she went to school with well, but she knew more about almost all of them than she did about Kyle Adams. Granted, she had seen him do one nice thing for someone, but who knew why? Maybe the only reason he'd done it was to impress impressionable girls like herself. What she was going to say to him when he came back at closing time, she couldn't imagine. How she was going to be able to get any work done in the meantime seemed equally uncertain.

"Hellooo," called one of the other waitresses who was standing almost on Lily's toes. "Do you think you'll be back down to earth in time to clock in and join us today?"

Lily wasn't sure if she would be or not.

Mason Stone paused just outside the door to Ramius King's study, taking a moment to focus his thoughts, to dismiss the lingering excitement he felt from his contest with the late Landon Lewis. Mason wasn't terribly worried about having to justify the action he'd taken. Mr. King trusted his judgment when it came to exercising his authority over the workers. The Tall Man respected him above any other among the ranks, he knew, which was why he was called first general. However, it was always sensible, even for him, to be careful. It wouldn't do to forget, even for a moment, who that was in the next room. When you worked for the most dangerous man in the world, it paid to tread carefully at all times.

Satisfied that he was ready, Mason knocked against the heavy wood, and almost instantly the door swung open, releasing a subtle waft of cinnamon and Pachelbel's Canon. Mason disliked the stuffy drone of King's classical music, but, of course, he'd never let it show. He never let anything show.

Mason moved deliberately into the study, pulling the heavy oak door closed behind him. Ramius King stood at the opposite side of the room facing away from his first general. He appeared to be examining one of the antiquities from his collection, and Mason waited in silence for him to finish, showing no hint of impatience or apprehension.

After a long minute, empty except for the soft dancing of the flute and violin, King finally turned, revealing the object which he'd been scrutinizing. It was the

Plume of Shu. The Tall Man's long fingers traced its obsidian edges lovingly, but his cold stare now fell upon the man across the room.

"Tell me, Mason, do I possess the qualities of a great leader?" he asked, sounding casual. "Am I the leader here because I inspire trust and devotion, or is it simply that the men recognize my power and fear the consequences of disobeying me? What do you think?"

Mason, instantly filled with suspicion, considered the questions carefully. Men like King never asked casual questions. He was never just making conversation. There was always judgment being passed, a constant testing of character, intelligence, boldness, and restraint.

"It is only because of your power that the men follow you," Mason answered honestly. "They do as you command them because they are afraid. But fear is enough. Their fear of you makes their obedience absolute, and maintaining absolute obedience is proof of great leadership, however achieved."

The Tall Man smiled coldly in response. Of course his leadership was based in fear, and of course the fear was enough, more than enough. He'd have been disappointed had his first general tried to make anything more of it than that. As usual, Mason had known the right thing to say, and as usual, it was impossible to tell what was hidden behind his cautious words. His answer might have been spoken in utter honesty or it might have been complete fiction. There was no way to be certain, and Ramius King did not like uncertainty.

Long fingers continued to caress the inky black talisman.

"You are a shrewd man, Mason. It is as much for that quality as for your strength that you became my right hand. It is that same quality that makes me confident in granting you the freedom to direct and discipline every soldier who serves me as you see fit. It is an immense responsibility that I've handed you, and thus far you've responded to it admirably."

"Thank you, Mr. King," Mason responded automatically in his low hissing voice. There was no hint of gratitude in his tone.

"However," the Tall Man continued as he began to pace across his expensive oriental rug, "the man who died this afternoon was one of my oldest and most talented soldiers. He died at your hands, and I think that you had better offer me an explanation."

Naturally, Mason had rehearsed his explanation long before he ever reached the door of Ramius King's study.

"Of course, Mr. King. I had just received your summons this morning and was on my way here when I came across the Monster battering one of the new lab techs and Dr. Simpson ..."

King sat back into the soft leather of his plush office chair and gently laid the Plume of Shu down upon the desk. He intently studied the little, gray-skinned man who stood before him rationalizing an act that had undoubtedly needed none. The Tall Man regretted losing one of his fiercest soldiers, but he understood that Mason's commands would not be questioned again for a long time. Losing one of his weapons in order to solidify the chain of command, and thus improve the functioning of the rest of his weapons, seemed a reasonable tradeoff.

King considered himself to have a superb ability to read the hidden intentions of the people around him. It didn't have anything to do with his command over the magic, it was just one of those little random talents that some people are born with and others are not. It was a very handy talent for him to have. The subtle blushing of a man's skin, a minor change in his posture, or an increase in his rate of speech could all be valuable clues if read correctly. The Tall Man had a gift for interpreting those little clues, and it served him well in facing both allies and adversaries.

At that particular moment, however, all of the Tall Man's instincts and insights were worthless. The man he studied wore a mask of hardened clay that offered no hints whatsoever as to the intents within. He stood there in perfect motionlessness, more like a marble statue than a living man. His hissing voice slipped out in a steady rhythm, never rising or falling, never hurrying or delaying. He was expressionless, seemingly emotionless. There was nothing to interpret beyond the words that Mason spoke, and those were always so carefully scripted. King did not like the way that his first general could remain so inscrutable. It almost gave the impression that he was not afraid.

"I understand your reasoning," King said when the explanation was complete, "and I accept what you considered to be the warranted response to Landon's behavior. I had shaped him into a very powerful creature of magic, one of the deadliest among my forces I should think, but he always lacked the intelligence to be a complete weapon. He should have known to respect the chain of command, and he should have known when to back down to a superior opponent."

Mason's face remained stoic, but deep inside, his heart rate quickened ever so slightly at his master's words. *A superior opponent.*

Once again, the room was left for a moment in silence except for the soft music. King appeared to be considering something important as his brow furrowed in an expression of … frustration? Mason couldn't be certain.

"Now then, on to the next piece of business," the Tall Man continued at last. "The reason that I summoned you to my study in the first place was to discuss the results of the tests that Dr. Simpson conducted at the school yesterday. It turns out that there are two students at the school, one girl and one boy, who both possess the talent. They are not related, which again increases the unlikelihood of the situation. The chances of finding one such rare individual in one little school is incredibly remote, but the chances of finding two are astronomical. I have considered these circumstances carefully and have decided that precaution must win out over opportunity. I assume that only one of this pair is the threat foreseen in the fortune teller's vision, but I will not risk the possibility of choosing incorrectly which it is. Therefore, I would like you to send men this very night to track them both down and eliminate them from my list of concerns."

Mason nodded once in response and then started back toward the door.

"And one other thing," King added, freezing his first general between strides, "do try and avoid killing anyone else in my service for the remainder of the day. That is all."

The Girl of His Dreams

To Kyle's surprise, Marion's horror, and Jerrod's delight, the 442 rumbled into the driveway at the house on Riverside Road with a little too much speed and slid the last couple feet before coming to a stop. Kyle tried, and almost managed, not to laugh.

After letting Kyle out from the back seat, Jerrod paused, not moving immediately toward the house as his wife did. "Us boys will be just a minute behind you, Marion," he said. "I want to show Kyle a few things about the car."

Marion looked suspiciously at her younger husband for a moment, but then continued on inside.

"I don't know too much about cars," admitted Kyle as his eyes traced over the smooth lines of the silver Oldsmobile. "My old foster father taught me how to change the oil and filter, but that's about it."

"That's all right," Jerrod responded sincerely. "It'll be my pleasure to introduce you to the craft, especially with an educational model as fine as my Betty. But maybe your first lesson could wait for another day, if that's alright with you?"

Jerrod peered over toward the house for a moment, his gaze shifting from one window to the next. Then, once he was satisfied that Marion wasn't keeping an eye on them, he started off toward a rickety, old shed that sat at the back edge of the yard, motioning for Kyle to follow him. Once they were both safely out of view from the house, Jerrod reached into his pocket and retrieved a soft pack of Marlboro Lights and a shiny Zippo lighter that said "The Doors" on each side. He offered a cigarette to Kyle, who refused, and then proceeded to light one for himself. His first drag was a deep one, and it was followed by an even deeper sigh of satisfaction.

"The old lady thinks I quit," Jerrod explained, "so keep your lips zipped, okay?"

Kyle nodded, and smiled.

"So, tell me what you really think of that little, blonde cutie you were talking to at the restaurant," Jerrod prompted.

Kyle smiled again, surprised anew at the behavior of his foster father. He was so laid back, even cool, so completely opposite of Marion.

"I think that she might be the girl of my dreams," Kyle admitted, fully aware that he was blushing again.

"Think you might ask her out?"

To that, Kyle didn't respond. His expression went blank and his stare distant. Something that he'd just said had sent up a flag in his mind, an alert to a connection that he'd nearly made, but not quite. He had the sense that somehow he should have just made an important realization, but it was kept just barely out of his reach. *The girl of his dreams.*

"You should," Jerrod continued finally, mistaking Kyle's distraction for consideration. "After all, you are the only city man in this town full of country boys. How could she resist?"

Kyle laughed at his foster father's encouragement, thinking that it was the sort of thing you'd expect to hear from a school buddy, not a parent.

"Actually, I'm supposed to meet her at the restaurant when she gets out of work this evening," Kyle said finally, breaking free from his reverie.

"Nice work. Want to borrow Betty for the night?"

"Hell yes!" Kyle blurted. "I mean, if you're sure that it's alright. If you don't think that Marion would ..."

"Now hold on just a second." Jerrod scrutinized Kyle for a moment as the mischievous grin crept back onto his face. "Who is it you think wears the pants in this family, anyway?" From the pocket of his jeans, Jerrod fished out the keys for the 442 and handed them to Kyle. "Take her out, show her off, let her work her magic on your girl, and then at the end of the night bring her on home to her daddy."

Kyle studied the keys reverently for a moment, and then jammed them into his pocket.

Jerrod dropped his butt into the grass, ground it with the tow of his shoe, and then motioned for Kyle to follow him back to the house. He tucked the soft pack back into his jacket pocket and pulled out two sticks of peppermint gum in its place. He gave one stick to Kyle and winked, seeming pleased with his own sly-ness.

Kyle accepted the gum and laughed in spite of himself. Judging by how care-fully Jerrod was hiding his smoking habit, it seemed clear enough who "wore the pants in the family." How in the world could they have ended up together?

Time was running short. It had been the fastest shift that Lily had ever worked. Eight hours had raced by and despite her almost continuous introspec-tion during that time, she still hadn't been able to figure out what in the world had come over her. As a result of her momentary slip into reckless impulsiveness, a boy that she'd just met, and knew hardly anything about, would be there to meet her in a matter of minutes.

It occurred to Lily that she hadn't eaten anything that morning before heading off to work. Perhaps that was the true explanation for her rash behavior. Maybe her momentary lapse in judgment had simply been the result of temporary mal-nutrition. If that was the case, was she really obligated to keep the date? Was she responsible for decisions made under the duress of low blood sugar? It was a cre-ative attempt to rationalize taking the easy way out, but it was hardly a legitimate excuse.

Lily couldn't remember being so excited and so full of dread in her whole life, except perhaps for the first time that she'd discovered her special talent. She let her thoughts drift back to that day as she began wiping down the table tops, happy to have stumbled onto a memory powerful enough to keep her distracted for a while.

She recalled the day in the stop-motion way all memories from early child-hood are kept. She retrieved pictures from the archives of her mind, white-flow-ered water lilies growing along a wide, slow moving section of the Brooke River and the little frogs and insects that warm themselves in the sun resting atop the floating leaves. She remembered how hot it had been that day, August in full bloom, swelteringly humid even in the shade. Her father had brought her up the river on his tiny motorboat to fish and eat a picnic lunch, and she'd been wonder-fully eager to go. She'd loved fishing at six years old, so long as she didn't have to bait her own hook.

They spread a blanket out over a flat, grassy spot in the shade of a weeping willow, but before they could spread the food or wet a line her father had fallen asleep. He'd worked so much back then and was always tired out. She hadn't understood then that all the overtime he put in had been for her. Lily's mother had died in labor, giving birth to her, and her father had done everything within his power to see to it that she didn't miss out on the things that he couldn't provide for her himself. She always had the best daycare and the nicest playgroups. He worked almost constantly so that he could pay for those things and everything else she'd needed, except for a mother. Those couldn't be purchased.

The way Lily's father had slept that day was a testament to his fatigue, leaned back against the ragged bark of the big willow with his chin at his chest. He surely hadn't meant to fall asleep and leave her unattended. She was only six.

Lily had chosen not to disturb his nap. She'd wandered down along the bank of the river, humming the songs she'd learned in playgroup for the turtles and birds and whoever else she'd thought to be listening. She'd come upon a sandy strip at an elbow in the river, a worthy beach to her young eyes, and she'd stopped there to cool her feet in the water.

She remembered how the hot wind had felt as it blew against her face and how the sand had felt as she let it slip through her tiny fingers, soft and warmed by the afternoon sun. She remembered being startled, but then refreshed, as she dipped her bare toes into the river's chill current. She remembered closing her eyes and allowing herself to become lost in the peacefulness, in the clean smell of the air and the lulling rhythms of the wind and the water. She didn't remember lying back on the sand or drifting off to sleep, but she had.

Lily had slipped away from the waking world, wandering in her subconscious from one secret adventure to the next. She'd dreamed that she was sailing across the ocean, crossing water so wide that the other side was out of sight. She'd dreamed of raging storms and lavender sunsets, of smiling friends and snarling enemies. Her last dream before waking had been a bad one. She'd dreamed about a snake, a giant serpent with unblinking eyes and a wicked forked tongue that flicked in and out threateningly. She had always been afraid of snakes. The snake was coming for her, to devour her. It slithered, no swam, toward her with frightening speed.

Then she'd awakened. Or had she? She had felt herself escaping from sleep, and her senses had flooded with vibrant perceptions to replace the fuzzy impressions of the dreams, but something was strange. Her thoughts drifted through that mysterious place where you can find yourself only for the moment between dreaming and waking, where the line that separates reality from fantasy is blurred beyond recognition. She could hear the river once again, and she could feel the heat in her cheeks from having dozed in the open sunlight. She must have been awake, but something from her dream was still there—the snake. It was a fat, black water snake, squirming its long body along the surface of the water in whiplash esses, headed right for her. She was so scared that she couldn't even scream.

Instead she threw her hands out before her, thrusting her palms forward defensively.

Water suddenly exploded up in all directions, blasted away from Lily so completely that for a moment a small section of the riverbed lay dry around her wrinkled toes. Who knew where the snake had gone. Wherever it had ended up, it certainly must have been afraid for its life.

The water had settled back into place a split-second later, covering her feet once again, and six year old Lily had been left there wondering what had happened. It had been like magic. That's when the old man had arrived.

Thinking back on it from seventeen years old, Lily had to wonder how much of her memory was genuine and how much was embellished or altered, or perhaps even fabricated altogether. It had all happened so long ago, when she was so young, and it had all been so mysterious.

The way she remembered it, the old man had been sitting there not ten feet from her when she'd first noticed him. It was like he'd been there the whole time. She couldn't imagine how that was possible, but that was how it had seemed. He'd complimented her on how she'd handled the snake. She thought that it may have actually been he who'd made it happen, but he'd assured her that was not the case. He told her that she had magic, and that if she practiced with it she could learn to bring it to life on command, whenever she wanted. He'd also told her that it had to be kept secret, that no one else, not even her father, could ever know about it.

In her memory the old man appeared like a fairy tale being, too wonderful and mystical to be real. As she'd watched him leave, strolling down along the bank of the river, struggling to ignite a corncob pipe, a black dog had materialized from the forest and followed him at a distance. She'd thought of it as a wolf at the time, but that was probably just her childish imagination. Surely, it was just a regular dog.

She'd gone back and found her father where she'd left him, napping against the big willow. She woke him because she was hungry, and then they'd eaten their picnic and enjoyed the rest of the afternoon like it was an ordinary day. She didn't say a word about her encounters with the snake and the old man.

Later that night, long after she should have been asleep, Lily sat atop the covers of her bed with the snowglobe set before her, shimmering in dim moonlight. She had willed the flakes to move with every ounce of strength and faith that she could muster, and eventually they had. It had barely been enough to notice at first, but the small success was encouragement enough to fortify her effort, and soon she'd held a miniature blizzard in the palms of her hands.

Lily finally surfaced again from the depths of her memories, prompted by a wispy voice from a nearby table.

"Lily, my dear, could you come here for a second?" the voice asked.

Lily couldn't quite read the expression that she saw on old Charlie's face. He looked uncharacteristically timid, perhaps even embarrassed. It was his second trip in that day for coffee and conversation, and he was the last customer left in the restaurant. He'd seemed his normal self up to then.

"You need something, Charlie?"

"Think that I made a goof-up, Lily," he continued hesitantly. "Think my bill-fold's still at home. I'm awful embarrassed. Do you think that I should …"

"I think that this cup's on me," Lily cut him off as she snatched the check from atop his table.

"No, no," Charlie immediately objected when he saw Lily reaching into her apron. "I couldn't let you do that. I know how hard you work for those tips."

Lily already had the right money for a cup of coffee counted out though, and was headed for the register. "You're all set, sir," she said over her shoulder. "Have a great night, and we'll see you tomorrow."

"Okay, I'll pay you back tomorrow then," the old man finally submitted as he slowly followed Lily to the front of the restaurant.

"It's not a loan, Charlie," Lily corrected, "it's my treat, and it's my pleasure. Doing a favor for someone as nice as you will be the highlight of my day, I'm sure. I mean it."

"You know, Lily," Charlie said, but then hesitated for a moment before continuing, "we're all awful fond of you around here, all us old coffee sippin' geriatrics. I've always thought that you had a sort of a gracefulness about you, and grace is a rare thing to find in someone so young."

Charlie seemed to catch himself suddenly, and his eyes cast down to his feet bashfully. He looked as though he might have more to say, but couldn't quite come up with the right words. Instead he just nodded, smiled, and headed out the door, bending over immediately to untie Black Dog's leash."

Lily watched after the slow moving pair as they shuffled across the dirt parking lot, and she smiled inwardly. Steel City didn't have much in the way of industry or entertainment, or even culture when you got right down to it, but it was a town full of honest, do-good folks. A town is its people after all, not its buildings or its streets or its businesses. Steel City had good people, and they made it a good town.

After paying for Charlie's coffee, Lily reached back into her apron and dug out the check for her own breakfast. She'd had her usual two-egg, cheese omelet on her break, and she knew its cost by heart.

"What do you think you're doing?" asked a voice from the dining room. It was Lily's boss, Aaron Ulrich, who owned and managed the Country Kitchen restaurant.

"I was just paying my break ticket, Mr. Ulrich," Lily explained.

"Oh, I don't think you are," he disagreed as he grabbed the check from the countertop beside the register. "It's my treat today, and it's my pleasure."

Lily started to protest, but didn't get far.

"Doing a favor for you will be the highlight of my day," Ulrich recited with a smile. "Now get out of here. The morning girls can finish your clean-up tomorrow since you had to finish theirs today–again."

Lily wasn't about to argue with that, so she thanked for her meal on the house and headed out the door.

A Dream Coming True

Rosa Sanchez had been waiting at the scene of her premonition for over two hours already, and during the last thirty minutes or so she'd been growing steadily more anxious. She'd obviously arrived way too early, but the dreams only gave her glimpses of the scene that would unfold and the actual time could only be estimated. She couldn't risk being late.

The place where the incident would take place was not difficult to find, and there was a little bus stop shelter and bench right across the street where she could wait in relative comfort until it happened. What she was waiting to do, she still didn't know. Hide and watch? Call the police? Run for her life? She couldn't decide.

Ordinarily, Rosa's response to a premonition was to make an anonymous phone call to the proper authorities and tell them when and where they would need to be in order to stop a tragedy. Her cryptic calls had prompted only casual responses at first, but soon, as the accuracy of her tips became apparent, the police learned to act upon her advice without doubt or hesitation. She always called the same station, and the officers had learned to take her tips very seriously. She never called from home, and she always kept the conversation short in order to ensure that her identity remained secret.

Thus far, Rosa's "heads up" calls hadn't been turned into headlines, apparently indicating that at least a few of the boys in blue were willing to take a good thing for what it was worth and not ask too many questions. Either that or they were unwilling to go public with a story about a young, Latino psychic who tipped them off about crimes that were yet to be committed. Whichever it was, one Miami police station was nailing the bad guys just in the nick of time with uncanny regularity, and unbeknownst to them, they had Rosa to thank.

"You still waiting out here, sweet-cheeks?" asked a by-then familiar voice. The man's face was peeking around the side of the bus stop shelter in which Rosa sat. He was a clerk from a nearby party store, and it was the third time he'd emerged to smoke and intrude since Rosa had arrived. Despite her efforts to deter his attention, he seemed to grow chummier with every cigarette. Rosa was hardly a flirty sort of girl anyway, and that day she had even less patience for cliché pick-up lines and pitiful come-ons than usual.

"I must say," the man continued after exhaling a long line of rancid smoke that blew right into Rosa's face, "it makes me awful sad seeing a foxy little thing like you all by yourself out here, all lonely and ..."

"Was I too subtle when I refused to talk to you an hour ago?" Rosa cut him off. "Should I have been blunter when I told you that I felt like being alone twenty minutes after that? Could you possibly have misunderstood when I told you to kiss off just fifteen minutes ago? I'd rather sit here by myself forever until I die and rot on this bench than spend another second breathing your poison cloud and listening to your bullshit. There, did you catch it that time? Leave me alone, jerk."

The man never bothered to answer. He flicked the butt of his cigarette down at Rosa's feet and tromped back toward the store, muttering under his breath as he went. The only word she could make out was "bitch."

It was a just observation, Rosa thought, a deserved insult, and even a good choice of words. She was a bitch, and she knew it. Most everyone around her knew it, too, although they didn't know why. Only she knew that.

Rosa had been twenty years old when she'd last gone on a date, three years past. She'd only just begun to understand the nature of her frequent and troubling dreams at the time, and she was still living under the assumption that she'd eventually find true love and settle down like a normal person to live a normal life. It was during the spring of that year that Rosa had her most disturbing and frighteningly authentic vision yet. She'd dreamed of a car-jacking, saw it happen along a street that she walked to and from work every day as clearly as if it were real. She'd awakened so upset that she hadn't been able to fall back to sleep all night.

The next morning, after dragging her unrested body out of bed and getting ready for work with her eyes half closed, Rosa headed out along her usual route. She walked without intent or anticipation, simply following her routine. A gut-wrenching wave of nausea and a bizarre sense of déjà vu swept over her though, as she neared a hauntingly familiar scene. The car was there, just as she'd dreamed it, and the same woman was sitting behind the wheel looking through the same purse in the same hurried manner. Then the same man with the green shirt and the tiny silver gun walked up and ...

To her horror, Rosa was forced to witness the same act of grotesque violence all over again. Only this time, there was no waking up at the climax of her fright. It was real, and there was no escaping it.

Rosa rushed back home in a state of shock, and only then, sitting alone in her apartment, did the true gravity of what had happened finally set in. She'd witnessed the future, peeked ahead into time, and done nothing to try and alter what she'd seen there. It was a devastating blow, a wound that would never completely heal. The face of that woman rummaging through her purse would haunt Rosa forever, not in her dreams, but in her every waking hour. Her ghastly premonitions, however, were not recurring as the daydream memory was. The night visions were always new.

Rosa never had another serious relationship after that. The visions became increasingly frequent, and her responses to them occupied an ever greater part of her time. Between them and the scratching out of some sort of living at whatever crappy job she could find at the time, there didn't seem to be much room left to fit in anything else, or anyone else.

Besides being undeniably attractive with her long, auburn curls and big, dark eyes, Rosa's spunky curtness usually backfired, drawing more attention than it warded off. She used to be flattered when she noticed guys noticing her, but it had become a nuisance. There was no point in playing that game if she could never play it to completion. Who could she ever allow to know her that well? She couldn't imagine someone who would be able to believe, let alone deal with, a girl who mystically foresaw the grimmest of what tomorrow had to offer and spent all her spare time trying to prevent those foresights from becoming reality. And yet she'd never really be close to someone if they didn't know. Twisted as is seemed considering their grisly nature, the visions were a vital part of how Rosa identified herself. Her foresight seemed as much a curse as a gift, but regardless, it was the centerpiece of her life.

Then Ramius King had come, and everything had changed again. Since his appearance, Rosa had lived with a whole new kind of fear, not just for the people in her dreams, but for herself. She didn't need a good friend, a confidant, or a sugar-daddy. What she needed was a rescuer, a knight in shining armor, but the world had run short on those a long time ago.

With every passing second, Rosa's fear increased. She was alone there on a dangerous street, and with the sky full of thick, gray clouds, evening was settling into place earlier than usual. Shadows were already stretching and the day's heat had almost completely dissipated. Not that she was afraid of braving the streets alone at night. Rosa knew that people like her, people without money, were rarely targets for the nocturnal predators. She was afraid because she knew that her waiting must nearly be over, and she was afraid because she still didn't know what she should do when it was.

It was almost as if her thoughts had summoned the man, because just then the tourist from her dreams rounded the corner at the end of the block.

Instinctively, Rosa hurriedly scanned around for the trio of muggers that she knew would be arriving next. She spotted them almost immediately, striding cautiously but intently toward the snowbird. None of them seemed to notice her tucked within the shadows of the bus stop shelter.

Rosa straightened up from her bench seat, ignoring the stiffness that had settled into her legs while she'd been waiting. The moment of truth had arrived, and she had run out of time to consider her options.

It wasn't too late to intervene. All she had to do was call out to the soon-to-be victim, tell him to turn around and run, to get inside, to call the police. But would that save him? Or would he just get run down from behind ten steps into his flight? Or would they make her their new target instead? If she sent up the warning signal right then, she might end up spending the rest of her life, all four or five minutes of it, face down in a dumpster in one of those shadowy alleys. After all, she didn't just suspect the nature and intentions of those three young men, she knew it. She'd not just seen what they were capable of, she'd seen what they were actually about to do, or at least try to do.

Her indecision seemed to become tangible, a heavy mass in her skull that crowded out all rational thought. A dozen unanswerable questions echoed in rapid succession in her mind, but there was one that sounded a level above the rest. When Redbeard arrived, who would he turn out to be? Would he be like Ramius King?

Within the halo of a streetlamp that had just kicked on, Rosa could barely make out a steady mist of tiny raindrops that had begun to fall. Had she not been able to see the rain in her vision, or had it simply become lost in her recollection? Could other details, perhaps less benign ones, have been misplaced in her memory as well?

The hoodlums and their intended prey had nearly come together across the street. A chillingly familiar look of terror crossed over the tourist's face as understanding finally came to him. He was a fly just feeling the sticky web of three thirsty spiders.

Testing the Limits of Restraint

Michael walked without purpose or destination, except to keep moving further from the scene of his crime. His thoughts wandered simultaneously with his feet. Up and down the streets and alleys he strode, barely noticing the fading of the daylight, or even the light drizzle that gradually darkened the shade of his khaki pants. He had only the ghosts he carried with him for company, and they were unwelcome company indeed.

The thoughts that arose unbidden within Michael that night were dismal even by his own piteous standards, which was saying something. The routine into which he'd fallen had grown nearly unbearable, but he didn't know what else to do. He needed change, but he needed to keep some sense of purpose as well.

The change might well come of its own accord, Michael reflected, thinking back to the suspicious look he'd seen on the face of the armored truck officer. As his reputation continued to build, the odds of his being captured rose as well. If it was the police that captured him, then they'd surely try and throw him into jail, and that wasn't an option. Michael wasn't the kind of man who could survive life in a cage. If one of the professional criminals he stole from caught him, then he'd be sentenced not to confinement, but to death. Would he still be able to restrain himself, even if they tried to kill him? He couldn't know.

If only he was still a Guardian. But he couldn't go back. Even if Grandma Jo permitted it, even if she welcomed him with open arms, he still wouldn't go. Not after what he'd done. Besides, the one thing that had made him useful to the Guardians in the first place was the one thing he could no longer offer.

No hint of the turmoil within him showed through in the features of his narrow face, now streaked with raindrops. The cool beads ran down across his pale skin and gathered in the shock of red hair that tipped his chin.

The alley through which Michael was currently walking was a particularly grungy one. Piles of trash were heaped here and there, and the building doors that he passed had been permanently sealed for years. It wasn't a nice place for an evening stroll by one's self, but all that was irrelevant to the long faced wanderer. Like Rosa, but to an even greater extent, Michael had nothing worth stealing, which didn't make him much of a target to *other* thieves.

Besides, people always tended to keep their distance from Michael wherever he went. He certainly wasn't practiced up on his social graces as of late, and he wasn't an overly friendly person to have to stand next to in line at Burger King, but it went beyond that. It seemed that in some subconscious, instinctual sort of way, people always knew that Michael wasn't just another guy. There was something very different about him, and it made people nervous, kept them at a safe distance. He was the man who could walk down the busiest sidewalks and never bump another shoulder. Even after the many years of his seclusion there was still that presence around him, undeniable and unforgettable. Someone else might have reveled in such a stately aura, but Michael yearned instead for the careless brushing of sleeves that others took for granted. He longed to be average, to enjoy the pleasures and endure the pains of an average man, but it could never be so.

The constant vigilance that was required of Michael to keep his secret hidden was proof that somewhere deep inside, he still carried the curse. Trying to wish the magic away was like trying to wish away his heart, his stomach, or his lungs. It was as integral a part of him as any of those.

As Michael approached the end of the alley, still slipping along with his fluid, but aimless steps, he became aware of a voice speaking from just around the next corner.

"What do you guys want?" the voice asked. It sounded like a middle-aged man, and his accent wasn't native. There was fear in his tone.

"Just give us what you got, man, and we don't have to mess you up," instructed a second man whose voice was full of youth and local flavor. "Come on, give it up, man. We're serious."

Michael's pace quickened. He scanned around the end of the alley as he passed it by, hoping to find something that could be utilized as a weapon, but there was only useless trash, either too big to handle or too small to be dangerous. He emerged into the street empty-handed.

A sinking feeling filled Michael when he saw the scene in total. There were three bad guys, not just one, and they were standing between the tourist and himself. Their postures told Michael everything he needed to know about their intentions. Startled by his sudden appearance, the nearest of the menacing trio reached automatically beneath the front of his shirt.

Knife or gun?

"Hey, there you are, Bob," Michael spoke casually, forcing himself to ignore the three young muggers and focus on the tourist. "I've been looking all over for you. You must have really gotten turned around to end up all the way over here. You're lucky I was even able to find you."

Michael walked nonchalantly past the three young men as he spoke, hoping beyond hope that they might reassess their odds now that it was two on three and decide to seek easier prey elsewhere. He reached the snowbird without being shot or stabbed in the back, which was encouraging, but when he turned again and met the eyes of the foremost mugger, he knew instantly that his performance hadn't been convincing enough. The greasy-haired teenager stood with his arms crossed over his puffed out chest, and his feet spread further than shoulder width.

He'd roar if he could, Michael thought.

"Know what I think?" the young man asked rhetorically. "I think that you're not really all that tight with Bob here, or whatever the hell his name is. I think that you're just some stupid jerk trying to be some kind of Good Samaritan. And I think that you'll end up regretting it. Now, let's have a little more honesty. How many credit cards you got?"

"None," Michael answered honestly. "I pay for everything with crisp, green bills."

"That's even better. I got a whole lotta love for cash carriers."

At that moment the tourist decided to make run for it. A deep seated urge to flee along side him washed over Michael, but as usual he didn't give in to it. Logic told him to stand his ground.

A memory flashed in Michael's mind, one from the childhood he'd shared with his twin brother. They'd decided to run track together in junior high, and during training runs down the country roads around their home they'd had several inevitable run-ins with dogs. He'd learned a lesson from those dogs about predators. Predators love to hunt as much as they love to kill. If you ran from a dog, he'd chase you for sure. Instinct would demand it be his response to seeing your retreating hind quarters. However, if you stood tall and stared the dog in the eyes he might just stare back. He might just sit there and wonder why you weren't running, why you weren't afraid.

The three young predators tensed in reaction to the sudden flight of the tourist, but none followed. All their eyes were locked on Michael.

Still without panic, Michael searched for options, for any possible means of escape or defense. Nothing. The tourist's footsteps faded away down the street.

"What's that, Bob, you'll go for help?" Michael called over his shoulder. "Good idea."

The trio only smiled in response, baring their teeth hungrily as if they really were a pack of wild dogs.

Michael gritted his teeth as two of the teenage muggers started slowly around his flanks. In another couple of seconds he'd be surrounded, and in the worst possible defensive position. He wouldn't wait for that. He took one big step forward and kicked the pack leader between the legs.

Knowing that attacks would already be on the way from the other two, Michael didn't wait to watch the young man fall. He spun around as fast as he could, which was just fast enough. A tiny glint of reflected streetlamp light flashed through the air. Michael reeled and heard the sound of a blade slash through the air beside him.

The third mugger stood motionless with his hands at his sides, apparently unsure for the moment about what he should do. He paid the price for his hesitation. Lunging forward, Michael threw a low, sweeping kick that completely undercut the teenager's legs, dropping him to the concrete with a thud.

Unfortunately, the kick also threw Michael momentarily off balance. As he struggled to regain his footing another swish sounded from behind him.

The short knife caught Michael in the side, not penetrating his rib cage, but slicing through enough flesh to trigger a wave of searing pain that dropped him to the ground.

Arriving simultaneously with the pain was another equally torturous sensation—temptation. The gash in his side had triggered to life a part of Michael's subconscious mind, the animal part that knows only to survive by any means necessary. To that self-preservation instinct, the cost of that survival was irrelevant, even if it meant sweeping away the lives of three young hoodlums.

Michael rose to his knees, teeth mashed together and fists clenched, shaking all over from the supreme effort of his inner battle. He forced his mouth open, gasping for air, desperate to vent the furnace burning in his chest.

It's mine to control! It's mine to control! It's mine to control!

Michael repeated the litany over and over in his mind, struggling to hear his own thoughts over the pounding of his blood. The pain of the knife wound still throbbed at his side, and its every pulse gave strength to the cause of his subconscious compulsion. If the magic was loosed, it would save his life, whether he wanted it saved or not. It would kill those young men if he couldn't hold it in check.

All three of the dog pack were back on their feet now, although the leader still hunched forward uncomfortably, obviously not yet fully recovered from the kick to his groin.

"What's wrong with him?" asked the kid with the knife as he studied Michael's shaking body and cringing face. "I didn't stick him that bad."

"I think it's a seizure," the leader offered weakly, his voice still high and frail. As he spoke, he reached into each of Michael's pockets in turn, disappointed to find nothing. "I seen my sister have a seizure once, and that's how it was."

The third teenager, the one who'd hesitated to join in the fight, had nothing to add to the discussion. Instead, he stepped forward and hit Michael with a stiff right jab, catching him at the left temple and sending him sprawling across the sidewalk.

"I don't give a shit if you're seizuring or what, jerk. You're about to pay up for kicking out my feet."

Michael didn't realize that it was a fist that had just slammed into his head. All he knew was that his pain had just increased, and his temptation along with it.

Mine to control! Mine to control!

Encouraged by their cohort's aggression, the pack leader and the knife wielder joined in, kicking Michael in the stomach and the back and the face.

CONTROL! CONTROL!

As the pummeling continued, Michael felt the reins begin to slip from his hands. Try as he might, he was losing his restraint. He couldn't concentrate through the pain. He had to get away. If he didn't escape right then, the magic would break free.

Summoning all of the effort he could spare, and still fighting frantically to keep the power at bay, Michael began to crawl. His body still trembled under the strain of his internal battle, but, shifting one limb at a time, he inched ahead. He knew when he'd reached the edge of the street only when he felt the curb beneath his hands, and finally the assault subsided.

The three teen muggers stood gasping, out of breath more from exhilaration than from actual physical exhaustion. They watched their wounded prey drag himself pitifully out into the street. The pale streetlamp light showed that his rain soaked shirt was smeared red with blood from the knife wound.

A car turned the corner at the end of the block. Cowering shyly from the exposing light of the approaching vehicle, the trio flattened themselves against the brick wall of an abandoned factory building, the nearest shelter.

With his eyes still squeezed shut, Michael wasn't even aware of the new danger until the sound of the car's engine reached his buzzing ears, too late to get out of the way. Michael opened his eyes, but was blinded instantly by the intensity of the halogen beams that were bearing down upon him. There was just enough time to realize that death had finally come for him. Strangely, he didn't spend his last moment thinking about his lost life, his unfulfilled dreams, or even his brother, Sean, and the tragedy that took his life. Instead, he thought about all that money hidden in the treehouse above Maverick's doghouse. What a waste.

The car's driver, who was simultaneously talking on the cell phone, smoking a cigarette, and scanning through his favorite radio stations, never saw Michael's dark form sprawled in the middle of the equally dark street.

Michael didn't flinch from the blinding brightness of the car's headlights, but stared straight ahead into his imminent death.

Then suddenly the light flickered. Someone had run out into the street between the car and himself, arms flailing wildly in the air.

The car's driver locked up the brakes and sent the car sliding across the other lane, missing Michael's savior by inches and smashing into a parked SUV. The SUV's alarm blared to life, scattering the mugger trio back into the alley from which Michael had come. The driver of the car stepped out into the rain and immediately began to inspect the damage to the front end of his vehicle.

"Are you okay?" the driver asked after a moment, looking first to Michael and then to the petite woman who'd just saved his life. "What the hell were you doing out in the middle of the street? Damn it! This is my company car!"

Pain still streaked through Michael's torso, but the anxious fire in his belly was beginning to die back. There was no apparent need for the magic now that the muggers had fled. It had been awful close to the surface, he knew. It had nearly gotten free.

Long, dark hair stuck across the girl's face in thick strands, partially hiding her features, but not entirely. What Michael read on her face was strange. There was shock in her eyes, understandably, but there was confusion as well. Perhaps she was trying to figure out why she'd just risked her life so recklessly for a complete stranger.

"I have to get out of here," Michael managed to say over the incessant wailing of the SUV's alarm.

"You're hurt," the girl responded after a moment. "I should call an ambulance."

Even as she spoke, Michael could see the persistent look of uncertainty in her expression. What was she trying to figure out?

"I can't go to the hospital. I just need to go. I can't be here when the cops arrive." As soon as the words were out of Michael's mouth, he realized how bad they sounded. How likely would she be to help him further after he'd just all but admitted that he was in trouble with the law?

The girl looked over at the crashed car, where the driver had climbed back in out of the rain and was making a call on his cell phone. Then she looked back at Michael, pushed the wet hair from her face, and froze, perhaps struggling to decide what to do.

To Michael's surprise, when the girl finally moved, it was toward him. She knelt beside him, draped his arm over her shoulder, and straining, pulled him to his feet. They started slowly down the street, not sharing another word, simply putting one foot in front of the other.

"Hey, the cops are on their way," the company car driver yelled from behind them. "They'll be here in a minute." Having said what he felt obligated to say, the man hopped back into the car, wiping the rainwater from his forehead, and started dialing again on his cell phone. Not only had he smashed up the company car, he was going to be late for his poker night as well. Maybe it was a sign. He'd only been losing money at the table lately anyway.

An Evening to
Remember

Mason Stone had considered the situation carefully before choosing which of his men would serve best in completing the task that Mr. King had assigned. Eliminating two high school students who were at best novices to the workings of their magic sounded like a simple enough matter, but doing it secretly, without drawing unnecessary attention or suspicion, was another. For obvious reasons, Mason did not readily permit the soldiers he commanded to operate outside of the old mill compound. It simply wouldn't do to have local rumors fueled by sightings of men with unnatural powers or inhuman forms. Such secrecy wouldn't be necessary much longer, but for the time being it was an unavoidable nuisance.

On one hand, Mason considered the targets to be readily accessible in the tiny town and basically unprotected. Any of his soldiers would seem to be adequate for the job, but then again, this was an order that had come down from the top, from Mr. King himself, which meant that even the slightest possibility of error was unacceptable. Ramius King was not the sort to tolerate failure, especially involving a matter that he considered to be potentially hazardous to the completion of his ultimate plans.

Mason considered sending Fat Man and Little Boy to carry out the assignment, but had eventually decided against it. Fat Man and Little Boy were his two most reliable soldiers. They were both exceedingly well trained, and both possessed the skill and power to carry out a forceful strike anywhere and against virtually any opposition on the planet. All they lacked was subtlety, but it was a trait beyond their reach. Fat Man and Little Boy would be a sight to behold once Mr. King's siege was underway and all secrets were revealed, but for now it was just too risky to allow them out unless it was absolutely necessary. They were overkill for the task at hand. Sending them to eliminate a couple of kids would be like swatting flies with a sledgehammer.

The first general felt confident that the decision he'd finally arrived upon was the correct one. He had sent out the Snapdragons. That was the name that Mr. King had given to them after their capture some years earlier. Unlike most of the talent that was recruited into the Tall Man's service, the Snapdragons' magic was already quite developed beforehand, having transformed them into things as much reptile as human.

The Tall Man discovered them by tracing back from a series of mysterious killings that were occurring in southern Florida, an area bordering Everglades National Park. Apparently they were siblings who had been outcast early in life because of the way that their magic was shaping their bodies and minds. They had lived in exile from all humanity in the wetlands wilderness for many years until new housing developments infringed upon the land that was their territory. They viewed the occupants as nothing more than new, easily captured prey items.

Mr. King lost three of his soldiers in the capture of the pair, but it had been a worthy expense. The Snapdragons had lost most of their humanity, even their ability to speak, but they were not unintelligent, and not beyond trainability when adequate rewards were offered and suffering inflicted. As long as they were fed and periodically reminded of their subservience, they were very useful tools. The Snapdragons were stealthy hunters, fast and efficient, perfect for the quiet taking of two unsuspecting teenagers. They would do the job and they would leave little evidence, a few tiny table scraps at most.

Kyle shifted nervously in the driver's seat of the 442 and then fiddled for the fiftieth time with the radio dials. He had been stupid for showing up at the Country Kitchen so early. He'd wanted to be sure that he was there right when Lily got out of work, but now he'd been sitting there in the car for twenty minutes, trying to distract himself and hoping that no one noticed him. Twenty minutes in the parking lot behind the restaurant had felt like an eternity with a new doubt surfacing every couple of seconds. What if she had finished work early and already gone home? What if she hadn't really expected him to show up at all? What if he still sounded like a brainless idiot when he tried to talk to her again? What if she found out that there was nothing special about him, that he was just a plain, average guy, and decided that she would be better off spending time with someone else?

Just then, the restaurant's door swung open and out walked Charlie. Kyle had seen Black Dog snoozing by the entrance when he'd first pulled in and known that the old man must be inside. Kyle hoped that he was back again, as opposed to still being there since the morning. That would have been an awfully long time for the sad-faced hound dog to lie there tethered to that spot. Kyle watched Charlie give Black Dog a thorough ear scratching before untying his leash and leading him across the parking lot, presumably toward his home.

Kyle thought back to the strange conversation that he'd had with the old man that morning in the restaurant. It felt like his new life was flooded with little mysteries. So many intriguing clues must all add up to something, but Kyle couldn't imagine what.

And there it was again, that feeling of dread and anticipation that had teased at Kyle periodically throughout his life, that sense of foreboding that hinted at events just beyond the horizon. The quiet, inner voice that used to whisper about doom and destiny was suddenly a scream echoing inside his skull. A realization struck Kyle like a blow, jarring him on the inside, rushing through him with such force that he couldn't resist it, couldn't even consider the possibility that it might be untrue. Whatever it was that he'd been waiting for all his life, it had finally arrived. He felt it instinctively and positively. Tonight was the night when everything would change for him, and there was nothing he could do to avoid or prevent it. His future, whatever it was, started now. The bigger world was about to be revealed.

Kyle reached down and turned off the radio, hoping that in the quiet he might be able to come to terms with the rush of emotions that suddenly threatened to overwhelm him. The wailing voice of an electric guitar was cut short just in time for him to hear the bell above the restaurant door jingle as Lily stepped out. She spotted Kyle immediately and started toward the car, waving shyly, and flashing her secret smile so sweetly that it froze him between thoughts. In the soft evening light, she looked like an angel.

Kyle stepped out of the car, still trying to shake free from the near panic that he was experiencing. As the door slammed shut behind him, a chill ran down Kyle's back, triggering all of his muscles to flex simultaneously, and with it came a whole new wave of trepidation. The feeling was different from what he'd sensed in the car, but it was familiar as well, and in a flash he understood why. It was the same sensation he'd experienced the previous day on the steps of the school.

Kyle scanned from one side of the deserted parking lot to the other, but there was no one else to see except Lily and himself. Then, as he scanned back again in the opposite direction, he noticed the look on Lily's face, an expression that mirrored his own emotion exactly.

"You can feel it too, can't you?" she asked in a voice so small that Kyle barely caught her words. "I've never felt anything like this before. What's happening?"

From the far side of the restaurant, the sound of an automobile door slamming echoed through the still evening air. A throaty, truck engine started a moment later, and its gruff voice began to move away almost immediately, fading within seconds. The kids just listened, never moving or responding in any way. They were too shaken by the sense of foreboding that flooded them to do anything.

"That was my boss," Lily whispered. "He was the last one to leave."

Kyle walked cautiously to where Lily stood and grasped her hand in his own. He could feel her trembling, and she looked as through she were desperate to find some place to hide.

Kyle continued to scan back and forth across the area surrounding the parking lot, certain that somewhere there was a tangible source of his intuitive fear. However, as carefully he thought he was watching, the first of the silently creeping, cloaked figures was only forty feet away when he finally spotted it. The dark form was all shadow and its movements were as fluid and measured as a python easing patiently toward its prey. A long cloak hung about the figure and an oversized hood hid its face in blackness, revealing only a pair of reflective points of light that were its lidless eyes. It was a darker smear among the shadows through which it crept, more like a gap in the light than a solid thing.

As the crouched form eased ever closer to the two teenagers, it managed to avoid making a single whisper of sound. Its progress across the dirt lot was dreadfully slow, but at the same time completely without pause or any shifting of weight. The motion was fluid to the point of being graceful in an eerie way, and as Kyle watched he found himself struggling to stay alert, as if he were being lulled into a stupor.

It was the increased trembling that Kyle felt beneath his grip that finally broke his gaze from the twinkling points of light that were hidden deep within the creature's hood. And "creature" was the right word, Kyle felt certain of that. No man or woman could ever move the way the cloaked figure moved, so stealthily and so perfectly controlled.

When Kyle looked back to Lily, he found that she was now facing away from him. He followed the line of sight from her blank, mesmerized eyes to the second shadowy form, creeping forward in the same deliberate manner as its counterpart. The crouch of the figure reminded Kyle of a compressed spring, and he suspected that whatever it was hiding beneath the cloak, it was a thing of great strength, and that at any moment it could lash out at snake strike speed. He couldn't afford to wait and find out for sure, he knew, but he couldn't imagine that they could escape by making a run for it either.

The Snapdragons continued their simultaneous approach from opposite sides until they were only fifteen feet away from the cowering pair, within striking distance. Their progress slowed to an even more excruciating crawl, so that their motion was almost beyond perception, and their crouch dropped another hair lower to the ground. Kyle realized that an attack was imminent. The slithery hunters' silent stalk was over, and now came the culmination of their patience. If Kyle didn't do something in the next few seconds, he and Lily were finished, but try as he might, he couldn't think of a thing. And then time ran out.

When the attack came, it came from a thick grove of spruce and fir trees that filled the lot adjacent to the Country Kitchen. The attacker sprung suddenly from the concealing shadows beneath the droopy branches of the trees, and the nearest of the two cloaked creatures had been so intent on its own hunt that it hardly even reacted to the ambush. There was a flash of blue light, and the Snapdragon was flung from its feet. It came down hard on its side, but recovered immediately, springing back to its ready crouch and beginning its stalk once again, this time toward its newly arrived assailant.

Kyle didn't wait to see what happened between the two. As soon as the inhuman pair of would-be assassins was distracted, he bolted away, dragging Lily along beside him. He didn't get far though. As he reached the edge of the restaurant's parking lot, Lily's hand tore free from his grip. He slid to a halt, but lost his footing in the loose gravel and fell to his knees. What he saw when he looked back horrified him. The hooded creature knelt over Lily, pinning her shoulders to the ground with two greenish reptilian claws that protruded from the loose sleeves of its long cloak. Apparently it was more intent on finishing its hunt than on defending its counterpart. Lily thrashed with all her strength under the creature's weight, but didn't utter a word of protest. Her voice had abandoned her. Kyle felt his stomach turn at the sight, and his head spun.

The streetlamp at the corner of the parking lot kicked on, and the scene was suddenly flooded in dim, yellow light. The lidless, slitted eyes of the creature reflected the light like golden marbles beneath its dark hood.

"Kyle," Lily managed, her voice a frantic whisper, and the creature immediately shifted one of its powerful green claws over her face, silencing her instantly.

The long, dark cloak of the figure hung loosely across the ground, hiding it and its victim in impenetrable shadow.

Although Kyle felt a desperate need to do something, anything to stop the monster from hurting Lily, his body simply would not respond to his mind's pleas. He was petrified.

With a lightning fast flick of its neck, the creature threw back its hood, revealing a face more repulsive than anything Kyle had ever imagined could exist. The shape of the Snapdragon's head was still mostly human, although somewhat elongated, but its skin had dried and hardened, and had the greenish-gray color of alligator hide. Its unblinking stare fell upon Kyle for a moment, and again he had the sense of being somehow transfixed, as if his focus was being forcibly dulled. The thing lowered its scaly face down to within inches of Lily's own, and out flicked its long, split tongue, probing for a first taste of its prey. Slowly, the creature drew open its huge, yawning mouth filled with row upon row on tiny pointed teeth. Kyle heard a distinctive pop when the jaw bones unhinged. Free of its skeletal restraints, the gaping maw stretched wider still until it spread cavernously over Lily's entire head.

Then Kyle was back on his feet, charging at the stooped form with a full head of steam. He was moving purely on instinct, having never made a conscious decision to take action. Rage filled him, rushing the blood through his vessels so forcefully that he could feel every hammering beat of his heart surge up and down his arms and legs. He lowered his shoulder, intent on slamming into the creature with all his momentum, but the lidless reptilian eyes found him at the last instant.

Powerful lower limbs launched the cloaked figure aside with speed that seemed to defy physics, and one of its wicked claws slashed through the air, raking down across Kyle's back as he sailed helplessly past. There was a tearing sound, and Kyle wondered if it was from his shirt or his skin.

The Snapdragon wasted no time, returning without hesitation to its intended victim, who had just risen to her hands and knees. A grip of cold, scaly fingers closed over the back of Lily's thin neck and forced her effortlessly back down against the ground. Once again, the creature worked loose its overgrown mandibles and prepared to feast.

Kyle picked himself up at the edge of the street thirty feet away, the place where he'd finally skidded to a halt after his failed blitz. He looked around frantically, searching for anything that he might be able to use as a weapon, but found nothing. His thoughts were in such frenzied turmoil that the familiar face doing battle at the other end of the parking lot didn't even register when he saw it.

The reptilian hide of the Snapdragon's face was stretched to its maximum, and sticky saliva dripped coldly onto the back of Lily's neck from the needle tips of its fanglike teeth.

"Kyle!" Lily cried out for help, finding her voice again. "Kyle, help me!"

The heavy weight of the creature's bulk crushed down abruptly atop Lily, pinning her against the ground so hard that she could barely move. It was difficult to pull any air into her lungs, and stars of light began to dance before her tear-filled eyes. Then, everything seemed to go quiet and dark.

A strange curiosity intruded into Lily's mind just as she was accepting the fact that she was almost certainly about to die. She wondered if the magic might somehow have been able to save her?

"Lily, please be okay! Lily, please!" Kyle's voice was a last flicker of hope, but Lily could find no voice of her own to respond.

Then the creature rolled away, freeing Lily's chest to draw breath again. Kyle was there, bending over her, checking her for injuries, begging her to be alright. When she sat up and smiled to reassure her rescuer, he hugged her like he was afraid to let her go. Over his shoulder, Lily could see the reptilian form of the Snapdragon lying sprawled on the ground beside them, motionless. Next to it laid a dirty metal disc splattered with wet, red blood. It was the thing that had saved her life, and in a flash of insight, Lily understood the connection between herself and Kyle Adams.

Kyle also stared down at the still figure, and the weight of what he'd just done slowly settled into the bottom of his stomach like lead. He'd heard the cracking sound of the impact, the sound of a skull caving in. There was no need to check for breathing or a pulse or any other sign of life. The creature wouldn't be waking up.

"Surrender is your only choice," spoke a strong, feminine voice from across the parking lot. "You must realize that you can't defeat me."

Only when he heard the familiar voice did Kyle finally remember the image that he'd glimpsed right after tumbling into the street.

"Lily," Kyle shouted with renewed panic, "that's my foster mother over there! That's Marion that the other creature is attacking!" But even as Kyle spoke the words, he saw the error in them. Actually, it had been Marion who'd attacked the creature, not the other way around, but that didn't make any sense at all.

Kyle started toward the remaining two combatants, still energized with something more than adrenaline, but unsure of what he could do to help his foster mother. Then all at once Kyle recognized the scene for what it really was. As Marion's confident voice floated across the warm night air again, Kyle realized that there was no trace of fear in her words. It didn't matter that he didn't know how to help her, because she didn't need his help.

"I know who sent you here," Marion said calmly, but firmly. "If you surrender yourself to me, and cooperate with my people, your life will be spared. If you continue on with this confrontation, you'll die at my hands. If you return to your master after failing this mission, you'll die at his hands. If you turn and run, he'll hunt you down. You must know that there's no hiding from Ramius King, ever. Our protection is the only thing that can save you."

The remaining Snapdragon and Marion stood twenty feet apart, both frozen in ready postures, looking like two gunfighters from the old-west, each daring the other to draw.

Everything was silent for a few seconds, and Kyle wondered if the creature was considering the options that his foster mother had offered, weighing one against the others, trying to reason for itself how best to stay alive. And then Kyle knew that its decision was made.

The shadowy figure lunged at Marion with frightening speed and force, dagger-like claws appearing momentarily, slashing through the air. The faint blue light that seemed to be emanating from Marion's right hand glowed brighter as she somehow deflected the creature's assault. The momentum of the Snapdragon's charge knocked Marion from her feet, but she was upright again in an instant and appeared to be unhurt. Something had kept the creature's claws from reaching her skin.

The Snapdragon was also poised again in its set crouch the instant it slid to a stop.

"I understand the decision you've made," Marion admitted, a hint of disappointment evident in her tone. "The options left to you were few and poor."

Kyle sensed more than saw the posture of the cloaked creature drop just a touch lower, and he knew that it was about to pounce again.

Before it could, Marion hurled the glowing object from her hand, sent it flying through the air on a line to the Snapdragon's hooded face. A major league pitcher couldn't have been so accurate, and an Olympic discuss thrower couldn't have generated such power.

With blinding quickness, the creature ducked to the side, barely avoiding the shining projectile. Then it straightened itself and started slinking forward toward its enemy, faster this time, anxious. Its opponent was finally parted from her strange and powerful talisman, and she was vulnerable.

Marion held her right hand extended before her, fingers spread out wide in a gesture that Kyle misread completely. If he had seen the calmness in her face, he might have realized his error. It appeared to him as though his foster mother was making a halting gesture, wordlessly pleading her foe to stay away, but that was not the case. A streak of blue screamed through the air, and suddenly Marion's hand was closed again and holding her mysterious weapon. The Snapdragon had gone still, and Kyle could barely make out a growing pool of dark fluid collecting between its clawed feet. The creature fell over a moment later, making no effort to catch itself, a dead weight.

Kyle approached the crumpled form cautiously, wary of the possibility that it might be playing opossum. The Snapdragon was lying face down in the gravel, and its blood, for Kyle could now see for certain that's what it was, had formed a puddle so dark it barely reflected the light from the streetlamp. There was a tear in the back of the creature's dark cloak, about six inches long and surgically straight. Kyle knew without looking that there would be another to match it in the center of the dead thing's chest, over what was left of its reptilian heart.

A strong odor penetrated Kyle's nose, musky and rotten, and he turned away from the carcass at his feet in response, fighting down an urge to vomit.

"I guess this means that we'll be having our first serious parent-child discussion, Kyle," said Marion in a humorless tone. "I'm sorry you had to find out this way. It certainly wasn't our intention. Hold on to your questions for now though, we need to get these two and ourselves out of here as quickly as possible. My car's parked just a little ways down the road. Stay right here while I go get it, and make sure she stays with you."

Kyle stared at his new foster mother as if seeing her for the first time. Had he really just watched her dispatch that vicious monster without so much as breaking a sweat? With all the profound questions that balanced at the tip of Kyle's tongue, the one that came out seemed somewhat superfluous.

"You're afraid of spiders?"

But Marion was already hurrying away, having either missed the question or chosen to ignore it.

Lily walked over to where Kyle stood and took his hand again. Kyle barely noticed, so intent was he on searching for a way to rationalize the impossible things he'd just witnessed. Only Lily's soft voice recaptured his attention, and to her words he had no response.

"Quite a first date."

Mason Stone hesitated. He squatted quietly beneath the limbs of a blue spruce that grew at the other end of the same grove of evergreen trees where Marion had hidden before ambushing the Snapdragon. He was caught in a moment of indecision, but it was also a moment of opportunity, and one that would be passed and gone in seconds. The first general had wanted to see for himself that the Tall Man's assignment was completed satisfactorily, and it was a good thing he had.

Mason had shadowed his own charge, the first Snapdragon, into Steel City to the Country Kitchen Restaurant, the place where the girl, Lily Goodshepherd, was supposed to be found. He'd watched the stealthy assassin settle into a shadowy corner at the end of the building, a spot where it could blend with the other shadows, go unnoticed by anyone who might happen by, and wait for its target prey. Then the strangest thing had happened, the boy had shown up as well, the one that he'd seen at the school, the second target. Not surprisingly, the second Snapdragon was already tailing him, having followed him into town from the house on Riverside Road, but then unexpectedly, someone else had secretly followed him. That someone had been a woman, but not just any woman.

Mason had waited there patiently, watching the boy in his car, both of his assassins, and the dark shape at the other end of the conifer grove which he knew was the woman. He had waited for what seemed like a very long time, but he was patient when patience was required. Then the girl had appeared at the door, and the Snapdragons had revealed themselves. The battle that had ensued from there resulted in the death of both of the Snapdragons. Worse, both of the kids had amazingly survived. In fact, the two seemingly helpless teenagers had come through completely unblemished except for a few scrapes on the boy's knees and back. But they weren't out of danger yet. Mason was in the perfect position to clean up the mess. The targets were both within easy reach, and their surprise protector had momentarily abandoned them, and yet he hesitated.

The sequence of the battle he'd witnessed played over again in his mind, and what he saw gave strength to a suspicion that was quickly becoming conviction. The woman who'd intervened just in time to save the kids had wielded a Gift of Nature, and that meant that she must be a Guardian, which led him to believe that one of two circumstances was true. First, there was the possibility that the Guardians had somehow discovered the talent in one or both of the kids for themselves and sent the woman to Steel City to recruit them. Secondly, and this was the really interesting prospect, it might be that the Guardians had somehow discovered King's new center of operations at the Mill and had brought their own ranks to hide somewhere nearby in response.

Finding out which of the two sets of circumstances was true had to be his priority, Mason realized. If the enemy had somehow snuck into their territory, then everything was suddenly changed, all plans suddenly placed into jeopardy. And so Mason decided that he would continue on a little longer with his reconnaissance.

He crept silently back out from under the prickly tree, carelessly dragging himself over a bed of sharp needles, and then snuck away to retrieve his black Towncar.

A FEISTY HOSTESS

Michael let himself come gradually awake, taking the necessary time to allow his memories to shuffle back into order in his mind. He flexed the muscles of one limb at a time, discovering pain and stiffness everywhere. A headache throbbed behind his eyes, and his right side stung sharply with every breath. Slowly, the memories began to fall back into place. He remembered the armored car, his day at the library, the muggers, and the girl. The girl had risked her life for him. Why had she done that?

"Am I supposed to believe that you're some kind of dangerous fugitive from the law or something?" asked a Latino accented feminine voice.

The sudden breaking of the silence startled Michael, who sat upright too quickly, amplifying the pounding in his head and pulling at the knife wound over his ribs.

"Shit. I hurt everywhere." They weren't the words that Michael had intended to speak, but they were the ones that came out.

"No doubt, I bet you do," Rosa quickly agreed. "That's what happens when you let a couple of little, teenage street thugs kick the crap out of you."

"There were three of them," Michael defended weakly after a moment's hesitation.

"I know how many there were," she threw back. "I was standing there watching the whole thing."

"Were you?" Michael's voice suddenly took on a harder edge in response to Rosa's attitude. "Well, I certainly hope you enjoyed the show. I hope you were

- 113 -

adequately entertained watching the little, teenage street thugs kick the crap out of me."

"Listen, jerk, I almost became a hood ornament on some yuppie's company sedan tonight, and all on account of me having to save your skinny, white butt. Now here you are, moaning and groaning and bleeding all over the place in my apartment. I'll have to sterilize everything you touched in here. I could have just come on home tonight, watched Pat and Alex, mixed me a cocktail, ate some ..."

"Why didn't you?" Michael asked, cutting her rant short. "Why did you do what you did for me? You could have been killed."

"Why did I do it?" she echoed, sounding incredulous. "What the hell kind of question is that? How about this, why did you step in between those hoods and that snowbird? Answer me that one, Redbeard." *Damn!* Rosa caught her mistake too late. She'd called him Redbeard.

Michael didn't respond. Instead, he just stared at the girl standing on the opposite side of the small, dimly lit room. His stare was full of suspicion and curiosity. He studied the girl's long-lashed brown eyes, her petite frame, her dark, curly hair, and her tan skin. He studied her intently for several seconds before deciding with certainty that he'd never seen her before that night, which raised questions.

For one thing, why was there that odd sense of familiarity in the way she spoke to him? Could it be that the girl recognized his face from somewhere even though she was a stranger to him? And there was still that peculiar look of expectancy in her eyes when he caught her gaze, he'd seen it out in the street, and he could see it there in the apartment as well. What was it that she expected him to do?

"What's your name?" he asked.

She hesitated for a moment as if unsure of how much she should divulge, but then answered, "Rosa Sanchez."

Michael didn't recognize the girl's name any more than he recognized the girl herself, and yet even in her introduction he could hear that same unmistakable tone of familiarity, like she was talking to someone she already knew, or at least knew by reputation.

"Well, Rosa Sanchez, my name is Michael Galladin, and I owe you my life. What you did for me tonight was one of the finest things that anyone has ever done for me. Thank you."

"You're just lucky I was there or you'd be grill grime on that shmuck's car now." Rosa cringed inwardly at the sound of her own words. Why did she always have to be so damn snotty? Not that she owed anything to Michael Galladin.

After all, she had saved his life, not the other way around. And yet, Rosa felt a little rush of excitement at finally having a name to put with the face that had frequented her visions for so long, and she hadn't expected that.

"I'm sorry to have interrupted your doubtlessly busy schedule," Michael apologized, a hint of sarcasm in his voice, "but I'm feeling much better now, and I think that I'll get going so as to not impose upon you any further." With that, Michael threw his legs over the side of the small bed, set his feet flat against the shag carpet floor, stood up unsteadily, and then promptly fell back onto the bed. "Shit."

"What you just did there, jumping out of bed like it's the top of the morning and you're headed out for a brisk jog, probably not the smartest choice, Redbeard," Rosa advised, cursing inwardly for letting the nickname slip out again. "You've got at least a minor concussion, a knife wound, and basically the crap kicked out of you all over the place. I'm thinking that you've got a few hours of bedtime ahead." Then, in a softer tone, she continued, "It should really be a hospital bed. You're pretty messed up, and I'm worried that I can't take care of you enough."

Michael looked into the girl's brown eyes and saw that, despite her sassy attitude, she was genuinely concerned about his wellbeing.

"I can't go to the hospital. There's a chance that someone there might recognize me, and that would be bad."

The room fell into utter silence as Rosa considered what that statement might imply.

"You're safe while you're here," she promised. "I live by myself. I don't have friends that stop by unannounced, and I never let in strangers."

"You let me in though," Michael pointed out. "And we're strangers, aren't we?"

"What?"

"Are we really strangers, Rosa? Because when you look at me and when you talk to me it seems like you know me. Do you?"

Uncharacteristically, Rosa paused to consider things carefully before speaking. Telling Redbeard the truth was out of the question, but she had the feeling that he would be able to see through any lie that she could fabricate on the fly.

"The cut on your side is bleeding again," she pointed out, choosing to simply change the subject rather than answer his question. "It needs to be cleaned, and then it needs to be stitched. I work at a veterinary office and know a little of that stuff. I can do it if you want, but it won't be a beautiful job, and I don't have any pain killers as strong as you would want."

Michael just nodded his head in affirmation, accepting for the moment that whatever it was that Rosa saw in him, it would remain her secret for the time being.

About a half an hour later, well into the night, Rosa trimmed the excess thread at the end of her stitching. She thought that she'd done a pretty neat job with it, but it still must have hurt like hell. Michael had never complained once. He'd never even flinched.

"I have to admit, you're tougher than me, Redbeard," she offered sincerely. *Damn, three times with the name!* "Makes me wonder why you weren't a little tougher out there with the criminal adolescents. It looked to me like you gave up on fighting back pretty quick."

Michael thought back to what had happened and what had nearly happened.

"You're wrong," he countered. "When you thought you saw me give up, that's when I was fighting the hardest, the hardest I've had to fight in a long time. You just saw me quit fighting against those boys."

The explanation made Rosa uneasy. It hinted at possibilities that she'd almost ruled out by then. Despite their both being regulars in her visions, Michael Galladin and Ramius King seemed nothing alike. If there was a monster hiding there in plain sight in Rosa's bedroom, then he was wearing a very convincing disguise.

By the time Rosa had concluded with what modest medical services she could think to offer to her uninvited guest, there were only a few hours left before sunrise. Her patient had fallen asleep quickly, no doubt exhausted from the beating he'd received and also from the multitude of over-the-counter pain relievers she'd fed him. Rosa, however, found sleep more difficult to achieve. For one thing, she was forced to lie in the reclining chair covered with a spare blanket since her bed was already occupied. It was worry though, more than discomfort that kept her from dozing off.

Rosa had walked in the cold shadow of a dark cloud every day since her first meeting with Ramius King. He had hurt her in a way that few other people could understand and left her handicapped by a fear of such sweeping and staggering influence that it infected every corner of her life. He'd given her a leash of perpetual dread to wear, but that was not nearly as terrible as what he'd taken from her. The worst of it by far was the realization that King had used Rosa's gift for his own evil purposes, extracting knowledge from her premonitions that could serve him in ways that were too terrible to consider. He had made her an unwilling servant to his own wickedness.

She'd thought of running a thousand times, of spending her last dollar on a plane ticket to somewhere far away and hoping that it would be far enough, but running from the Tall Man, she knew, would be like trying to stay ahead of the sunset. He'd told her what he'd do if she fled. He'd told her that he could find her anywhere, and that if he had to track her down he'd make her pay for it in ways she couldn't imagine. She never doubted that it was the truth.

Ramius King was one of the three people who had shown up repeatedly in Rosa's visions. He had appeared to her so often that she'd memorized his face even before their first meeting. When they finally did come face to face, he'd turned out to be the most malevolent person she'd ever dreamed of, let alone met. And now there, on the other side of the very room in which Rosa was contemplating sleep, lay one of only two other recurring characters from her premonitions. There was a link between Michael Galladin and Ramius King, but there was no way to be sure of what it was.

By caring for Michael as she had, Rosa had taken an awful, but calculated risk. She'd seen what Michael had done that night, how he'd rescued a complete stranger with no expectation of reward and no consideration for his own safety. He'd done the right thing for its own sake, just because it was right, and that was something that Ramius King would never do. Michael had saved that man because it was in his nature to do so. He was a protector. And maybe, just maybe, Rosa hoped desperately, he could protect her.

Then again, he did get the crap kicked out of him by three little, teenage street thugs, which didn't inspire much faith.

Rosa's mind was finally easing out of focus, drifting toward sleep, when a mumbled voice pulled her back, denying her still the rest she badly needed if she was going to make it in to work the next day.

"Hey, you all right over there?" she whispered experimentally through the darkness.

The mumbling continued, half formed words that Rosa recognized as the accidental speech of a dreamer. Michael was talking in his sleep. She sat perfectly still in the old recliner, ignoring the urge to push away a dark curl that hung before her eyes and to wiggle the foot that had fallen asleep without her. She listened as carefully as she could, knowing that unconscious men weren't good at keeping secrets. There could be valuable clues to the mystery of Michael Galladin right there for the taking if only she could understand.

Suddenly, the sleeping man's voice became louder, revealing not only his words, but also the desperation with which they were spoken.

"Not you! Please! It can't be you!"

Michael was so consumed by the horror of his nightmare that he barely even noticed the pain that was triggered throughout his battered body as he sprung upright in the bed. As the familiar images of his nightmare began to fade away, Michael realized that he'd been calling out in his sleep, probably loud enough to wake the girl. After a few deep breaths to steady his mind and voice, he spoke into the night.

"I'm sorry if I scared you," he apologized softly, willing away the tightness in his chest. "I have bad dreams sometimes, but I'm fine." He waited for a response, but none came. He could hear the girl's breathing across the room, sharp and quick, definitely not in the rhythm of sleep. What else to say?

A lamp clicked on beside the reclining chair, a three-way bulb whose first stage barely produced enough light to reach the four corners of the small room. Part of the girl's long hair hung in a dark spiral before her face, hiding her expression, but Michael could sense the girl's fear nonetheless. It was there, unmistakable in the stoop of her shoulders and the strained grip with which she held the chair's worn arms.

"Was it him in your dream?" Rosa asked in a mouse's voice. "Was it the Tall Man?"

Had the light been just a touch brighter, Rosa might have been able to watch the color drain from Michael's face. Very slowly, he stood up next to the bed, strode soundlessly across the room, and knelt down on the shag carpet at Rosa's feet.

"Who do you mean, Rosa?" he whispered secretively. "Do you see a tall man when you dream at night?"

Michael's eyes were still calm, but there was a deadly seriousness in his face that showed through in tensed muscles around his mouth and jaw and over his eyes. His voice had frosted over, and it made Rosa afraid. The man kneeling at her feet had undergone an abrupt change, no longer the Good Samaritan in the street or the needy victim in her bed. All of a sudden he'd become something much more formidable, more dangerous.

"You have to tell me, Rosa," he pressed, taking her trembling hands in his own. "I have to know."

Rosa couldn't find her voice. She already knew that she would tell Michael everything, the whole of her life as she'd never shared it with anyone else. She could feel all of her long guarded secrets surging up into her throat from the deepest pit of her stomach, eager to finally be set loose. It would be terribly exposing for her, but perhaps in the end, relieving as well. She didn't know where to start, how far back to go.

"You don't have to be afraid," Michael reassured, squeezing her hands just a little tighter. "I'll protect you. I swear it."

Rosa, trusting instinct over reason, chose to believe that he was telling the truth.

"Do you know the Tall Man's name, Rosa? Is it Ramius King?"

Rosa shuddered visibly in reaction to hearing the name, all the answer that Michael required.

The drizzling rain from the evening had died away, and in its place a misty haze had settled down into the streets and alleys of Miami. As the higher clouds broke apart, a first view of a bright, round moon opened, offering anyone still awake to see it an enchanting spectacle. A brilliant corona of oriole orange enveloped the earth's barren orbiter, giving the impression that a master artist's creation hung in the sky rather than the actual nightscape. Rosa and Michael stared up at the image through the sole window of her tiny apartment, bewitched by its beauty and appreciative for a distraction worthy of delaying conversation.

Still unsure of how to begin, but tired of waiting for inspiration, Rosa threw caution to the wind and offered up her biggest secret first.

"I've never told another person, not once, but I can see the future." *How was that for diving right in?* She waited a few seconds before continuing, allowing enough time for Michael to think back over the words once, make sure he'd heard her correctly. "I usually dream about a dog I helped at work last week or a day my family spent at Epcot when I was little or a boyfriend I had in the eighth grade. My dreams are like anybody else's most of the time, but not always. Once in a while, I wake up in my bed drenched in sweat and shaking, like it is with a nightmare, but worse. I'm so afraid that it feels like I'm dying, and in my head there's a memory of something that hasn't happened yet. It's like I get to see the replay of the ballgame before it's been played. I usually see things that'll happen soon and close by, someplace I could get to that following day. And it's never anything good. In fact, it's just the opposite."

"You mean like what happened tonight to the tourist?" Michael asked gently, sensing how vulnerable Rosa was leaving herself by opening up so completely. "You see something bad that's going to happen, and then you get there first and try to intervene?"

"I just call the cops," she clarified, making light of the part she played. "I tell them when and where to be, and then I let them deal with it. I didn't make the call tonight on account of you showing up in my dream. I wasn't sure ..." She left the thought unfinished.

Michael heard the suspicion return to Rosa's voice once again, and finally he understood its source.

"You'd seen me before, hadn't you? That wasn't the first time I'd appeared in your premonitions, was it?" He'd worded it like a question, but it came out sounding more like a statement of fact.

Rosa cringed as she continued on, feeling her invisible armor peeled away as more of her coveted secrets were bared.

"There're only three people who have ever shown up in my visions repeatedly, you and two others. Those are also the only visions where I see places other than right here in Miami."

"Tell me about the other two," Michael said, his voice soft, but irresistible.

"One's the Tall Man, Ramius King." She whispered the name as if afraid to speak it too loudly. "I guess you already know him, huh?"

"I know him," Michael admitted gravely. "I've spent the last fifteen years trying to forget him and what he did to me. And what he made me do. Because of him, I changed, and for the worse. Now I can never change back. I can never undo what I did or be who I was."

Michael noticed the look in Rosa's eyes as he spoke the words. In them he saw a mixture of pain and pity that went so deep it was bottomless. There was too much sympathy there to be all for him, some had to be for herself as well. His words had touched at something dreadful inside her.

"The third is a woman," Rosa continued. "She's old, kind of hunched over, but she's not a care home resident, that's for sure. I always get the feeling that she's in charge of the people around her. I could be wrong though, it's just glimpses I get, barely enough to make impressions. I call her Grandmother because she's so old, but I don't have the faintest idea who she is."

"Actually, your intuition landed you awful close to the mark. Everybody calls her Grandma Jo, and despite her age, she is a very powerful woman. She's the leader of the Guardians." Michael watched Rosa's reactions carefully as he spoke. She showed no sign of recognition when he mentioned the Guardians.

"Is she ... like him, like the Tall Man?" Rosa asked hesitantly.

Michael caught the underlying question beneath the spoken words. Rosa naturally assumed that there was a connection between the three recurring characters of her visions, but she was unsure of its nature. She wanted to know about the old lady she'd never met, but probably not nearly as much as she wanted to know about the man kneeling right there at her feet.

"No, she's not," he assured, "and neither am I."

"I didn't mean that. I didn't think you were ..." Rosa fumbled for the right words to form an excuse, but they eluded her. "I saw what you did tonight for that man on the street," she continued after a moment. "I was afraid before that you might turn out to be like King, but I'm not anymore. I trust you."

The statement caught Michael off guard, froze him between breaths. A tiny part of him that had lain dormant for years was suddenly reanimated. He was happy that she trusted him, though he didn't know exactly why, happier than he'd been about anything in quite a while. It was a fairly pathetic admittance.

Rosa noted Michael's pause and insightfully interpreted it.

"Where are you from, Michael Galladin?" she asked, hoping to have a slightly different question answered by a somewhat roundabout means.

"I've been traveling a lot lately," he half lied in answer. "You know, just throwing up my sail whenever I get the urge and letting the wind ..." He left off, losing the inclination to continue on with his euphemism. "I've been wandering. I've been alone for a long time." Michael hated his words even as he spoke them.

"Well you don't have to be alone tonight," Rosa said comfortingly, her voice dropping down to the lowest audible whisper. "You're all beat up and need taking care of, and I'll do it, because I really do trust you."

Michael nearly shuddered from the impact of her words. It seemed ironic that *she* should be taking care of *him*, particularly considering what her visions suggested about the nature of his dormant power. Why else, after all, would she see him along with the two most powerful wielders of magic in the world?

Michael felt off balance as he moved back to the bed to try for some more sleep, following Rosa's semi-professional advice, but it had nothing to do with his injuries or fatigue. Rosa's openness, her quick faith, had moved him and left him with an unfamiliar sense of urgency. He, too, needed to share his terrible secrets. Finally setting them free might be the first step toward freeing himself, and Rosa, it seemed, was the one with whom he could share. She had to be. There was no one else.

Just that fast, Michael's mind was made up. This one time, he would allow his guard to drop, let his demons loose, and Rosa would be his confessor. He would tell her everything, just as she had done for him.

Little did Michael know, however, that Rosa had not yet told quite all there was to tell. Her darkest secret remained between Ramius King and herself.

MAGIC?

Marion didn't say a single word as she drove back to the house on Riverside Road. Neither did any of her passengers, not the living ones in the back seat nor the dead ones in the trunk.

Kyle looked over at Lily sitting beside him. The look on her face was difficult to read. There was fear there, no doubt about that, but there was something more as well. It might have been recognition, some sort of understanding. That didn't seem very appropriate considering the circumstances. It would have made a lot more sense if she'd looked as if she were struggling to make herself believe that the last ten minutes of her life had really happened. Then again, that's what Kyle should've been doing as well. After all, he'd just had a run-in with a pair of scaly-skinned mutants, one of which tried to bite the head of the girl he had a crush on, and the other died from a wound inflicted by his foster mother's glow-in-the-dark boomerang. To say it was out of the ordinary was a gross understatement. It didn't even sound sane. So why not think instead that he was having some sort of hallucination, a psychotic break or something? Wasn't that in actuality more plausible?

Another person might have done just that, hidden the terrible memories behind self-imposed walls of mental bullshit. Kyle, however, didn't need to lie to himself, didn't need to chalk the experience up to fantasy because logic said it wasn't possible. He knew that it was possible. Somehow he'd always known that there was more going on in the world than what everybody saw everyday at school and at work and on the evening news. He'd always felt that it was just a matter of time before he would be plunged into a whole new world of impossibility made reality, and obviously he'd been right. At long last, he'd taken that plunge.

Jerrod was there to greet the three warmly when they reached the house, but Kyle could sense immediately that his usual joviality was absent. After satisfying himself that both of the teenagers and his wife were okay, Jerrod stepped outside the door, but reappeared again in seconds. Kyle supposed that he'd been checking to make sure no one was following behind them.

"Where the hell is my car?" Jerrod asked, his voice edged with concern.

"Don't even start, Jerrod," Marion cut him off sharply. "This is not a good night to mess with me." No one in the room seemed to doubt the truth in that.

"What's happened?" Jerrod asked more seriously. Clearly, something in Marion's voice or expression had impressed upon him how serious the situation truly was.

"Kyle," Marion said in what sounded like a deliberately passive tone, "Jerrod and I need to have a private discussion, so why don't you take Lily into the living room for a few minutes. Turn on the TV and just relax for a bit. Okay?"

Okay? Of course it's not okay! Kyle thought to himself.

"Sure," he said instead. He was frustrated at being dismissed at this point and anxious for an explanation, but he wasn't about to argue with Marion, not after what he'd seen her do outside the restaurant.

Jerrod listened without interrupting as Marion gave a hushed account of their confrontation with the Snapdragons. From the next room, he could hear tinny voices from the television, but nothing from the two kids sitting on the sofa. They were side by side with their heads dipped close together. Obviously they were whispering, but he couldn't make out a word of what was being said, which was good. They wouldn't be able to hear him either.

"And you're certain that they're both dead?" Jerrod asked when Marion's recap was complete. "You're absolutely sure?"

"Would you like to check for yourself?" Marion responded, dangling her car keys in front of his face. "Their scaly corpses are locked in the trunk of my car."

"Of course I don't need to check in your trunk," Jerrod answered harshly, his whisper nearly becoming something more. "I'm just trying to make sure that we're covering all our bases here. You know as well as I do that what's happened tonight changes more than just how we're handling Kyle. This changes everything."

Marion paused for a moment, thinking through the implications of the night's events for the tenth time, searching for angles she might previously have missed.

"I know," she continued. "The creatures were King's servants, and even though they won't be going home to report seeing me themselves, it won't really matter. When they don't return, King will know that they must have encountered a Guardian. His hunters wouldn't have been knocked off in a chance skirmish with local authorities or anything like that, and we all know that his men never go AWOL. He'll know that there's at least one of us around, and you're right, that changes everything."

"Plans will have to be accelerated," Jerrod said, thinking aloud. "Our next course of action needs to be decided immediately. Do we attack while surprise is still on our side, or do we flee before King's hunters sniff out our lair and we become vulnerable?"

"Jerrod, why did Ramius King try to kill Kyle tonight?" Marion asked suddenly, struck by what should have been an obvious question.

"Are you sure the creatures weren't just trying to capture Kyle? Maybe King identified him just like we did, and tonight he was trying to recruit him."

"No, that's not what it was," Marion said shaking her head. "King wouldn't have sent the Snapdragons for a kidnapping. They weren't big and overpowering, they were fast and stealthy. They were predators. No, they were there to kill Kyle, I'm sure of it, and when the girl showed up and got in the way, she had to get it, too. They couldn't leave a witness."

"That's another thing. What do we do about the girl?" Jerrod asked.

Marion shook her head in frustration. It seemed like all they had were questions, but no answers.

"She'll have to stay with us for now," she answered finally. "We can't risk having an outbreak of local paranoia before we decide on our next move. Of course if we decide on an immediate strike against King's compound, then there's going to be a whole lot more than just one girl's crazy story to worry about. It won't be a quiet incident."

Jerrod tried to imagine it, a battle to end the silent war. Twenty-four hours from then, he might very well be taking part in a historical event. Twenty-four hours! He needed more time, more training, and ... and ... a cigarette. Never in his whole life had he needed to smoke so badly.

As Kyle sat down next to Lily on the sofa, it occurred to him that as thrown as he was feeling, she might well be in worse shape yet. Not that he really understood any of what had happened, but he'd already been suspicious about things because of the peculiar circumstances surrounding his move to the new foster home. And he knew from that feeling of dread he'd always had about the future that this was the big thing he was destined to be a part of. His destiny, not hers. Lily was an innocent bystander, caught in the wrong place at the wrong time, and forced to endure the horror of that night. And it was his fault. Kyle didn't know why the creatures had come after him, but he knew that if he hadn't been meeting Lily at the restaurant, then she wouldn't have been caught in their path. *Although, it had been Lily, not he, whom the creatures attacked first, hadn't it? Even when he had charged the one, it had brushed him aside and gone right back after Lily. Why would it have done that?*

"I can't believe that just happened" whispered Lily's gentle voice, interrupting Kyle's train of thought. "That was the most amazing thing that I've ever seen."

"Look, Lily," Kyle began, not having paused to consider her words, "I'm so sorry that you had to go through this. I hope you believe me when I tell you that I had no idea that being around me might put you in danger. I don't even know what those two creatures were, and I certainly don't know why they were after me. If I could go back somehow and keep you out of all this ..." *Did she say amazing?* "Did you say amazing?"

"Of course! Kyle, you need to understand that before tonight I thought I might be the only one."

"The only one what?" Kyle asked, confused.

"The only one with magic. I thought I might be the only one in the whole world who had it."

Now Kyle was more than confused. Had Lily been so traumatized by the encounter at the restaurant that she'd completely snapped?

Lily must have been able to see something in the look on Kyle's face and recognized what it was that he was thinking.

"Kyle, you must know about the magic," she urged. "You have to realize that what we saw tonight was magic, those creatures and your foster mother, too. And you."

Kyle was at a complete loss for words. What Lily was saying was ridiculous, and yet it had started a tingling in the back of his mind, an uncomfortable feeling of suspicion that was all too familiar. He had always known that eventually he'd experience something extraordinary, that he'd discover the range of possibility to be broader than what most people believed, but magic? That was a concept for fairy tales and daydreams. Magic couldn't be real.

"What do you mean *and me?*" Kyle asked, bewildered.

"How could you have saved my life the way you did without magic?"

"Lily, I hit the thing with a manhole cover. That's how I saved your life. There was nothing mystical or magical about it."

"You mean that one-hundred pound manhole cover that you threw from thirty feet away and hit the monster right in the head with?" Lily clarified. "That's right, those things weigh a hundred pounds. You couldn't have done it on your own. It had to be magic."

Kyle's mind was racing. How could he have thrown a hundred pound manhole cover thirty feet through the air? And what were those creatures anyway, some sort of genetic mutants, some mad scientist's experiment gone awry? Was that any more believable than the explanation Lily was offering?

"Look at me, Kyle," she practically pleaded, "look me in the eyes. I know that it's true. I know that magic is real, and I can prove it."

Lily stood up from the sofa, clicked off the TV, and walked over to a window that faced out toward the woods behind the house. A windchime hung just inside the window, a dozen or so tiny glass fish that hung beneath varying lengths of fishing line. When the window was open, the fresh air that was drawn in through the screen would swing the little fish around, and their collisions sounded like twinkling jingle bells. Right then, the window was shut, and the fish were still.

Kyle picked himself up from the sofa as well and followed Lily over to the window, curious to see what she was going to do.

Lily cupped her slender hands around the tiny school of glass fish, almost touching them, but never quite. She closed her eyes and thought about her snow-globe, how it felt under her invisible touch, how she felt when she willed it to life. Thin, invisible fingers of energy reached out from Lily's open palms, caressing the glass pieces, stirring them from rest.

As Kyle watched in awe, the windchime started to move. The glass fish swayed only the tiniest bit at first, but they gradually gained speed, swinging further and further at the end of their lines until at last they could reach one another. It was as if a gust of wind had just swept through the room and set the chime into motion, only Kyle didn't feel any such breeze. Each meeting between the little glass pendulums produced a beautiful ring, and together the rings made a chorus of sound that filled the otherwise quiet room.

Kyle couldn't believe what he was seeing.

The first thing Lily saw when she opened her eyes was Kyle's foster parents staring back from across the room, drawn by the chiming of the glass fish.

"And the surprises just keep on coming," Marion said with a sigh.

The Local Authorities

The first general of Ramius King's forces sat in the driver's seat of his black Lincoln, perfectly silent and perfectly still. Mason had chosen to park the car across the road and down a ways from the house where the woman Guardian's car had pulled in. There was a dirt lane there, nearly overgrown with weeds and tree saplings. It obviously hadn't been used in quite some time. Mason assumed that it was probably someone's lane to get back to their favorite hunting spot during deer season later in the fall.

From where he parked he couldn't even see the house, just the end of the driveway another couple hundred feet down the road. He knew that he was taking a risk by concealing himself so far off, but as always he'd given careful thought to choosing the spot. Granted, he wished that he could observe whatever was going on in and around the house right then, but he couldn't risk being away from the car in case everyone decided to leave, as he suspected they would. If the Guardians were there, somewhere close by, then what mattered above all else was finding them. That little house clearly couldn't be their new base of operations. It was much too small and unprotected. For the moment, the best thing to do was continue to be patient.

The woman Guardian knew that the house was compromised, so she'd have to return to their home lair soon, if in fact it was nearby. She wouldn't expect anyone to miss the Snapdragons yet, so she wouldn't suspect that she might already have a tail. She wouldn't count on someone being as careful as Mason Stone was.

A car drove by just then, only the second that Mason had seen since he'd been waiting. He noted the star painted on the door and saw the brake lights flash red as the car passed the lane where he was parked. It was a cop, and he'd noticed the Lincoln.

Officer Bart Packard was at the end of his shift and headed back to town to meet the guys at The Bar, hopefully in time to see at least half of a great hockey game. The boys had all decided to play the tape of the final game of the previous year's Stanley Cup playoffs that night, and they'd surely started already without him. It had been a long, boring day as usual, and he was definitely ready to crack open a barley pop and toast the Redwings.

When he saw the black Lincoln pulled off the road, Bart had an urge to pull over and check it out. There'd been lots of rumors around about the sleek Town-cars that came into town from the old steel mill. Nobody knew the people who'd reopened the mill, and folks around town were thinking up all sorts of crazy stories about what they were doing out there.

He'd hit the brakes instinctively when he'd spotted the parked car out of the corner of his eye. It was a golden opportunity for him to check out one of those guys for himself, to satisfy his own curiosity. Maybe he'd even find the guy spilling chemicals from the mill back in the woods or something. He hadn't written a ticket all week, and the Chief had been bitching about a lack of productivity. Tagging somebody for illegal dumping would surely get the Chief off his back for a while. It might even be worth missing a few minutes of the Wings game.

Bart made a u-turn that required him to drive off the road on both sides and headed back toward the lane where he'd spotted the parked Lincoln. The Town-car had been backed in far enough that Bart could pull his cruiser in front of it without having his rear end hanging out in the road. When his bright head lights washed over the front of the sleek luxury car, he could see that there was someone sitting in the driver's seat. If they were dumping chemicals, they'd either finished already or hadn't gotten to it yet.

Bart stepped slowly out of his cruiser, pushing back his broad shoulders and sucking in his fat belly. He unsnapped the strap from over his 9mm pistol as he approached the car, leaving his right hand there just in case. It never hurt to be cautious. There were nut-cases turning up all over the place these days, even in quiet little towns like Steel City.

The Lincoln's window slid down just as Bart reached the car and aimed his flashlight at the man in the driver's seat. When he saw the man's face, Bart's fingers tightened reflexively over the grip of his service pistol. Was the guy wearing a mask?

"Can I help you, officer?" asked a slow, hissing voice from inside the car.

The hair on the back of Bart's neck stood on end and out came the gun. He was suddenly humming with adrenaline. He'd only ever drawn his 9mm once, an incident involving some poachers three years back.

"Please remove your mask, sir," Bart ordered. "Take it off very slowly."

The voice floated out from the driver's seat again, just as soft and slippery as before.

"It's not a mask, officer, it's my face. I have a skin condition."

The man in the driver's seat leaned slowly over until his head was part way out the window, giving Bart a clearer view of his face. Could that be the result of a skin condition? The man's face looked like it was made out of dried clay, gray and smooth. He didn't think it was a mask. There weren't any seams around the eyes or nose or anywhere over his bald head. But the mouth didn't look right. There weren't really any lips, just a slit in the skin.

"I'd like you to step slowly out of the vehicle, sir. Do it very slowly." Bart could hear fear in the tone of his own voice, and he inwardly chided himself for it. "What are you doing out here tonight, sir?"

As the man stepped deliberately out of the driver's seat, Bart realized that he wasn't very big. In fact, he couldn't have been more than about five-six, most of a foot shorter than himself. Nevertheless, something in the way the man moved hinted at tremendous physical strength hidden in his smallish frame.

"I had a call on my cell phone," the man replied in his quiet, hissing voice. "They say it's safer if you pull off the road while you talk."

"Well, that's very conscientious of you, sir. Either that, or it's bullshit. Now I'll ask you one more time, what are you doing out here?"

The smaller man just stared back with his lifeless, gray eyes, but didn't answer. He didn't even move, not a bit. He stood there like a statue, so still that Bart couldn't even see his chest swelling as he breathed.

"Look, sir," Bart pressed, consciously trying to sound authoritative, "if you're not going to cooperate with me, then I'll have to take you in and try again later. And I'll have to impound that fancy car of yours." That sounded more like it. Suddenly, Bart was feeling better about the situation, more in charge. He could hear his own voice smoothing out and gaining confidence, sounding more like the cops on the TV shows. Whatever it was he'd stumbled onto, he could handle it. He was the law.

The sound of a car door slamming somewhere down the road reached them just then, and a moment later an engine started up. The gray-skinned man finally moved, shifting his gaze over toward the sounds from down the street.

"I am sorry, officer, but I'll have to be going now," he announced with chilling calmness. "And since you've parked me in, I'll be taking your cruiser."

The words hardly registered with Bart until the shorter man started moving toward him.

"Hold it right there, buddy!" Bart practically shouted, steadying his gun in the palm of his free hand. "I'm serious, stop right there!"

But the man didn't stop, didn't even hesitate. He just kept coming, and Bart began to backpedal to maintain the distance between them. He could see the 9mm shaking in his grip as he tried to aim it steadily. Why wouldn't the guy stop?

"Come on, I'm not screwing around, buddy!" Bart yelled as the man increased his pace. "Don't make me do this!"

BANG!

Bart had never fired his service pistol at someone. He hadn't fired it at all in quite a while. The concussion of the shot was so loud in his ears that it nearly loosed his bladder, but that wasn't the worst of it, not by a long shot. Bart stared blankly at the gun in his hands as the ringing in his ears started to wane, and slowly the realization of what he'd just done set in. He'd shot a man at point blank range. He'd probably just killed someone who, to the best of his knowledge, hadn't really done anything wrong.

Another grim thought occurred to Bart. Why hadn't the man fallen down? He was just standing there doubled over, gray hands pressed into his stomach where the bullet had struck. Could he be dead on his feet, stuck in that position? Bart wished desperately that the man would just fall over so that it would be done with.

Then, with his claylike fingers still pressed into his stomach, the man straightened. That same blank expression still spread across his mannequin face, cold and emotionless.

"Was that really necessary?" the little man hissed, a slight hint of impatience sounding through in his tone. "As I said, I'll be taking your patrol car. Oh, and I'll be taking you as well. I am sorry to have to do that, but it wouldn't do to have you telling the boys back at the station some crazy story about a bullet-proof man. I'm sure you understand."

The man pulled his hands away from his stomach, held out the ruined 9mm bullet in his palm for Bart to see, and then dropped it at his feet. He then took

Bart's pistol and escorted him to the back seat of his own cruiser, locking him inside like a criminal. Bart didn't resist, didn't even consider resisting.

Through the grill that separated him from the front of the cruiser, Bart watched the car that he'd heard starting up across the street pull out into the road and head toward town. After a few moments passed, his captor started up the cruiser, backed out onto Riverside Road, and followed. There was moonlight enough to drive without lights, and with no streetlamps and next to no other traffic, they would be virtually invisible.

A poacher? It had been a good explanation to offer to the kids when they'd heard the gunshot, but Marion knew that she hadn't sounded very convincing. The look on Jerrod's face plainly showed his own misgivings. Some hillbilly hunting with a spotlight would have sounded rational on another night, but after everything else that had happened in the last hour, it was a little too simple. And unless she was mistaken, that had been a police car she'd seen parked just off the road, and only a couple hundred feet or so down the road from their house. That was also a strange coincidence, and as Marion knew, too many coincidences usually added up to something more than just coincidence. Maybe it had been a local cop who was bored and hadn't got to shoot his gun in a while, and then again, maybe not.

A little smile crossed her face as the house disappeared from sight in her rearview mirror. It hadn't been a bad place to live for a little while. Even Jerrod hadn't turned out to be as completely annoying to live with as she'd expected. He was young and crass and hardly took anything seriously, but he was a good man deep down, and his power had tremendous potential. The council had been right in choosing him to be next in the line of succession for a Gift of Nature. By that same time tomorrow night, Jerrod would be her equal and no longer her pretend husband. Marion was surprised to feel regret at having the charade come to an end. She had never even bothered daydreaming about it before, but a simpler life might have been nice. She might have made a good wife had things turned out differently, maybe even a mother. It was a bitter-sweet fantasy.

GRANDMA JO

No one spoke during the short ride into town from the house on Riverside Road. It was clear that neither Jerrod nor Marion was willing to discuss scaly-skinned monsters or killer boomerangs or magic, but any of the more day-to-day topics would have seemed trivial beyond tolerance under the circumstances. So they all rode in silence, left to their own broodings.

Through the backseat window, Kyle stared out at a large, bright moon. As the evening had turned over to night, the yellow sphere had risen from behind a bank of low, wispy clouds, casting amber light over the little town and the forest that surrounded it. The air was cooling off quickly, dropping down so much that Kyle's breath fogged the chilly glass. The first frost usually wouldn't arrive for another month or even two, but it felt that night as if fall might be making an early appearance.

Jerrod brought the car to a stop at the flashing light in town, right beside The Bar and just a short ways down from the Country Kitchen. He waited for what seemed to Kyle to be a very long time, checking his mirrors over and over, before finally flipping on his blinker and making a right turn. They drove a little ways, made a right, drove a little ways again, and then made another right, and yet another after that. When they'd completed a lap around the block, arriving back at the flashing light where they'd started, Jerrod paused again, checking his mirrors repeatedly just as he had before.

Kyle wondered how Jerrod could possibly have gotten turned around so completely. How could anybody ever get lost in a place like Steel City? And then he got it.

Before turning right *again* and driving past the front of The Bar *again*, Kyle's new foster father exchanged nods of satisfaction with his wife. He didn't look confused or lost, but serious, as serious as Kyle had ever seen him. He was being careful, making sure that they weren't being followed.

Jerrod drove the car straight on this time, passing by The Bar, a couple of small homes, and one large corn field. At the end of the cornfield was Steel City's abandoned firehouse. Jerrod killed the headlights just before they reached the drive and then pulled in.

Kyle wondered if the firehouse might turn out to be somewhat less abandoned than it appeared. After the things he'd seen already that night, he wouldn't have been shocked to find a herd of pink elephants hiding inside.

Sure enough, the firehouse was far from empty. Although the building's exterior was in shambles, the interior had been refurbished completely. Crumbling walls had been repaired and repainted, corroded fixtures had been replaced, and the smell of mildew was almost completely smothered by vanilla scented air freshener. From the road it looked like a condemned structure, but inside it was livable. In fact, there were three people living there.

The main space of the firehouse, the room into which they entered, was the old parking structure for the sole truck that had serviced Steel City in its more prosperous days. Buzzing fluorescent bulbs gleamed down from a high ceiling, flooding the entire room with the same sort of artificial feeling brightness that you find in supermarkets and hospitals. The large, open space that was left in the absence of the truck, which was many years sold and gone, had been transformed into a fitness room, one unlike any other Kyle had ever seen. Two of the firehouse's three inhabitants were "exercising" in that room when Kyle, Lily, Marion, and Jerrod arrived, and they, too, were unlike anything Kyle had ever seen.

Jerrod would later introduce the pair as Ivan and Petra. They were brother and sister and spoke with strong accents that Kyle thought to be Russian or Austrian. They sounded sort of like Arnold Schwarzenegger. They sort of looked like him, too.

As Jerrod held the door, Kyle had been the first of the four to enter the firehouse and the first to witness the spectacle of the siblings' workout. Petra was holding onto the old slide pole that came down from the second floor with both hands, suspending her body out erect and motionless in the air, parallel to the floor several feet below her. She held herself in that impossible position seemingly without effort and simultaneously studied the flashing screen of a nearby television where one of the old black and white Zorro movies was playing.

Ivan was standing in the middle of the room holding three straight bars, each of which held immense stacks of iron weights at each end. At least Kyle thought he was holding all three bars. Two of the bars were held in the man's two hands, each extended straight out to his sides. The third however, didn't appear to be in direct contact with anything. It floated above Ivan's head, resting so still in the air that it might have been dangling from some piano wires mounted to the rafters above. But Kyle knew that no thin wires could ever support the massive weight of that bar and its load. What Kyle was seeing was magic, no strings attached. What other explanation could there be?

Ivan and Petra were further evidence that what Lily had said was the truth. To call the siblings' physiques unnatural would have been an understatement. No amount of weightlifting, no exercise regimen, and no growth enhancing substance could possibly account for how they were put together. They looked more like comic book heroes than real people, muscles on top of muscles.

"Follow me," Marion had instructed once everyone was inside. She and Jerrod led the kids through the fitness room, momentarily distracting Ivan and Petra from a particularly dashing swordfight.

Kyle stared openly at Petra as they passed by, unable to look away. A part of him still wanted desperately to find some clue that might indicate that the seemingly superhuman feats he was witnessing were more magic trick than actual magic. When Petra recognized the look in his eyes, she released the slide pole with one hand, and though she trembled ever so slightly under the increased strain, she held her pose.

Beyond the converted truck garage, the foursome passed through a room with a refrigerator and a microwave. A folding table was set up in the middle of the room, and the remains of a dinner for three spread across its surface. There was a hallway beyond that, lined with small living quarters, and at the end of the hallway there was a final door made of lightly stained oak. The door was closed, but soft light flickered through the crack of space beneath its base.

Marion rapped gently against the heavy wood when they reached it, and an old lady's voice responded immediately.

"Come on in, Marion dear, and bring Jerrod with you."

Marion opened the door and stepped into a small candlelit room, and Jerrod followed at her heels.

"You kids wait outside though, if you please," the old lady continued, speaking from behind a large, cluttered desk. She had white hair neatly pulled into a bun at the top of her head, and a heavy crocheted shawl was wrapped tightly around her sagging shoulders.

"Why don't you two go relax back in the kitchen," Jerrod suggested. "There's soda and beer in the fridge. Help yourselves."

"To a soda!" Marion specified as Jerrod swung the door shut, his mischievous smile in place.

Kyle and Lily walked back to the room with the refrigerator and opened two cans of ginger ale. They sat down on a tattered vinyl sofa that obviously must have been leftover from the firehouse's original décor. They drank the sodas quickly, listening to a defiant speech from Zorro that echoed in from the next room.

"You don't have to feel bad if you're pretty freaked out," Kyle offered after a bit. "Anybody would be after what we've gone through tonight."

Lily looked back at him with a somewhat puzzled expression.

"You're the one who didn't even know about magic until tonight. You're probably freaked out a lot worse than me."

Kyle swallowed that down with a gulp, and the taste it left in his mouth was sour. She was right, of course. In truth, Lily appeared much calmer than Kyle felt.

"But just like you said," she continued, "you have every right to feel that way. Don't worry too much though, I can tell your foster parents are good people. I'm sure they'll take care of us."

As Lily spoke, Kyle was reminded of the first time he'd seen her in the hallway at the school. Her gentle voice was the same now as it had been then, charming and disarming. There was such perfect sweetness in her that it shamed him for feeling so afraid. Then he remembered the Snapdragon poised over her in the restaurant parking lot. He remembered feeling certain that the creature's intents were deadly, and yet for long and precious seconds, he'd been unable to muster the courage to even try to defend her. He'd been too scared to move. She could have died, and it would have been his fault. *Never again,* he vowed silently.

Marion and Jerrod reappeared then, emerging from the hall that led to the old lady's room.

"Grandma Jo would like to see you, Kyle," Marion said. "You can just go on in, she's waiting for you."

Marion then walked to an old-fashioned rotary phone and began dialing a call. Jerrod walked straight to the fridge and retrieved a beer, cracking it open immediately. Apparently, neither of them thought that Kyle needed any further information from them at the moment. He wasn't so sure.

As he walked again past the small living quarters, Kyle wondered what to make of the elderly woman he'd glimpsed in the room at the end of the hallway. Marion had called her Grandma Jo, but the way she'd said it sounded a little too formal. He didn't think that the old lady was really Marion's grandmother. But what was she then, and why did she want to see him but not Lily?

Kyle took a deep breath when he reached the heavy oak door at the end of the hallway, which was left ajar, and then he pushed it open and went inside.

"Come on in, Kyle Adams," the old lady called from behind her cluttered desk, her voice cheerful and sweet, grandmotherly, "and call me Grandma Jo." She was facing away from the door, rummaging through a drawer behind her. "Oh," she said when she finally turned, "you're in already. Good. We need to have us a little rap, Kyle, just you and me." As she spoke she cleared a small area atop her desk and poured several fingers of amber colored liquid from a flask into a short glass. "Isn't that how they say it these days, a *rap*? It's hard to keep up on the new lingo when you're as old as me. I'd like to hear you try to guess just how old I am. That'll be your first test."

Kyle was confused. He hadn't known what to expect from the old lady, but he surely hadn't expected casual conversation. Also, he remembered his second foster mother teaching him never to guess at a woman's age or weight. It was never a safe thing to do, she'd said.

"Eighty-four," he guessed anyway.

"Eighty-four?" she repeated, sounding amused. "Hell, I can barely even remember being eighty-four it was so long ago. Try ninety-nine. Mmm-hmm, that's right, next April, God willing, I'll hit the century mark. You never know though, that's a milestone that not too many reach. Hell, I don't even bother buying green bananas any more. There's no telling if I'll still be ready for them by the time they're ready for me." She laughed at herself and then took a big gulp from the tumbler.

To that, Kyle had no response.

"It's fine if you prefer to stand while we talk," she assured in her sweet, grand-motherly tone. "I don't care at all."

"Oh, I'm sorry," Kyle apologized, thinking that he'd made a breach in etiquette. He moved toward the chair on the opposite side of the desk from where the old lady sat. "I should sit down?"

"Should you sit down?" she asked, sounding amused once again. "What the hell did I just say two seconds ago?"

"That you don't care at all," Kyle answered.

"Mmm-hmm, that's right, I said I don't care at all. Just two seconds ago, I said that. I haven't changed my mind in those two seconds, so do what you want." As she swirled her liquor over the candle that burned at the edge of her desk, she grumbled in a much lower voice. "Damn kids never listen anymore. It's because of all them video games and all that thug music, all full of the f-word and busting caps at police officers."

Kyle laughed. He couldn't help it.

Grandma Jo fell instantly silent, her grumbling abruptly halted, and her eyes sharpened to a hawk's stare, so intense it seemed dangerous.

"I'm sorry," Kyle apologized immediately. "I didn't mean to laugh. I'm a little thrown, that's all. None of this is what I'd expected."

"Mmm-hmm, that's right, you should be sorry," she agreed, though her features softened as she spoke. "I didn't mean to give you such a harsh look, but you threw me a little, too. It seems like nobody around here's got the guts to laugh at me, even when I'm being my funny old self and deserve a little chuckle."

Kyle thought about who the people around there were. He thought about Marion offering to spare the life of the reptile-man behind the restaurant and then killing it when it refused to cooperate. He thought about Ivan and Petra bench-pressing uncounted tons of steel weights down the hallway. He thought about those people lacking the guts to laugh at the little old lady on the other side of the desk.

Apparently, she could guess at what he was thinking.

"Mmm-hmm, that's right, I'm a tough old bitch," she confirmed proudly. "When I got something to say around here, people listen. But listen to me ramble on about myself like this, wasting precious time. That's just plain silly. You should stop us old folks when we get going like that. Anyway, the reason I asked for you to come in here is because I want to know about you."

Kyle said nothing. He just sat there, trying to sort out all of what he'd just heard.

"Well, come on," she prompted. "Hell, I only got about a thousand other things that need doing, let's have it."

"I'm not sure how much you already know," Kyle hesitated, uncertain of where to start. "I grew up in Chicago, lived with four different foster families while I was there. I was just a regular kid, nothing special. Then, some genius at the agency decided to ship me up here into the middle of nowhere for my senior year. They never even bothered to offer me any kind of explanation, and I can't imagine ..."

Kyle never bothered finishing his thought, because a new and more interesting thought had just come to him. Of course there'd been a reason for sending him there, a good one. It had been arranged. He'd been brought there because someone had discovered his secret before he'd discovered it himself. Lily was right about how he'd thrown the manhole cover. It was the reason he'd been moved to Michigan. It was the reason he'd never quite fit in with the other kids. Somewhere inside him, somehow, there really was magic.

Kyle looked up at the old lady across the big, cluttered desk, and what he found in her stare was recognition. For the second time, he had the distinct feeling that she was looking right into his mind, reading his thoughts.

"So, it's true," Grandma Jo said gravely. Suddenly her voice was hard and serious, far from grandmotherly. "You really had no idea, not until this very night. That's fairly remarkable."

"What is?" Kyle asked. "What's remarkable? I don't understand any of this, and I don't know what to believe. I feel like someone's playing a trick on me." His head spun. Suddenly nothing was certain, no belief safe. The ground was crumbling away beneath his feet.

"What's remarkable," Grandma Jo explained calmly, "is that you're damn near eighteen years old, and you're only just finding out about yourself. There aren't many of us around who can use magic, not many who even know about it. Usually, if someone with the talent hasn't discovered it by the time they're half your age, they never will."

"Why?" Kyle asked. "Why couldn't they find out later on? Does it go away if you don't use it?"

"No, that's not exactly it. At least that's not what I think. I think that by the time people are grown up, they're so settled within the limitations of what they will and won't believe to be possible that they just can't accept something like magic. And we're all bound by our beliefs, sure as shit."

"Then how come I was able to do what I did tonight?" Kyle pressed. "I've never believed in magic. I'm not completely sure I do even now."

Grandma Jo thought about this for a moment before continuing. Then she asked, "Are you sure you never believed in it? Not even in the possibility that it was real?"

"Of course not," Kyle answered as if it was obvious. "Who would unless they were crazy, or if they'd seen the crazy stuff that I saw tonight."

"You never had the feeling that there was something secret just beyond the edge of the everyday world," the old lady prompted further, "something wonderful and powerful that most people never get to see?"

Kyle was all ready to go on with his denial, but this time the words stuck in his throat. Her question resonated with him, strangely familiar.

"You've never heard that little voice in your ears, whispering to you, guiding you, giving you insights that your normal senses never could?" She looked confident, like she already knew his answer and it hardly mattered whether he chose to speak it aloud or not.

Kyle kept quiet. Involuntarily, he drew back in his chair, distancing himself from something that suddenly felt perilous. *A secret world? His quiet, inner voice?* It was all too familiar. There could be no passing it off as coincidence.

"Mmm-hmm, that's right," Grandma Jo agreed with Kyle's silent confirmation. "I can see it in your eyes right now. You believed it all along, believed that it was possible at least, even if you didn't know exactly what *it* was."

Kyle just sat there, stunned, thinking about what the old lady was saying, knowing deep down that it was true, but fearing what that truth would mean for him.

A knock at the door interrupted his thoughts. It was Marion.

"I just talked to Raymond," she said. "He'll be here by morning, with everyone."

"Then the ceremony'll be first thing in the morning," Grandma Jo responded, "as soon as they get here. And after that, we bet it all on one hand. Get some sleep, Marion."

Kyle's foster mother nodded and turned to leave.

"And Marion," Grandma Jo added, "better tell Jerrod to get some sleep, too, if he can."

Kyle couldn't be sure, but he thought he saw a tiny smile spread across Marion's face, there for a single moment and then gone. And then she was gone as well, and once again Kyle and the old lady were left alone.

"I like the candlelight," Grandma Jo noted absently. "All those fluorescent bulbs all over the rest of this place give me a headache. Then again, sourmash gives me a headache, too, but I seem to have an easier time giving up the fluorescent light."

The apparently idle chit-chat seemed dreadfully out of place to Kyle. Was she testing him, checking to see how he'd respond? Or was she just giving herself time to think?

"What happens to me and Lily?" Kyle asked. "Do we have to stay here?"

"Mmm-hmm, that's right, for tonight and tomorrow at least. We'll make a call to Lily's father, or have her make one. We'll tell him she's staying at a friend's house or something. That'll have to do for now. Tomorrow, we'll make the rest of the decisions that need to be made. Or else they'll be made for us."

Her words made Kyle shudder, because in them he could hear a hint of the old lady's apprehension. What roused fear in the woman who inspired fear in everyone else? Kyle didn't even want to guess.

A TEST

Kyle couldn't get to sleep that night, and understandably. The firehouse's small living quarters contained only four beds, and they were already spoken for by Marion, Jerrod, and the muscle-bound siblings. Kyle deferred the old vinyl couch by the kitchen table to Lily and settled as best as he could on an army-style folding cot nearby. Without any extra cushion, the cot felt hard beneath his shoulders, and it sagged deeply under his butt. It was far from comfortable, but that was a moot point anyway. He could have tossed and turned between silk sheets atop a king-sized waterbed just as easily.

Grandma Jo never emerged from her office after she and Kyle had talked. He assumed that she slept in there, and considering the cramped size of the room and the lack of other furniture, he assumed that she slept right in her chair.

It was nearly 4 o'clock in the morning when Kyle finally decided that he might as well get up. His mind was still reeling over the events and revelations of the past two days and also over the possibilities of the new day that was almost ready to begin. The firehouse was utterly dark, and it seemed that no matter how long he waited, his eyes couldn't adjust enough to let him see more than a few faint shapes. He could just make out the white of the refrigerator, the black of the tabletop, and the gentle rise and fall of Lily's chest as she slept mouse-quiet on the old couch. How she managed to slumber away so peacefully, he couldn't imagine.

For a short while, Kyle entertained a hope that the headlights of a passing car might give him a quick glimpse of his surroundings, just enough to remind him of where it was safe to step. Then he remembered where he was, and it was a good thing he did. He might have been waiting on traffic for a long time. Nightlife in Steel City was nonexistent.

Kyle thought about the other people sleeping just down the hallway, Ivan and Petra and his so-called foster parents. While Kyle had been talking with Grandma Jo, Lily had been talking with Jerrod, and she'd shared the highlights of that conversation with him before turning in for the night.

Jerrod had told Lily about magic, about Grandma Jo and the Guardians she led, about Ramius King and his hunters, and about the centuries old secret war. He'd told her that Kyle's ability to use magic had been discovered at his old school by means of a mock psychology experiment. He'd been brought to Steel City to live under the scrutiny of the Guardians who would then decide whether or not to recruit him into their ranks. So in reality, Marion and Jerrod weren't Kyle's new foster parents at all, but soldiers in some secret militia. In fact, after a little consideration, Kyle decided that they probably weren't even husband and wife. They had always struck him as incompatible, and so they probably were.

The smooth, tile floor of the firehouse was cold beneath Kyle's toes, but bare feet made soundless steps, and he didn't want anyone else to have to share in his insomnia. He headed slowly toward the only object in the room which he could make out with any sort of clarity, the refrigerator. He was thirsty, and sometimes a cold drink helped him get to sleep, cooled him down and heightened the appeal of warm covers.

Just as Kyle reached the fridge, he paused. A very faint glimmer of light had caught his attention. It stretched delicately down the hallway, offering just enough illumination to reveal the doorways of the rooms where the Guardians slept. Leaning out into the hallway, Kyle could see that it was from the crack beneath Grandma Jo's office door that the flickering glow emanated.

The old lady must still be up, Kyle thought at first, but then reconsidered. More likely was the possibility that she was fast asleep in that chair as he'd pictured her and had simply drifted off before extinguishing the candle. He wondered though.

Prompted by his curiosity, Kyle tip-toed down the hallway, past the small living quarters, to the door of Grandma Jo's room. He leaned forward and held his ear up against the door's cool, wooden surface. He listened as carefully as he could, but wouldn't have needed to. He'd have heard her anyway.

"Come on in if you want."

"Mmm-hmm, that's right," Grandma Jo said as Kyle slipped into the office and immediately sat down, "the old lady's still awake."

Kyle laughed a little, and she smiled in return. A glass of steaming hot tea had replaced the whiskey atop her desk. There was no microwave in the room that Kyle could see, and he knew that she hadn't left the office all night. Could that little candle have been responsible for heating the drink? He didn't think so.

"Funny you should find your way back to my office like this, Kyle Adams," Grandma Jo said. "As it happens, I was just thinking about you."

"I couldn't sleep," Kyle explained. "I didn't mean to bother you."

"No bother at all," she assured him. "In fact, I could use some company and you're just the man for the job. Hell, you'd better be, the whole rest of the world's asleep, I think."

Kyle laughed again, but this time she didn't smile back. She looked very serious and thoughtful.

When she spoke again, she did so hesitantly, choosing her words with care. "The reason I was just thinking about you is because there're a few things that I was tempted to tell you when you were in here before, but I didn't. I wasn't sure that I should."

"If it's about the Guardians of Magic or the man called King and his hunters, then I already know," Kyle offered. "Lily told me about it before we went to bed." He didn't mention who had told Lily, afraid he might get Jerrod into trouble for being too casual with privileged information. "I know about why I was brought here to Steel City, too, and that Jerrod and Marion aren't really my foster parents. They aren't even married, right?" he added as an afterthought, hoping to settle his curiosity.

"No, they definitely are not," she confirmed, "not your foster parents and not married. I paired them together to act as your foster parents because I thought it might do them both some good. Thought he might loosen her up or she might straighten him up or maybe even some of both. You probably know what I'm talking about, yes?"

Kyle smiled and nodded in confirmation.

"Mmm-hmm, I imagine those two worked each other's nerves up pretty good. But what I was thinking about telling you was something else, something that Lily doesn't know and neither do you."

She paused again then, staring at Kyle expectantly, as if waiting for him to tell her whether or not to go on. But how could he do that when he didn't know what it was she was going to say?

"Ordinarily, I wouldn't tell someone in your place what I'm going to tell you," she went on, "at least not so soon. I'm worried though, that if I don't say it now, it won't get said. Tomorrow's going to be a big day, historical big, although

I doubt it'll get written up in any of the history books. It might just be that right here and right now will be the last chance you and I get to talk, so I think I'd better go ahead and say what I've got to say."

The implications of the old lady's words shocked Kyle like a face-full of cold water. The hair along his forearms stood in response.

"We don't ordinarily go through all the hoopla that we did with you, with Jerrod and Marion and the house and all. Usually, it's a much simpler matter when we find somebody with the magic, somebody we'd like to teach. Most of the time we do our looking with the younger kids, more like elementary aged than high school. When we do test the high school aged kids, we're mostly looking for the ones who refuse to take the tests, who are too nervous to try because they already know they might make something happen. We've hardly ever found anyone like you, who's nearly grown up and still hasn't discovered the magic. Your situation is a rare one, and we mean to be careful with how we handle it."

"Why?" Kyle asked sharply, feeling suddenly defensive. "Why do you have to be careful? Why is my situation so rare?"

Kyle felt fully the terrible disadvantage he was at, knowing virtually nothing about the issues that now seemed most pertinent to his future. He was scared that after all the excitement of the past days, he still might end up being dismissed by these mysterious people, sent away to be plain, average Kyle once again.

"It's harder for somebody like you, who makes the discovery so late," Grandma Jo explained. "Often times it's impossible. People usually think they got things all worked out by the time they're old enough to drive. They think they know the whole spectrum of what's possible and what isn't, and if somebody really doesn't believe in magic, not even deep down in their guts where other people don't get to see, then they'll never be able to make it happen, not consciously. By that time their potential has already been wasted, they've grown out of it."

Kyle thought back to the restaurant, when he'd thrown the manhole cover at the creature to protect Lily. If it had truly been magic that had enabled him to save her, then he had used it unconsciously, without even realizing what it was.

"If it's harder for people like me, then I'll just work harder," Kyle reasoned determinedly. "I'll study twice as hard and practice twice as long. You must think I can. If you didn't, then why would you have gone to all this trouble to check me out? Why would you have set up the whole pretend foster home and everything if you didn't think that I could cut it as one of your students?"

Grandma Jo hesitated again. "It's not as simple as your making it out to be. We're not only concerned with whether or not you'll be able to learn to use the magic. We're also concerned with whether or not you should learn to use it. It's not a given. Just because you have the talent doesn't mean that we're obligated to nurture it. For someone like you it could be … dangerous."

"Are you saying that you don't trust me?" Kyle asked, sounding hurt. "You don't think I'd be responsible with the stuff you'd teach me? Please, I've always felt like I was meant to do something bigger, to be someone important. I know I can become one of your Guardians. I think it's what I'm meant to do. Can you at least tell me that you'll give me the chance to try?"

"We found a pair of twin brothers one time, a little younger yet than yourself, and they, too, were late bloomers," Grandma Jo said, choosing not to answer his question straight away. She tilted her head and closed her eyes as she spoke, thinking back. "They had just discovered the magic for themselves, and we were quick to recruit them. They showed great potential and were both anxious to learn. We thought that together they might finally give us a distinct advantage over our enemies, enough to let us move against them. The magic in them grew quickly. In retrospect, I suppose I'd say too quickly. One handled it okay, but the other didn't. It ended badly." The old lady opened her eyes again, and found Kyle's own staring back. "It was a mistake that we mean not to repeat."

"I'll take my time," Kyle promised, sounding nearly desperate. "Just teach me a little bit at a time. Just let me watch. I'll stay out of everyone's way. I promise I won't want more than what you think I should have."

"Mmm-hmm, I know you mean what you say, but I also know how promises work with people your age, and I know that there are some things that just can't be promised. We all want what we want, and you can't know what you might want a month from now or a year from now, after you've gotten a taste of some stronger magic."

"Please," Kyle begged, "I can't go back to the life I had, not now that I know what else there is."

Grandma Jo sighed, took a sip from her tea, and then stared intently at Kyle, as if studying him. The look on her face told of the sympathy she felt.

"I tell you what, I'll give you another test," she offered, "and if you pass, then I'll promise you can stay with us. I won't say in what capacity, but I'll say you can stay, if you pass my test."

"Okay," Kyle agreed quickly, trying to steady his breathing and ready himself for whatever test he would face.

Grandma Jo noted his focus and nodded approvingly.

"I haven't even told you what the test is and already you're doing the right thing."

Kyle didn't have a clue what that meant.

"When we talked earlier, I mentioned a little voice," Grandma Jo said, "and I could see by the look on your face that you knew what I was talking about. You've heard that little voice before, only you didn't know what it was."

"It was the magic?" Kyle guessed.

"That's right, it was. The magic can speak to us in a way. It can whisper to us when we're frightened or shout through us when we're angry. That voice inside you, your magic, it's only ever whispered so far, but that might not always be the case."

"If it got louder, I'd be more powerful?" Kyle guessed.

"Mmm-hmm, that's right, but that's a dangerous road. As the voice rises, it gives you power, but it also gains power over you. The magic could end up using you instead of the other way around."

"Is that what happened to the twins?" Kyle asked.

"That's what happened to one of them," she amended. "I don't know what happened to the other."

"And is that what happened to the man named King?"

Grandma Jo considered that for a moment, and then answered, "No, that's not what happened to him, but that's what's happened to most of his followers, the ones he calls hunters. He teaches them to let it happen, because when they lose control over themselves, they're easier for him to control."

Kyle noted the twinge at the corners of the old lady's eyes. He'd seen it before when he'd mentioned Ramius King.

"There's another way though, to increase the strength of your magic, and it doesn't require you to sacrifice your control over it. If you can learn to listen carefully enough, then you won't need the magic's voice to do more than whisper. If you can hear it clearly, then it can be powerful, even when it's quiet. It's harder to gain the power that way, and it's harder to maintain it, especially when you're in a tough spot and you need it most, but it's the only way I'll teach you, the only option I'll offer. I expect my people to be responsible with the skills I give them. No one should wield power that they can't control."

"Am I going to be tested over this?" Kyle asked.

Grandma Jo laughed, sounding grandmotherly again.

"Damn right you are. If you want to become a Guardian, then you'll be tested over that again and again for the rest of your life. But the test I had in mind for you tonight is a harder one. Are you ready for it?"

Kyle took a deep breath and said, "I'll do my best."

"If you want to stay here with us," the old lady explained slowly, deliberately, "then what you need to do for me is put out that candle burning on my desk. Extinguish it using only your magic."

Grandma Jo's words settled over Kyle like a cloud of noxious gas, suffocating him. When he replied, his words came out between gasps for air.

"That's my test? Why not ask me to raise the Titanic instead? My odds would be just as good."

"I've thought about trying that, but I'm afraid it'd be a little indiscrete." Grandma Jo laughed at herself, seeming genuinely pleased with her own wit.

"Why present me with a test you know I can't pass?" Kyle asked bitterly. "Why not just send me away and be done with it?"

"The task I've given you is very attainable, I promise," she assured. "In fact, putting out that candle with magic like yours can be effortless. If you truly believe that you can do it, then you will do it. On the other hand, if you tell yourself it can't be done, you'll still end up being right, sure as shit."

Kyle took a deep breath, trying to calm himself, trying to quiet his own doubt.

"Will you help me?"

"I will."

Grandma Jo leaned forward in her chair and slid the burning candle to the middle of her desk balancing it atop a tall stack of books and folders. Its flame flickered precariously, but it burned on.

"You see what a fragile thing that fire is, Kyle?" she asked. "It won't take much, but you have to believe."

"I'm trying to believe. I'm trying to picture the flame dying down."

"No, don't do that," she corrected. "Picture it already out, and when you see it clearly, then we can make it happen." She paused a few seconds, scrutinizing him. "Can you see it?"

"Yes."

"Okay, first thing you need to do is slide around in that chair a little until you find a nice comfortable spot. Then I want you to close your eyes and relax. Take a few deep breaths, and let all the muscles in your body go loose. Feel all that excitement from the last couple days just leak right out."

Kyle relaxed immediately, effortlessly. Being in dire need of sleep made it easy.

"That's it. Good," Grandma Jo encouraged. "Slow your breathing. Don't try to fill your lungs all up or completely empty them either. Keep them half full. Keep enough air moving in and out to stay sharp, but not enough to hurry your heart. Little breaths. Slow, little breaths."

The flickering light of the candle still registered with Kyle's closed eyes, barely penetrating his lids, but unmistakable.

"Now I want you to tell me everything you can hear," Grandma Jo continued. "Start with the loudest sound and move down to the faintest."

Kyle sat like he was made of stone, motionless and silent. He fell into that sessile mode easily, almost instinctually, and then he listened. The room was very quiet, but not without sound. The first thing he heard was the ticking of a clock. He hadn't noticed it before, but it sounded like it was probably hanging on the wall behind Grandma Jo.

"I hear the clock," he said.

"Mmm-hmm, I should think so. What else?"

Kyle focused harder, but without exertion. Instead of straining, he allowed himself to relax even further, quiet his breathing just a little more so that there would be that much less interference.

"I can hear a whistle," Kyle continued. "It's distant, but obvious now that I'm aware of it. It's only now and then, not steady. It sounds like somebody blowing over the mouth of a pop bottle."

Grandma Jo nodded her head in approval and said, "I hear that just about every night here. One of the old fireman's ladders is leaned up against the back of the place, right behind my little office, and when the wind blows through its rungs, it whistles. What else?"

"A scratching sound?" Kyle offered uncertainly. "I think so. It's also coming from outside, from up above us."

"Mmm-hmm, the lowest branches of that old Basswood tickling the roof," the old lady clarified.

"I think that's it," Kyle said after another moment. "Other than that it's perfectly quiet."

"No, there's more," she insisted. "Block those other things out, find a way to make yourself ignore them completely, and then you can reach further."

Kyle held his breath, and his heartbeat slowed as if half-frozen. He blocked the room's sounds from his mind one by one, first the clock, then the whistling ladder and the scratching branches. He concentrated so deeply and listened so carefully that soon the entire room seemed to buzz with its own ever-present voice, a steady drone coming from all directions at once.

Ever so gently, and unseen to Kyle, Grandma Jo blew out a tiny gust of breath across the surface of her desk. She directed the air so softly that not even the faintest sound escaped along with it.

"I heard it," Kyle whispered excitedly, "I heard what you just did. I mean, I know what you must have done, because I heard the flicker of the candle. You blew across its flame."

"Very good," Grandma Jo whispered back, genuinely impressed. "Think about the sound it made. Think about the exact spot where it came from, the exact pitch and color of its voice. If you listen carefully enough, you can hear it still, even as it burns steadily. Can you hear it?"

Kyle sifted through the faintest differences in the room's steady buzzing, and there on the desk, just an arm's reach away, he heard the candle. It was such a miniscule vibration above the room's drone that it was barely there, but once he found it, he held on, honed all his thought on it until there was nothing else in the world to touch any of his senses. It was an amazing discovery, a treasure found within himself.

"I hear it," he whispered so softly that he wasn't sure Grandma Jo would hear.

"Stay focused, don't let it slip away, but let another sound back in. Let yourself hear the branches on the roof again and then the wind through the ladder."

Kyle opened himself just slightly, letting those outside sounds register again, and instantly the candle was silenced to him. He froze, halting his breathing once again, struggling to reconnect with that delicate channel of sound from the flame. He found it again, and with difficulty he held it along with the scratching and the whistling.

I have it, he mouthed, but did not speak aloud.

"And now the clock," she whispered.

The ticking from the wall returned to Kyle's consciousness immediately, and this time he maintained his focus enough to lose none of the smaller sounds beneath it. Each jerk of the second hand was now a miniature gunshot in his ears. He could hear the echo of each tick reverberate back from the wall behind him.

"Mmm-hmm, that's right, that's just where you need to be. When you're completely calm and completely concentrated, that's when you can hear that little voice inside yourself most clearly. That's when you can bring that magic to life and control it."

Kyle still sat like a statue, barely breathing. He'd forgotten completely what it was that he was meant to do.

"Now open your other senses back up," Grandma Jo instructed. "Feel the arms of the chair beneath your hands and the floor under your feet. Smell the candle's smoke. Taste it in the air. Feel its tiny warmth against your face. See it."

Kyle opened his eyes and found them already focused on the candle. He could smell it and taste it and feel the heat that radiated from it. He could even hear it burning.

"Imagine that energy being sent to you from the candle, the heat and light and sound. Reach back to the candle through the same lines that energy is tracing to you. Push your own energy back into the flame and ..."

Suddenly, the room fell into darkness.

Kyle gasped, jerked out of his near-trance by the plunge into utter blackness.

Then, just as abruptly, the flame was relit. Grandma Jo held her crooked-knuckled fingers over the candle. The fresh light seemed to penetrate through the tissue paper skin of her hand, setting jagged blue veins into contrast. A proud, grandmotherly smile spread across her face.

"Mmm-hmm, you can stick around then I guess," she said.

"It was so hard to reach the candle," Kyle blurted excitedly, "but once I got there it went out so easily. I whispered to it and it died cold in an instant."

Everything grandmotherly evaporated from Grandma Jo's face, and suddenly she was dangerous again.

"They say that the life in every man and woman is like a flame," she warned in a grave tone. "Someday, your magic could snuff a life as easily as it did this candle."

Her words sank in slowly for Kyle, gnawing away at every part of him that was still more child than man, marking him permanently with a new definition of responsibility. They were words he'd never forget.

"I can see that idea scares you," Grandma Jo noted. "It had better. If it didn't, then this night's lesson would have been your last from me."

After sending Kyle back to bed with strict orders to get some sleep before morning, Grandma Jo sat once again in the stillness of her office, staring into the candle's flame and thinking about the future. She could sense a nearby power that had not been there the previous night when she'd sat in that same place. There was an undiscovered potential bound up within one of those young people sleeping down the hallway. She'd felt it the moment they'd arrived, the instant they'd rode up in Jerrod's car. One of those two had it in them to become something very special, something extraordinary even among the ranks of the Guardians. She was excited at the thought, but anxious as well. She had to assume that the power she felt was in Kyle. His were the extraordinary circumstances, growing nearly to adulthood without discovering the magic, but still being able to bring it to life. It was so rare for such a thing to occur, and such cases were not well explored. Perhaps his belated discovery was somehow responsible for the quiet growth of an immense reservoir of untapped strength.

Discovering the girl right there in Steel City was certainly auspicious, but she seemed more or less typical of the recruits they usually found, a young person who'd spent years coveting their secret power.

The old lady took a long, deep breath and then exhaled it slowly. She could worry about the kids after tomorrow. After tomorrow, she might not have much else to worry about. It was such a seductive thought, but she was afraid to embrace it too tightly. Even if everything went according to plan, there was still a high probability that people whom she cared deeply for would not survive. Tomorrow would be a great and terrible day.

SUNDAY, SEPTEMBER 3

Working for a Living

At seven on Sunday morning, the clock radio flipped on atop Rosa's dresser, jar
ring her from sleep. She turned her head and showed her teeth in the direction of
the radio, practically hissing at the crass voices of the morning talk show that
delayed the playing of her modern rock. She found their overzealous laughter
intolerably grating, which was exactly why she never changed the station. She
might be tempted to roll over and ignore anything else, but the talk show hosts
were impossible to block out. It forced her out of bed to turn it off no matter how
tired she was, and once she was up, she was up to stay.

Michael, who was awake when the radio came on, chose to keep still and let
his eyes stay closed a little longer. He ignored the vile personalities that invaded
the apartment via the radio and pretended to slumber on as Rosa got up, turned
off the radio, and treaded softly into the bathroom. As the sound of the shower
reached his ears, Michael rolled over onto his back, wincing as the stitches tugged
at his side, and stared up at the ceiling with tired, but thoughtful eyes.

Actually, Michael had already been awake for nearly three hours, ever since
Rosa had lain down on the bed beside him. She probably couldn't sleep a wink in
the chair, but regardless, lying down next to a near stranger for a couple hours of
shut eye seemed an outlandish alternative to a restless night. Quite frankly,
Michael couldn't understand why she'd done it. For just shy of three hours, he'd
feigned sleep beside her. He should have spent the time trying to decipher Rosa's
extraordinary gift for foresight or her curious behavior in the street the previous
night, but try as he might, he couldn't manage to think about anything other

than the soft looking curls of dark hair that lay temptingly across the edge of his pillow.

When Rosa emerged from the bathroom, Michael let his eyes fall closed again and consciously slowed his breathing to mimic the sleep rhythm. He could hear Rosa yawning almost constantly, proof of her fatigue. It had been a busy evening and a short night, and she had a right to feel spent. A part of him wanted to sit up right then, to stop pretending to be sleeping in, but for some reason he couldn't bring himself to do it. All he could do was lie there and think about what had happened and about what might happen next. He wanted some time to think things through before he and Rosa spoke again.

There was the sound of a pen scratching hurriedly across paper, and then Rosa was out the door and everything was quiet again.

Michael stepped out of bed and stretched, feeling a great deal of stiffness, but very little pain other than the twinge at his side. Lifting up his shirt, Michael peeled back a dry, red bandage and saw that Rosa's neat sewing now covered an ugly, purple scar. The scar was indisputable proof that no matter how hard he tried, Michael could never truly deny the curse he carried. Even if he chose to lock it away and ignore it completely, somewhere deep down inside him, at least a remnant of the magic remained. Nothing else could explain his speedy healing.

It took less than a minute for Michael to remove the stitches from his side once he found a sharp paring knife in the tiny kitchenette which also appeared to serve as dining room, living room, and entryway in Rosa's apartment. A closer look around confirmed the first impression that Michael had made the previous night. It was not the sort of place where someone chose to live if they could afford to live somewhere else.

The scribbling that Michael had heard that morning turned out to be a note. It was stuck to the doorknob with a bit of tape where he couldn't possibly miss it on his way out. It read:

> *Michael,*
>   *I feel bad leaving you here alone, but can't afford to miss another day of work. There's not much in here to eat, but help yourself to whatever you can find. Hope you're still here when I get home.*
>   *-Rosa*

It was such a simple message, and yet it prompted a powerful stir of emotions in its reader. Michael simultaneously felt guilt and gratefulness and also a bit of something else, something that he hadn't dared to feel in a very long time.

After splashing some cold water over his face in the bathroom sink, Michael examined his image in the cracked mirror doors of Rosa's medicine cabinet. His long, narrow face looked dreadfully pale, a testament to how infrequently he spent time in the sunshine. He had turned into a recluse, a hider, and since it was hard to hide in broad daylight, he mostly avoided it. The dark rings around his deep-set eyes were more pronounced than he remembered ever seeing them before, but then again, it had been a while since he'd cared to inspect his own appearance. The fiery goatee that tipped his chin with red was in desperate need of a trim, a sad end to a sad face.

There was nothing in the mirror that struck Michael as attractive, and he didn't see how anyone else might see otherwise. Once again, he thought about Rosa, and once again, he failed to make any sense of her. She was full of life and energy, and she was kind beneath her brash exterior, and she was beautiful. She wasn't the kind of girl who you'd expect to be alone.

"So why is she?" Michael asked himself aloud. "And why is she so willing to take me into her home and take care of me like this?"

There were so many peculiar circumstances coming together, so many coincidences. Michael knew he had to be careful. Although he tried to deny it, he was not just another wandering vagrant, and there was always the slim, but dreadful possibility that even after all the time that had passed, his old life could still catch up with him. It certainly felt closer than it had in a long time.

He could leave, walk out the door of the tiny two-room apartment right then and never come back. A part of him pleaded the case for that very course of action, argued that he should keep on running before things became more complicated. He should go before anyone could get hurt because of him, because he could never go through that again. It was the logical thing to do, he decided, so he would do it, but not before one last little thing got taken care of. Regardless of what Rosa's motives might be, she had helped him, cared for him, even risked her life for him, and her deeds deserved compensation.

Going back to retrieve the armored car money ahead of schedule was a little risky, but considering the circumstances, it seemed like a risk worth taking. Michael would get the money, leave the most expensive dog-bone the supermarket carried for Maverick, leave some cash for Rosa, and then he would leave, himself.

"Then I'll drop off the rest of the money at the first soup kitchen I find, minus enough for a bus ticket to anywhere, wherever fate leads me next." Michael spoke the words in the hopes that hearing them might add some strength to his conviction.

He was surprised to hear himself use the word "fate." It wasn't something he would usually say. Fate was a concept he'd never accepted, at least not for the last fifteen years, not for the second half of his life. The idea that there was a path for everyone to follow, a series of events they were destined to live, was hard to swallow. It sounded like a trap. Michael preferred to think in terms of logic instead. People did the things they did because they sought to fulfill their own selfish desires, or because random chance forced them in one direction or another, or more rarely because they were obeying their personal sense of morality. There was no logic in the idea of preordination. It was unthinkable that he might have been meant to do what he had done.

Rosa was five minutes late for work, which was nearly prompt compared to the ten or twelve that were more her usual. However, her boss, a recent college graduate and licensed veterinarian for less than one year, failed to see her tardiness in quite that same light.

"My office, Miss Sanchez," he called out immediately as Rosa walked through the door. "Let's have our talk so we can get to work, shall we?"

Rosa clenched her teeth, fighting down the urge to spout off. This was her third job for the year, and finding work was getting harder all the time. She couldn't afford to quit again, no matter how much she despised her pretty-boy, preppy boss. Nor could she afford to get fired. Over the years she'd acquired something of an affinity for both, not a financially responsible habit to develop.

"Close the door behind you," the young doctor said as Rosa entered his spacious, immaculate office.

Rosa remained standing as he walked casually around to sit behind his orderly desk, pausing briefly to straighten his degree, which hung framed on the wall. Along with a "puppy love" calendar, it was the room's only decoration. A small, vanilla scented candle burned at the corner of the desk, the ultimate proof for Rosa that she worked for a complete pansy. What kind of veterinarian had to hide from the smell of his own clinic?

"I imagine that what I'm about to say will sound familiar," the doctor began, retrieving a lint brush from a desk drawer and cleaning animal hair from his khaki pants. "That's because it's the same speech I've already had to present to you several times over the past month. This isn't volunteer work that you do here, Miss Sanchez, this is your job. I pay you for doing this job and therefore expect you to do it diligently, which means being here for the start of your shift every day and not calling off every time you're not in the mood to work."

Blah, blah, blah. Rosa thought that the little sissy was probably secretly glad when she showed up late, because it gave him an excuse to perform one of his little reprimand spiels and prove that he was the boss.

"As you know, there are other people out there right now looking for a job just like yours, people who could do your job just as well as you. If you want to keep this job, then things need to change. You've had plenty of warnings, so I'm making this your last. If you continue to be late and unreliable, then you will be replaced. Now, I'm sorry that I have to make it be like that, I really am. I really like you and want to be able to keep you on, but my first responsibility is to keep this clinic running smoothly. You understand that, don't you, Miss Sanchez?"

I understand that you'd miss staring at my ass when I clean the kennels, she thought.

"Yes sir, I promise it won't happen again," she said instead.

"All right then, let's go to work, shall we?"

As the two walked out of the office, they met an elderly woman holding a tiny white poodle. She was standing just outside the door of an examination room across the hallway.

"I'm very sorry, Doctor, but Pippy just made a little piddle in there," the woman apologized.

"That's quite alright," the doctor assured her, "this young lady will clean that up for you right away."

Young lady? The doctor was four years older than Rosa at most. *What a jerk.*

Cleaning up Pippy's piddle didn't turn out to be much of a job, not surprising considering the feeble stature of the "toy dog."

Rosa walked out of the examination room when she was done, never having shared a word with the old lady that owned the poodle, which was just fine. If she was required to do such demeaning tasks as wiping up the urine of someone else's undergrown pet, then at least she could be left alone while she did it. It didn't seem like too much to ask.

Since she was already in the mode, Rosa decided she might as well go ahead and get her dirtiest work of the day over and done with, so she headed back toward the kennel room. She only made if half way there though, before the doctor pulled her aside again and gave her a different assignment, one that made mopping puppy pee sound almost pleasant.

"Are you Mr. Dunn?" Rosa inquired as she entered another of the examination rooms a minute later.

"That's me," answered the impatient looking man sitting in the room's only chair.

"I'm Rosa Sanchez, and the doctor has asked me to talk with you about your Golden Retriever, Duke. As you know, Duke's degenerative hip has continued to cause him a great deal of pain over the past several months despite the increased medications that we've ..."

"Listen, love, I'm kind of in a hurry, so if you could cut to the chase I'd appreciate it."

"Excuse me?" Rosa asked. *Love?*

"Not to sound insensitive or anything, but I have a tee time this morning. Can you fix my wife's dog, or is it time to pull his plug?"

Rosa just stared at the man without answering, aghast at his casual disregard for the animal's future or lack thereof.

"Come on, love, out with it. I haven't got all day to waste here."

It took all of the self restraint that Rosa could muster to hold her tongue. She forced herself to think of the money. No matter how lousy the work and how stupid the people she had to deal with, she needed this job because she needed the money. Swallowing her pride and choking back her anger, Rosa answered the man as calmly and professionally as she was able.

"I'm sorry, sir, but the doctor has recommended that it would be best to bring an end to Duke's suffering at this time."

"Damn it, my wife's going to be ticked. Oh well, at least I'll be done paying these outrageous veterinarian bills."

"At least there's that," Rosa agreed sarcastically as she turned to leave the room.

"Hey," the man called out as she reached the door, "do you think that we could wait about a week before we do it? I just bought a brand new bag of that expensive dog chow. I'd hate to have it go to waste."

Rosa's response was not calm or professional. Along with an impressive string of expletives, she also thought to suggest that Duke, the Golden Retriever, was not the one who ought to be "put down." It was, actually, more of a tirade than a response. It was enough to send the man into a retaliatory tirade of his own, and it was enough to get Rosa fired.

As she walked back to the tiny apartment that she called home, Rosa did something that she hadn't done in years, something that she'd suspected she might never do again, she cried. After the years of emotional abuse that she'd suffered from her grim visions, a thick callus had developed over Rosa's heart. She'd seen so many terrible things, and not just in the movies, but in real life, things done by real people. She'd grown cold in a way, removed from the suffering to which she was a reluctant spectator. It was a necessary defense, and without it she might have gone insane long before then from the strain of her secret service. That's why it seemed so strange that after so long and so much, the tears would finally come again right then. It was more than just losing another job that had evoked her deep sentiment. In fact, losing a job was a blow that she could take easier than most people since she'd lost so many before. It wasn't just the stranger sleeping in her apartment either, but he was definitely a larger part of it.

What was she doing playing this game with Michael Galladin anyway? She'd saved his life, tended to his wounded body, sheltered him in her own home, and even shared her precious secrets with him. She'd done it all with the intention of earning his trust, hopefully even ensnaring his affections, and all for the prospect that he might be someone who could protect her. It sounded fairly ridiculous when she thought it through, seeking protection from someone she knew basically nothing about, someone who she'd seen pummeled by a couple of punk kids.

What if her instincts were wrong? If Michael turned out to be just another man who happened to show up in her dreams from time to time, then she'd have saved his life only to place him in harms way again. If the Tall Man returned tomorrow and found Michael there in her apartment, then she wouldn't really have saved his life after all, but merely delayed his death, and only briefly at that.

By the time Rosa reached her apartment, she had calmed down for the most part, soothed herself with a self-directed suggestion that there was probably nothing more to consider in regards to Michael Galladin anyway. In all likelihood, he'd left as soon as he'd awakened, and she'd never see him again, except maybe in her dreams.

The knob of Rosa's front door turned on the first try, but she clearly remembered locking up on her way out that morning.

"So it turns out you were just a regular guy after all," she reasoned aloud. "You didn't even have the consideration to lock the door behind you. Typical."

As Rosa passed her miniature dining room table, she noticed the note she'd written for Michael that morning lying there. She grabbed it up quickly, turning it over, searching for a reply. There was none. He was gone, and he wouldn't be back.

"So there's no point in wasting any more time thinking about him," Rosa advised herself. "He was hardly your knight in shining armor anyway, was he?"

She thought over her own question for a moment as she walked into the bed-room, collapsing atop the tousled sheets. Michael Galladin was moneyless, home-less, and hopeless. But still, there was something else to the man that wasn't so obvious at first glance, something mysterious that Rosa had only just begun to investigate. It might have been anything or nothing at all, but she hadn't had enough time to figure it out, and now it seemed that she never would.

Rosa's thoughts were interrupted suddenly by a faint, but familiar sound from the other room. It was a quiet click that she'd heard a thousand times before, so often that she couldn't possibly mistake it for anything else. Someone had just locked her apartment door–from the inside.

EDWARD CHARLESTON YORK

As quietly as she could, Rosa picked herself up from the rumpled bedsheets and crept over to her bedroom door. Cautiously, she peeked around the doorframe into the kitchen. A man stood next to the apartment's locked entrance, the only way in or out of her third story apartment. He saw Rosa the same instant she saw him, so she didn't bother trying to pull back out of his view.

As the two stared silently at one another, the middle-aged man struck a match and proceeded to methodically tickle the end of a very thin cigar. He rolled the cigarillo expertly between his thumb and forefinger, permitting only the very tip of the match's flame to reach the pungent smelling tobacco that immediately scented the room. He had a pinched rat's face and a sharp nose that pointed pretentiously skyward.

"Whoever you are, you're not allowed to smoke in this building," Rosa said, hoping that she didn't sound or look as scared as she felt.

"Oh, that's funny, dear girl, much funnier than you realize actually, but we'll get to that later." The man's voice was high pitched and aristocratic, with a pronounced British accent.

"Look, jerk, my husband's coming right behind me, and he's a cop, so you'd better get the hell out of here!" Rosa winced inwardly. Not only was that an unconvincing lie, she could hear panic in her every word. Undoubtedly, the man could as well.

"Really, Miss Sanchez, such silly banter will serve you no purpose this morning. Now come out from there so that I can introduce myself properly." The man seated himself at the little kitchen table as he spoke, carefully crossing his legs and smoothing the wrinkles from his neat gray suit.

Rosa retreated another step back into the bedroom, unsure of what to make of the strange intruder and of what to do about him.

"Fine then," the man continued after a moment, "remain cowering in there like a frightened child if you prefer. In truth, I hardly expected you to be a civil hostess. Be warned though, if you fail to demonstrate any courtesy, then in like fashion you shall receive none. Do I make myself clear?"

"I understand you just fine, shithead," Rosa responded, peaking back around the edge of the door frame. She was pleased to see the man wince at her vulgarity. "What I don't understand is who the hell you are and what the hell you're doing in my apartment."

"I see. I suppose that should be my cue to advance this conversation on to the heart of the matter." The rat-faced man took a long drag from his thin cigar, apparently collecting his thoughts before continuing. "My name is Edward Charleston York, and I am an associate of someone with whom you're already familiar, Ramius King."

"Oh, God." All the air was sucked out of Rosa's lungs as she whispered the quiet plea, leaving her breathless.

"No, not a god, although I suspect at times that he perceives himself as such. In truth, Mr. King is but a man, albeit an extraordinary man if ever there was one. He wields power that few people could imagine, and he possesses ambition and ruthlessness in quantities that I personally suspect to be unhealthy."

It seemed to Rosa that the man's bravado faltered somewhat as he spoke of the Tall Man, his so-called associate.

"But enough about Mr. King," he went on, brushing away a few crumbs from the tabletop before him, a cringe of disgust crossing his face. "As I said, my name is Edward Charleston York. I hate that we have to meet under these awkward circumstances, but clearly that cannot be helped. It might surprise you to know that I always regret meeting new people when such is the nature of the day's business."

"Are you going to take me to him?" Rosa whispered.

"To whom do you mean, my dear? To Mr. King? My goodness no, I'm not taking you anywhere. Indeed, I must apologize for I have gotten quite ahead of myself, haven't I? Allow me to clarify. I work for Mr. King in the capacity of a hired assassin, a hit-man if you prefer a more American phrasing. Do you understand?"

Rosa understood perfectly. She understood the word assassin, and she understood why there was one in her apartment. For whatever reason, Ramius King had decided that she was a tool whose use he no longer required. Apparently she'd served her purpose to him, and so here was Edward Charleston York to tie up the loose end that she'd become.

Rosa didn't bother to answer, nor did she wait to hear another word from the killer in her kitchen. As quietly as she could manage with her every muscle quivering, she crept across the shag carpet of her bedroom to the nightstand next to her bed. The phone on it was dead, its cord severed. Next she moved to the window. She looked outside, down at the sidewalk below, far below. It would be a drop of thirty feet. It she jumped, she'd end up a pile of broken bones at the street side. She might even die, but she might not. If she spent another minute in the apartment, she'd die for sure. Any chance was better than no chance, she reasoned as she flipped the catch to release the sliding pane. She took several deep breaths in a desperate effort to still her shaking body and quiet her buzzing mind, but she'd have been better off had she not hesitated.

The assassin pulled Rosa back away from the window with such force that she actually left her feet, flying through the air and finally crashing back down atop her bed. Before she could even utter a cry for help, a wet rag smashed down over her face, covering her nose and mouth, cutting off her air. Rosa held her breath, knowing full well what the wetness and the sudden stinging in her eyes meant.

With a strength that could be summoned only by the fear of death, Rosa struggled against her attacker, thrashing wildly and striking out with her hands and feet, but it was all to no avail.

Edward Charleston York was well acquainted with death and the desperation of the dying. He knew that the struggling would subside momentarily, just as he knew that so long as it took place atop the bed, it would stay relatively quiet. He accepted blows to his face and torso stoically, never losing concentration enough to ease the pressure from the girl's face. All he had to do was wait a few more moments.

Again and again Rosa stuck out at the man, but her breath was running out and her time along with it. As she thrashed, one hand found a grip on the man's dress shirt and tore it open, sending buttons flying through the air.

At last, Rosa's strength gave in. As she neared the point of blacking out from oxygen deprivation, her autonomic controls took over, pulling in the breath she so badly needed and along with it the toxic fumes of the poisoned cloth. The chloroform worked quickly. Within seconds Rosa's flailing arms and legs dropped motionless atop the bedsheets.

The last thing that she saw before drifting off to sleep was a glimpse of Edward Charleston York's chest. From one shoulder to the opposite side of his stomach ran the ugliest scar that she had ever seen, jagged and wide and black like a charred piece of steak forgotten atop a hot grill.

Rosa revived gently, bit by bit, so that she could recall the dream out from which she'd just been drawn. It hadn't been a premonition, but the opposite, a remembrance of a time long since past. It was a good memory, a happy one, from Rosa's childhood. There had been a camping trip with friends. They'd caught fish with an old fashioned cane pole, painted each other's faces with mud from the riverbank, ate a dinner of candybars, and then stayed up all night telling scary stories beside a flickering campfire. It was such a vivid dream that it seemed as though she could still smell smoke from the fire, even as she came fully awake.

But it was more than a phantom perception, she quickly came to realize. The smoke was real. At the same moment she also became aware of the gag in her mouth and the twine that bound her wrists and ankles, holding her immobile atop her own bed.

"Ah, there you are, my dear," spoke an uppity and all too familiar voice. "I was growing concerned that you might actually slumber on right through to the very end, the finale. As it is, you've regained consciousness in time to permit tremendous anticipation before the conclusion of our regrettably brief acquaintance. And you can take it from an expert, my dear, the anticipation is what it's all about."

Rosa tried to thrash, to tear loose from the bonds that held her, but was unable to do so. She couldn't move, she couldn't scream, and she couldn't think of anything to do to try and save her own life. All she could do was wait, breathe in the increasingly smoky air, and listen to the assassin ramble on, seemingly for his own amusement.

"Right now the fire is following a trail of slow burning fluid that I laid down shortly after our little skirmish. It came to life in the dining area, if that's what you'd like to call the only other room in this pitiful urban dwelling, and very patiently it's been creeping toward the cornerpost of your unmade bed. I wish that you could see it right now, creeping resolutely forward across the carpet, as if it has a mind of its own and knows its destination. It's hungry you see, as fire always is, but so far I've given it very little to eat. Restrained as you are, my dear, I'm not sure that you've even noticed, but I've saturated your bed with two gallons of food for the fire. In another minute or two, when it reaches you, it will have enough sustenance to grow from the flicker that it is now into a monster capable of consuming this entire building and unhappily, yourself along with it."

As Edward Charleston York prattled on, Rosa took a moment to consider the circumstances of her imminent death and the quality of her fading life. The situation seemed cruelly ironic. Her premonitions had given her forewarning of so many other people's approaching deaths and presented her with the opportunity to save them, but there she was in the end, utterly blindsided. She'd never had a clue that death might be coming for her so soon. She wondered if she might have been able to glimpse this scene ahead of its time had she slept more the previous night. Might she have been able to escape this fate if she'd spent the night alone, as she had every other night for so long?

Rosa remembered hearing once that no one was supposed to be able to dream their own death, that if they did, they'd actually die. Maybe it was true. Then again, the scenario didn't leave much room for credible witnesses. What she could be sure of was that no one was there for her at her death, just as no one had been there for her all through the last years of her life.

"You might be interested to discover that I was a professional killer long before I became intimate with fire. It was a decade and a half ago, and I recall the scene most vividly. I had already been in the service of Mr. King for most of two years at the time. I found myself unwittingly caught in the midst of an engagement of combat where I honestly had no place being. Though I am abhorred to admit it, both of the combatants were quite clearly out of my league. One of them, a young apprentice of Mr. King's most dangerous enemy, gave me the scar that I saw you take note of earlier, my reward for getting in the way. He was only sixteen years old, and with a single stroke of the weapon he wielded, he very nearly killed me. He burned me with a fire hotter than any I could ever produce myself, and the pain it caused me ... Well, I dare say, my dear, that you cannot imagine the agony that I suffered. However, that is about to change. In a moment you will not only imagine that suffering, you will live it for yourself—to death."

Rosa's breaths became pants, and beads of sweat stood out on her forehead, glistening behind a loose curl of her dark hair. She tugged against the thin ropes again, causing them to dig painfully into her wrists and ankles, but they wouldn't budge.

"My dear," York continued after a brief pause, "are you listening to me? You seem oddly indifferent to what I'm saying. This would be an unfortunate moment for a communication breakdown?"

Indeed, Rosa had stopped listening. She was concentrating instead on another sound, a fainter one mostly masked by the assassin's voice. It was a sound that she heard infrequently, except when she was making it herself. It was the creaking of someone climbing the metal stairs outside, the steps that lead to her apartment. Her heart leapt, pulling taught within her chest a last thread of hope. Maybe it was the police. Maybe they knew about Edward Charleston York. Maybe they'd been tracking him for months or even years, and now they'd finally caught up with him, just in time to save her.

Suddenly, the room went quiet. York had heard the steps as well.

"My dear, are you expecting company?"

The knob on the apartment door rattled once and then again.

"Rosa, are you in there? It's me, Michael. There's something I have to give you."

Just as swiftly as they'd risen, Rosa's hopes sank. It wasn't the police. It wasn't the SWAT team. It was Michael, the man who she'd seen pummeled by three half-grown delinquents. Not only would Michael be unable to save her, he probably wouldn't even have the sense to run away and save himself. He'd try, and almost certainly fail, to rescue her, and he'd end up next to her on the bed, finishing his day right where he'd started it. He'd be just another log on the fire to Edward Charleston York.

"Ah-ha, I knew that such a lovely girl couldn't be as all alone as you appeared," spoke the prissy voice of the assassin. "This will be a glorious end for the two of you, reminiscent of the great tragedies of old Greece. That is your sweetheart at the door, isn't it? Let's invite him inside, shall we? When I see him see you, all bound up as you are, then I'll know what there is between you."

Edward Charleston York practically skipped over to where Rosa lay atop the bed. She winced in anticipation of what he might do and was surprised when he pulled the gag from her mouth.

"Michael, get out of here!" The words came out between gasps as Rosa struggled to find her voice. "Go!"

"Well," the assassin chuckled as he replaced the gag, "apparently you don't have a tremendous amount of faith in your man's ability to defend himself, or you for that matter. Oh, well. His addition to the funeral pyre won't be quite as sweet if he turns out to be a sniveling coward, but I'll manage the disappointment. Maybe he won't even come in. Maybe he'll actually flee as you've instructed him to, which would be pointless, of course. By the time he could summon any help, I'll be long gone, and so will you."

Wham!

The apartment door burst open, and in stepped Michael. Rosa strained to lift her head high enough to see what was happening. The room was filling with wispy, gray smoke, and it obscured her view so much that Michael's face was barely recognizable.

"Welcome, young man," greeted Edward Charleston York who stood patiently at the end of the bed. "Come join us." His voice sounded as clear as if he were breathing the freshest of air. The thickening smoke didn't seem to bother him in the slightest.

As he spoke, Rosa noticed the man's hands. In his left, held out before him, an uncut cigarillo tumbled rhythmically across his fingers, and in the right, held behind his back, a long, thin blade reflected the flames that crept across the floor beside him.

"Wait here, my dear. I'll be right back," the assassin promised before stepping out into the other room to meet the newcomer.

The smoke suddenly became completely opaque as the flames around the bedroom door jumped higher, nearly closing off the passage between the rooms. Rosa heard the sounds of a commotion, but strain as she might, she couldn't see what was happening.

The air in the room had become oppressively hot, and the sheets beneath Rosa had become soaked with sweat. Her lungs stung sharply with each breath as she pulled in more and more of the noxious fumes. Her brown eyes filled with tears.

Then the strangest thing happened. It was so strange that Rosa wondered if she might be hallucinating, losing her grasp on reality as she became asphyxiated by the poison gases from the blaze. Through the smoke and the tears, she saw Michael step through her bedroom doorway. The flames which had completely engulfed the doorframe seemed to bend away at his approach, as if making room for him to pass. He made his way immediately to her side, where he tore free her restraints and picked her up into his arms with seemingly impossible ease. She buried her face into his chest and didn't open her eyes again until she tasted fresh air.

A few moments later, as gently as if she were made of glass, Michael set Rosa down on the sidewalk. She opened her eyes and looked up at her home, realizing that she'd been carried all the way down the staircase to the street side. Black smoke billowed out the door of her apartment which had been left open behind them.

"Can I save any of my things?" Rosa whispered between coughs.

Michael only shook his head in response.

An alarm sounded, and Rosa's neighbors began emerging from the shabby old building, staring up at the billowing black smoke. She counted them off mentally, satisfying herself that everyone was safely out. Then she looked back to Michael, who was scanning the street intently.

"Is he dead, the man who started the fire?"

"No, he's not," Michael answered flatly. "He left ahead of us."

"Then he could still be out here," Rosa said fearfully, starting to get back onto her feet.

"No, no," Michael reassured, "he's gone, hurrying back to his master even as we speak. We need to leave, Rosa. I know what that fire means. I know what you've lost, but you need to get away from here, and now. The man who started the fire is a killer, and he's a servant of Ramius King."

"But you said he's gone. Maybe he won't come back."

"He won't come back," Michael affirmed, "but others will, maybe even King, himself."

Rosa didn't respond to that. It was too terrible a thought even to consider at the moment.

As Michael helped Rosa to her feet, the sound of the first fire truck's horn sounded from down the street. Slowly, they moved away, holding each other's hands because they had nothing else to hold. In fact, they had next to nothing else period, just the clothes they were wearing and a brown paper bag that Michael retrieved from the base of the staircase.

Rosa looked curiously down at the bag, then at the man holding it. A strange thought popped into her mind and along with it an even stranger memory. She stopped, and Michael stopped with her.

"Why aren't you burned?"

Michael only stared back at her, his brow furrowed as if he didn't understand the question.

"The doorway between the front room and the bedroom was full of fire. Why aren't we both burned?"

Michael looked down along his own arms, seeming to notice for the first time the truth of what she was saying.

"When we get somewhere safe, I'll tell you. I'll tell you everything."

RITE OF SUCCESSION

Lily awoke early that morning feeling surprisingly refreshed. The old vinyl couch was more comfortable than it looked, and she'd slept mostly uninterrupted through the night, disturbed only once or twice by dreams of scaly-skinned monsters. Strangely though, she found herself as excited about the dreams as she was afraid of them, which was just how she felt about the events of the previous evening. Yes, she had seen terrible things, and she was certainly apprehensive about what else might be yet to come, but without doubt the adventure she'd been waiting so long for had finally begun, and that was a very exciting prospect.

She could see Kyle in the dim morning glow, still asleep on the little folding cot. She was surprised that he'd been able to sleep at all. The cot didn't look at all comfortable, and more importantly, he'd just found out about his magic. She remembered struggling to find her way to sleep for many consecutive nights after she'd made the discovery for herself.

It seemed that all was quiet in the firehouse. Either no one else was awake yet, or else they were being very considerate to those who were still asleep. She guessed that it was probably the ladder. The people she'd met the previous night hadn't struck her as late risers.

Lily picked herself up from the couch slowly, trying to minimize its squeaks for Kyle's sake. On cat's paws, she slipped from the room and into the hallway.

"Ho! You scared the crap out of me," Jerrod gasped as he and Lily practically collided. They'd both been sneaking and had accidentally snuck up on each other.

"Sorry, I was trying to be quiet so I wouldn't wake Kyle," Lily whispered.

Jerrod glanced back in at the occupied cot and nodded. I was on my way out for a breath of fresh air. Join me?"

Lily nodded that she would, and they headed out the firehouse's back door together.

"Where're the others this morning?" Lily asked once they were outside, the hush eased from her voice.

"Marion's meditating with Mr. and Mrs. Universe," Jerrod answered. "That's how they *gather themselves,* whatever that means. I guess it's supposed to be relaxing."

"I suppose everybody could use some relaxation after last night," Lily suggested.

"For sure," Jerrod agreed, "but some of us know easier ways than stretching ourselves out over the astral plain." As he spoke, he retrieved a brand new soft pack of Marlboro Lights and started packing them habitually against his palm.

"So much for the fresh air," Lily noted when she saw the cigarettes.

"Sorry, sweety," Jerrod apologized, "but this is going to be a big morning for me, and these are the only medicine my nerves respond to."

As Jerrod fired up a smoke with his trusty Doors Zippo, Lily looked out over the cornfield that stretched away behind the firehouse. It was a beautiful morning. The air was still and warm, the sun was just peeking over the horizon, smearing the sky peach and orange, and the songbirds were doing what they did best from every direction.

After the first long drag off his cigarette and the following sigh of exultation, Jerrod said, "So, I guess Kyle must have been pretty disappointed last night. It was pretty untimely having all this other stuff pop up on the night of his first date with the girl of his dreams. I'm pretty sure that's how he put it, the girl of his dreams." Jerrod's mischievous smile curled into place.

"I'm sure he just said that to be nice," Lily responded. She could feel the roses blooming in her cheeks. Her bronze skin mostly hid the embarrassment patches, but she could see in Jerrod's expression that they showed through at least a little.

"To be nice to who, me?" Jerrod asked, looking sly. "No one else was there. No, I imagine he said it because he meant it. I'm surprised to see you surprised. I'd have guessed that a pretty girl like you'd be getting hounded after by every boy in town."

"Not really," she admitted shyly. "Actually, not at all. I mean the boys notice me, but that's it. I don't think I've ever been *hounded after.*"

"Let me guess, they treat you like you're different," Jerrod said in a more serious tone. "No wonder, you are different–from them. We've all been there, everyone you'll meet in this place, even Grandma Jo. I still feel it from time to time, sitting in a restaurant or standing on a street corner. People don't know what it is they sense about us, but they sense something. They get a little nervous feeling when they're close, and it keeps them from ever getting *too* close."

"And there's no way to fix it?" Lily asked doubtfully.

"Fix it?" Jerrod asked, the smile back on his face. "Nothing's broken, sweety, it's just the way it is. It's even harder for the older Guardians who have more power. You should see Grandma Jo walk down a crowded sidewalk. They part in front of her like the Red Sea before Moses. It's hilarious, watching everybody ducking out of the way of a hobbling old lady. Their instincts tell them to scoot, and they do it. They're just obeying their gut."

Jerrod saw the corners of Lily's small mouth dip, and he knew that he hadn't offered the answer she'd been hoping for.

"But you don't have to worry about that any more," he reassured her. "You're going to meet a whole bunch of people this morning who are like you, who will never make you feel like an outsider. And, as chance would have it, there just happens to be a strapping young lad here about your age, and he just happened to have mentioned to me that he totally has the hots for you. Well, that's not exactly what he said, but that's what he was trying to say. Trust me."

Lily's blush deepened another shade.

"I'm sure that if we become students of the Guardians, like you said we might, Kyle and I'll be awful busy with studying or training, or whatever," Lily said, searching for the right words. "I doubt that there'll be time for much of anything else." She almost looked hopeful that it would be true.

"No you don't," Jerrod stopped her. "I won't let you excuse yourself so easily because you're nervous about letting someone get to know you. Besides, no matter how busy you are, you're never too busy for some things. When you've got it for somebody bad, the whole world can be crumbling away around you and you'll barely notice. Sounds crazy, but it's like that sometimes. If you're lucky."

Just then, as Lily stared out over the golden corn fields stretching away behind the firehouse, something caught her attention. A line of dust was peeling up from one of the dirt roads in the distance, and whatever its source, it seemed to be headed in their direction. Nearer and nearer the smoky plume drew, and soon it became clear that more than one vehicle must be responsible for kicking up so much dust, quite a few more.

When Jerrod noticed the approaching caravan he threw down the butt of his cigarette and headed back into the firehouse without another word. Lily could only assume that these were the people Jerrod had mentioned, the ones like her.

"Well, Lily," she whispered to herself, "here comes that adventure you've always wanted." With that she turned and headed inside to wake Kyle. It was hardly the right morning for lounging late in bed.

She found Kyle already awake, stirred by Marion in time to be ready when their guests arrived. Lily wished that Marion would have told her to get ready, too. She hadn't even brushed her teeth yet or fixed her hair or changed her clothes.

At that moment, the first of the new arrivals came walking in through the door, and Lily instantly forgot all about her teeth and her hair and her clothes. He was a broad-shouldered, dark-skinned man in a sleek, pinstripe suit. His head was covered with a thin layer of black hair, and there were lightning bolts shaved over his ears. His face was nearly covered with dark-ink artwork, tattoos that looked like some sort of archaic writing. He was a striking figure to say the least.

Jerrod met him at the door, but the man only briefly acknowledged him and continued on. To Lily's great surprise, he continued on directly to her.

"Is your name Lily?" the man asked, his voice as smooth as the edge of a Samurai sword.

"Yes," she answered so timidly that she could barely even hear herself.

The man smiled in response to her bashfulness and said, "There's a man outside who says he's your father. He told me to send you out."

Lily hurried over to the door and peered outside. Sure enough, it was her father, parked on the street in front of the firehouse in his F-150. He didn't see her right away though, being fairly distracted by the steady stream of people coming around from the side of the building where the caravan had parked. The ranks of the Guardians would have qualified as a conspicuous group anywhere, but in Steel City they were absolutely remarkable, and the look on Lily's father's face reflected his astonishment.

Lily raced out to the pick-up truck, going straight to the driver's side where her father threw open the door and hugged her tightly. He was happy to see her, but not nearly as upset as she expected, especially considering the continuing flow of strange and even dangerous looking people who were filing into the firehouse.

"Come on," he said calmly, "we're going home. Right now, get in the truck."

Obediently, Lily walked around and opened the passenger's side door. She was just stepping up into the truck when a voice called out her name.

"Lily, wait," Kyle called from the door of the firehouse. He ran out about half-way to the truck and stopped. "You can't just leave, not now."

I'm sorry. She mouthed the words, but did not speak them. She slammed the door shut behind her, faced forward, and didn't look back. Then the truck pulled away, headed unhurriedly back toward town.

Kyle turned back to the firehouse, intent on finding Grandma Jo and telling her what had happened, but he didn't need to. She was there already, just stepping out the door.

"Grandma Jo, we've got to go after them" Kyle implored. "We'll explain everything to her father, convince him to bring her back."

The old lady smiled her grandmotherly smile in response and said, "We're not in the business of kidnapping. If she wants to go, then she goes. If she wants to come back, then she'll come back. Be patient. Give her a chance to work it out."

"But it might not be safe for her at home," Kyle argued. "That's why she and I had to stay here last night, right?"

"Mmm-hmm, that's right," she agreed, "but in just a little bit all that trouble might be getting resolved anyway."

Kyle wasn't sure what exactly she meant by that, but as he watched the last of the Guardians enter the firehouse, each looking just about as jovial as a candy addict in the dentist chair, he started to have some strong suspicions. Clearly, they weren't merely stopping by for brunch or anything like that.

Without any pageantry or pleasantries, the Guardians marched through the firehouse, passing by the kitchen table and depositing one item apiece. The objects they set upon the table were strange leftover pieces of plants and animals of all sorts, all as black as tar and as lustrous as colored glass.

Kyle didn't know what to think at first, but then Marion cut into the procession, and as he watched her lay down a familiar black leaf, he suddenly understood. They were disarming. Not a single Guardian, save one, passed by the table without adding to the collection, and before long nearly twenty of the strange talismans covered the tabletop. At the end of the line came Grandma Jo, moving with her light, quick steps, not old-ladylike at all.

"Would you come here for a moment?" she asked, turning to Kyle. "I'll need your help."

"Of course, whatever you need," Kyle assured, not understanding what help he could offer.

Slowly, almost reverently, Grandma Jo lifted a necklace over her white hair. It must have been hidden beneath her clothing before, because Kyle hadn't noticed it. It was a long string of bone-white beads and in the front, spaced out with several beads in between them, were four enormous, jet black teeth

"This is the Bear's Tooth Necklace," Grandma Jo explained. "It is one of the oldest and most powerful Gifts of Nature that we know, and until the time comes when I pass it on to my successor, I lead the Guardians of Magic."

She spread the necklace out delicately in the center of the table, filling a space which had obviously been left just for her. She left one hand rest atop the necklace for a moment, breathing deeply, seemingly hesitant to give up that final bit of contact. When at last her hand withdrew, she hunched forward awkwardly, as if from back pain.

"Are you okay?" Kyle asked, taking her elbows supportively.

She smiled up at him in her wonderful grandmotherly way and said, "I'm still a tough nut to crack, but a hundred is pretty old."

With Kyle's help, Grandma Jo continued on across the room and into the hallway. A door near the sleeping quarters that had previously been closed now stood open, and they headed toward it. The door opened to a stairway which descended to a large basement. It took what felt to Kyle like a very long time to reach the bottom of the stairs, and every unsteady step that Grandma Jo took the whole way made Kyle cringe.

"Have a seat, y'all," the old lady said when she reached the bottom of the steps. Her voice sounded terribly frail now, matching her new posture.

The Guardians sat down in folding chairs which had been arranged in a large circle that more or less filled the single room sublevel. Except for a large pile of dusty boxes and crates piled haphazardly in one corner, the room was otherwise barren.

"Remember what I told you," Grandma Jo said to Kyle in her new old voice, "just watch and keep quiet." Then, she stepped gingerly into the circle and settled, with some difficulty, into the last unoccupied chair.

Kyle considered getting one of the crates to sit on, but decided against it, figuring that he'd be able to see more if he remained standing.

"Mmm-hmm, it's good to see everybody," Grandma Jo addressed the seated Guardians. "I know it's a difficult thing to ask, but I'd like you all to put the rest of today's plans out of your minds. The two men being honored in today's ceremony deserve your undivided attention." She sounded very tired.

Kyle wondered again about *the rest of today's plans*.

"Raymond, would you continue on for me?" Grandma Jo asked.

Immediately one of the Guardians rose from his chair. He was the well-dressed, black man who'd been first into the firehouse, the one who'd talked to Lily's father. Raymond was also the name Marion had mentioned to Grandma Jo after making her phone call the previous night. Kyle assumed that he must be second in charge after Grandma Jo, and looking at him, it was no wonder why.

The room was lit only with candles, and the dim glow they produced was barely enough to make the man's rune tattoos discernible. As he looked over the ranks of Guardians seated around him, he radiated authority and confidence. He looked like he was in charge.

"Fellow Guardians," he began, his silky voice filling the small space effortlessly, "we are gathered here this morning to stand as witnesses to one of our most sacred ceremonies, the passing of a Gift of Nature. Clayton, Jerrod, please step forward."

As Kyle watched on intently, Jerrod and an elderly Guardian who'd been seated next to him rose and moved to the center of the circle. The old man, the one called Clayton, had an incredibly wrinkled face and eyes that were set so deeply, it was impossible to tell which way he was looking.

Raymond nodded to them both curtly and said, "Clayton, you've proven yourself worthy of the Gift of Nature you carry for more years than most of us have walked this earth. You've fought our enemies for the sakes of your fellow Guardians and for the sakes of all people protected by our vigilance. You have been a friend and teacher to each of us gathered here, myself included, and even Grandma Jo. You have upheld our ideals and preserved our secrets throughout your time of service. For nearly eighty years you have held one of our sacred talismans, and you hold it still. You alone in this room are so armed. Our lives are in your hands. Tell us, what will you do with this power you hold?"

The old man hiked one sleeve up over his thin arm and showed a silver bracelet into which were set four giant cat claws, long and sharp looking, and shimmering like black obsidian.

"I choose to lay the power down, to pass it on to my deserving successor." His voice was soft, but full of pride.

Very slowly, he slid the bracelet from his wrist and held it out before him, offering it to Jerrod.

"You've been a patient student, Jerrod," the old man continued. "This ceremony is overdue for you. It's overdue for me, too, but letting go isn't easy even when you're as old as I am. Promise me that you'll only ever wield this weapon justly, and it's yours."

"I promise," Jerrod whispered.

Even as Jerrod reached up and grasped the bracelet gently between thumb and forefinger, and the two men briefly held the thing together, the old man's failing was already becoming visible. The grimace on Clayton's face reminded Kyle of Grandma Jo's apparent degeneration when she'd set down the Bear's Tooth Necklace, and that recognition sparked understanding. Perhaps the old lady's vigor and clarity at nearly one-hundred years old was the result of something more than good genes or a healthy lifestyle. Perhaps her longevity had more to do with the necklace she wore than it did with vitamins or exercise.

"I imagine that I will be seeing some of you again very soon," Clayton offered gravely as he scanned around the room. "Know that I'll be there to welcome you on the other side. Remember, the sacrifice I make now, and the sacrifices that others among you will yet make before this day is through, are in service to every man, woman, and child living here on God's earth who cherishes their freedom. And so I'll say goodbye now, and good hunting to you all."

As Clayton took his hand away from the bracelet, his knees gave way and his whole body went limp, appearing almost to shrink in upon itself. He fell as lightly as if he were reduced to the clothes that he wore, but he never reached the ground. As he collapsed before the watery eyes of the collected Guardians, a hand streaked through the air, caught Clayton's lifeless form by the back of his shirt, and held him there with impossible ease.

Like a mother with her newborn, Jerrod cradled the old man's lifeless form, and then he gently eased him down to the cold, concrete floor. He knelt there beside his fallen mentor for a moment, his eyes squeezed shut. He might have been lost in prayer, or he might simply have been struggling against a rush of emotions.

When he did finally stand, he looked more than recovered. He looked, in fact, reborn. The jovial young man who had posed as Kyle's foster father had vanished, and in his place stood a figure who possessed the imposing stare and regal posture of a pride leader. He exuded confidence and power in the way he held himself, and when he spoke, his voice was almost melodious in its purity.

"Clayton is gone. He lived his life and gave his life for the ideals of the Guardians, for honor and freedom."

"For honor and freedom," the gathered Guardians echoed in unison, their collective voices startlingly loud in the confined space. A chill raced down Kyle's spine.

Everything but the flickering candles fell still for a moment, and then Raymond's commanding voice called out, "Jerrod, in this room, you alone hold a Gift of Nature. The lives of your fellow Guardians are in your hands. Tell us, what will you do with this power you hold?"

"With the sacred talisman that has been passed to me," Jerrod vowed, "I will uphold the ideals of the Guardians even to my death. I will keep our secrets safe and fight for the freedom of ..."

Jerrod paused suddenly, and a look of deep concentration came over his face. Kyle wondered if he might have lost his place in the recitation.

Heads were turning all around the room. Everyone seemed to be trying to figure something out, perhaps straining to make out a faint sound, buy Kyle didn't hear anything.

"No," a voice gasped, breaking the silence. Kyle saw that it was Marion, and she was looking up toward the ceiling.

Raymond sprung into action from the center of the circle, rushing toward the stairs, shouting, "The Gifts! We have to get to the Gifts!"

"Raymond, stop!" ordered another, softer voice, freezing the Guardians' second in command with one foot already lifted to the first step. "They already have the Gifts. I could feel the power of their group increased when they were taken up. It's too late." Grandma Jo grimaced painfully. "We were so close."

"Kyle," called Marion, "go hide in those crates over there, and don't come out no matter what happens. Just stay hidden."

Kyle did as he was told, found a crate that was big enough and then climbed in and pulled the lid down over his head. As the darkness enveloped him, there was a crashing sound, and the whole room rattled. Kyle watched the events that transpired in the following moments through a thin crack in the side of his crate. The images he saw would haunt him for the rest of his life.

As Kyle disappeared down into his hopeless hiding place, Grandma Jo looked over toward him, wondering at the improbability of his finally finding the magic and coming to the Guardians, and just in time to witness their destruction.

Right at that moment, the old lady had a strange thought. She didn't have time to consider the implications of her realization, but it was curious. She hadn't noticed it before, but now that she was so intently honed in on all the nearby sources of magic, it was obvious. She realized that one distinct aura, one that she'd felt first when Kyle had entered the firehouse, was now strangely absent. She didn't understand how that extraordinary potential she'd sensed earlier could be gone from him now, but there was no more time to ponder it. There was no more time for anything.

The Fall of the Guardians of Magic

The crash that Kyle heard was the sound of the basement ceiling caving in. A flare of blue fire erupted down through the gaping hole, and when it died back, everything was left in relative darkness. The concussion of the blast extinguished the candles in the room, leaving only a diffuse stream of light from the first floor to see by, and it was heavily clouded with dust and debris.

Through the crack in his crate, Kyle watched as a man fell down through that hazy band of illumination from above. It was certainly a fall, Kyle thought, and not a jump. Someone had misjudged how large a hole was going to be opened up by the blast, and that someone had been standing a little too close when it had happened. The man's arms wind milled as he fell, an instinctual attempt to try and right his compromised balance, and he might actually have been able to land on his feet had he actually reached the floor.

The man fell to within inches of the basement floor before being struck in the middle of the back by an incredibly athletic roundhouse kick from the Guardian's second in command. The falling man was caught completely off guard by his premature drop into the basement and had no opportunity to raise his defenses, to make use of the stolen talisman he held. When Raymond's foot struck him, he lurched sideways through the air and landed in a motionless heap.

Without any hesitation, Raymond dove to the ground after the man, and when he stood up again, he held a depthless black Sycamore leaf, Marion's Gift. He turned toward Marion, ready to return the weapon to its rightful owner, but then he paused. Marion stood with one hand opened flat before her, a stop sign holding Raymond back from what he'd intended to do. With her other hand she pointed across the room to the other side of the circle of Guardians, to Grandma Jo.

Raymond flung the strange leaf through the air, and it shimmered like black glass through the streaming light. It flew through the air like a missile, but just before it reached its target it started to slow. The talisman seemed to drag against the air until it was barely moving any more, and then it settled ever so gently into the open hand of the old lady, where it immediately glowed blue.

Grandma Jo's back straightened, her head lifted, and her eyes sharpened into a predatory stare. Kyle watched her change from elderly and decrepit to powerful and dangerous in a heartbeat, but even as she transformed another of Ramius King's hunters leapt down into their midst.

This time, Kyle knew that the man had jumped rather than fallen from the first floor because he'd landed in balance. He didn't land gracefully, however, but hard, without any effort to bend and absorb the force of the impact, and the concrete floor cracked beneath his feet.

Jerrod stepped toward the center of the circle, a ball of blue light encompassing his fist. By the time he reached the intruder that light had grown in intensity and stretched out into a fiery bar, a weapon formed purely of magic, sprung forth from the power of the Gift of Nature that was bound around his wrist. Very few Guardians could have been able to produce such a weapon so soon after receiving their talisman, but it was an achievement that Jerrod had no time to take pride in.

With a broad sweep Jerrod swung his ethereal weapon, striking his enemy in the side, but its flames died instantly when it reached its mark. A burned-edged tear in Mason Stone's shirt and a faint black stripe across the smooth, gray flesh of his torso was the only proof that the fire had reached him at all.

Jerrod backpedaled, shocked at the utter ineffectiveness of his attack, but determined to try again.

Mason Stone just stood there, giving all the Guardians a good look at him, allowing them a moment to appreciate what had just happened. Then the others came, dropping down one by one through the hole in the ceiling. Ramius King's entire assemblage of hunters poured in, many twisted and inhuman looking, all dangerous, and all armed with Gifts of Nature. Only Fat Man and Little Boy, Mason's most trusted soldiers, failed to join. They, as ordered by the Tall Man himself, stood as sentries at the door by the stairs and at the hole in the floor to make sure that not a single Guardian could sneak away and survive.

Kyle watched on in horror as the previously dark room filled with firelight from dozens of flaming weapons that sprung magically to life. The room filled with screams of rage, groans of pain, and some sounds so wild and guttural that they bore more resemblance to the roar of a lion or the squeal of a boar than to human speech.

Having nowhere to run and no way to defend themselves from such an assault, most of the Guardians' ranks were cut down in seconds. None of King's hunters seemed able to reach Grandma Jo and a few who hid behind her, but everywhere else they ravaged their unarmed opposition in a bestial frenzy of violence.

Kyle wanted to turn away, to close his eyes and cut off the feed of gruesome imagery, but he couldn't. He saw the tattooed face of Raymond, his cheek pressed against the cold concrete of the basement floor and his eyes glazed over. The expression on his face seemed inappropriately peaceful amidst the chaos.

He saw Jerrod smashing his way through a wave of brutish forms, sending enemies to the floor with every swing of his reformed bludgeon of azure fire. His lips were curled back and his clenched teeth were bared. He was fighting for his life. Then the gray-skinned man was before him again, his lifeless eyes as calm as ever. With a shout of primal fury, Jerrod attacked the smallish man again, but the result was the same. As Kyle watched in stunned horror, the fire of his foster father's weapon was extinguished, and then a moment later, so was his life.

Try as he might, Kyle couldn't find Marion anywhere in the melee, but she had been on the far side of the ring when the fighting began, far from Jerrod and Grandma Jo, the only armed Guardians. Her fate had been sealed from the beginning.

Until then, Kyle had sat in silence and stillness, barely even breathing, but suddenly the power of his grief overcame his shock. Tears streamed down his cheeks, and his whole body shook feverishly. Could this really be happening, he wondered, or might this be the awful dream from which he always awakened? He closed his eyes and prayed frantically that it might be so, that he might wake up with a bloody lip or his fingernails imbedded into his palms, but with Jerrod and Marion still alive.

Try as he might though, Kyle couldn't manage to escape the reality of what was happening. He couldn't wish away the carnage that filled the room in which he hid.

When the sound of the slaughter finally dimmed, Kyle pried his eyes back open, afraid to see what was happening, but unable to stop himself from looking.

To his relief, Grandma Jo remained standing, Marion's Gift still glowing brightly in her blue-veined hand. She was panting heavily though, obviously feeling the effects of exerting herself and her magic so furiously. Bodies were strewn all around her, and to Kyle's amazement, he realized that many of them were King's hunters. As far as he could see, no other Guardian remained on their feet, but a large part of the Tall Man's attack force was down as well.

There were at least a dozen hunters still standing as well as Mason Stone, who stood facing Grandma Jo, but clearly keeping their distance. All of them but Mason began to backpedal cautiously toward the stairway, their eyes never shifting from the little, old lady who'd cut down so many of their comrades.

"Mmm-hmm, that's right," Grandma Jo hollered after them, "running away from a white-haired geriatric. Cowards! You can run as far as you like, but I swear I'll find you no matter where you go. I'll kill you sons of bitches for what you've done!"

She sounded absolutely ferocious, and it made Kyle shudder.

"Maybe you should save your strength, *Grandma*," hissed Mason softly as he, too, began to fall back. "We all have our orders to follow, and my orders were to leave you for Mr. King. That is, if you managed to survive the initial onslaught."

"And I survived just fine, didn't I? So go on, fetch your master for me," the old lady ordered defiantly.

Stone and the others disappeared up the stairway, and when they were out of sight, Grandma Jo exhaled painfully. Her shoulders dipped and her chin fell to her chest. She'd been holding a lot in while in sight of her enemies.

Kyle was about to give up his hiding spot and rush to her side when she turned suddenly in his direction and whispered, "Stay put and keep quiet."

He did.

Then the sound of footfalls reached his ears, unhurried steps creaking down the stairs toward the basement. The Tall Man was coming.

"It's been a long time, Grandma Jo," King greeted cordially when he reached the bottom of the stairs. "How I've missed you."

"Mmm-hmm, I bet you have," replied the old lady sarcastically. "You best wipe that shit-eating grin out from under that crooked nose of yours. What's happened here today was a battle, not the war. You won't have a free pass, even with us gone. There'll always be somebody to block your path. I did it for my time, and now somebody else will."

"And who might your replacement be, old woman?" King asked sharply. "My soldiers have just butchered every last one of your potential protégés. No, I think that my path is quite clear now. Who's left to stop me? The armies with their guns? I'm impervious to anything they call a weapon. Or might the masses rise up against me once I've made myself their emperor? No, I don't think so. I think it much more likely that they'll worship me. As they should. Those who do resist will be dealt with in the same way I've always handled dissidents under my command. They'll be *purged*."

"In case you haven't noticed, half of your hunters are now stinking up this basement, and it's the last thing they're ever going to do," Grandma Jo pointed out. "If you think that you and your last dozen thugs can control the world, then you've got shit for brains."

"Oh, that's right, you haven't heard. A scientist friend of mine has recently discovered a means of giving the ability to use magic to those who were born without it. That's what we've been working on down at the Mill. My first engineered magicians are nearly ready, and now, thanks to you and your recently departed Guardians, we'll have Gifts of Nature for the best of the batch. The *first* batch, that is. So, here at the time of your death, you can be assured that this world *will* belong to me, and quite soon. I'll grind up every head of state and every army general under the heel of my ..."

"Enough yapping," Grandma Jo interrupted. "I'd rather go out fighting than have you talk me to death. Shit for brains."

"So be it," King responded with a disgusted sneer.

The explosive blue flash that followed was so intense that even the thin bar of light that reached Kyle's eyes through the crack in his crate was painfully bright. Stars danced before his blinded eyes. Electric sounding screeches filled the room, high-pitched and agonizingly loud. It was the sound of massive energy arcing through the air. Every hair on Kyle's body stood on end, and he could feel his teeth vibrating in his mouth like he'd just chewed into a high voltage line.

And then everything was quiet again.

Kyle tried to peer out through the crack, but his sight was still horribly out of focus, and he felt so dizzy he could barely hold himself still. When the lid of the crate was lifted off from over his head, he cowered into the corner.

"Well, fancy finding you here," the Tall Man said evenly, sounding almost amused. "No, we haven't actually met, but we nearly did. It was I in the black Lincoln outside the school the other day. I'm sure you must remember. It was right before you scampered away across the parking lot like a frightened rabbit."

"I remember," Kyle mumbled between sobs, "and I know who you are. You're Ramius King, and you're the enemy of the Guardians."

"The Guardians? What Guardians? Haven't you been watching?" King asked smugly.

Kyle hated the man standing before him as he'd never hated anyone or anything before. He wanted so badly to strike out against him, but he knew that it would be pointless. Against Ramius King he was absolutely helpless, a mouse caught in the inescapable grip of a hawk's talons.

"What to do with you?" King wondered aloud. "I suppose that there are two options. One, I lay you down here beside the old lady and her departed followers, or two, I draft you into my own forces, groom you to become one of my hunters."

"I'll choose death over life as your prisoner," Kyle shouted bravely, struggling to keep Jerrod and Marion's faces out of his mind.

"I'm sorry, I wasn't really asking you as much as I was thinking aloud," the Tall Man apologized mockingly. "And another thing, if you come with me it will be as a student, not a prisoner. As you can see, I'm going to be a little short on naturally qualified help for a while, and so I'll be needing some new recruits. Yes, that sounds logical," he reasoned to himself. "You'll come with me."

Kyle was about to protest when one of the Tall Man's long-fingered hands flew out toward him. There was another flash of blue light, and then everything went dark.

A Secret Heritage

Lily's father didn't say a word during the car ride home from the firehouse. He was a quiet man in general, but it was rare for him to disregard his daughter completely when she was sitting right beside him. The look on his face said that for once he had plenty to say, but he was holding it in, holding it back. His expression showed more fear though, than anger, and that was confusing to Lily, and unnerving. Wondering how her father had managed to track her down at the secret base of the Guardians amplified those same feelings.

"Have a seat, Pumpkin," her father had said when they'd made it home and walked into the house. He motioned toward the loveseat, and she went to it. He hadn't called her Pumpkin since she was ten years old.

Lily sat as she was told and watched her father kick off his shoes and check the answering machine for messages. There weren't any, but if there had been he wouldn't have heard them anyway. His feet were just carrying him through his routine while he built up the nerve to say the things that needed to be said.

When he finally came over and settled himself onto the loveseat beside his daughter, his face was so full of anguish that Lily leaned over and hugged him reflexively.

"I'm so sorry, Daddy," she whispered. "I know you must have been so worried, but I didn't know what to do." Lily hadn't called her father Daddy since he'd called her Pumpkin.

Still he said nothing. His lips moved slightly, as if there were words right there at the threshold, on the verge of spilling out, but he remained quiet.

"How did you find me?" she asked timidly, not really expecting an answer, but needing to ask.

Slowly he turned to her and said, "Someone left me a note. I stayed awake all night worrying about where you really were if you weren't really staying with a friend, because I didn't think you really were. I felt like I should make some calls, but I didn't know who to call. I don't really know the families of any of the other kids in your class. I was tempted to call the police, but I had a feeling that they wouldn't be able to help. By this morning I'd decided that I'd just get in the car and start driving around looking for you, or for some sign of you. I knew it was probably a pointless thing to do, but I just needed to do something. Anyway, on my way out to the car I found the note tucked inside the screen door."

"And the note said that I was at the firehouse?" Lily asked, feeling more confused than ever. Who could possibly have left the note? The only people that knew where she was were there with her.

"Yes," her father confirmed, "it said you were at the firehouse. Listen, Pumpkin, we need to talk. There're some things that I've been meaning to tell you for a long time, but it's just never seemed like the right time. You need to know about your mother."

Lily was stunned. How in the world could all of this have anything to do with her mother? After all the years of avoidance, why would her father finally choose to broach the topic now in the middle of all this other stuff?

Her father sighed deeply, and then continued on. "I know that I've never talked much about your mom, but you have to understand how painful it is for me, even after all this time. It was such a long time ago, but it still hurts when I think of her, when I remember how it was when we were together. I loved her so much, and I'd made her everything in my life, so when she died I lost it all, everything except for you. If it wasn't for you I don't think I'd have made it through that first year. I could see her in you, even when you were very little, and much more now that you're grown. I found it comforting, like part of her was still with me."

Lily felt tears welling up in her eyes. She'd never seen her father even approach anything like deep sentiment before, and now there he was baring his soul. The thought of being very much like her mother was wonderful, but every reminder of how she'd died sparked secret agony. Lily had never really blamed herself for her mother's death, and her father surely didn't either, but there was guilt nonetheless. Even if it was unfounded, it was there, and from time to time it took hold, and when it did, it was excruciating.

"Your mother was very special," Lily's father went on once he'd steadied his voice, "and I don't just mean special to me. I don't just mean special how everybody's special in their own way. I mean she was really different, but in a good way, a wonderful way. And you are, too, Pumpkin. I know that not all the people around you can see it, but it's there. Your mother passed it on to you, how ... special she was."

Suddenly, Lily got it. It dawned on her all at once, and just like that she understood why her father was stumbling so badly through his words. She also knew why he'd sheltered her so much throughout her life and why he hadn't been more stunned by the sight of the Guardians. He knew.

"Mom could do magic, couldn't she, Daddy?"

Lily's father slumped back into the love seat and sighed.

"She was magic, Pumpkin," he answered, sounding nostalgic. "She was so full of magic that you could hear it every time she spoke and feel it all around her when she was close. She could do things, make things happen, that should have been impossible. And now, unless I'm mistaken, so can you, at least a little."

Hesitantly, Lily nodded in affirmation.

"I've been able to feel it around you for a long time," her father admitted, "most of your life by now, but I was always too afraid to do or say anything about it. Other people can sense it in you, too, I'm sure, but they just don't know what *it* is. I do though, because of your mother."

"Was she a Guardian?" Lily asked. "Was she like those people we saw this morning?"

"No, she wasn't one of them. In fact, until you said that, I wasn't even sure that those people were the Guardians. I know something about them, but not much. Your grandfather told me about them once."

"My grandfather?" Lily asked, sounding exasperated. "My grandfather knew about magic, too? Why don't I know anything about him? Why don't I know anything about any of this?"

Lily's father faltered visibly, fighting down a fresh wave of regret.

"Maybe you should have known," he conceded. "Maybe I should have told you about your grandfather and your mother and your heritage a long time ago. I don't know, but I know that I can't go back now and do things differently. I had no idea how to be a good father for you, Lily, but I did the best I could. I knew that I couldn't fill the void that was left in your mother's absence. There was so much I didn't know about babies, and then about little girls, and then about young women. It was so much harder for us than it was for other families, and I just didn't think that you needed any extra burdens."

"Maybe it wouldn't have been a burden," Lily suggested. "Maybe knowing about my mother would have comforted me. Until yesterday I thought that I might be the only one in the world who had magic. It's so lonely to think that there's no one else like you. I've felt like that my whole life."

Twin tears balanced at the rims of Lily's lower eyelids.

"I'm so sorry," her father apologized desperately. "I'm so sorry, Pumpkin. I just wanted to protect you. Everything I've done for the last eighteen years, I've done to keep you safe." He took Lily's hands in his own and squeezing them until his knuckles turned white, he asked, "Can you forgive me?"

"There's nothing to forgive, Daddy," Lily whispered, forcing her soft voice to even out, demanding herself to be strong. "Protecting me was exactly what you were supposed to do. You're a very good father."

In response to her words, Lily's father dropped his head into his hands. He remained silent, but a steady, subtle trembling revealed how delicately his composure was held.

Stricken by the sight of her father in such a state, Lily reached over and hugged him tightly, laying her head against his shoulder like she used to when she was a little girl.

And then the front door came crashing in.

Fat Man was a fitting name for one of Ramius King's most dangerous hunters. He stood nearly seven feet tall, and his bulk was immense. Any man his size could have kicked down an average wooden door easily. Fat Man, not only huge, but also imbued with devastatingly powerful magic, could have kicked down the vault door in any bank. When he kicked the front door of Lily's house, the hinges popped free from the wall cleanly, and the door itself flew all the way to the opposite side of the room where it completely smashed a floor lamp, a bookshelf, a framed picture of Lily and her father fishing, and a Chia Pet shaped like a troll. Fat Man himself, having grossly overestimated the resistance of the door, lost his balance and ended up on his face in the middle of the living room.

Even as the behemoth was stumbling past the loveseat, Lily and her father were already springing to their feet, scrambling for the front door. That is, where the front door had been. Lily made it through in time, but her father did not. Just as he reached the threshold, a fat-fingered hand grasped him about the ankle, a death grip from which there could be no shaking free.

"Lily, run!" her father screamed as he struggled uselessly against the giant man's hold. "Just go!"

All her life, Lily had always done what her father had asked of her, and so, without even thinking about it, she ran. She ran toward the woods behind the house because that's the direction she happened to pick, and she didn't even slow down until she was thirty feet into the densely growing trees. Then, when the reality of the situation finally hit her, she stopped. They had her father!

Lily set her jaw and spun around, fully intending to run right back to where she'd just run from. She didn't know what she could possibly do to help her father, but she'd do something, anything. Somehow, she was going to find a way to save him, but she never got the chance to try.

It wasn't a bone-crushing grip that halted her, but a gently whispered voice. Lily hadn't noticed anyone when she'd run into the woods, or when she'd stopped, or when she'd turned back toward the house, but suddenly someone was there, right beside her, whispering in her ear.

She froze, terrified. She didn't even hear the words that were spoken to her at first, just the voice. The second time, however, she heard him perfectly.

"Stay still, Princess. If you stay still and stay quiet, they won't find you."

Lily did what she was told, too afraid to do anything else. She stood there like she'd become one of the trees, not even glancing back over her shoulder to see whose instructions she was following. Horrified and helpless, she watched the giant man who'd kicked in the door emerge from the house. Her father was still caught in the brute's grip, but he wasn't fighting back any longer. In fact, he wasn't even moving.

"He's dead!" Lily whispered urgently.

"Hush!" hissed the voice from over her shoulder. "You don't know that. He might just be knocked out. Anyway, you can't help him, so keep still and be quiet."

"Hello, Lily Goodshepherd," called a new voice from somewhere nearby. It was a man's voice, but not a familiar one. It was deep and strong, full of testosterone. "Grandma Jo sent us to get you. She's really worried. Come on out."

Lily saw the man then. He was the size of a small child, as small as the other man was large. He looked completely unfitting for the voice that he spoke with. He walked along the edge of the woods, peering intently through the trees, trying to spot her. "We need to get you back to the firehouse right away. It's not safe for you here."

Lily kept still. If the old lady had sent someone to retrieve her, surely they would have knocked on the door instead of kicking it in.

The tiny man with the deep voice continued along the edge of the yard until he was directly between Lily and the house, just thirty feet away. It was thirty feet filled with leaves and vines and tree trunks, but Lily's red shirt couldn't possibly be hidden from the man's view, she knew.

"I know you're in there. Don't make me come in after you," Little Boy threatened, continuing to scan the woods.

Lily kept still. Why didn't he see her?

"Okay, so the old lady didn't send me, Ramius King did. You don't know him, but he's the guy that just sent Grandma Jo to her next life. Even if I can't find you, he can. There's no hiding from him, and if he has to come out here to fetch you himself, he'll probably be pretty annoyed. He'll probably take it out on your helpless father."

Lily reacted instantly to the threat, started forward, toward the little man, but was held back by a pair of strong hands that settled firmly over her thin shoulders.

Little Boy's attention seemed to be drawn by the movement for a split second, but then his gaze drifted on. He couldn't see them. After a few more seconds, he turned and headed back toward the black Lincoln parked in front of the house. Fat Man was already there, tossing Lily's father into the back seat with less care than he'd have shown a bag of golf clubs. The hulk followed him in, and as his girth settled, the car's rear end sagged visibly. Little Boy disappeared behind the far side of the sleek car, and only the sound of another door slamming shut indicated that he, too, was inside.

"Mr. King isn't going to be happy if we show up without the girl," Little Boy grumbled over his shoulder as he climbed up into the driver's seat. "I don't know how she could have disappeared like that. I couldn't sense her at all. She's just a novice. I don't think she could hide like that by herself."

Fat Man's eyes narrowed at the possible implications of his tiny counterpart's words, but he said nothing. There was nothing else to say, and there was nothing else to do, so away they drove to deliver the bad news. Their only hope was that the greatness of the day's victory over the Guardians would overshadow their relatively insignificant failure.

Lily watched the car speed away down the street. Her father was gone, stolen away by men who claimed that the leader of the Guardians of Magic was dead. For all she knew, her father might be dead as well. They were such awful thoughts, so imposing, that Lily wasn't even considering the stranger whose hands still rested upon her shoulders. When she finally turned and saw him though, he captured her whole attention.

"It's you," she gasped. "You're real. You're the man from the river, the one who told me about magic."

"That's right, it's me," wheezed the old man through a series of raspy smoker's coughs. "It's your granddad, Princess."

"My grandfather?" Lily asked, hardly able to believe that she'd heard the man right. "It was you at the river, wasn't it? You're the one who saw me use the magic the very first time, right? And you're my grandfather?"

"Yes, yes, and yes," the man answered. "It was me at the river, I saw you use magic, and I am your granddad. Once upon a time, your mother was my little princess, my pride and joy."

"And you've stayed away all this time, all my life? Why? Why would you let me see you that one time and then leave for all these years?"

"I never left, Princess," he corrected as he retrieved a corncob pipe from his worn denim jacket. "I've always watched over you from a distance. I'm the one who left the note for your father this morning."

"Why did you keep your distance?" Lily pressed. "You could have helped me so much. You could have helped me with the magic."

"You're the princess of our tribe, Lily, even if you are half your father. Magic is one thing that you shouldn't need any help with."

Lily meant to push on, to plead her sense of loss further, but her grandfather's last statement brought her up short. *Princess? Of our tribe?*

"We have a tribe?" Lily asked, feeling silly as she spoke. Suddenly, she was painfully aware of how little she really knew about her own heritage, about herself. "I'm the princess of a tribe?"

Lily's grandfather laughed hoarsely in response to her question, but the laughs changed over almost immediately into raspy smoker's coughs.

"Yes, you're the princess of our tribe," he confirmed, "but don't get too awful excited about it just yet. I'm the chief of the tribe, and that means I pretty much get to make all the big decisions for us. And besides that, you're only the princess of you and me, because we're the entire tribe. We're all that's left."

Lily's heart sank. It was like she'd just been told that she'd won the lottery, and then found out that her winnings could only be spent on fast food hamburgers.

"How could the whole rest of the tribe have died?" Lily asked, not really all that sure she wanted to hear the answer.

"They didn't all die," the Chief answered. "No, mostly they just moved on and moved away."

Lily considered this for a moment, and then asked, "So why am I still part of the tribe if they're not? I didn't even know that I had a tribe until just now. I certainly haven't been keeping up any of the old Indian traditions."

"First of all," the old man practically snarled, "Indians live in India. We're Native Americans. And secondly, you've maintained one of our oldest legacies, one that most of our people don't even believe in anymore. You have the magic."

"But the magic can hardly do anything," Lily argued.

"Wrong again," said the Chief as he fumbled through the pockets of his jacket, searching for matches. "You've hardly done anything with the magic, but the magic can do great things. The magic of our people used to be widely dispersed, but now it's been funneled down with our dwindling numbers. What was once a small talent in many is now a large talent all in you."

Lily didn't have anything to say to that. She certainly didn't believe that he was right, but she didn't know enough about the magic or the people it supposedly descended from to offer any sort of justifiable argument. She could use the magic to send the flakes aflutter in her snow globe and perform some other similarly worthless tricks, but that was it. If it could do more, she would have known. Wouldn't she?

"The magic was always strongest with the women of our tribe," Lily's grandfather explained as he carefully ignited the contents of his pipe. "My daughter, your mother, could have been the most powerful magician in the history of our people. She could have done so many things for our tribe and our ancestral land, but no, she preferred to leave that life behind. She decided to get married to some blonde-haired, blue-eyed, pasty-skinned Euro-American who should have been living in Scandinavia."

"My father is a good man!" Lily declared with such force that she surprised herself. "He's a hard worker and a responsible father, and no matter what color his hair is or where he …"

And all at once, Lily remembered the events that had just transpired. Her father was gone. She gritted her teeth, cursing herself for losing track of things. Nothing was more important than her father, not ever. Her magic, her heritage, her alleged title, and even her grandfather could all wait, indefinitely if need be. All that mattered was finding her father and making sure he was okay.

Just for the briefest moment, Lily allowed herself to consider the possibility that her father might not be okay. She began to shake all over and her throat felt dangerously constricted, making it difficult to swallow. Tears sprung from her chicory blue eyes and streaked down over her cheeks as if racing to her slender chin.

"Oh, Princess, I am sorry," the Chief whispered hoarsely, forgetting for the moment about the pipe he'd been so intent on. "I haven't been around people for so long. I've forgot all my manners. I've watched how your father's cared for you all these years, and I know he's a good man. It wasn't right of me to say nothing bad about him, especially just now. I hope you'll forgive me. I always was a horse's ass when it came to being proper and doing all the niceties."

Despite everything, Lily giggled in response to the old man's curse. She could see a charm in him as he apologized that hadn't been there before, and it was a relief. She could live with her grandfather being bitter, but not if he was too bitter to help her.

"Please help me find him," Lily pleaded, her voice filled with quiet desperation. "Grandfather, please."

"I'll help you do whatever I can help you do," he vowed. "But before we do anything, we need to get someplace safer than here. I don't know if them boys' boss would really come back here to collect you himself or not, but if he did, I might not be able to hide you. My magic might not be enough."

"You mean you have magic, too?" Lily asked, sounding the tiniest bit hopeful. Maybe the Chief really would be able to help rescue her father.

The old man sighed deeply and said, "Oh, I got a little bit left, but not much. I can still use it to keep hidden, but that's about it. And it's getting so I can only even do that very well when I'm here in the woods."

"Will I be able to come back to the house later?" Lily asked, considering the proposition of leaving all her things in a house with no door. "Can I run in and grab a few things before we leave?"

"I can't hide you outside the woods," the Chief answered, shaking his head. "As far as later is concerned, it might be a lot later, but I'm not so worried about that house and the stuff in it as I'm worried about you."

Lily just nodded, accepting his decision. She had no idea how to go about finding her father, and if what those two men had said was true, her grandfather might be the only one left to help. She looked back at the house, seeing it in a way she never had before. There were so many memories there, so many special times shared between her father and herself. The idea that their sweet and sour conversation on the loveseat that morning might turn out to be the last of those special times was almost unbearable.

The touch of the Chief's rough fingers against her cheek jolted Lily back from her grim reverie. When she looked back, she found that he was smiling. All the considerable wrinkles in his leathery face stretched with the expression, and left him looking something like a giant dried fig with teeth. Not that many teeth though, she noted.

"I didn't mean to startle you, Princess," he apologized softly, "but I've wanted to do that for such a long time. That hair and those eyes are from your father, but you've got so much of your mother in you, too, and even after all these years I miss her terribly. If not for you, I'd be all alone, the last of us."

Lily didn't know what to say, so she said nothing. She just smiled back, that shy, secret smile that she shared so rarely, a genuine treasure for anyone who could find it.

The Chief headed off then, trudging through the woods with an old man's swaying gait, and Lily followed. Periodically, she noticed him peering fixedly into the trees to one side or the other, seemingly searching for something. She didn't even bother guessing at what it might be.

Any Average Couple

By late Sunday evening, Michael and Rosa had rode the city bus to the far side of Miami, picked up fresh clothes and a few hygiene necessities at a dollar store, checked into a two-bed room at a chain hotel, and found a nearby sports bar where they could catch their breath and eat some supper. Michael insisted on paying for everything, and he did so entirely with cash. Watching him produce one crisp Grant after another from the pocket of his new utility pants roused suspicion in Rosa, reminding her of how anxious he'd been to avoid meeting the police the previous night. However, she wasn't about to decline the offer to be treated, especially when everything she owned had literally just gone up in smoke. She couldn't even offer to go Dutch.

It was a relief for both Rosa and Michael when their meals were served. Eating was a good excuse not to talk, and a good excuse made the silence between them more comfortable. Rosa ate quickly, which she'd grown accustomed to doing during her short lunch breaks at work, and finished first. She watched Michael intently smearing ketchup back and forth across his plate with a greasy fry, his expression melancholy as always. Finally, inevitably, she broke the silence between them.

"So, I'm thinking that you've had plenty of time now to organize your thoughts or whatever, so let's have it already."

"Have what?" Michael asked, looking up from his plate at last.

"Have what?" she repeated in disbelief. "What the hell do you think? An explanation for all the crazy shit that's happened to me since I met you last night, that's what. I can't believe that was only last night! I've known you twenty-four hours and in that time I've nearly been killed–twice, run over by a yuppie first and then burned alive by an arsonist maniac. I lost my job and all my shit got torched and my apartment with it. I'm thinking that some sort of explanation is in order. I'm sure you agree."

Michael winced in response to hearing the last twenty-four hours' events in a nutshell. Everything she'd said illustrated exactly why it was so important for him to keep his distance–from everyone. His was a cursed life, and it wasn't fair to share that curse with anyone else.

"You're right, of course. I owe you that much and more. I guess before I say anything else, I want to say that I'm sorry. I certainly never meant to cause you any trouble. I wish that I could undo …"

"You're sorry?" Rosa asked, sounding amazed. "That's what you wanted to say first, that you're sorry?"

Michael was stunned by her response. He felt suddenly wracked with guilt.

"I don't know what else to say," he admitted miserably.

"How about "you're welcome," you might want to say that."

Michael bit back what was going to be a continuation on his apology, floored all over again by her suggestion.

"I mean granted," she continued, "it's been a pretty shitty day for me, one of the worst I've ever had, but it could have been worse. It would have been worse if not for you. The guy that started the fire, he came for me, not you. He came to kill me. And he would have if you hadn't shown up and chased him away. You rescued me, and it was the most amazing thing that anyone's ever done for me. You were like my knight in shining armor. You don't need to apologize for anything, you just need to catch me up on what the hell all this is about."

Michael just stared at her as if dumbstruck. Under the weight of Rosa's praise, his defenses were buckling. The high wall around his heart was nearly breached.

"I hate to have to admit this," Michael said hesitantly, "especially now, but I didn't really chase him away. He just left."

Rosa looked at Michael as if he'd just said something that struck her as very stupid.

"You see, I met that man before," Michael went on, "a long time ago. There was a fight, and I hurt him–badly. I might have almost killed him, but I'm not really sure. When he saw my face this afternoon he must have recognized me, even after all these years, and then he just left."

Rosa pictured Edward Charleston York in her mind, pictured the wicked black scar that crossed his torso. Could Michael have done that? It was hard to imagine.

"How did you hurt him, Michael? Did you burn him somehow?"

Quite inopportunely, the waitress stopped by their table just then, offering refills on their drinks.

When she was gone, having left the bill on the table, Michael reached into his pants pocket and retrieved enough money for the meal and a generous tip.

"There're people waiting at the door," he noted. "We should probably get going so they can have our table."

"Sorry, my attention span's not that short, Redbeard," Rosa said, letting the nickname slip again. "Will you answer my question or not?"

"I will," Michael affirmed with a small nod, "but let's get out of here first."

Without anything further, they rose and left, looking all the part of any average couple out for a casual dinner. How deceiving looks can be.

It was turning into an unseasonably cool night as the two strode back toward the hotel. High, thin clouds moved rapidly across the dark sky, offering intermittent glimpses of a round moon that was as yellow as a cat's eye. With the crowd, the noise, and the smoky air of the sports bar left behind, it seemed that an appropriate moment for the sharing of quiet secrets had finally arrived. It was Michael who began.

"It's a bigger world than what most people see everyday on their drive to work, Rosa. There are things that most people don't know anything about and that nobody can really explain. There's magic."

Rosa paused between strides, looking up at Michael through a dark curl of hair that hung down over her face.

"You've got to be kidding me? This is my explanation? I can chalk my recent run on sour luck up to mystical forces? Or is David Copperfield plotting against me? For his next big trick he made my job and my apartment disappear?"

"No tricks," Michael responded calmly, apparently not surprised by the sarcastic response. "I mean real magic, the kind that lets you glimpse the future."

"Don't even go there. They always told me that my grandma was some kind of gypsy psychic or something, not that I ever really believed them then, but hey, considering how things are for me now, I guess she probably was. Anyway, my visions came from her. Maybe me and her got some special brain waves or something, but it's not magic. Who even talks about magic like it's a real thing anyway? It's crazy talk. Maybe the only explanation I need is that you're a little loco, Redbeard."

"Are you finished?" Michael asked when he could. Once again, he was amazed at how quickly Rosa could switch back and forth between solemn and sassy.

"Look at me, Rosa," Michael pressed, "and listen to what I'm about to tell you, because it's something that you need to hear. I'm not crazy, and I'm not an idiot, and I'm telling you that magic is real. It's not like magic you see at kiddy birthday parties or Vegas stage shows, it's not card tricks and illusions. Magic is a force of nature and a powerful one. Very few people are aware of its presence in our world and fewer still are able to utilize its power. It's magic that makes Ramius King the most dangerous man alive, and it's magic that's responsible for your premonitions."

Rosa paused momentarily in thought and then started again down the dark sidewalk toward the hotel. Michael hurried to keep pace, trying to catch her eyes.

"I don't think that you're crazy, Michael, and I don't think that you're stupid either, but you're asking me to make a big leap here."

"Why? Why is it such a big leap? How many lives have been saved because of your foresight? Rosa, you can do something that other people can't do, and it's because you have a gift that they don't have. You have an ability that ninety-nine percent of all people don't even believe to be possible. Don't you feel that separation between you and the people you meet on the street and at work and in restaurants and movie theaters? Isn't it why you live alone?"

Rosa kept walking, kept staring straight ahead. The idea of magic being real was outrageous, and yet it came from a man whom she trusted. Although she'd know him only a day, Rosa trusted Michael as much as anyone she knew. She could hear the integrity in his words and see it in his deeds. He wouldn't lie to her, which meant that either he was wrong or else it was true. Could it be true?

"You have to believe that magic is real, Rosa. There's more that I need to tell you, but I'll be wasting my breath if you don't believe me about magic. That has to come first. So tell me right now whether or not there's any point in me going on."

Rosa stopped again, fighting back a sick feeling in her stomach. She dared herself to believe that it was true.

Looking up at Michael in the half light, she was struck once again by his oddly combined features. There was a remarkable strength in him, she sensed, but it was hidden deep beneath calluses of loneliness and regret. And there were his eyes, so filled with sadness and fatigue, as if they'd been stolen from a man twice his age.

"I trust you, Michael, and I'll believe what you tell me."

Michael hoped that it was too dark for Rosa to read his face. He hoped that she couldn't see how much her words affected him, how deeply he appreciated her trust.

"There are people in the world who posses the ability to use magic, and there have been such people for a long time, thousands of years. Some of the fairy tales that you were told as a child, stories about sorcerers and spellcasters, some of them are based on truth, on real people from the past. A thousand years from now there may be legends based on the life and deeds of Ramius King. He's the most powerful wielder of magic in the world today, one of the most powerful there's ever been, and eventually he will share with the world the secret that I'm sharing with you now. He's a potent and ambitious man, and the life of underground plots and covert operations that he lives now will never satisfy him. He's intended to live a life of mythical proportions from the day he killed his father for the Gift, maybe even before."

"How could he have taken the gift from his father?" Rosa asked, confused. "I thought it was something inside of you, like a talent from birth."

"That's not what I meant. King was born with the ability to use magic, just like you say. What he took from his father was a Gift of Nature, a tool that magnifies his strength tremendously. They're incredibly rare, and those who hold them can't be challenged by those who don't. Ramius King's father found a Gift at an archaeological dig near Cairo sixty years ago, one that had been wielded by a magician in ancient Egypt millennia ago. It's the oldest Gift we know of and the most powerful, and it's King's. As long as he has it, he's top dog."

Rosa shuddered. Some of what Michael was saying was hard to follow, but that last part she understood perfectly well. There was a man who was evil in a way she never imagined anyone could be, a man who had hurt her beyond healing, and according to Michael, there was no one alive who could stop him from doing it again.

"King isn't without opposition though" Michael continued, starting back down the sidewalk again. "There are the Guardians, a group of people who also have the ability to use magic. For hundreds of years they've sought out magicians and Gifts of Nature to add to their strength. Time and again they have served as a counterforce in opposition to those who would use magic as a means to oppress and dominate others."

Michael looked down at Rosa and read the question in her eyes.

"I was one of them," he confirmed, "but it was a long time ago. I don't carry a Gift of Nature anymore, and I can't control the magic like I used to."

"What do you mean you can't? You lost the knack or what?"

"Something like that," Michael answered, just audibly.

"Something like that or that?" Rosa demanded, not willing to let him off the hook so easily. "You almost killed King's assassin when you were only a kid, but now you can get whipped by a few junior street thugs? Come on, seriously, what's the deal? Did you get hurt and now you can't do it anymore?"

"No, I hurt somebody else, and now I can't do it anymore!" The words were out before Michael could stop them, and there was no taking them back.

Rosa heard it in his voice even before she saw the clenched muscles in his jaw and the worry lines at the corners of his eyes. It was the final answer to all her questions about Michael.

"What happened?" she whispered.

Michael didn't answer, and Rosa didn't ask again. They kept walking, Michael looking more like an apparition than a living man. His steps were silent as always, and his face was a stony mask of detachment. He'd gone away from himself, from a dark street in southern Florida and from a night in the late-summer of his thirty-first year. He'd gone to the time and place of his nightmares, to his last day as a Guardian, the day his brother died.

They entered the hotel in silence, passing a few late arriving guests carrying their suitcases, a group of businessmen headed to the lounge, and three small children chasing each other around in bathing suits dripping with pool water. Rosa noted how everyone that went by took note of Michael. Even the chlorine scented children slowed briefly and quieted their giggling until they were past. It was as if everyone sensed something in him, some invisible aura of authority. Or danger.

While Rosa showered, Michael stood at the hotel room's only window, staring out into the blackness. He knew that neither the soft pillows nor the warm blankets on the bed behind him could offer any comfort. Out there in the night was where he would be most at ease, where he could feel the breeze blowing across his face and smell the salt spray it carried. He'd spent too many nights on the streets, and the tiny hotel room felt oppressively claustrophobic.

So much had happened in the last day, and consequently Michael's mind raced along several lines of thought at once. He thought of Edward Charleston York, a figure from the past that he'd left behind. He thought about the fire in the apartment, trying to recall exactly how it had looked. Everything had happened so quickly. He'd been in and out of the burning bedroom in a matter of seconds and had acted mostly on instinct during that small window of time. He honestly couldn't remember how close the flames had been, but he suspected that they were very close. He wasn't sure why he hadn't been burned, but he had suspicions about that, too.

Michael was thirty-one years old and had spent the last fifteen as a wanderer, almost half his life. His childhood had already been completely behind him by the time he set out on his own at the age of sixteen, but he hadn't been a grown man yet. During his years of roaming, it seemed that he'd not only finished growing up, but already grown old. He'd wasted a decade and a half, but there were worse things than wasting time. Better to do nothing than to do wrong. And maybe not all of the dirty money he'd commandeered for the shelters and soup kitchens had gone to waste, maybe some of it had actually helped someone to get back on their feet and improve their life. He hoped so.

He'd saved Rosa, too. At least there was that one good thing that he knew he'd done right. What he should do for her now that he'd saved her, he wasn't sure. Rosa's assessment of Edward Charleston York had been correct. If King had sent him for her, then she wasn't supposed to have survived the day. York wasn't a kidnapper or an intimidator, he was a killer. If someone needed to be removed and that someone wasn't a wielder of dangerous magic, then it was a task for York. The Tall Man preferred not to expose his more powerful agents unless it was absolutely necessary. York, though he commanded no magic, was cunning and professional and almost always completed his assignments.

Michael imagined York standing before his master, briefing him on the failed mission to Miami. He imagined the look on King's face when he heard that Michael Galladin was still alive. His response would be immediate and definitive, and it wouldn't be a return trip for Edward Charleston York. Knowing Michael's history full well, King would take no chances. If he didn't come after them himself, he'd send someone in whom he placed a tremendous amount of confidence. The next attack wouldn't involve fire or firearms, but magic. If one of the Tall Man's agents was able to track them down, then it would take magic to save them, but the most solemn oath of his life prevented Michael from using his own magic, if it was even still within his reach.

Turning away from the dark window and the sounds of the city night outside, Michael strained to hear the shower still running in the bathroom. How would he be able to save her if she needed saving again, he worried? *If she needed saving?*

A new and startling possibility suddenly presented itself. What if Rosa didn't need saving? He had never known magic to be expressed in anyone else as it had in her, and he had no idea how frequent or how clear her visions of the future were. If she could see the imminent deaths of complete strangers, didn't it seem likely that she would be able to see her own approaching demise? Who could guess at the true motives of a person who acts in response to events that haven't yet taken place? Was it possible that she might be using him? Might she have saved his life the night they met because she already knew that he would later save hers? Might she have let herself be captured by York only to be saved by Michael, already knowing how things would turn out?

Michael shook his head, erasing the speculations from his mind. He had considered the possibility of his being used, and that was cautious. To dwell upon those theories without further evidence would be paranoia.

Michael yawned deeply, a reminder of what a busy couple of days it had been. Pulling an armchair next to the open window, he sat down, folded his arms across his chest, and stretched out his legs. He was still thinking of Rosa as he drifted off to sleep with uncharacteristic swiftness. He wasn't thinking about how she might betray him if her apparent intentions were false, nor was he thinking about how he might protect her if she turned out to be genuine. Instead he was thinking about how it might feel to run his fingers through her beautiful, dark curls.

"What's that?" Rosa called from the bathroom.

She'd just emerged from the shower and could have sworn that she'd heard Michael's voice from the next room. It didn't seem likely that he'd be making a phone call to some buddy who lived nearby, so she assumed that he must be talking to her.

She heard it again, undoubtedly Michael's voice, but his words were spoken too softly to understand.

"Can't you wait a second?"

Still she could hear his mumbling. Rosa wondered if someone might have shown up at the door. Maybe Michael had ordered a pizza or something. It wouldn't be a bad move on his part, she thought. He could stand to pack on a couple extra pounds, but something told her that he wasn't likely to invite a delivery boy or anyone else to come to their room.

Wrapping a towel around herself, Rosa opened the bathroom door a crack. In an instant she understood what it was she'd been hearing. Although she still couldn't make out Michael's words, she recognized the way they were being spoken immediately. Michael sounded exactly as he had the previous night in her apartment on the other side of town—when he was dreaming. The difference was that this night the lights were still on and Rosa could plainly see Michael's face and the horror that was written upon it. He looked like a small child who desperately needed his mother to wake him, to save him from the monsters in his nightmares. What could be so terrifying to a man who walks in and out of a burning building without breaking a sweat?

"It can't be you," he mumbled through quivering lips, tossing his head to the side.

"Michael," Rosa whispered, hesitant to disturb him while in such a state. "Michael, can you hear me?" On her toes, she crept across the room.

Michael didn't respond.

Very gently, Rosa reached her hand toward his, which was holding the arm of the chair in which he sat in a white-knuckle grip. Her fingertips brushed against his wrist.

A bright light flashed behind Rosa's eyes and a chill rushed up her spine, curling her toes and sucking all the air from her lungs. She backed up a step from the still sleeping form of Michael, gasping and fighting to regain her balance, struggling just to stay on her feet.

As the wave of vertigo passed, Rosa realized that the flash in her head had been more than just light, it had been an image. In the instant when she'd touched Michael's wrist, she'd seen a picture, a still frame of Michael, or rather what Michael must have looked like when he was only a teenager. The perpetual sadness that she was accustomed to seeing in his eyes had been absent as had his beard, but there was no mistaking his angular face, even at the much younger age. She felt sure that it had been him she'd glimpsed, but if it was, then how could the image have come from where she suspected? If she'd just peeked into Michael's nightmare, then he was doing something that no one was supposed to be able to do, dreaming his own death. That's what she'd seen, a young Michael Galladin laid dead upon the ground.

"Somebody help me!" Michael begged in a much stronger tone, but still without waking himself.

Rosa winced at the agony that was obvious in his voice. She wanted to help him desperately, but how could she, except to wake him up and release him from the dream's grip. Clearly that's what she needed to do, and yet she hesitated, tempted by the draw of another possibility. Could the nightmare divulge the secret that Michael hid? Could she have her explanation at last? Perhaps if she better understood his situation, she would be better able to help him.

Once again, even more slowly than the first time, Rosa reached unsteadily toward Michael's restlessly sleeping form. When she gently cradled the side of his face in her small hand, the light behind her eyes returned in a surge, growing rapidly brighter until its intensity drowned her actual vision. The hotel room, along with all its sounds and smells, was smeared from her awareness and in its place a whole new world materialized, the world of Michael's nightmare.

Michael's Nightmare

Rosa struggled against the disorientation that seemed to be gumming up the gears of her brain, slowing the pace of her thoughts to a crawl. It felt as though her body had just been flung a million miles in a heartbeat, and it was taking a few seconds for her mind to catch up and get settled back into place.

The new world that surrounded her was more or less as she'd glimpsed it before, but now she could truly appreciate the vividness and detail of its features. In every breath drawn in over her lips she could taste the flavors of late evening in the woods, musty air seasoned with rotting leaves and mildew. She could feel the cool and dampness of the breeze and smell a hint of some unknown wildflower's sweet fragrance. It was all so real! She could see the stars just becoming visible in the fading twilight and the shivering needles of some nearby pines. She could hear a horribly familiar voice.

"I'm sure you think that I'm a monster for doing this, but you really must understand that in the end we all do only what we are naturally suited to do, what we are *meant* to do. Other men are born with affinities for building, cooking, painting, playing golf, and so many other such talents, but I was not. My innate skills are in killing, and I do it very well. And I'm paid very well to do it. I do detest in a way being commissioned for a target so young as yourself, but if it were not me, then it would be someone else, someone with less consideration in all likelihood. In fact, I have to admit that I am somewhat surprised to be the one who found you first. Mr. King's new prodigy, the one they call the Guardian Hunter, has been seeking you out as well."

Although the speaker's face was hidden mostly in shadow, there was no mistaking his prim, arrogant voice. The man stalking young Michael Galladin through the forest of his dream was the very same man who'd tried, and nearly succeeded, to kill Rosa earlier that day, Edward Charleston York.

As Michael's younger self backed steadily away through the dusky woods, York paced him nonchalantly, appearing completely unhurried. A glint of the evening's ambient light caught Rosa's attention. A knife had suddenly appeared in the assassin's hand. In fact, unless she was mistaken, it was the very same knife she'd seen before. Or had she seen it later? Seeing the past, for she was now almost certain that's what the dream was, and seeing it "live," made things confusing.

"You might be interested to know that I acquired this knife from the home of a Senator, my first prestigious target. I was hired to eliminate ..."

Young Michael, apparently more afraid for his life than captivated by the killer's rambling, bolted at the sight of the weapon and was pursued immediately. As the two men charged headlong through the dark forest, Rosa somehow kept a steady view of the action, seeming to fly along beside them, slaved to their motion.

It was like watching a nature special on TV, a big cat chasing down a calf buffalo, enjoying the hunt before savoring the kill. That's just what it looked like, right up to the point where young Michael looked back. It was nothing more than a quick glance over his shoulder, a check on the progress of his pursuer, but in that split second Rosa saw his face clearly, and what she saw there made her reconsider her take on the situation. Michael looked calm, without any trace of fear. He didn't look like a fleeing prey, like a calf buffalo. He looked like a big buffalo, a bull, a creature that had long ago outgrown the need to run away from or be afraid of anything.

Through the Woods Rosa flew, watching the two men weave and dodge between the trees while she seemed to pass right through them. She should have felt terrified, frightened beyond reason, but that's not what she felt at all. Instead she felt calm, a calculated, steady coolness that seemed wholly inappropriate under the circumstances.

Then Michael was in the open, suddenly emerged from the forest into the dead end of a small, dirt road. A large black van was parked along side the road, its back doors opened wide, and next to the van stood another man, old enough to be Michael's father. The van's parking lights bathed the area in a soft glow of orange light, making it easier for Rosa to see, but still not revealing anything beyond thirty feet in front of the vehicle.

Michael slowed as he approached the van, nodding to the other man who casually tossed him a strange looking black object. It was solid black and curl shaped, and it ended in several sharp looking points. Rosa wasn't sure what it was, but at the instant when it landed in Michael's hand, her chest seemed to fill with a strange warmth.

Then Michael turned back to face the direction from which he'd come. He still looked completely collected, not winded in the least from his flight, if that's truly what it had been. Rosa had her doubts.

In fact, the more she thought about it, the more certain she became that she knew what it was she was really seeing, and it wasn't Michael Galladin fleeing for his life. It was a trap for the man chasing Michael, for Edward Charleston York, Ramius King's assassin. She knew it. She knew how they'd lured the killer to that spot and baited him into pursuing Michael. She knew what they planned to do in a moment when York materialized from the dark woods. She even knew the name of the man standing next to the van, although she'd never seen him before. She knew everything that Michael knew.

Thinking back again to the out of place sense of calmness that Rosa had felt as she'd flown along side the running men, things suddenly clicked. It was Michael who'd stayed calm, not her. Not only was she seeing his past, she was hearing his thoughts and feeling his emotions. She was truly experiencing the memory exactly as Michael did.

Edward Charleston York reappeared, still running at a near-sprint and still holding the thin silver blade before him. When he saw the van and the two men, he immediately stopped, dropped the knife, and falling to one knee, he drew a small black pistol from the inside of his jacket. He didn't bother with threats or ultimatums, he just fired, and he kept firing until every shell was spent. Then he calmly replaced the weapon back into his jacket.

Neither of York's targets fell back from the gunfire, nor did they even flinch. They stood side by side, each with one arm extended forward, one palm held flat toward York, looking as if they were shielding their eyes from a bright light.

It was difficult for Rosa to see exactly what happened to the flying bullets, whether they were stopped short of their targets, redirected, or completely disintegrated. One thing that was perfectly clear though, was that none of them reached the men they were intended to kill.

Rosa could still sense the concentration and confidence of Michael. He knew, and so she did as well, that the gun couldn't hurt him. Shared memory confirmed that his defense against such an assault had been tested before.

"Now you know what I really am, Mr. York," young Michael said, his voice cool, but cautious. "I'm no longer a student as you were led to believe, but a graduate, a Guardian of Magic." He held the strange, black object before him as if offering proof that could confirm the truth of what he said. "I know that you're a killer for Ramius King, and I also know that you don't wield any magic. You're powerless to resist me. Get into the back of the van quietly, and you have my word that no one will hurt you."

Edward Charleston York didn't look frightened as much as he looked furious, at the brink of rage for being deceived and belittled by the much younger man. He looked like a cornered animal, desperate and dangerous. Just when Rosa was sure he was about to fight or flee, his shoulders sagged. He exhaled the breath he'd been holding, unclenched his jaw, and started slowly toward the van, apparently accepting the inevitability of his defeat. Ten feet short of his soon-to-be captors, York stopped, his eyes darting to the shadowed space behind Michael and his partner.

Instinctively, the two Guardians spun around, raising their magic in defense with a sweep of their hands. For Michael it was a reflex action, like a karate master blocking a punch, and still he shielded himself with no time to spare. His partner was only momentarily slower, but it was a moment too long.

Blinded by an explosion of light, Michael didn't actually see his partner engulfed in the blue flames which seemed to be erupting from the extended hands of their sneak attacker. It took only a split-second though, for his vision to clear, and when it did, the damage that had been inflicted was all too plain to see. The other Guardian lay across the ground, literally smoldering. His eyes were wide and panic stricken, and his body was fixed in an unnatural pose of frozen motion, limbs fixed at sickeningly awkward angles.

Suddenly Rosa was afraid. The calm which had permeated her before was gone, and in its place came terror. Young Michael's perfect composure had slipped. More than that, Rosa was terrified because she knew who the new threat was. Although his face was totally hidden behind a red mask, she knew, because Michael knew. The shared memories told her that this was Ramius King's newest and deadliest agent, the one they called the Guardian Hunter.

Young Michael stepped back unsteadily, keeping his eyes locked on his new enemy instead of his dying comrade. As he retreated, he held his empty hand before him in a tight fist, squeezing his fingers together so intensely that Rosa could see the muscles in his forearm quaking from the effort. Had his hand been wounded in the attack? Rosa didn't think so, but couldn't be sure.

The Guardian Hunter stepped forward, and bending over, he grabbed his wounded victim by the charred remnants of his shirt and hauled him harshly back up to his feet.

"Don't touch him!" Michael yelled, the rage in his voice blatant. Still his clenched fist trembled before him, apparently straining to crush some invisible object in its grasp. "Leave him alone!"

The Guardian Hunter seemed not to respond to Michael's demands. If there was any reaction to his words, it was hidden behind his demonic, crimson mask. He looked like a horror movie come to life, and Rosa didn't think that she would ever be able to look away no matter how badly she wanted to. The man held a black object just like the one Michael held, and as he brandished it before him, Rosa cringed, terrified to see what he was going to do, but she couldn't risk taking her eyes off of him even for a second. Only when the aura of blue light surrounding Michael's shaking fist became impossible to ignore was she finally able to shift her attention.

It looked as though he was holding the world's brightest firefly, and its light was bursting out through the cracks between his fingers, but she knew that couldn't be so. Young Michael couldn't be holding any firefly or flashlight or anything else, because only moments before she'd seen that his hand was empty. The light was his own, his magic coming to life.

Brighter and brighter the blue glow grew, illuminating Michael's face from below, creating sharply contrasting shadows over his nose and eyes, making his features look eerily skull-like.

The light emanated most strongly from the top of his fist, where it began to stretch out into a thin beam, and then a gently curving arc, a blade. Wisps of blue fire danced over the surface of the condensed light. Only when the radiance of the beam had become too bright to look upon directly, forcing her to look away, did Rosa hear its song. She knew instantly that's what it was, the song of Michael's sword. The blazing shape that had sprouted mystically from his fist was the young man's weapon, a sword built of magic, substanceless energy forged into something corporeal. The sword's song was high and clear and beautiful, like the humming of a fine crystal goblet tickled by a moist fingertip. The image of the weapon was inspiring and terrifying, and in seeing it Rosa truly realized the power and potential of magic for the first time.

The song of the flaming blade was enchanting, and Rosa felt herself lulled by its beauty and its comforting familiarity, for some part of its voice was Michael's. It was not so much the tone or timbre with which he spoke that she recognized, but the pure sincerity that was woven into his every word.

The clarity of the song lasted only moments though, before another sound was competing with it in Rosa's ears. It was another steady humming, but a very different one from that of Michael's sword. This second hum was a deep growl, electric and dangerous, the sound of something lethal to the touch.

Rosa looked back to King's man, the Guardian Hunter, already suspecting the nature of the menacing new sound. The man stood where he'd been, still holding Michael's wounded companion, keeping him on his feet.

"Where did you get that Gift?" Michael asked, his voice laced with panic. He pointed his ethereal blade toward his enemy's talisman, a twin to his own. "How did you get it? If you hurt him, I'll kill you!"

The Guardian Hunter turned his eyes to the limp form he held beside him, offering no response to Michael's inquiry.

As Rosa looked on helplessly, a point of light appeared amid the chest of the fallen Guardian, shining with the same blue brilliance that emanated from Michael's sword. Slowly, so slowly that Rosa could barely wait to breathe again, the point of blue light extended, lengthening into a blade, one shorter and stouter than Michael's, piercing the helpless man's frame like a hot poker through a sheet of candle wax.

"NOOO!" Michael roared with so much savage anger that if caused Rosa to shudder.

With an indignant shove, the Guardian Hunter deposited the body of his most recent victim to the ground beside him, where it settled in an awkward position that no living creature would have tolerated. The masked killer stepped forward then, his stride careful and ceremonious. He raised his own fiery sword before him and made a shallow bow, a gesture of mock courtesy that invited violence.

Michael's response was immediate. Like a projectile fired from a giant sling-shot he lunged forward, seeming to fly through the space that separated him from his adversary. The voice of his sword rose in volume and pitch, no longer beautiful, but shrill and grating like the squealing tires of a speeding car sliding out of control. With equal speed, the Guardian Hunter reacted to the attack, throwing up his own blazing weapon in defense, and when the two blades struck, their collective blue light flashed blindingly bright. The energy released at the swords' impact threw the men back apart, repelling them from one another like two magnets meeting with the same pole.

When only a moment before Rosa had struggled to pull a single breath into her lungs, now she panted furiously, almost hyperventilating. She could feel every hair on her body standing on end, reacting to the static energy that saturated the air. Of course it was only what Michael was feeling, she knew. Every ounce of his fear and anger was hers to experience, and it was nearly overwhelming.

Again and again the two men brought the fiery weapons together, and again and again they were flung back apart, flashing like lightning and crying out in their own inhuman voices. Where Michael's sword continued to sing out in an ever higher pitch, the growl of the Guardian Hunter's blade rumbled ever deeper, its bass voice so low that it was felt as much as heard. All along, Michael's face showed the anguish that Rosa felt. The masked face of his enemy showed nothing but the wickedness that was most certainly the intent of its design.

Surely, Rosa thought, neither of the two conjured blades possessed any actual mass, but whenever the two came together there was the definite appearance that the Guardian Hunter's blade, the shorter and broader of the two, carried the greater force. And the longer it went on, the more clear the difference seemed to become. Michael was gradually being beaten back, worn down by a stronger opponent.

It seemed to Rosa that the battle had been waging for a long time, but a part of her knew instinctively that it wasn't so. In reality, this entire sequence of events was playing out before her in seconds, at the speed of streaming energy–dream speed.

The two men fought savagely, chopping and slashing at one another with unfaltering determination. Their engagement was so transfixing that at first Rosa didn't even notice the shadowy outline of Edward Charleston York when he crept into the small circle of light that had become a miniature gladiator's arena. Michael didn't notice him until he was a mere two steps away, but he noticed in time. The prissy assassin had snuck up from behind with his favorite knife cocked above his head, ready to strike, but he never got the chance. Without ever looking away from the deadlier of his foes, Michael swept his ghostly sword through the air, blue flames trailing behind it. The arc was wide, deflecting an attack from the Guardian Hunter and then continuing around his body where its point traced a black line across the torso of Edward Charleston York. It looked like a fatal blow, but Rosa knew otherwise.

York fell to the ground, and to Rosa's horror he began convulsing violently, kicking and clawing in all directions, screaming with the guttural, primal voice of a dying animal.

Although the assassin's knife never found its mark, the attempt turned out to be effective nonetheless. The extra long swing that Michael had made to ward off the secondary attack had taken a split second that, despite its briefness, couldn't be spared. Suddenly the disadvantage that Rosa had been suspecting became more significant. Michael was backpedaling, struggling frantically to keep his enemy's blade from penetrating his defense.

With the overhead chop of a lumberjack, the Guardian Hunter brought his weapon down upon Michael like a splitting maul, his most vicious attack yet. Once again, Michael was able to raise his own blade in time, but the weight of the blow was too much, and his footing was lost. Down he went, landing flat on his back, the flaming sword still held out before him, but the intensity of its fire waning visibly and the purity of it song faltering audibly. It seemed that the young man's strength was nearly spent, and with it the magic that fueled his only means of defense against the Guardian Hunter.

The man behind the red mask stepped back several paces, looking down upon young Michael like a big game hunter over a trophy kill. He raised his weapon high, its blue flames lashing out so wildly that the sword's shape was lost within the blaze, and he paused there, poised for the deathblow. Then, for the first time, he spoke.

"Now I'm one of a kind."

The Guardian Hunter's voice filled the chambers of Rosa's heart with ice water, freezing her insides stiff. She felt Michael's fear doubled in response to his enemy's words. He sounded so cold, so bitter, so wicked … *so familiar.*

Without further hesitation, the Guardian Hunter rushed forward, ready to bring his weapon down one last time and claim his victory.

In what seemed to be a futile display of desperation, Michael raised his own conjured blade over his head. With what must have been his last reserve of strength, he heaved forward, flinging the sword at his charging foe.

Suddenly, everything seemed to lose its momentum. The Guardian Hunter's attack became a snail's crawl, and Michael's flying weapon appeared to hover in midair. Everything progressed in super-slow motion, and it was at that speed that Rosa was forced to watch.

The instant that Michael's sword left his hand, its fire began to die and its voice to fade. Its blue flames shrank away until only a thin, dim bean of light was left, a fading glow in the dark evening.

Just before the Guardian Hunter could reach Michael, Michael's sword reached him. At least Rosa thought it did. Still watching in torturous sluggishness, she saw the last glimmer of the fire that Michael's magic had ignited vanish, just as it reached the masked man's chest, just as his blazing weapon bore down over Michael. Then everything went black.

Rosa had the sense that time sped back up to the normal pace, but for several long seconds she couldn't see anything as her eyes adjusted. When her vision did return, what she saw both shocked and confused her. The shock would stay with her, but the confusion would last but a moment.

She was back at the scene she'd originally glimpsed when she'd first touched Michael's dream. There, lying lifeless upon the ground was young Michael Galladin, his limbs gone limp and his pale, green eyes staring blankly into eternity. The strange black object he'd held lay nearly lost in shadow on the ground beside him. He wore the clothes of the Guardian Hunter.

If it weren't for her emotional connection to Michael, Rosa's confusion may have continued, but what she felt through him was an instant solution to the mystery of what she saw. Even before she looked up to see Michael staring down, seemingly into his own eyes, she understood what had happened. The gaping emptiness she felt opening in her chest and the staggering self-hatred that threatened her very sanity made it clear, his victory over the Guardian Hunter had been the death of someone with whom Michael shared an exceptionally close bond. He'd killed his own twin brother.

And then Michael changed, the young man he'd been melted away before her eyes, aging years between heartbeats. His familiar sad eyes looked up and found her gaze, apparently able to recognize her presence in the dream at last, and in his stare Rosa found the final answer to all her questions.

Wracked with pity and revulsion, Rosa wanted desperately to reach out to Michael, to comfort him, but instead of holding him, she let him go. Her hand fell away from his trembling cheek, and their link was severed. Rosa felt herself hurdling through time and space again, and this time when the disorientation receded, she was back in the little hotel room in Miami, and there, waiting for her, was Michael.

With My Life

Michael came awake knowing full well what had happened. What he didn't know was what he, or she, would do next. Would he ever be able to look Rosa in the eye again now that she knew what he'd done? Would she be horrified of him? Would she run from the room afraid for her life? He suspected that she might and wouldn't blame her if she did.

When Rosa's eyes finally opened, she took a deep breath, as if she'd been holding her air for a long time. Her brown eyes blinked rapidly, and when he caught her gaze he saw that they were filled with tears. A single salty drop slid down the curve of her cheek, settling at the corner of her quivering lips. He had his answer. He could see it plainly in the lines of her brow. She was filled not with horror, but with sympathy. She hadn't just seen what had happened fifteen years ago, she'd felt it, the shock he'd suffered then as well as the remorse that had been corroding his spirit ever since. Her tears were for Michael, not his dead brother.

With a trembling finger, Michael wiped the tear streak gently away. Her skin felt as soft as brushed suede, and he found, unexpectedly, that he couldn't pull his hand away. He found that he didn't want to.

Michael's stomach lurched and his head spun. A rush of alien emotions threatened to completely undermine his equilibrium, leaving him feeling as though the ground underfoot was crumbling away. But strangely, the feeling was not upsetting. Not even unsettling. As the sensation of falling grew stronger, he fought against it less and less, gradually giving himself over to it, relinquishing control completely. It didn't feel like he was falling to his death, but to his life, to the parts of life he'd done without for so many years.

At long last, all of his precious secrets were out, replayed in living color. After guarding those secrets so closely for so long, he would have expected to feel a greater sense of loss, even violation at having them broadcasted through his dream, but what he felt instead was relief. For the whole of his adult life, Michael had walked the earth a tortured soul, like Atlas with the weight of the world upon his shoulders. Suddenly, that weight was no longer his to bear alone. Someone else knew what had happened, what he'd done. His secret tragedy was a secret no more.

There was more to it than that though. The unexpected joining had done more than just unburden Michael of his festering past, it had also whittled away a good part of his carefully maintained loneliness. For a decade and a half he had never once been close with another human being, shared anything beyond casual conversations, and even those had usually occurred under some pretense. Now the streak was broken, a seemingly endless winter finally arriving to the spring thaw, and all as a result of the slightest touch from a girl he hardly knew. Of course that wasn't the case any more. Now he knew her very well indeed, perhaps better than any one else did or ever had.

It was Rosa's magic, Michael knew, and not his own that had built the bridge between their minds. It may be that such a bridge could only have been formed with someone like him, someone with magic, but she was the key, the one who made it possible. Her gift of premonition was obviously more than just that. When she'd entered into his dream, she'd not only seen what he'd seen, she'd actually felt what he'd felt, all his hope and doubt and despair. And whether she'd been aware of it or not, he'd experienced all of those things through her as well. He'd experienced her every reaction to the dream as it unfolded. Every bit of her fear and confusion had been his as well, and most importantly, her sympathy.

As he stared into her eyes, he realized that she, too, understood the depth of what they'd shared.

"I never knew two people could share something like that," Michael whispered, still struggling to catch his breath. "I didn't know it was possible."

"I did," Rosa whispered back, her voice frigid and frail.

Not only was Michael more than a little disappointed at hearing her response, he was also confused. The inflection he'd heard in her voice didn't seem to fit with what she'd said. What he and Rosa had just shared was an incredible bonding, an encounter than transcended any in his previous experience. It had been a connection of pure honesty, shameless and blameless sharing. Why would she go cold on thinking back to another similar encounter?

"Something like that's happened to you before?" Michael asked hesitantly. "With someone else?"

Rosa took another deep breath.

"One other, yes," Rosa confirmed, "but it wasn't like what just happened with us."

Michael didn't ask for a further explanation. He'd wait for her to elaborate if she chose to, but he wouldn't make it a request. He didn't have to wait long.

"It was the Tall Man," she hissed through clenched teeth as a new welling of tears sprung forth from the corners of her eyes. "It was Ramius King."

Michael was aghast. The revulsion he always experienced from hearing the name was increased tenfold by the thought of King being that close to Rosa.

"It wasn't sharing how we just shared," she continued unsteadily. "It was ..."

Rosa stopped, dropped her tear-blurred gaze to the floor, and forced herself to take a long, deep breath. She had just learned Michael's deepest, darkest secret, and now she was ready to share her own with him. She knew that he would keep her secret safe. She no longer merely suspected his qualities, she knew them beyond doubt. She knew him better than most people would ever know anyone.

"I knew he was coming the first time," she began, her voice still a frail whisper. "I saw him in a premonition the night before. That was the first time that one of you three who I've seen more than once was somewhere I recognized. He was standing next to an old warehouse right down the street from where I live–where I lived. I decided that I'd hide nearby and wait for him to arrive. I wasn't going to call the police, because I didn't know what I could tell them. I knew he was a dangerous man, but I hadn't actually seen him doing anything illegal in the premonition. I was just going to watch from a safe distance, see him for myself, with my own eyes in the real world. It didn't work out. Two of his men showed up at my apartment before I could leave, and they took me to the warehouse that I'd seen in my vision."

Michael could see Rosa's discomfort growing, heightening as the memory replayed itself in her mind. He could sense the agony that the discomfort would soon become. A part of him wanted to stop her where she was, tell her that he didn't need to hear the rest, but that wasn't true. He did need to hear, for himself and perhaps countless others.

"I didn't know what he'd do, but I knew what he could do, what he was capable of. I knew the sort of man he was from the glimpses I'd seen of him in my visions." She paused, shaking her head regretfully. "I was so stupid. It never even occurred to me that I might be the reason he was in Miami."

"What did the other men look like?" Michael asked gently, hating to interrupt, but needing to know everything he could.

"One was huge, and I'm talking like five-hundred pounds huge, and the other one was tiny, a little kid's body with a grown up face. After they took me to the warehouse, to King, they just kept watch while ..."

Rosa shuddered visibly, as though something vile had just risen up into her throat.

Impulsively, Michael reached out and took her hands in his own. A rush of warmth washed over him, and he could see that she felt it as well. A glimmer of the connection that they'd shared remained. He couldn't hear her thoughts or feel her emotions exactly, but there was still a bond beyond their closeness in the physical sense, an empathy that was more than what other people could achieve.

"It's okay, Rosa," Michael assured, squeezing her hands tightly. "You don't have to be afraid anymore. I won't let him hurt you ever again. I'll protect you with my life."

Rosa was awestruck at his declaration. How could he possibly mean it? How could he be ready to face Ramius King, and probable death, on her behalf when he'd only known her for two days? It *was* true though, she knew. He hadn't made it a promise, but he hadn't needed to. She knew the kind of man he was. Everything he said was a promise.

With renewed strength in her voice, Rosa continued, saying, "King tied me to a chair in the warehouse, tight enough so I couldn't move anything but my head. I was terrified, thinking back to all the mobster movies, all the guys getting their fingernails pulled out until they spilled their secrets. I didn't know what secrets I could have that he'd want, but that's what I thought was going to happen. I wish that's what had happened, because what he did was so much worse."

Michael felt her grip tighten around his fingers.

"While the other two kept watch, King came and stood in front of me. He had a box, real fancy looking, gold and jewels and everything. He opened it, and inside there was a sort of a crown. It wasn't fancy like the box it came out of, but when he picked it up and put it on, he treated it like it was precious. Anyway, it was just a black, leather headband really, and mounted right in the front of it was a black feather, not a real one, but a sculpture or a carving. It looked like it was made of that glassy, black rock that comes from volcanoes, shiny and hard edged like that. When he put the thing on, it was like the whole room started to buzz. All the air felt charged up, like how it feels right before a thunderstorm. He ... he touched my face, like I did yours while you were sleeping, and he ... got into my mind. It was like it was with us, but different, more forceful."

Things should've started coming together for Michael right then. He should have been able to reason out how King had used Rosa's gift, how he'd manipulated her talent for his own dark purposes. He might have even been able to guess at why she'd now become a target for King's assassin, but he didn't. He was so full of anger that there was no room left for reason. The thought of Ramius King being as close to Rosa as he had been was unbearable.

"It wasn't sharing like it was with us, it was just taking. He took everything from me, and there was nothing I could do to stop him. He could read my thoughts like they were written out on paper, and he could feel everything I was feeling. He could feel that I was too scared to fight back. I was so scared that I couldn't even try to stop him, and he knew it, and he loved it, and I hated him for it. He violated me so completely. I hate him so much, and it's like being poisoned, having that kind of hate inside you."

Michael fought to keep himself still, to maintain control. He knew of the hate that Rosa spoke of. He remembered touching it in their memory sharing, a black shadow in the back of her mind that was never forgotten altogether, even for a moment.

"Michael, you still don't understand, it's not just what he did to me, it's what he made me do. When he touched me, when he forced himself into my mind, he used my gift, my visions. He stole away my ability to see things that haven't happened yet. Who knows what terrible things he did because of what I showed him?"

"Don't do that Rosa," Michael stopped her. "You can't carry that kind of guilt around. Trust me, if you try to it'll …"

For just a moment, Michael had forgotten. He didn't need to explain. She knew everything.

"I know that it wasn't really my fault, Michael," Rosa whispered, "but the guilt stays with me anyway, just like it does with you. Deep inside, you must realize that what happened to your brother was his own fault, not yours. He's the one who forced it. He deceived you, and he would have killed you if he could have."

Michael gritted his teeth as she made the accusation against his brother. He did know that it was the truth, but his conscience still tortured him, demanded that he defend his brother's memory. However, when the truth is known absolutely, there is no defense for the guilty.

"You're right," he agreed reluctantly. "Sean was the one who hid his identity and left the Guardians, but it was Ramius King who took him from us. It was King who made him into a traitor. It wasn't just that Sean turned away from the Guardians, he betrayed them utterly, hunting them overtly, under the pretense of friendship, and then killing them for his new master. The Guardians almost lost the war that year because of what Sean and I did."

"But you said it yourself," Rosa protested, "it was Sean's fault, not yours."

"That's not what I meant. I did something else. Or rather didn't do something else."

Rosa shook her head, confused.

"I wasn't sure if I'd be able to go back to the Guardians after what Sean had done to them, and after what I'd done to him, but I did know one thing, I knew that I'd never use the magic again. And I never have. I went back to our secret base of operations that night after Sean's death. I kept hidden outside our perimeter, trying to decide if I could go back inside or not. A pair of King's servants snuck through our defenses that night and ended up killing a Guardian who was on sentry duty. That man had a son, Jerrod, who was a close friend of mine. Jerrod was still in the first phase of his training with the Guardians. Anyway, I watched the creatures sneak in from where I was hiding. I knew who they were. We called them the Snapdragons. I was strong enough to stop them. I could have stopped them, but not without the magic, and I just couldn't ..."

"I'd destroyed the lives of the two people I cared most about in a single night. I couldn't think of anything else to do but run, so I ran. I ran and I ran, and I've never stopped."

"Maybe you can stop now." Rosa's whisper had dropped another level, barely strong enough to be heard. "Running is something you do by yourself, and now you're not by yourself anymore, because now I'm with you. Do you understand what I'm saying? I don't just mean here and now, I mean that I'm *with you*. You get it, Redbeard?"

He got it. He could hardly believe that it was true, but he got it.

For the second night in a row, neither Michael nor Rosa managed much of any sleep. Instead, they sat there waiting for the dawn together, trading stories like old friends. With their biggest secrets out, everything else came easily. Rosa told Michael about the campouts she'd enjoyed as a child, the football Dan Marino had tossed her at the sidelines of a Dolphins game, and the clarinet that she'd learned to play in junior high and secretly still practiced with on occasion. Only after admitting this did she remember that the clarinet had been in her apartment. She also thought to mention, quite casually, that she'd once saved the life of the President of the United States. She'd tipped off the police about an assassination attempt she'd foreseen during his tour through Miami surveying hurricane damage.

Michael told Rosa about growing up with his brother, about how they'd wanted to become secret agents, how they'd secretly raised a stranded litter of baby raccoons in the shed behind their house, and how they'd owned two of every Led Zeppelin album, a complete set apiece. He also brought up the time when he stole over a million dollars from the most notorious illegal weapons trafficker on the west coast."

"It was a good month for the L.A. homeless shelters," he'd added nonchalantly.

Monday,
September 4

A Rude Awakening

The following morning, five states to the north, Kyle Adams resurfaced from the depths of a long, dreamless sleep. Before opening his eyes, he listened carefully to the sounds that surrounded him. He could hear the whir of electric motors and the steady hum of a large ventilation system. There were voices as well, but they were too faint to understand or even judge as being either familiar or foreign. He could smell a strong scent of disinfectant that reminded him of the science lab at school.

Reaching a fingertip to each of his temples, Kyle gently massages both sides of an ear to ear headache. Not only did the ritual gesture fail to ease the pain, it gave new cause for concern. His arms felt so heavy that only with great effort did he manage to heave them up from their resting positions.

Still without opening his eyes, Kyle rolled his head to the side, searching for a position where the throbbing behind his eyes would be eased. As he moved, something pulled uncomfortably at his neck.

Kyle popped upright in the bed like the thermometer in a cooked turkey. As his hands reached to the plastic collar around his neck, his eyes popped open, but things did not become clear. The room seemed to swim around him, walls rushing in and then falling away, assaulting him with alternating sensations of being trapped and then falling.

One bright, bare bulb filled the room with glaring light from above the bed in which Kyle sat. When he looked up, the single point of brightness split apart and spread out across the ceiling until it became thousands of dancing sparkles. Kyle's stomach heaved precariously, but he didn't vomit.

Try as he might, Kyle couldn't think where he was, nor could he remember where he'd been before falling asleep. He had a vague sense that something terrible had happened, but what exactly it was, he couldn't recall. He willed his legs to swing over the side of the bed, but they didn't respond. The sheets were too soft, too comfortable. It was as if the bed was a giant magnet and his legs were made of iron. He was pinned in place by invisible bonds.

When the other man entered the room, Kyle didn't even notice. He believed himself to be alone right up until the man yelled into his ear from just an arm's length away.

"Goodmorning!" the man shouted, startling Kyle so badly that he actually pulled the bedsheet up to his chin, cowering behind it. "How's our new guest feeling this morning?"

Kyle said nothing. He was terrified at how helpless he felt. He had no idea where he was, no idea how he got there, and no idea as to the identity of the stranger shouting at him. He also had no idea why he felt so completely disoriented. He couldn't think clearly about anything. All he wanted to do was hide. *Hide.* The word struck a nerve, nearly sparking a memory, but not quite.

"You don't know what's going on, do you?" the man continued. His grin was broad, nearly connecting two long sideburns that skidded down the sides of his face. "I'll refresh your memory. You were spending some time over at the old firehouse with the Guardians. Mr. King and General Stone and most of the others went over there and sent everybody packing for the great beyond. Everybody except you, that is. You were the sole survivor of the assault. Don't feel too proud though, you're only alive because Mr. King decided to let you live." The man's voice turned into wicked laughter.

Tears gathered at the corners of Kyle's eyes. He did remember. He remembered hiding in the crate. He remembered Marion and Jerrod and Grandma Jo. He remembered the Tall Man standing over him.

"Not very talkative are we?" the man asked sarcastically. "You'll start talking soon enough if I want you to, you can be sure of that. In fact, you'll do anything I ask. Do you know why?"

Kyle stayed quiet, still struggling to decide for sure whether the horrific images in his mind were real memories or gruesome hallucinations.

"I asked you a question. Answer me!"

A blast of pain exploded at the back of Kyle's neck, sending streaks of searing energy down his spine and over his skull, triggering his teeth to clench and his toes to curl convulsively.

And then it stopped. Kyle was left breathless, unable to move or even cry out.

"I asked if you know why you'll do whatever I want. Answer me."

With all the strength he could muster and all the haste he could achieve, Kyle sputtered, "I don't know."

The man's grin widened even further, actually wrinkling the skin beneath his giant sideburns.

"You should have said that the first time," he advised mockingly. "I bet next time you'll answer right away, don't you think? Don't you think?"

"Yes," Kyle blurted quickly. "Yes, I will."

Kyle's head throbbed. His thoughts were still hard to hold on to for more than a moment, and his entire body still tingled with the pain that had come from his collar. It felt like he was dying.

"Now that I know I have your full attention, I'll introduce myself. I'm Mr. Choplin, and you are my prisoner. Everything else you need to know, you'll pick up as we go along. I'm sure it won't be a problem now that I have your full attention. Don't you agree?"

"Yes," Kyle hastily concurred.

"Good. Then drag yourself out of that bed. You have an appointment that you won't want to be late for."

Ramius King stood at the center of the expensive Oriental rug that covered the center of the floor in his office. He faced away from the door, his eyes closed, his tall frame rigid. Beethoven's Ode to Joy blared from speakers placed at each corner of the room, engulfing him completely, swallowing him up in its power. It was victory music.

With the music playing so loudly, the Tall Man barely heard the knock against the heavy oak door. Without so much as opening his eyes, King pointed one long finger in the direction of the CD player, and instantly the volume dial spun counter-clockwise, softening the music to a level better suited to accompanying conversation.

"Come in," he said when he was ready.

The door swung open, and in stumbled Kyle. His feet were beneath him now, but his balance was only somewhat recovered.

A step behind Kyle came Choplin, his head bowed low, chin to chest. He waited in the doorway, saying nothing.

"Did you have something to report, Mr. Choplin?" King asked, looking to his warden. His stare was contemptuous.

"After the Doc shot him up last night, I let him sleep it off in the old janitor's closet, just like you said to. And then this morning the Doc gave him a shot of something to perk him up for talking to you, just like you wanted. I gave him a little taste of the juice this morning, too, just to let him know what he can expect if he …"

"That's enough," King cut him short. "Leave."

For the tiniest second, Choplin looked offended at the abrupt dismissal, but he quickly remembered his place and scurried from the office, easing the heavy door closed behind him.

"I'd ask you to sit, Mr. Adams, but you're head will clear more quickly if you stay on your feet." King walked casually to the back of his desk and sank stiffly down into his plush office chair. Its leather groaned under his weight. "I want you to tell me about how you feel and about what you can remember. Are you lucid enough for conversation?"

Kyle didn't answer right away. The gears of his mind were still turning as though clogged with sand, and he didn't want to say the wrong thing before he could think better of it.

"I feel pretty woozy," Kyle admitted hesitantly. "I can't seem to remember anything from the last few days. I can remember being in Chicago, ready to move to my new foster home in Michigan, and then … nothing." It was a bold lie to offer under the circumstances, especially considering who it was that he was lying to.

For a moment, only Beethoven sounded through the room, and then King said, "That was a very careful answer, young man. I applaud you. Most people wouldn't have had the sense to try that even with their full wits about them, let alone half recovered from a deep drugging. If you were just a little further recovered from the narcotics that were administered to you yesterday, you might have convinced me. You might have, but probably not. Anyway, the drug obviously didn't succeed in wiping away your recent memories, so go ahead and tell me what you really remember. I'm curious about your impressions."

Kyle thought back once again to the battle in the firehouse the previous evening. But as his mind continued to clear, he realized that wasn't right. The battle in the firehouse had been in the morning, not the evening. He must have been asleep for the rest of that day and the entire night after that.

"I can see you're trying to sort things out," King observed. "Take your time."

As his head continued to unfog, Kyle was at last able to recall exactly what had happened, every horrid detail.

"I remember it all," Kyle said, sounding suddenly more angry than afraid. "I remember what happened to Jerrod and Marion and the others. I remember what happened to Grandma Jo, what you did to her. I remember your ugly face last of all, staring down at me just before everything went dark."

"You remember all that?" the Tall Man asked, sounding surprised. "You must have quite a strong constitution. The treatment you underwent seems to have failed in erasing any part of your memory whatsoever. It's a credit to you. I'm genuinely impressed."

"Like I give a shit," Kyle sneered. "I don't want to impress you. I just want to get the hell out of here so I don't have to look at your ugly face anymore!"

Very slowly, King rose from his chair, and in four long, graceful strides, he rounded the desk. He came to a halt standing practically on Kyle's toes, towering over him.

"That's twice you've insulted me, young man," King whispered coldly. "That's something most men would never have the opportunity to do. I'm trying to be patient with you, but two insults is your limit. I'm quite sure of it."

Kyle's lips parted, but no words came out. He couldn't even manage to meet King's stare.

"My father gave me this face," King continued, his voice still menacing, "this crooked nose and two false teeth. He also gave me bruises beyond count and several broken bones. He gave me all that, but I wanted more, so I took his life. I was even younger than you when I killed my father. I removed him from the path that I needed to follow, as I've done with everyone who's ever blocked that path, including Grandma Jo and her Guardians."

"Not all the Guardians," Kyle interjected, "just the ones who were at the firehouse." He tried to steady himself, his eyes and his voice. He hoped it was a more convincing lie than his first had been.

The Tall Man stared down on him for a moment, his dark eyes as sharp as a circling raptor's.

"No, I don't think that's the case. I do think that now you've not only insulted me twice, but lied to me twice as well. I'd hoped that we could be reasonable this morning. I thought that I would be able to get what I needed from you without having to assert myself *forcibly*. I prefer to leave those more barbaric tactics to my barbarian-like servants, like Choplin. However, if you persist with these insults and lies, you'll leave me with little choice. I *will* get what I want from you. Your cooperation or lack thereof will determine how I get it."

Kyle shivered in spite of himself, having no illusions about how defenseless he was against the man who'd killed Grandma Jo.

"So where were we?" King asked casually as he returned to his chair.

"The last thing I remember was you uncovering the crate I was hiding in," Kyle answered dispassionately.

"Yes, that's right. You remember everything. That's unfortunate for you. The old lady and her private army put up quite a fight yesterday considering the fact that they were caught off guard and without their Gifts of Nature. Many of my hunters didn't survive. Therefore, I'm left a little shorthanded right now. Fresh talent is terribly scarce where magic is concerned, and searching it out is quite time consuming. That is why I decided to let you live yesterday. You are my newest recruit."

Kyle cringed, but said nothing. What could he say? He'd never join the man who was responsible for the deaths of the Guardians, of Jerrod and Marion, but what good could it do to say as much right then and there? To do so would be to invite punishment.

"It would have been a simpler matter had you forgotten what you saw," King went on, "but you will become one of my hunters nonetheless, have no doubt about that. You are an untrained boy, and I have broken the spirits of many powerful men, Guardians among them."

"Is that why you were at the school that day?" Kyle asked. "Were you there for me?"

King's long, stoic face flinched ever so slightly. It was a question he'd not anticipated, and he thought he'd anticipated everything.

"As a matter of fact," he explained coolly, "I wasn't. I was at the school for someone else. I didn't even know who you were then. Someone was working for me at the school that day, testing the students for potential talent."

"Mr. Simpson, right?" Kyle asked.

"Yes, that's right, it was Dr. Simpson," King confirmed, again angry with himself for failing to foresee this line of conversation. "His tests identified you and the girl. Someone told me that there might be a dangerous person in Steel City, and I thought for a moment that it might be one of you two. I knew better though, as soon as I discovered that your foster parents were actually Guardians of Magic. Have you realized yet, I wonder, that it was because of you that the Guardians were destroyed? When you were whisked away to the firehouse, the first general of my forces was following you. I didn't even know the Guardians were here until you led me to them. I suspect they were probably planning an imminent attack against me, and I just beat them to the draw. I suppose that I should thank you, Mr. Adams."

Kyle began to shake. His lower lip pulled up between his teeth, and tears formed once again at the corners of his eyes.

"Now that I've identified and eliminated the real danger that was here in Steel City, I see no reason not to use you and the girl. As I said before, our numbers are down and need replenishing. That's why I brought you here, and that's why I've sent men to retrieve your little girlfriend."

There, hidden in the Tall Man's vile words, Kyle found a faint glimmer of hope. Wherever he was, he'd already been there for a full day, and for whatever reason, they still didn't have Lily. Maybe her father had somehow realized the danger she was in and whisked her away to a safe place far away.

"What I want you to do now," King instructed, "is return to your bed and sleep off the lingering effects of your drugging. When your faculties are fully recovered, I'll give you your first lesson in real magic. Now go."

Numbly, barely feeling the ground beneath his feet, Kyle turned and started toward the door.

"And one more thing, Mr. Adams," King added, stopping Kyle between strides, "it would be wise to behave for that buffoon that I've made your keeper. He lacks my tact and will simply electrocute you if you displease him."

When Kyle was gone, King pointed again at the CD player, and this time it died completely, plunging the room into silence. He wanted to take a few quiet moments to consider the impressions he'd just gathered. Young Kyle Adams had potential, but perhaps of a dangerous sort. The magic was there within him, ready to be developed, but he had another sort of potential as well. He was clever. Even in a half stupor, he'd thought to attempt two cunning misconceptions. That sort of guile could be very useful, but it could also be dangerous. Sly men were needed for sensitive tasks, but sly men were difficult to read and difficult to control. Mindless brutes could always be beaten into submission, but a thinker might let you believe he'd submitted when he still resisted in secret. A thinker might someday think to rebel.

King's pondering led him back once again to his first general. Mason was by far the finest soldier he'd ever produced, very powerful and very clever. And with that damn stony face, he was impossible to read. There was no way to judge his true strength or ambition, and those were dangerous bits of information to have withheld.

Kyle felt dazed as he headed away from King's office. His body still shook all over, but he wasn't sure why. There were a variety of good guesses he could make, including his recent exposure to electric shock and some strong narcotics, his witnessing of a mass murder, and the proposition of being forced into a life of servitude to Ramius King. If he never stopped shaking, it wouldn't come as much of a surprise.

What was a surprise was that Kyle's captors were allowing him to roam through the place, wherever it was, without an escort. If he was a prisoner, it seemed like he should be accompanied by a guard. As he wondered about that, Kyle scanned the hallway through which he strode carefully and immediately found an explanation. At the very end of the corridor, nestled in the corner between the wall and the ceiling, was a video camera. So he was alone, but not truly unattended. Still, even if they were watching, no one was right there with him. If he tried to make a run for it, how quickly would King's men descend on him? It wasn't something to test right then, not in his current state, but it was something to keep it in mind.

At the end of the corridor, Kyle passed by an open door beyond which an extensive laboratory spread. He paused, peeking in through the door, and found himself face to face with a madman.

"What are you doing to me?" the man screamed at the top of his voice.

Kyle stumbled backward, nearly falling.

"You're making me crazy!" the man screamed again as he lurched forward after Kyle.

The man's eyes were severely bloodshot, and although he looked as pale as if he were freezing to death, beads of sweat streamed down his face. He truly looked insane.

With a hard knock, Kyle's shoulders struck the wall behind him. He had retreated as far as he could, and still the man staggered ever nearer. Kyle wanted to run, but had no idea where to run to. He didn't even know where he was.

Just as the madman's hands stretched out before him, reaching for Kyle's throat, he jerked back. The man straightened up rigidly, his arms and legs sprung out to full extension. Then, with agonizing slowness, the man fell backward. He landed flat on his back without making even the slightest effort to right himself or ease his impact against the floor. He lay there without moving, and as Kyle watched, revolted, foam began to form at the corners of his mouth. The man's eyes gaped open, bulging from their sockets like barely restrained ping pong balls

Dr. Spencer Simpson appeared at the door to the lab holding a small remote control in one latex gloved hand. He hit a button on the remote, and immediately the madman's eyes closed. The foam from his mouth ceased its flow, and his body went limp.

"I'm sorry you had to see that," the doctor apologized. "I, ah, I hate having to do that, but I, ah, I don't really have much of a choice. Do I know you?"

"I'm Kyle Adams," Kyle barely managed. "You taught my biology class. The test you gave me is the reason that I'm here."

The doctor's eyes dropped to the floor, and he sighed deeply.

"I, um, I'm s-sorry about that," Simpson stuttered. "I really am. I, um, I suppose I did a terrible thing to you."

Kyle considered that and said, "Maybe not as terrible as what you just did to him."

The man on the floor lay motionless, the froth still clinging to his face.

"Don't, ah, feel too bad for him," the doctor advised coldly. "He'll be a powerful man very soon. I know he doesn't, ah, look like much now, but he will. I just need to adjust his, um, dosages a little."

A college-age lab technician appeared at the door, and with Dr. Simpson's help, he drug the unconscious madman away, back into the workroom. Kyle continued on his way.

Between the lab and the room where he'd awakened that morning, Kyle walked past several figures who were so overgrown and disfigured, they could have passed as horror movie stars in full costume and makeup. He was careful to meet none of their gazes as he hurried past them in silence.

At the doorway to his room, Kyle found Choplin, his wide grin in place.

"Glad to see you remembered the way back," he said. "I wasn't all that sure you would."

Kyle had nothing to say. All he wanted was to get back in his room where he could be alone, where he could think.

"Mr. King told me to get some rest," Kyle offered, "so you'd better let me get to bed."

Very slowly, the toothy grin melted away from the face of Kyle's jailor, dissolving into a sneer.

"Let's be sure you got the right impression of how this is going to work," Choplin practically hissed. "Mr. King thinks that he's going to turn you into one of his magician soldiers, but that's a long way off. Right now you're nothing but a shitsmear on the sole of my shoe. Mr. King's left it up to me to decide how to keep you quiet and keep you out of the way. I figure that collar's as good a way as any. Every time you look at me wrong or cough without covering you mouth I'll light you up like the evening sky on the fourth of July. You get me?"

Remembering vividly the terrific pain the collar could generate, Kyle nodded obediently in response. His gaze fell to his feet and stayed there.

Satisfied that his point had been adequately made, Choplin stepped out of the doorway and motioned for Kyle to go inside, which he did.

"By the way," the grinning jailor added as an afterthought, "I saw that little incident down there at the lab, watched the whole thing on one of my little computer screens. That poor sucker you saw go stiff and start foaming, he got zapped at setting eight. That little poke I sent through your collar this morning was only a four. If you tamper with your collar, it'll trigger a continuous current at ten, max voltage. Just thought you should know."

Just before he slammed the door shut and locked Kyle inside, Choplin pointed two fingers to his own eyes, and with the other hand he pointed at the swiveling camera mounted high in the corner of Kyle's room. It was a gesture that required no explanation.

A GRIM THEORY

Michael and Rosa finally managed a few hours of sleep after sharing the sunrise together. They awoke to the knocking of the room attendant, who reminded them of the ten o'clock check out time.

Rosa suspected that they'd be headed out of town on the first bus north, or maybe even the first boat south, but Michael seemed to have a different plan in mind. From the hotel they headed down the street on foot, passing by several delicious smelling restaurants despite Rosa's requests to stop. Each time she asked if they could just run inside for a quick bite, Michael would say only that he needed to pick something up before they did anything else. What that something might be, she couldn't guess.

Not until they actually walked into the showroom did Rosa finally believe that they were car shopping. She'd only ever owned two cars in her whole life, and both had been junkers that were nearly as old as she was. She was half way thrilled when Michael told her that buying new was the only way to be sure of dependability. She made it the other half of the way when he told her that she should pick it out, it would be hers. She came back down a notch though, when he disapproved of the sporty red convertible that was her first choice. Apparently, he thought it was a little too flashy for people on the run from evil, magic-wielding killers. Eventually they decided on a black Monte Carlo SS. It was fast, which Rosa liked, but understated enough to satisfy Michael as well.

The salesman nearly choked when Michael said he'd be paying in cash, all up front. His suspicion was obvious, but he couldn't resist taking the money.

Rosa drove the first shift after finally eating some breakfast, and the thrill of driving a brand new car was enough to keep her from wondering about their destination for an hour. Michael sat in the passenger's seat, staring out the window, apparently lost in some very deep thought. He spoke only periodically and only to tell Rosa to slow down. He said that they couldn't afford to get pulled over. It was possible she might already be on the missing persons list, and it would be preferable if she just stayed missing, at least for the time being. He also mentioned that there was a possibility of him showing up on a different list, another that the police might have seen. After hearing some of the stories he'd shared the previous night, she didn't need to ask for any elaboration.

"So where we headed anyway, Redbeard?" she asked finally after setting the cruise control at just slightly over the speed limit.

Michael looked over to her, but didn't answer immediately.

"Well, to be honest, I can't decide," he admitted at last. "I've been thinking it over this whole time while you've been driving. I guess I've got it narrowed down to two options, but I keep flip-flopping between them."

Something in Michael's voice put Rosa on edge. He was so hesitant, afraid to hear how she would respond to what he was thinking. He obviously wasn't going to suggest that they run away to Hawaii and live happily ever after sipping little umbrella drinks on the beach.

"Whatever it is you're so nervous to tell me, just tell me," Rosa suggested. "It'll take a lot to impress me after these last couple days, know what I mean?"

"My first idea was to head north until we're out of Florida and then get west as far as we can as fast as we can. King's hunters will come to Miami first since that's where York saw us. If they're headed here, then we should be headed away from here."

"I like your first idea," Rosa approved. "Let's go with it. I don't even need to hear number two. I don't need to hear *the but.*"

"*Buuut,*" Michael continued anyway, "the more I think about things, the more I think that maybe you were right when you said I've been running for too long. Maybe instead of running away from King, I should be running toward him. Maybe ..."

"Oh, hell no!" Rosa cut him short. "No way in hell you're going to give me any kind of credit for a stupid idea like that."

"Will you just hear me out, Rosa?" Michael asked less calmly.

"Hell no! Are you serious? Going looking for Ramius King is like trying to catch the plague or Ebola or the flesh-eating virus. If you're serious, then you're a moron."

"That sign said that there's a rest area in a mile. Pull off there and hear me out. Okay?"

"Fine, I'll pull off, and I'll hear whatever bullshit you've got to say, but I'm telling you right now that there's no way in hell you're going to convince me that you're not a moron for even thinking about going looking for Ramius King."

"I can't imagine how all that attitude fits into one little girl," Michael whispered through a small, crooked smile, stifling a laugh.

Rosa wasn't offended. In fact, all she could do in response was smile back. She'd never seen Michael with anything close to a happy expression on his face before, let alone heard him laugh. She decided that it was a pretty nice smile and secretly hoped that she'd be seeing more of it.

"Anyway," Michael continued, missing Rosa's reaction completely, "my idea wasn't for *us* to go looking for Ramius King."

And just like that, Rosa's smile vanished.

When the car came to a stop and the engine died, Michael hesitated. He needed to be sure that he said what he needed to say in just the right way. To Rosa's credit, she didn't say anything either, but waited for Michael to start when he was ready.

"I don't need to tell you what kind of man Ramius King is, Rosa," he began. "In fact, you know better than me. He doesn't want what other people want. His aspirations don't include more money or a bigger house or a nicer car. What he wants is the whole world and everyone in it. And you might think that I'm embellishing, but there is the real possibility that he could have it, the whole world for himself. I know how far-fetched it sounds, but it's not. Ninety-nine point some percent of the billions of people on this planet don't even know that there's real magic. All the politics, all the science, and all the technology are based on rules that don't apply to him."

"You can't seriously believe that he could defeat every army from every country, can you?" Rosa asked, unable to keep quiet any longer. "That is the number one, all-time stupidest thing I've ever heard in my life."

"He wouldn't have to defeat every army. He wouldn't have to defeat one. All he'd have to do is survive. If one army's weapons couldn't stop him, neither could any other's."

"Look, Michael, I saw through your own memories that magic can stop bullets, but before one man declares himself emperor of the world, he's going to have to deal with a lot more serious shit than that."

"Let me ask you something, Rosa, how heavy of a hammer would you need to cut down an oak tree? Or how many, if you think having more than one would help? Isn't it true that you could hammer against the trunk of an oak all day long with the heaviest mallet you could swing, and at the end of the day all you'd have managed to do is chip away a little bark or shake loose a couple acorns?"

"It sure didn't take very long for you to beat out your own record," Rosa noted, confusing Michael momentarily. "All that bullshit you just said, now that's the new number one, all-time stupidest thing I've ever heard in my life."

"I'm telling you, Rosa, it's exactly the same thing. Attacking King with any police or military weapon would be just like pounding against the tree with a hammer. It wouldn't matter how many weapons you had or how powerful they were, they just wouldn't be the right tools for the job."

"So you're trying to tell me that you think they could drop all sorts of bombs and rockets and tear gas and laser beams on top of Ramius King and he'd be fine afterward?" Rosa asked, her voice filled with disbelief.

"There's no reason to think he wouldn't be," Michael answered. "And I'm not sure they'd even think to try laser beams."

"Why don't you leave the sarcasm to me," Rosa snapped. "You knew what I meant."

"Here's the thing, Rosa, King has spent his whole life building and developing the magic he commands. He's had every opportunity to learn how that magic can be used to negate modern science and technology. On the other hand, the people who have built and developed the science and technology have no idea that magic even exists. They won't have any idea how to deal with it when the time comes."

"You mean *if* the time comes?"

"I meant exactly what I said."

"All right, let's pretend for a second, even though it's stupid even to pretend, that you're right and Ramius King couldn't be stopped by normal people with normal weapons. Even if that was true, which it isn't, aren't the Guardians supposed to protect against just that sort of thing. Isn't that what you were telling me all about last night. Aren't they the people who are supposed to protect the rest of us from a guy like King?"

"Yes, they most certainly are," Michael assured her, "if they're still alive."

"And why in the hell would you think they might not be?" Rosa sounded nearly hysterical. "Why has it always got to be the worst of the worst with you, Redbeard?"

"I've been thinking about how King used you," Michael continued, "about how he exploited your ability. I've been thinking about what he wants and what he'd do to achieve it. And about what he'd do *if* he achieved it."

"And you decided what?" Rosa asked. Some of the snotty attitude had drained away from her voice, replaced with mostly concealed trepidation. She wasn't sure yet what it was that had Michael so worried, but she did know how serious it must be. She had only to look him in the eye to know that.

"There's nothing Ramius King wouldn't do to get what he wants and no one he wouldn't kill. He'd eliminate his every enemy and sacrifice his every ally along the path to his ultimate victory. He'd employ any weapon. Among the weapons at his disposal, perhaps one of the most dangerous, is you."

Rosa cut in, her voice shaking. "I swear, Michael, I couldn't stop him. I tried so hard, as hard as I could, but ..."

"Oh, Rosa, I know," Michael stopped her quickly, unable to bear hearing her apologize for evil that had been visited upon her, not by her. "I know it wasn't your fault, not at all. In truth, I can barely keep myself still when I think about what he did to you, but that's not really what I was thinking about. I was thinking about his sending York after you."

"You mean you've been thinking about why he decided to kill me?" she asked rhetorically. "I've thought about that, too. I've always been more scared about him kidnapping me, but I hadn't thought much about him killing me. I don't know why he decided to."

"I don't know anything with certainty, but I have suspicions. Knowing what I know about Ramius King, I can pretty much guess why he never bothered taking you with him. He is an incredibly prideful man, and relying on someone else's help, especially someone else's magic, would be extremely distasteful to him. I imagine that it grated on him terribly every time he came to utilize your talent. Not that it's any consolation to you, but I imagine that's why he left you in Miami. He wouldn't want his people to know how he depended on your ability. Besides, running and hiding from him is not a simple task for anyone not schooled in magic. I'm sure he made mention of that to you."

Rosa only nodded to confirm that what Michael said was true.

"I can't say that I completely understand your gift, Rosa, even after our memory sharing, but I recognize its potential. I also don't know how much Ramius King could see ahead by channeling his power through you, but I'm sure it was somewhat limited."

"How do you know that?" Rosa asked.

"Because if he'd been able to see everything you could see, then he would have known about me."

Rosa shuddered, considering anew the possible ramifications of what King might have been able to do because of her gift.

"I'm sure King suspected, as I suspect, that your true potential has never been approached. As long as King could use you, then he'd never dream of having you killed. You were too valuable an asset to his plans. As long as he had a single enemy left to threaten him, then he'd need every weapon in his arsenal readily available. But if those enemies were destroyed, then his way of thinking might change."

"But that can't be true, Michael," Rosa argued. "King can't have defeated all his enemies. If he'd attacked, then we'd have heard about it. It'd be the biggest news ever."

"He would defeat his enemies before he made a move like what you're think-ing of. Remember, the army generals of the world aren't his real enemies. The militaries probably can't hurt him. His enemies, the ones who've prevented him from making a move already, are the Guardians. If they were gone, then there'd be no one left with magic enough to stand against him, except maybe you."

Rosa was appalled. "Me? What the hell are you talking about? I couldn't do anything to stop him. I couldn't even stop him from making me his puppet." Her voice was desperate.

"I can think of only one scenario where King would decide to have you killed, and it's if the Guardians were destroyed and if he perceived you as a possible threat."

"How in the hell could I be a threat to him? All I can do is predict muggings and car-jackings."

"There is a way." Michael's voice dropped to a whisper, as if he was nervous someone might be listening in on their conversation. "That feather in the head-band you saw Ramius King wearing, that was the Gift of Nature he killed his father for. It's called the Plume of Shu. It's the oldest and most powerful Gift we know of, but it's not the only one. If you somehow managed to get your hands on one of the others ..." Michael didn't bother finishing. Instead, he let Rosa think over the possibilities for herself.

"How much would I be able to see if I had one, one of the Gifts? What would I be able to know?"

"Who knows?" was all the answer Michael could offer. "If it's true, if the Guardians are annihilated, then I have to go after him now, before he begins his conquest. Once he's entrenched in power, he'll be unreachable. Besides, he prob-ably already knows from York that I'm alive, so he'll be after me anyway."

"Maybe he'll wait to do anything since he knows you're still around," Rosa proposed. "You were a Guardian once. He won't want to do anything until he knows what you're about, right?" She sounded doubtful.

"I can't take that chance. I have to find out if my suspicions are true. If it is as I fear, that the Guardians are lost, then I have to try and stop him while there's still a chance."

"What the hell chance are you thinking there is? Are you totally loco? You told me yourself he's the baddest man on the planet, and you got whipped by street thug trainees. What was all that stuff about you promising to take care of me, was that bullshit? Because if you go pick a fight with Ramius King, he's going to bury you, and then you're not going to be able to keep your promise. You don't know where to find him anyway, do you? It's not like you could just ..." Rosa stopped mid-rant, struck with an idea that she didn't care to share.

"There might be a way," Michael whispered, looking away from Rosa, "and I think you already know what it is."

The two sat there in the car for a while, considering what they'd said and what they might yet say. Out the driver's side window, Rosa watched a dirty station wagon park a few spots over. The wagon's license plate said Illinois. A young girl with a long, brown ponytail sprung from the back seat and rushed to touch the trunk of a royal palm that was growing next to the entrance to the restrooms. She looked thrilled beyond words, and her mother promptly took her picture. The girl looked so completely happy, so carefree. Rosa couldn't remember what care-free felt like.

"That girl's future could depend on you, Rosa," Michael said, breaking the silence. He had also taken note of the newly arrived family of tourists. "I know it sounds hard to believe, but it really could be true. King has the potential to reshape this world and the lives of everyone in it. Think about it. And while you're thinking, I'll drive for a while. Regardless of what we decide to do, I know where we need to go next."

They drove on for nearly three more hours, most of which passed in silence. Small talk about the weather or traffic seemed a little silly after what they'd dis-cussed at the rest area. At one point Rosa surprised Michael with an out of the blue tirade about how incredibly stupid some of his ideas were, but he offered no defense. All he did was laugh a little and smile at her volatility, which was exactly what she'd been hoping for, the reason she'd said it.

Still behind on sleep after consecutive short nights, Rosa drifted off eventually, snoring lightly in the passenger's seat. Michael didn't mind. He certainly didn't need a navigator to get him where he was headed. He felt like he could have found his way with his eyes closed, the pull was so strong inside him.

As he drove, Michael found that he could barely concentrate on the tasks and choices that lay before him, and that was quite disconcerting considering that in all likelihood they would be the most important of his life. When he should have been contemplating the possibility that he might soon be forced to face off with the most dangerous man on the planet, he was almost constantly distracted. In fact, he could barely even focus enough to keep his eyes on the road. He tried and tried to do just that, but his gaze was constantly drawn to the girl napping beside him.

As Rosa slept, all the impatience and hostility melted away from her face. The worry creases in her forehead smoothed over, and her lips, usually so tightly pursed, fell apart just slightly. From time to time her eyes would flutter gently. Just a dream or something more? Michael could only wonder. An endlessly defiant curl of dark hair still hung loosely over her face, dancing in the tiny gusts of her breath. At that moment, she was the sweetest thing he'd ever seen, angelic, and he could hardly manage to take his eyes off her. Nor did he want to.

A Grand Design

Despite the Tall Man's instruction, Kyle did not fall back to sleep. Instead, he lay quietly atop the small bed in his small quarters with his eyes closed and tried to think about what he should do. His head cleared completely as he rested, and the numbness gradually drained from his limbs.

A high pitched beeping sound startled Kyle free from his introspection after a bit. The sound was muted, no louder than the beeping of a watch timer, but it sounded like it had come from within a foot of his ear. Instinctively, he threw the pillow from under his head down to the floor beside his bed where he watched it cautiously, half expecting it to start spewing smoke or poison gas. It didn't though. It just laid there on the floor, looking very much like an ordinary pillow.

Then the beeping sounded again, and this time, being more alert to his surroundings, Kyle recognized its true source—the collar.

Kyle froze, praying that the beeps were not a prelude to activation. Unbidden, an image formed in his mind, a picture of his own body sprawled over the top of the bed, his limbs out stiff, his eyes rolled back, and tiny bubbles of spit seeping from the corners of his mouth.

Torturous seconds of silence slipped by, but nothing happened.

"You should see the look on your face," spoke a static-filled voice from a small speaker mounted near the room's video camera. It was Choplin. "I thought you might piss your drawers."

Kyle's jaw clenched, but he stayed quiet. He replaced the pillow at the head of his bed and pulled the covers up over it, flattening their wrinkles and hoping that his face wasn't in the camera's view. He hoped Choplin couldn't see how rattled he still felt.

"When you're done tidying up," the jailor's voice crackled, "get yourself to the main lab, the room where you saw the Doc this morning. Mr. King will meet you there for your first lesson."

Ramius King was already in the main lab when Kyle arrived. He stood beside Dr. Simpson examining a series of computer generated graphs.

Just as it had been in King's office, Kyle was struck by the presence of the Tall Man. He was indeed tall, but certainly not the tallest man that Kyle had ever seen. However, his actual height seemed always to be exaggerated by the light and the shadows around him. He seemed always to be looming overhead, huge and powerful, ready to crush anyone with the intensity of his stare, or if need be, the power of his magic. The man's deep, sharp eyes, his high, pale forehead, and that long, horribly crooked nose all added to his aura of wickedness. Nowhere in the man was there a shred of anything soft or warm, no trace of the more gentle elements of humanity.

The effect of King's presence was not merely a result of his intimidating physicality though. In fact, that was only the smallest part of the whole. It was chiefly the magic that announced the Tall Man's coming and warned of what could be expected for anyone who blocked his path. The power he exuded was so pervasive that it flooded whatever room he occupied, a stifling pressure upon anyone sharing his space. It could paralyze anyone who stumbled into the depths of his long shadow and drive those who dared meet his gaze to despair.

Kyle, however, did not let himself become daunted by the aura of Ramius King, not right then. Earlier that morning when Kyle had been summoned to the Tall Man's office, the last gusts of what had been a hurricane in his head were still swirling. He'd been halfway out of his mind and so disoriented that he'd been left with only raw perceptions to rely on for guidance. Every thought that grew in him then had its roots anchored in fear, but that was no longer the case. There was still fear, of course, but it wasn't predominant among his emotions anymore. Anger had become his new chief motivator.

As Kyle had feigned sleep after returning to his room from the Tall Man's office, he'd struggled to focus on constructive planning. Every time a worthwhile idea formed in his mind though, it was pushed aside by intruding memories of Jerrod or Marion or Grandma Jo. Their images flashed before his closed eyes in rapid succession, and each one was a log on the fire that was his anger.

That anger was displayed as obviously across Kyle's face as chicken pox. No one with even a small fraction of the perceptive abilities of Ramius King could have missed it.

At Kyle's approach, King dismissed Dr. Simpson with a wave of one long-fingered hand. Kyle heard only the very last comment that passed between them.

"Get it under control, whatever it takes," King demanded as the cowering doctor slunk away. Then, turning to Kyle, he said, "Good that you got here promptly. I don't tolerate tardiness."

Kyle gritted his teeth and said nothing. Being so close once again to the man who'd murdered Grandma Jo was sickening. His anger boiled.

"Are you rested now and ready to begin your training?" King asked.

With great effort, Kyle forced the anger in his belly to stay where it was. He couldn't afford to let it out. He had to play along with King's agenda for the time being, because there was nothing else he could do that would do any good. Not yet. When the right time came though, he'd be ready. Eventually an opportunity would present itself, a moment when he could attempt escape or sabotage King's operation, or perhaps both. He might die in the effort, but that didn't seem like such a terrifying proposition. His greater fear lie in what King would do to him in the mean time. Kyle would never dishonor his murdered friends by serving the Tall Man or his designs in any way, no matter what he was forced to endure, but if the appearance of cooperation could save him some suffering, then he'd play along.

"I'm rested up fine," Kyle answered coolly, "so we can start whenever you want."

King smiled faintly, apparently pleased with Kyle's calm response.

"In that case, we'll begin now," King suggested as if he'd only just decided so. "Walk with me a while, Mr. Adams. I'd like to show you something."

The Tall Man started across the main lab, not waiting to see if Kyle followed, but trusting implicitly that he would. He'd read the boy's eyes and in them his intentions. He knew that Kyle's apparent obedience was only for show, and that when a proper time came to rebel, he would. That was just fine. Such a time would never arrive, and soon it wouldn't matter anyway. Soon, Kyle Adams would be so emotionally crippled and hungry for power, he'd forget all about his desire to escape. He'd forget all about the Guardians, the missing girl, his hobbies and dreams, and every other part of his former life. Soon, he'd think only of magic, of how to make greater use of the magic he had and of how to acquire more.

The lab through which they walked was immense and impressive. The equipment that covered each table and lined each wall was all state-of-the-art, and the combined electric humming of the many machines filled the cavernous space with sound. Dr. Simpson stood before a large computer monitor in one corner of the room. He wore a pair of bulky black gloves from which a series of long cables ran, and as he moved his hands carefully in mid-air, a complex model of a DNA strand rotated synchronously on the screen. He looked steady and sharply focused, more confident than he'd seemed in casual conversation. He was clearly in his element.

There were a dozen other computers scattered around the huge workspace, some set alone and others packed into tight formations. Intricate series of chemistry apparatus were assembled atop several counters, some being monitored closely by young people in white coats, all equipped with plastic collars like the one Kyle wore. There were twin stacks of small-animal cages atop one counter filled with mice and rats and guinea pigs. A closed door on one side of the room had a large radiation symbol painted on it in blaze-orange. The smells of chemicals, cleaning agents, and ozone were everywhere, and the bright glare of the fluorescent lights shining down from above was oppressive.

King watched as the young man beside him took it all in, noting especially his reactions to the lab assistants, his slaves. He could assume that Kyle realized that's what they were, but he wouldn't. He wasn't the type to assume anything. He wanted to know everything his new pupil knew and everything he didn't.

"What you see around you, what you're having the privilege to witness here, are the labors of the greatest scientific discovery in history," King began, not trying to keep the pride from his voice. "Edison's lights, Ford's cars, and even Oppenheimer's bombs can't compare to the breakthroughs that have been realized in this facility. Those men were great inventors and innovators, and their work produced stepping-stones in science that dramatically changed millions of lives. This work is a milestone, not a stepping-stone, and it will completely reshape the life of every man, woman, and child on this planet and the lives of all their progeny."

The Tall Man's presentation had a practiced sound to it, and no wonder. He'd been practicing it in his mind even before he'd built the facility in Steel City, before his plan had even begun to unfold.

"With the products yielded in this laboratory, I will be able to claim dominion over every country on the face of this planet," King boasted, catching the look of disbelief that his young recruit tried, but failed, to hide. "And I'll do it easily. Within the span of a single year, everyone you know and everyone you don't will be ready to kneel at my feet. I see the doubt in your eyes, but you'll soon change your mind. Not only will you believe in what I've said, you'll help me make it so."

When Kyle and the Tall Man had passed through the main working space of the lab, a long, wide hallway stretched away before them, lined along both sides with white, cloth partitions. Between each partition was a hospital bed, and upon each bed was a man. All the men were still and quiet, although some had wide, staring eyes. Heart monitors and IV drips were in place beside each unconscious or semiconscious man. It was like the catatonic wing of some psychiatric hospital, except that the patients were all young and strong instead of old and infirm.

Once again, King noted the twinge that Kyle couldn't completely avoid. Clearly, he was afraid that he might end up in one of the beds himself, drugged beyond rational thought with spittle trickling down his chin. That was fear that could be utilized.

"Would you like to know how I intend to accomplish my grand ambition?" King asked, but then continued immediately without waiting for an answer. "I will begin by showing magic to the world. I will demonstrate the undeniable reality and the devastating power of magic to a populous that is as ignorant about it as were the ancient Greeks about the shape of an atom or the composition of the sun. Even the world's greatest scientists know nothing of magic and therefore have no base of knowledge to design a defense against it. I, on the other hand, have spent my entire life mastering the manipulation of magic, and I also ride the crest of the highest wave of modern science. I alone know how little separates the two. I alone understand that in truth, magic is simply a word we use to signify science that is yet to be explained. Stone-age man saw magic in fire and lightning. I will be viewed with exactly that same fear and awe."

"Imagine if Hitler could have taken his troops and their weapons back in time one hundred years and then launched his siege against Europe. That's how it will be for me. That's how ill-prepared this world is to defend itself against my power. Not that many will stand against my ascension anyhow. Most will view me and treat me as a god. Those who do resist will be dealt with by my governors."

Kyle's eyebrows knotted at hearing the word "governors." King, catching the look of confusion, was quick to explain.

"They lie all around you. These privileged men whom I stole away from their ordinary, pitiful lives are in the process of becoming extraordinary. I'm making them into supermen."

King held his young recruit's stare for a moment, allowing the full weight of his confidence and ambition to be felt, and then he turned and walked to the side of the nearest bed. Kyle hesitated, but eventually followed. Recognition showed in his young features when he saw the face of the man in the bed. It was the same man who'd charged out of the lab earlier that day in a state of complete mania. He now lay in complete stillness, his wide eyes staring off to some place higher than the ceiling above him.

King smiled wickedly when he saw Kyle's reaction to seeing the man again, and in such a state. It was good that he had thought to stop at that particular bed. It would add to Kyle's fear.

"This man was a construction worker when my recruiter found him," the Tall Man remarked passively. "He was a peon. Now he's one of my experiments, a rat in a maze, and if he finds his way out of the maze, he'll emerge a whole new rat, one capable of serving as governor over millions of *my* people."

"Even if you could give him powers like you say you can, what makes you think that a former construction worker will be fit to lead anybody?" Kyle asked, unable to stay quiet any longer.

"I didn't say he would lead anyone, only govern over them, and he will be able to do that because I will give him the power. After I show the world the devastating power of my magic, all my governors will have to do is demonstrate that they possess even the tiniest fraction of those same abilities, and people will cower. They'll fall to their knees and beg for mercy."

Kyle's face was a mask of strain. King couldn't be sure whether it was fear, anger, or simply disbelief that he was struggling against so intently.

"What you need to understand, Mr. Adams, is that you're not quite as special as you've previously been led to believe. You think that you have a gift that very few others in the world have, and that's true, but not for long. Very soon, I will give that gift to whomever I choose. I'm giving it to these men right now. The power to manipulate magic is stored in every cell of every person alive, an untapped reservoir of potential beyond imagination. Tell me what you learned in school about DNA, Mr. Adams."

Kyle didn't have an answer right away. It had been a long summer, one devoid of academic attention, and it took a moment to switch back to that mode of thinking. In fact, it was a struggle to shift his focus back to anything from what he now thought of as "normal life," anything before the past few days.

"DNA is the code for how a person is put together," Kyle offered at last, fumbling a little to find the right words. "It's the really long list of letters that's crumpled up in the nucleus of each cell."

"True enough," King conceded, "though not so eloquently phrased. DNA is a code, a secret code, and one that has only recently been unraveled, and only to a small degree at that. The code is for instructions, but only little bits of those instructions, pieces called exons, ever get used in most people. The rest, vast sections called introns, are left dormant, unused—in most people. The textbook they gave you in school probably referred to introns as junk DNA, because they never get sent out of the nucleus to be interpreted. How incredibly arrogant for people to think that anything in nature is junk. In truth, the code stored in those introns contains evolutionary possibilities that would stagger every scientist on earth, save one. Among those possibilities is the ability to manipulate magic. Only a tiny percentage of people are born with those particular pieces of code turned on, and even among those few, many never realize their own gift. But as it turns out, that dormant code can be brought to life in anyone with just a little genetic tweaking. Such is the case with this former construction worker. The secrets of his silent letters have been revealed, and soon he will learn those secrets for himself."

King studied Kyle's reaction, curious not only to see if he believed what he was hearing, but also if he truly grasped the magnitude of what it meant for the future of his world.

"Believe it, young man. The future is mine. And so are you."

A Hard Lesson Made Easy

The lab tour and the discussion on science and magic turned out to be only the prelude to Kyle's real lesson. After leaving the lab and the rows of occupied hospital beds behind, King led Kyle to a small room at the far end of an adjoining hallway. The room was dimly lit with a single overhead fluorescent bulb, and its walls were all bare. A long table was set along the wall opposite the hallway door, but there were no chairs. Atop the table were three large cardboard boxes.

Kyle remained standing just inside the door as King crossed the room in half a dozen long, graceful strides. When he reached the table, the Tall Man picked up the boxes one by one, setting them on the floor beside his feet, and then from one of the boxes he retrieved a white light bulb which he placed in the center of the table. He stepped back to the center of the room, ten feet in front of the table, and beckoned for Kyle.

"Come here, Mr. Adams," he commanded. "I've just prepared your first test."

Kyle moved to the side of his self-appointed mentor, suddenly able to feel every beat of his heart. He had next to no experience using magic and zero confidence that he could pass whatever sort of test was about to be assigned to him. How would Ramius King respond to his failure? Harshly, to be sure.

"I want you to use your magic to smash that light bulb," King instructed. "I hope you don't think it's demeaning, assigning you such a dreadfully simple task to begin with. After all, my first general saw you kill one of my hunters with a manhole cover that weighed most of what you weigh, and that certainly required power adequate for smashing a thousand light bulbs."

Kyle remembered throwing the manhole cover, but in the fuzzy way one remembers a dream or a memory from early childhood. He knew that the manhole cover must have been very heavy, and so he believed that it must have been magic that had allowed him to hurl it as he had, but how he'd done it, how he'd mustered that power, he hadn't a clue.

Kyle stared at the little sphere of glass intensely, willing it to break. He pictured in his mind how it would look shattered into a hundred tiny pieces. He clenched his teeth and balled his fists, desperate to make something happen, terrified of what punishment he'd face if nothing did.

"What's the problem, Mr. Adams?" King asked after watching Kyle strain for a few moments. "Someone like you should be able to crush that fragile little thing with a thought. It should be nearly effortless."

Kyle struggled harder, feeling the heavy burden of the Tall Man's presence beside him and the fear of his own imminent failure. He thought about the candle in Grandma Jo's office, how he'd felt it from a distance, how he'd snuffed its light with a touch of his magic. With all his strength he tried to extend himself out toward the light bulb in that same way, to feel its smooth surface, to bear the weight of his will down upon it and crush it.

Suddenly the light bulb moved, loosened ever so slightly from its resting position. It rolled over the tabletop, tracing a small semicircle before settling again to stillness.

Kyle gasped. He'd been holding his breath for too long, and his body's pleading for fresh air finally overrode his concentration.

"I can't do it," Kyle muttered between deep gulps of air. He didn't say anything else. He just waited for whatever reprimand was coming.

The Tall Man allowed Kyle to squirm under his silent stare for a moment, and then with a thin, wicked smile spread beneath his long, crooked nose, he said, "I can see that. Perhaps I've overestimated you somewhat. But fear not, for I am an excellent teacher, and I guarantee that your progress will be quick. I'll give you what you need to excel, what your first instructor denied you."

Then, from an inside pocket of the finely tailored suit coat he wore, Ramius King produced the Plume of Shu. He carefully unfolded the headband attached to the strange, black fossilized feather and placed it ceremoniously upon his head as if it were a crown of gold and jewels.

"Even without this talisman, I could shatter a million light bulbs with a single sweep of my magic," the Tall Man boasted, "but I couldn't do this."

King held one long-fingered hand out before him, and instantly the light bulb flew from the table top, falling up through the air as if gravity's force had suddenly been reversed. The bulb floated across the room and came to a halt in mid-air a foot short of King's extended hand, and there it hung, suspended by his magic.

"Without the Plume of Shu," King continued, "I could never maintain the sort of control needed to do something like this."

Kyle was mesmerized by the floating bulb. It rested in the air so perfectly still, like it was actually settled into King's palm instead of floating before it.

The long fingers of the Tall Man's hand curled just slightly, and a cracking sound broke the silence of the room. Another miniscule curl at the fingertips followed a moment later, and another series of cracks and pops sounded.

Kyle saw the jagged break lines as they spread across the delicate globe. He watched as the cracks spread out in every direction until there was no section of the sphere larger than an apple seed left intact, but somehow the thing held its shape. Not a sliver of glass fell away, and the bulb as a whole never quavered.

"You'll sooner be able to uproot trees and topple two story buildings before you'll be able to achieve this feat," King predicted. "Power comes much easier than control."

Kyle could still hear quiet crackling from the bulb, though he could no longer see the damage being done. The glass appeared uniform once more, its color now a dull yellow instead of its original bright white.

"Many of my men possess tremendous power, but my control is unparalleled. That, Mr. Adams, is why they are my men to command, and it is also why I am subject to no one's command."

The Tall Man's hand dropped to his side then, releasing his invisible grip. The metal plug of the bulb dropped to the ground with a tinny clang, and the glass scattered apart like dust, forming a cloud of tiny particulate sand that floated slowly down through the air.

When King's hand came back up, one long finger pointed to the first of the cardboard boxes sitting on the floor. Out from the box sprung another white bulb, which flew through the air just as the first had, but came to rest in midair not before King, but before Kyle.

"Take it," King said. "Run your fingers over its surface."

Kyle did as he was told, grabbing the bulb from the air and inspecting it.

"Now take this," King went on, handing Kyle a leather glove, "and smash it. See how it feels and how it sounds."

Again, Kyle did as instructed. He slid the glove over his right hand, and with a single squeeze the bulb succumbed to his grip, breaking apart into sharp white shards which he sprinkled onto the floor at his feet.

Another point from the Tall Man's finger brought out another white bulb, and this one settled to rest atop the table.

"Now take this," King said, making it sound almost like a dare, "and direct its power to that brittle little orb of glass."

Kyle heart quickened again as he watched King produce a second Gift of Nature from inside his jacket. It might have been a salamander or a small lizard. The black obsidian body of the little animal was twisted into an s-curve, and its legs were thrown straight out to it sides. It had the look of a dead thing still caught in the pull of rigor mortis, frozen in a posture of agony. A thin, silver chain was clasped about its neck.

Kyle stared at the talisman with a mix of wonder and horror. He was being offered one of the weapons that Jerrod had earned only after many years of training. Jerrod's Gift had come from a dead Guardian, and maybe the one being offered to him had as well.

"Don't worry," King offered in a mock-soothing tone, "this talisman belonged to one of my own soldiers."

Kyle started at the comment, unnerved at how accurately the Tall Man read his fears.

"Why do you hesitate?" King asked, sounding impatient. "What I'm offering you is one of the rarest treasures on earth. Whether you do it to serve me or to betray me, take this weapon. Without it you are weak. Without it you are helpless."

But still Kyle hesitated, not because he doubted what King was saying, but because he believed it. His only hope of escape was through magic beyond what he was as of yet capable of. Logic said it was so, but his instincts told him that King was playing him like a musical instrument, plucking the strings of his will with a master's subtle touch.

King's voice slowed and dropped to a whisper, and he said, "I tell you now, Mr. Adams, I will kill you where you stand if you do not take this talisman."

Kyle's breath caught in his throat. He looked into the dark, sharp eyes of Ramius King, and there he saw the doubtless sincerity of the threat.

Kyle's right hand shook as he reached forward, and when his fingers closed about the twisted black creature, a wave of heat raced down the skin of his arms and legs. An electric buzzing filled his ears, and a tiny vibration rattled through his teeth. His free hand sprung open wide without his telling it to do so, and his fingertips tingled with power.

"Now the light bulb," King reminded.

Kyle looked at the bulb lying atop the table. He remembered how it had felt to crush one just like it in his gloved hand. He remembered how easy it had been, how little resistance the thin glass had offered. He reached his free hand out toward the tabletop, and when he felt the invisible arc of energy race to his target, he squeezed his fingers into a white-knuckled fist. The glass shattered instantly, and the bulb's plug crumpled in on itself, reduced to a tiny, round wad of metal that rolled across the table, and then fell softly to the floor.

King asked Kyle to repeat the act three times in similar fashion. Each time the glass shattered immediately and easily, and each time the secret rush that Kyle received from the act grew slightly.

The Tall Man asked Kyle to close his eyes at one point, and when he reopened them there were two bulbs on the tabletop, one white and the other painted red.

"Break only the white one, Mr. Adams," King instructed.

On his first attempt Kyle broke both, but on his second effort he left the red one whole.

The next time Kyle opened his eyes there were three bulbs on the table, two white and one red. Again, he succeeded in breaking only the white ones. Then there were two white and two red, and then one white and three red, and so on and so forth. Kyle continued to perform flawlessly, reaching out with the magic that pulsed through his fingers with the ease of thought, smashing every sphere of white glass the moment he saw it and leaving all the red ones unharmed. He worked faster and faster, his confidence and enthusiasm building quickly.

Kyle was hardly even thinking about the exercise after a while, just opening his eyes and unleashing the magic. The reptilian talisman now hung around his neck, and each time he summoned its power it burned satisfyingly against his chest. For what must have been the twentieth time, Kyle closed his eyes. He heard the faint tinkling of the light bulbs as King spread them across the table top. He tried to picture them in his mind, how they might be arranged this time, red and then white, white and then red.

"Now!" King called again as he had each time when the targets were in place.

Kyle's eyelids snapped apart, the magic already poised at his fingertips like water against a dam, anxious to be loosed. There were more targets this time than there had been yet, perhaps ten in all, about half white and half red. Without even taking in the whole arrangement, Kyle let the magic go, allowing his intuition, his inner voice, which spoke with volume and authority like never before, to guide the energy by itself, to seek out only the white targets and destroy them. And it did. With reflex quickness, the magic swept across the table, utterly demolishing four white light bulbs and one white rat, King's surprise from the third box.

Kyle froze, revolted at what he'd just witnessed. No, what he'd just done! It hardly even felt as if he'd killed the rat, but he knew he had. It had been as easy as smashing another light bulb, and it had given him the same rush, the same thrill. But now, looking at the bloody mess splattered over the table, he felt very differently. He felt sick, like he'd been poisoned. His stomach turned over on itself, pushing bile up into his throat, which had gone suddenly dry, causing him to cough and struggle for breath. The anger that had boiled in him so hotly before returned now, but it wasn't just for Ramius King anymore, it was for himself.

"Just your first lesson and already you've killed for me," King noted, sounding satisfied. "That will be all for today, Mr. Adams. Return to your quarters until I call for you again. I'll have Choplin bring you some supper. He should start getting used to serving you anyway. You're on your way to becoming one of my hunters. When you are, you will be his master instead of the other way around."

Kyle turned away from the Tall Man, still fighting the urge to vomit, still cursing himself for having been played so easily.

"Don't forget the talisman," King reminded as Kyle approached the door. "Leave it on the table."

Kyle walked back across the room and lifted the chain over his head. He slowly lowered the strange, black fossil down until it touched the table's surface, but then he hesitated. His inner voice screamed anew, pleading with him not to let go.

"Go ahead, Mr. Adams," King prompted, "set it down."

Kyle willed his fist to relax, but it didn't respond. He couldn't let go. He still felt the tingling at his fingertips and still heard the comforting drone of the magic's buzzing in his ears. He still felt the seductive warmth of the power.

"You will set the weapon down or you will turn and test your strength against mine," King dared. "Choose quickly or I will choose for you."

Kyle gritted his teeth, strained to regain control over himself, and finally his fingers loosened.

As Kyle shuffled through the hallways back toward his room, he felt as drained as he ever had in his life. He hardly even noticed the people he passed. He felt like there was a great gaping hole right through the middle of him, and he knew that there was only one thing that could fill it. What he didn't know was how long it would take before that empty feeling went away, if it ever did.

Buried Treasure

The last four miles of road leading up to the house were still unpaved and rutted with washboard ripples, just as Michael remembered. Somehow, Rosa managed to keep on napping as they bounced along, a testament to her fatigue. Even when the car finally came to a stop and the engine died, she slumbered on. It was Michael's voice that finally roused her.

With an uncharacteristic edge of anticipation in his voice, Michael told Rosa that this was his home, the place where he and his brother had grown up. There was something he'd left behind, something he needed to retrieve, and she needn't accompany him. That was all he said before stepping out of the car and walking away, throwing the driver's side door shut behind him.

Rosa watched as he moved past the obviously abandoned house without ever looking at it. He continued on through a small grove of citrus trees behind the overgrown yard and was gone from her view in seconds. She didn't know what to think, but she knew she wasn't about to wait in the car as he'd suggested. Patience had never been among her strongest virtues.

Though her curiosity begged her to go inspect the house, Rosa continued past, keeping to Michael's path. The yard, just like the house, had clearly been neglected for many years. Nearly hidden in a waist-high carpet of palmetto and tall grasses, she could see the remnant of a children's sand box, and there was a tire lying beneath the branches of a tall pine that must've been a swing once, its rope long since rotted and broken. It was difficult to imagine Michael as a child, playing in that box or on that swing with his twin brother, doing the things any child does. Judging by his disregard, it was also a difficult thing for him to recall. Rosa knew why. Everything there would remind him of Sean.

Beyond the small grove of what Rosa now realized were grapefruit trees, a boardwalk trail headed into a swampy, low growing forest behind the house. The boards of the trail were rotting and completely overgrown in many places by shrubby grasses and palmettos. Rosa followed the trial with some difficulty for at least a hundred yards, at which point she became aware of the rhythmic sound of waves ahead. Around the next bend, the scrubby forest trees gave way to mangroves.

The boardwalk continued on through the sprawling knobby-kneed roots of the mangroves, but its deterioration there was more advanced, having reduced it to wood scraps covered with skittering silverfish and clumps of barnacles seeded by the high tide. Fiddler crabs peeked cautiously from the mouths of their finger width holes, having already fled for shelter at Michael's passing. At the end of the trail there was a small stretch of dingy beach and beyond that the Gulf of Mexico. A jagged line of mostly broken seashells ran along the water's edge, dotted here and there with bits of withered seagrass and several dead Mullet. A small group of Ibis picked curiously through the debris, their white feathers as flawless as freshly fallen snow. Standing ankle-deep in the water, his cargo pants soaked from the knees down, was Michael. He stood facing out over the vast water with his arms crossed over his chest, breathing in deep mouthfuls of the salty air.

"So this is what you needed to do while I waited in the car?" Rosa asked indignantly.

"We used to fish here," Michael said, clearly unsurprised to hear Rosa's voice despite his having asked her to remain behind. "We caught Sheephead, Mangrove Snapper, Spotted Seatrout, sometimes Redfish, and an occasional Snook. We caught the Fiddlers that live under those mangroves and used them for bait. We fed our fish cleaning scraps to the same Blue Heron with a crooked beak for five years in a row. We came out here every morning and sifted through whatever the tide had carried in during the night, picking out the prettiest shells to give to our mother."

"I know it must be hard remembering how things were back then, and how things turned out," Rosa offered sympathetically.

"It was on this beach that Sean and I first realized that we could do things other people couldn't do," Michael went on, his gaze still fixed over the blue expanse of the gulf. "We learned to draw lines in the sand without touching it and to smash seashells without lifting a stone. We were on this very beach one evening when a deer came walking down our boardwalk, a buck. We were thirteen at the time. He had to have seen us by the time he was in the mangroves, but he kept on coming like he wasn't afraid."

Finally, Michael turned around so Rosa could see him. His eyes seemed to be looking for something miles away. He walked up onto the beach next to her and extended one hand nervously into the empty space before him.

"It walked right out onto the beach where we were standing, right here. I couldn't imagine why it wasn't afraid, unless it was somehow because of our magic. We were still just beginning to understand what it could do. At the same time, Sean and I both reached out to it."

"You petted it?" Rosa interrupted.

Michael ignored her. "The instant we touched it, the deer burst into flames. It literally caught fire and burned right there before our eyes. It thrashed like it was in agony, but as hard as we tried, neither Sean nor I could get away from it. We were stuck to it, attached to a flailing mass of blue fire. And the pain, Rosa, it was indescribable. Think of a time when you touched your fingertip to a hot stovetop or a clothes iron. It hurt like that but everywhere at once, every inch of my body, inside and out. I thought that I was dying, but then suddenly it was over. The fire disappeared as completely as if it had never been there at all and so did the deer, and my brother and I were left there, completely unhurt. All that was left of the buck were its antlers. They laid there, one at Sean's feet and one at mine. They had turned pure black. When we picked them up we could feel the power that channeled through them."

Rosa listened, hardly able to imagine the scene that Michael was describing.

"Later on, when we joined the Guardians, we were the only two who'd received first generation Gifts of Nature. The other Gifts had all been handed down from previous generations. There're only a handful of Gifts in the world, and that handful has been discovered over the course of thousands of years. That animal was so extraordinarily rare, and it produced the only twin gifts known to history, and they were given to us, the only twins in history who both possessed the ability to use magic. We thought it was our destiny. We thought we were headed for glory. But now I wish it had never happened."

Rosa was stunned. How could any of what she was hearing be possible? That the world could be so different from what she'd always believed was terrifying.

"So what'd you guys do then, when you had your Gifts?" Rosa asked. "You went out into the world to battle evil wherever you could find it?"

"Not exactly," Michael answered, the slightest flicker of a smile flashing across his face. "With our fantastically enhanced powers and immeasurable new confidence, we decided to steal a car and drive down to the keys. We'd always wanted to go there and try to catch a Tarpon. They're supposed to fight like hell."

Rosa's jaw literally dropped. "Is that you trying to be funny? If it is, you missed by a long shot."

"No joke," Michael assured, the smile reappearing briefly. "That's what we decided to do. We were only thirteen years old, just junior high kids. Sean decided that our Gifts elevated us above the rules of ordinary people. He was always the leader, not me, and I always followed his lead. Anyway, a state trooper tried to pull us over in our stolen car, apparently because he didn't think Sean looked like he was old enough to drive."

"No shit," Rosa agreed.

"We tried to make a run for it, but it was Sean's first day of driving, and we didn't get too far. About a half a mile into the chase, if you could call it that, we went off the road doing over ninety. We slid for about fifty yards and then hit an oak tree nose first. Sean stayed in the driver's seat and ended up with the engine block in his lap. I went through the windshield and landed in a mud puddle another forty yards away from the highway, still holding my half of the deer's Gift."

"Lucky you weren't killed," Rosa whispered, aghast.

"That's the thing about it, we weren't even hurt. I mean not a scratch or a split lip, nothing. But I wouldn't say we were *lucky*. I don't think luck had anything to do with it. Needless to say, the state trooper and everyone else that soon followed found our remarkably good condition more than a little peculiar. Some reporter interviewed the EMT who found me in the mud puddle, and he wrote an article in the newspaper about it. Two days later, Grandma Jo came for us. Looking back, I think that was probably the last day of our childhood."

Michael imagined all of the questions that must have been forming in Rosa's mind. He supposed that she'd be wondering about what training was involved in becoming a Guardian, about how Sean and he had learned to use their Gifts, about the secrets that were revealed to them and the powers that were developed in them. For some reason, he didn't anticipate the question that she actually asked, although it was a logical one.

"So why the hell were you standing out there in the water when I walked up here?"

Michael didn't answer right away. He'd been so engrossed in reliving the past that he'd completely lost track of the present, of what he'd come back for, what he'd tried unsuccessfully to do already.

"Rosa, will you do something for me?" Michael asked.

The deadly seriousness in his voice demanded a serious answer.

"Of course. Anything," she promised.

"There's a group of coconut palms over there beyond the mangroves, the ones with the charred trunks. There's a flat, gray chunk of limestone lying beneath the tallest one, and buried underneath that rock is a wooden box. The Gifts that Sean and I were given on this beach are in that box. I buried them there fifteen years ago after Sean died, after I killed him." Michael looked back out across the wide, blue water, which was catching the glare of the afternoon sunlight. He seemed afraid to look at the place where he'd instructed her to go.

"You want me to go dig them up? I don't get it. If they're the reason you came here, why don't you go get them yourself?"

Michael turned back to face her, trying to think of how he could make her understand, searching for the right words.

Then, for the first time, Rosa noticed the beads that had risen on his forehead. She remembered back to the fire in her apartment, how he'd never even appeared flushed, even after carrying her through the flames. He didn't need to answer her question. Seeing him there, trying to douse his own internal fire in the seawater, she understood exactly what help he needed. She also realized at last what he'd meant the first night they'd met, when he told her how hard he'd been fighting as the muggers had beat him in the streets. He'd been fighting himself, fighting the temptation to defend himself with magic.

"I'll get them for you, Michael," she said solemnly. "I'll get them, and we'll put them in the trunk where they'll be out of sight and …"

"But don't touch them!" he cut her off, sounding as close to frantic as she'd ever heard him. "Just leave them in the box. Don't even open it."

Rosa sounded a little annoyed at what she took to be a lacking of trust from Michael as she suggested, "Maybe we should just take a peek. What if somebody found them? What if they aren't even in there anymore?"

"They're in there," he assured her. "You'll know it, too."

Rosa wasn't sure what that meant, and was not at all anxious to find out.

Michael had been right. Even as Rosa approached the cluster of palms where the Gifts were buried, she could already feel what Michael could obviously feel even from the greater distance. She noted that the trunks of the palms were only charred on one side. She wondered if it could be scarring from the fire all those years ago that produced the twins' Gifts?

The sensation of being a conduit of energy increased the nearer Rosa came to the place that Michael had chosen to be the antlers' grave. Her muscles actually started to twitch when she dug her fingers into the cold, wet sand that was packed beneath the limestone slab, which she'd found lying there right where he'd said it would be. As she lifted out the rotting wood box a minute later, she could see her hands shaking involuntarily. The whole way back to the car, it felt like she was carrying the live end of a power line, and it was flooding her body with electric current. Yet her urge was not to throw the box aside, to distance herself from it, but to open it up, to see for herself the source of the energy she felt.

Michael followed silently behind her, keeping a distance of some thirty feet between them. It occurred to Rosa that if both he and the Gifts were going to leave in the same car, they would have to be much closer together than he seemed comfortable being.

Rosa placed the box into the Monte's trunk and climbed into the driver's seat. She didn't think that Michael was in the right state of mind for driving and doubted equally the possibility that he would be interested in spending any more time at the house. And she was right. They set off immediately when Michael caught up and settled himself unsteadily into the front passenger's seat beside her. He didn't offer any instructions, so Rosa headed north, figuring that any other direction on the peninsula couldn't take them very far.

Never once while they traveled that evening did Michael appear to even approach a state of ease. The beads of sweat that Rosa had noted on his forehead earlier persisted, and every so often he'd run his hands over the legs of his cargo pants to dry his palms. More subtly, he also peaked over his shoulder from time to time, presumably in the direction of the trunk and its contents. He never spoke, and neither did she.

When the failing afternoon waned toward dusk, Rosa took it upon herself to decide that it was time to stop. She bought sandwiches at a fast-food drive-through with Michael's money and then pulled into the first hotel she saw to get a room for the night.

When she got out and moved to the trunk, Michael finally found his voice.

"Just leave them in there," he instructed.

She knew exactly what "them" he was referring to, but had her doubts about leaving such rare and powerful things unattended in the parking lot all night. She supposed that if they'd survived being buried in the sand for the last fifteen years, they'd probably be able to make it through one night in the trunk.

To Michael's relief, Rosa didn't seem interested in asking any more questions that night or prodding for any more details or explanations. It was probably due in greater part to fatigue rather than consideration, but he appreciated it nonetheless.

When they got into their room, Rosa clicked on the TV, maybe for some distraction or maybe just out of habit, and then they dug into their sandwiches. Rosa finished first again, and thus she got first crack at the shower. When she was finished, she emerged from the bathroom to find Michael sitting next the window, which he'd opened, pulling in deep lungfuls of the cool, salty air.

She was struck once again by the odd combining of young and old features in his face. There was the strong, angular chin, tipped with that vibrant flash of a red goatee. His nose, cheeks, and hair, and even the set of his jaw, all spoke of youth and vigor, but then there were his eyes, the eyes of an old man. His eyes were so sad, so lonely. How much guilt and despair must it have taken for someone so young to end up with eyes like those?

A memory flashed unbidden within Rosa, a recollection of the pain and sadness she'd felt through Michael as he'd slept and dreamed of his worst day. It had affected her so strongly, and yet for her it had lasted only moments. For Michael, those feelings had persisted for a decade and a half.

Just then, Michael rose from the chair, perhaps having sensed Rosa watching him. He started for the bathroom, but Rosa stopped him on the way by.

"You shouldn't spend so much time worrying, Redbeard," she advised gently. "You're a good man. We got some bad stuff to deal with here, but you'll do the best you can, and if that isn't enough, then tough shit. You can only do what you can do."

Impulsively, she rose to her tiptoes and kissed him on the cheek.

It happened so fast that Michael never even moved in response, not a muscle. It looked like the touch of her lips had frozen him, but that was hardly the case. Just the opposite, in fact.

Rosa moved past him then, laying out a pair of pajamas that were courtesy of the hotel across her bed.

"Well, you getting in that shower or not?" she suggested more than asked. "I need to change, and I don't need an audience."

Michael just smiled and headed into the bathroom.

Rosa turned around as the door shut, finding her refection looking back from a mirror mounted on the opposite wall.

"What the hell was that?" she asked herself in a sharp whisper. "Did you just kiss him?"

To Break a Promise

By the time Michael was finished showering, Rosa was already fast asleep. She lay curled up beneath the bedcover with one arm tucked under her pillow. On her face, Michael saw that same perfect sweetness he'd studied so intently as she'd slept in the car. An angel. He stared for a long time again, memorizing the shape of her eyelashes, the curve of her small nose, and the slight parting of her lips, like she'd just blown a kiss to some lucky guy–maybe him. He remembered how those lips had felt against his cheek, soft and warm. Once again, he was stunned at how easily and how powerfully she affected him. She could ask anything of him and he'd do it in a heartbeat, without any hesitation. It was a completely exhilarating and slightly terrifying realization.

He knew he shouldn't feel so worked up. After all, it was just a kiss on the cheek, a harmless and probably meaningless gesture. And yet all the logic in the world couldn't settle the stirring in his stomach.

Michael walked quietly back to the chair he'd placed beside the room's sole window and settled back into place. He shifted around a couple of times, but for some reason he couldn't seem to find a comfortable position. He tried crossing his legs and then uncrossing them, slouching down and then straightening up. Nothing worked. Finally, he decided to abandon his post at the window. He crept back to the bed and very carefully eased onto the opposite edge from where Rosa lay. He stretched himself out, feeling more comfortable than he'd expected. Even if he couldn't sleep, he reasoned, he could at least rest his limbs and think about what would need to be accomplished the following day.

Before the passing of a single minute, he was asleep. And for the first night in a very long time, it was a peaceful sleep. His ghosts, it seemed, were taking the night off. In the place of his recurring nightmare, he dreamed about Rosa. He dreamed about taking her fishing and dancing and sailing. He dreamed about taking her somewhere far away and never coming back.

Rosa's slumber was less peaceful. She kept waking up, and each time she did she had to decide all over again if she'd really kissed Michael or if it had only been a dream. Falling back to sleep was difficult as well, because her mind was filled not only with anxiety over what she'd done, but also with apprehension over what she hadn't done yet, but knew she would. She was going to follow Michael wherever he went, even to Ramius King.

When Rosa awoke at midnight and found Michael lying beside her, she decided to get up for a while and try to clear her head. As slowly and quietly as she could, she slid out from under the sheet and tiptoed across the room. She rummaged through the pockets of her shorts until she found the keycard for the room and the keys to the car, thinking that she might go distract herself by listening to the radio for a few minutes, and then she crept out the door.

The hallway outside their room was empty as was the staircase leading down to the ground level. The parking lot, however, was not completely abandoned, despite the late hour. As Rosa stepped out into the night, she caught a brief glimpse of two young kids who'd been squatted between two cars parked just a little ways down from the Monte Carlo. They scooted away when they heard the hotel door swing shut, but Rosa couldn't tell if they kept going or simply ducked out of sight.

"Better stay away from my new car, punks," Rosa hissed under her breath.

Without hesitating, she strode over to the Monte. She quickly looked it over, and when she was satisfied that it was fine, she unlocked the driver's side door, climbed in behind the wheel, and started it up. She backed up and drove the car part way around the lot, reparking it in a spot that would be visible from the window of their room. It was probably an unnecessary precaution, but it couldn't hurt. There were certainly fancier cars in the lot, more obvious targets, and besides, there was almost nothing in the Monte to steal. *Almost.*

As soon as Rosa popped the trunk, she could feel the same static buzz that she'd felt carrying the old, wooden box up from the beach. The temptation to open it and peek inside was intense, but resistible. The box's contents weren't hers, after all, and Michael had specifically asked her leave them alone, and she'd agreed. For once in her life, she wanted to have a completely honest relationship with someone. She knew she could count on honesty from Michael, and she was going to do her best to reciprocate it.

Back in the room, Rosa slid the still-damp box gently beneath the bathroom sink and then slid herself into the chair that Michael had set beside the window. She noticed that although he slept on, he did so fitfully, perhaps affected once again by the proximity of the Gifts.

The chair wasn't very comfortable, but Rosa figured that she wasn't going to be able to fall asleep anyhow. Not only had stepping outside failed to clear her mind, it had actually added to her list of concerns. Parked outside was the only new car she'd ever owned, the nicest thing that was ever really hers, and most importantly, a present from Michael. If those little punks even touched it, she thought, she'd kick their asses so hard their mothers would feel it.

Before Rosa had really even settled into place, one of the kids reappeared in the parking lot below. He walked without hesitation past a dozen other cars and went straight to the Monte Carlo. He gave the parking lot a quick once over and then squatted down beside the driver's side door.

Damn it! Rosa swore to herself. She looked back at Michael who seemed to be sleeping a little more peacefully again for the moment. She didn't need to wake him, she decided, not for one or two little punk kids. They'd probably take off again as soon as she stepped outside.

So, for the second time that night, Rosa snuck out of the room. She charged down the stairs, skipping over two with each stride, and when she reached the bottom she rushed outside, making her presence known immediately.

"I know you're not breaking into my car, punk," she shouted as she started more slowly toward the Monte Carlo. The boy seemed not to hear her. He didn't even look up from his work. "I'll whip your ass if you don't get the hell out of here," she tried again, raising her voice another notch. "You hear me, punk?"

Rosa was only ten feet from the boy when he finally looked up and showed his face.

"Did you just call me a punk, fortune teller?"

It wasn't one of the kids Rosa had seen snooping around earlier. It wasn't a kid at all. It was a man, a child-sized man, but a dangerous man nonetheless. Surely, Rosa knew, his much larger partner wouldn't be far away.

"Don't bother trying to run, Rosalind Sanchez," Little Boy instructed in his oversized voice. "You know I command magic. You can't escape me. And yes, Fat Man is here with us," he answered her unasked question.

"So you guys are King's relief pitchers?" Rosa asked, secretly proud of how brave she thought she sounded. "I hope that prissy Brit got whipped for blowing the game in Miami like he did."

Little Boy grinned wickedly and said, "I'm not sure what Mr. King did to him. As soon as he reported the news about your new friend, we were sent south. If you're genuinely curious about Mr. York's fate, then you can ask about him when we …"

Without finishing his thought, Little Boy sprung forward, grabbed Rosa about the hips and spun her around to face back toward the hotel. A short blade appeared from nowhere in one of his tiny hands, but not an ordinary blade. It was made of dancing blue flames, just like the weapons that Rosa had seen in Michael's nightmare. He held the fiery knife's point inches in front of her stomach, close enough to let her feel its heat and close enough for one quick flick of his wrist to mean her death.

"Come out, come out," the tiny man shouted, scanning over the parking lot intently. "You know that men like us can't hide from one another. I know you're here."

Then, to Rosa's delight and despair, the hotel door pushed open again, and out stepped Michael Galladin. It was delight that Rosa felt first, seeing that her knight had arrived to rescue her, but the despair came with her very next breath. This wasn't a hired hit-man with a fire fetish. This was Ramius King's number one team, his favorite killers.

Michael strode over the asphalt lot toward Rosa and Little Boy, one hand swaying loosely at his side and the other held awkwardly behind his back.

Rosa meant to call out to him, to warn him of the danger he was in, but her voice caught in her throat. Something about Michael was different. His tired, shuffling gait was gone. In fact, he hardly even bobbed between steps, as if he were weightless, barely touching the ground beneath his feet as he passed across it.

"I'm going to have to break my promise," Michael said aloud, perhaps to Rosa or perhaps to himself. "There's no other way."

"Stop where you are or I'll kill her right here," Little Boy threatened. He brought the flaming knife another inch closer to Rosa's stomach, darkening the fabric of her pajamas and causing her to gasp in pain.

Michael stopped.

"I doubt Mr. King would be very happy with you if you did that," Michael responded, his voice cool, but his eyes intense. "I assume that you're here to collect her, not to kill her. I assume that Mr. King has reconsidered her usefulness now that he knows about me."

"Mr. King has serious doubts about the Brit's story, thought he might be making it up as an excuse for missing his hit. But he's a careful man, so he sent me to be sure, and sure enough, there you are. After all these years, the lost Guardian of Magic is found. I'm sorry, did I say the *lost* Guardian? I meant the *last* Guardian."

Michael tried, but failed, to keep his expression stoic.

"I guess you really have been out of the loop, haven't you?" the tiny man continued, his gruff voice projecting out through a tight smile. "The Guardians are all dead, Michael, every one. Even the old lady."

The flame that had been relit in Michael's chest exploded into an inferno, and it took all his strength to hold it in. He couldn't even speak.

"I was sent here to retrieve the fortune teller, just like you say," Little Boy confirmed, "but since you're here, maybe I'll just kill you both and be done with it. I'm sure Mr. King wouldn't mind. He only needed her to find out about you. If you're dead, then she's useless again."

"If you think you can kill me, then why don't you quit hiding behind the girl and come do it," Michael dared, his voice frosty.

"Michael!" Rosa screamed, but too late to make any difference.

Fortunately, it didn't matter. Michael had been waiting for Fat Man to appear and sensed his approach even before Rosa spotted him.

As Rosa watched in horror and then disbelief, Fat Man rose up behind Michael, towering over him like a giant. But just as the brute lunged at his would-be prey, Michael spun around on one heel, a movement so smooth and perfectly balanced that it could have been a ballet step. He grabbed the much larger man with his free hand and literally threw him across the parking lot. Fat Man, caught completely by surprise, was off his feet and without leverage before he realized that his sneak attack hadn't been sneaky enough.

The behemoth's enormous mass struck the back of a conversion van parked right next to the Monte Carlo. His momentum was enough to snap both of the back doors cleanly from their hinges. The whole vehicle bounced on its overstressed shocks as the man, and the back doors, went crashing into the van's dark interior.

"Like you said, Little Boy, it's not easy for men like us to hide from one another," Michael reminded smugly.

A creaking sounded from the van a moment later, and from the cave that Michael had made of the vehicle's back end, Fat Man emerged, apparently unmarked except for the redness of his face.

Michael found the goliath's eyes and promised solemnly, "The next time you touch me, I'll kill you. No other warning and no hesitation." Then turning back to Little Boy, he asked, "So what do we do now?"

"I see two options," the tiny man reasoned aloud, his deep voice still calm, but edged with new tension, "either we fight or we don't. If we do, tubby and me might kill you, and then we could kill the girl while we were at it. That would be real good." As he spoke he motioned toward Fat Man, who had moved beside them, shaking with rage and humiliation. "Or else you might kill us both, which would be real bad. If we don't fight, I'll still deliver the fortune teller here to Mr. King, which is good, and there's no chance of me dying, which is also good. I guess that's the option I'm leaning toward."

When Michael responded, his voice had dropped yet another degree, iced over completely. "You're a coward, Little Boy, and so are you, Fat Man, if you follow him when he runs back to his master with his tail between his legs. You're both veterans of this war, and I haven't been tested in fifteen years."

"That's true," Little Boy agreed, "but your last test was a big one, and you passed it with flying colors. You killed Sean, after all, and he was pretty powerful. He had to have been in order to kill ... Oh, it's hard to remember. How many Guardians did your brother kill for us, anyway?"

At that point, it became physically painful for Michael to suppress the fire raging inside him. He wanted to let it out so badly, but he was also terrified to do so. Could he contain a fire that was built on ground soaked with gasoline? Could he control it once it was started, even when it would want so desperately to spread?

"I can tell that's a touchy subject with you, so I'll drop it," Little Boy offered in mock consideration. "We'll be leaving now, and you won't try to stop us, because I'll kill her if you do. You know I will."

"If you take her, I'll hold you responsible for anything *he* does. I swear it." Michael's voice came out in unsteady blurts as he continued to struggle against the burning in his chest.

Little Boy started away, still holding Rosa at the point of his fiery knife. At first, Fat Man didn't follow. He just stood there staring at Michael, clearly struggling to restrain himself as well. Only after another prompting from Little Boy did he break his stare and depart. He pointed one bratwurst sized finger at Michael as he moved away, a wordless promise that needed no translation. They'd finish later.

"Michael, I ..." Rosa's voice called out, but was abruptly silenced.

"I know," he whispered back through clenched teeth.

Michael just stood there, shaking with frustration and anger, and watched them go. What else could he do? Every possible course of action that he could take right then might end up resulting in Rosa's death. As long as he was alive, then King would keep Rosa alive as well. The only thing to do, he decided, was to let her go for then so she would survive to be saved later.

Finding them wouldn't be a problem. Michael had originally planned on asking Rosa if he could utilize her unique talent in order to find King. She'd known that's what he intended. Now, finding the Tall Man was a simpler matter. Rosa was on her way to him, and the bond that she and Michael shared was strong enough that she could never truly be lost to him. They could try to hide her on the other side of the globe, and still he would find her. Even then, as the sound of a revving car engine reached his ears, Michael could still feel Rosa's presence in his heart. He could feel her speeding away.

Rosa sat in silence in the back of the car into which she'd been loaded. She kept her eyes closed because it was her only way to hide. The man sitting beside her filled the rest of the back seat so completely that she was pinned against the door every time he filled his lungs.

As she sat there, she thought about what had happened. She dared not think about what might happen next, when they reached the Tall Man. She thought instead about what Michael had done, and what he'd said. He'd actually thrown that brute beside her across the parking lot, and with only one arm. There could only be one explanation for that. The same explanation would account for how Little Boy had known when Michael was coming, and how Michael in turn had known when Fat Man was coming. It also explained what Michael had meant when he said he'd have to break his promise.

At the time, Rosa had thought that Michael was saying he couldn't protect her, which he'd promised to do, but that wasn't it at all. He had promised to protect her, but he'd also promised never to use the magic again. One of those promises couldn't be kept without breaking the other, and he wasn't about to forsake her trust in him, of that she felt certain. King's men had stolen her away, but she wasn't abandoned. Sooner or later, Michael would be coming.

As Michael climbed the stairs back to the hotel room, he passed several people who he supposed had been awakened by the confrontation outside. He never met any of their eyes, and most ducked timidly back into their rooms as he approached, like rabbits hiding down their holes from a prowling fox.

Just one man stood fast as Michael passed by, unable to move at all because his fear was so great. He hardly even breathed as he watched Michael retreat down the hallway with what appeared to be a blackened deer antler gripped tightly behind his back. What a strange thing to see.

TUESDAY, SEPTEMBER 5

The Hunger

Sleep did not come easily for Kyle during the night after his first lesson with Ramius King. His body shook in little spasms from time to time, whenever the hunger for the talisman's magic grew strong enough to trigger a physical response. He'd held the Gift of Nature for a single hour only, and he'd only used its power to accomplish relatively simple tasks, but none of that mattered in the slightest. His need to hold it again, to use its power again, had already been made absolute. The Tall Man had snared him with an addiction. Kyle understood that perfectly well, but understanding didn't ease the hunger. Only one thing could do that, and Kyle was certain that one thing would be offered to him again. He knew, too, that when it was, he wouldn't refuse.

As he lay restlessly in his bed, Kyle spent nine of every ten minutes thinking about how it had felt to wield the strange black weapon that the Tall Man had lent him. During the remainder of the time, he thought about how it had felt when he'd killed the rat, or rather how he'd felt right afterward. It surely had been a lab specimen, bred to die in the name of experimentation, but that had not been its fate. Kyle had killed that animal just as surely as if he'd stomped it to death beneath the heel of his shoe. It was only a rat, but it was dead because of him, and for no other reason than to tighten the noose that Ramius King had so tactfully slipped around his neck. Kyle hated King for tricking him, and he hated himself for being so easily tricked.

Kyle was caught firmly in the grip of a dream early the next morning, having finally drifted off for a couple of hours. It was his dream, the one he always

- 271 -

dreamed, but never remembered. Its images were so real, so compelling to his subconscious mind, that even the beeping of his collar couldn't pull him away. Not until Choplin came and physically pounded against the door did Kyle finally awake, bathed in sweat and dazed by the intensity of the vision he'd just escaped and that had, he realized, just escaped him as well.

"Out of that bed!" Choplin shouted as he barged in through the door into Kyle's room. "You're lucky I didn't just wake you up with my trusty bug-zapper. Only reason I held back is because you probably would've pissed yourself, and I hate the smell of piss."

The strong emotions that always lingered when Kyle awoke from the dream were already fading to nothingness, but the feeling that something important had just slipped away from him remained. Fatigue was like a physical substance for him that morning, something that had been injected into his veins and now circulated throughout his body, carrying soreness and stiffness from his fingers to his toes. And the painful hunger that he'd gone to sleep with was still there as well. He was starving for another taste of the Gift's power. Instead of dreading being called for his next lesson, he was anxious for it. In fact, getting his hands back on the little obsidian reptile was all he could think about.

"If you've got a message to deliver from your master, then do it," Kyle suggested to his jailor, inwardly surprised to hear the words that were coming from his mouth. "Otherwise, why don't you and your stupid Presley impersonator sideburns get the hell out of my room."

Choplin just stared back, obviously fuming at being spoken down to by his own prisoner.

"You might want to watch your mouth, boy. I could just start lighting you up and not quit until you pissed yourself dry, and then I could make you wipe up the mess with the shirt off your back. The smell'd be awful, but it might be worth it to hear you sizzle."

Kyle's teeth ground harder with every word Choplin spoke. He imagined how it would feel to reach out and loose the magic against him, to set it free and let it do what it would with him. If only he had the talisman right then, he'd listen to Choplin sizzle for a while. Someday, when he'd earned the right to carry a Gift of Nature all the time, when he'd become …

No! Kyle caught himself before the thought was complete. No, he'd never be one of King's soldiers. He was only playing along for now until he found a way out. He was learning how to use the weapon because it might prove to be his only means of escape, that's all. Without it, his own magic would never be enough. He needed the Gift, but only to save himself, not to hurt anyone else. All he wanted was to get free.

He could almost convince himself that it was all still true.

"I think I'd like you to apologize," Choplin said thoughtfully. "I think that would be a real nice gesture. Stand up and say you're sorry."

Kyle stood, stared his jailor in the eyes, and said, "I'm sorry your stupid sideburns remind me of a Presley impersonator."

The words were barely out of Kyle's mouth when the collar came to life, firing white-hot spears of energy down the length of his spine. His legs went numb, and without any attempt to catch himself, he collapsed to the floor, landing as hard as a chopped tree. His eyes sprang wide open, forcing him to endure not only the excruciating pain, but also the delight that was plainly written in Choplin's expression. The jailor's smile was so wide that once again it nearly managed to connect the sideburns that framed his face.

"All you had to do was apologize," Choplin reminded, keeping his thumb pressed into his remote control. "A few brief words of sincere regret, and I'd have spared you all this pain."

On and on the pain came until Kyle's vision started to dim. It felt like he was dying, like his insides were being cooked.

Behind the jailor, the door burst open, and there was Ramius King.

"That's enough, Mr. Choplin," he said flatly.

Just as Kyle felt his bladder start to give, the collar disengaged. His eyes were still frozen in an unblinking gape, and his breath would only come in the tiniest gasps.

"Leave, Mr. Choplin," King ordered.

Kyle's jailor smiled down at him for another moment, relishing the sight of what his smart-mouthed captive had been reduced to. Then, he turned and started to leave as instructed. Just as he reached the door though, he paused. Glancing back over his shoulder, he hit the remote one last time, sending a brief, but agonizing jolt through Kyle's already racked body.

With an almost casual wave of one pale-skinned hand, Ramius King's magic sent Choplin flying across the room, where he struck the wall head first. The jailor collapsed into a heap following the impact, knocked instantly unconscious.

"I said that's enough," King reminded needlessly. Then, turning to Kyle, he said, "I know it's horribly degrading to be subjected to the torments of such a disgusting man, but I need someone to keep track of my employees in the lab and also my guests like you. And my soldiers don't tend to make good keepers. They tend to view it as demeaning work, and they tend to take out their frustrations at being assigned such duties on their detainees."

Kyle didn't fail to note the Tall Man's careful word selection. Those assistants in the lab were no more employees than he was a guest. Surely King didn't really expect him to believe that either euphemism was true.

"If it helps you to more easily tolerate this situation for the time being," King continued, "then trust that the situation could soon change. The progress you made yesterday was more than I had hoped for, and if you continue to surpass my expectations, then I may soon give you the means to command Choplin, instead of the other way around. Every time you prove yourself to be proficient during your lessons, you will hasten the arrival of that transition."

Kyle felt the attraction of the proposal. It was exactly what he wanted, and maybe, just maybe, it was also what he needed. Nothing in the world sounded sweeter at that moment than the idea of using the magic against Choplin as King just had, to repay some of the suffering he'd endured for the sake of the jailor's amusement. And wouldn't it also improve his chances of escape if his skills with the magic and his status in the compound were advanced? For the moment, it seemed that what King wanted from him paralleled what he needed for himself, so he'd continue to play along.

Kyle hesitated though, wondering about the twisting feeling in his stomach. Why did it seem that he was having to try so hard to convince himself that his rationale for being cooperative was a legitimate one?

"Get dressed and meet me in the room we used for yesterday's lesson," King instructed before turning and gracefully sweeping out of the room.

Kyle didn't need to ask when he was to meet Mr. King. It would be as soon as he could possibly be ready. Mr. King wouldn't expect, or tolerate, any delay.

But even as Kyle rushed to the sink to wash his face, he wondered if that, too, might be just an excuse. Was he really hurrying to get ready because he was afraid to make the Tall Man wait, or was it just because he was so anxious to get his hands back on the Gift of Nature?

The Only One Alive

Kyle thought of Choplin as he walked through the halls of the Mill, pictured him still lying unconscious on the floor of his room. Perhaps he'd suffered a concussion. If he had, he deserved it. And more.

Even as Kyle pushed open the training room door, Choplin's overly delighted face was still grinning gleefully in the back of his mind, which is why it was so startling to find that same face staring back at him from inside the room. There was the despicable jailor, as if summoned by magic, his smug grin stretching from one sideburn to the other.

But no, it wasn't really Choplin after all, Kyle realized almost immediately. What he was really looking at was a cardboard cutout of the man, life-size, full color, and startlingly realistic.

"Go ahead," said Ramius King as he stepped out from behind the cutout, "tear it apart. I'm sure you want to, and we've got plenty of copies."

Despite himself, Kyle smiled, but wished immediately that he hadn't. Playing along with King's games was one thing, but he certainly didn't want to make the impression that he was enjoying himself.

"I had a whole stack of these made up for my last recruit," the Tall Man explained. "He felt similarly toward my jailor as you do. Having a target that provoked some emotion seemed to help him focus during his lessons, and I thought it might do the same for you. It was quite a generous thing of me to do, don't you agree, Mr. Adams?"

Hearing his name, Kyle forced himself to tighten his focus. He needed to be careful to pay attention. He needed to remember that his instructor was not renowned for his patience, or his tolerance. The difficulty at the moment was that somewhere in that room, perhaps even back in King's jacket pocket, was the talisman. He knew it had to be close, almost within reach. He could almost hear it calling to him. He needed to find it, to put his hands on it again and feel its power.

"Yes, Mr. King," Kyle agreed eagerly. "I appreciate you going out of your way like that. I'm sure the cutouts will be helpful."

"I'd prefer proof to your assurance. So, whenever you're ready. You don't need to wait for me to say when."

Kyle hoped he didn't look anxious, but suspected that he did. He held out his hand to the Tall Man, expecting to be offered the thing that he'd been craving so desperately. He could see the quivering of his own extended fingers, but seemed unable even to diminish their motion, let alone still them completely.

The only thing King offered was a thin, cold smile. He tilted his head back, allowing the fluorescent light from above to fill the sharp grooves of his long face. He looked down on Kyle over the rims of his lower lids, past the long, crooked nose. To Kyle, he appeared seven feet tall.

"I'd like you to deal with this first one unassisted," King explained, the words sliding out through a tiny part in his thin smile.

"But I couldn't even break a light bulb without the Gift," Kyle reminded, feeling suddenly panicky. "There's no way I can …" Kyle caught the look on the Tall Man's face and swallowed down the remainder of his objection.

"Turn this flimsy piece of cardboard into ruins, or else I will never permit you to use my talisman again," King threatened. "Is that clear?"

Kyle's panic came into full bloom as King's words struck him. He felt like crying, like dropping down to his knees and begging to have the thing that he so urgently desired. Not until right then, when the idea of never having it again first formed, did Kyle truly understand the depth of his dependence.

Kyle turned and faced the cutout of Choplin, struggling to concentrate on anything other than the possibility that he might never feel whole again. He picked a spot right in the middle of the jailor's chest, fixed his stare there, and tried to block out everything else in the room. Grandma Jo had relit the candle he'd extinguished effortlessly. If he tried hard enough, maybe he could start the thing on fire. All he would have to do was get it started, and then the flames would spread and eventually destroy the whole thing. And then King would give him the Gift!

But try as he might, Kyle couldn't make it happen. It seemed like the harder he tried to concentrate, the harder it became to concentrate. His panic rose even further, pressing in painfully at his temples, making him dizzy, threatening to topple him right off his feet.

King looked on curiously, studying his young student's every movement and expression. He knew that the timing would have to be perfect.

Kyle gasped for air, tiring quickly from his fruitless exertion.

"You do understand what I said, don't you?" the Tall Man asked, adding pressure that he knew Kyle couldn't bare. "I will lock you away in that room forever. I will allow Choplin do whatever he wants with you. I will make sure that you're never in the same room with a Gift of Nature again."

"I can't do it," Kyle practically screamed. Tears were forming at the corners of his eyes. "I need the Gift!"

"I'll give you the talisman when you've destroyed this cutout," King repeated, his voice hardening. "If your feeble magic is insufficient for the task, then might I suggest you resort to more rudimentary methods? Do whatever you have to do to make it happen." King had slipped the Plume of Shu upon his brow as he spoke, and his voice became like channeled thunder, electric and irresistible, imbued with the power of the relic.

Kyle didn't hesitate. He dove at the cutout, throwing it to the ground as if it was a real man and he truly meant to kill him. He tore at the thing with all his strength and all his desperation. He kicked it and tore at it with his hands. He even tried biting a chunk away, but nothing worked. The cutout remained intact.

In his frenzy, Kyle didn't even realize that it was a thin sheet of plastic weave that he was attacking, not cardboard. The stuff was light and pliable, but far too strong to tear without mechanical assistance.

Oblivious to how completely ineffective his efforts were proving, Kyle struggled on, slamming the mock-up of his jailor against the floor over and over, begging for it to yield to his fury. He would never get to hold the talisman again, that was all he could think about, and it was fuel enough to spur him on well past the point of exhaustion.

As Kyle continued to thrash across the floor, Ramius King glanced away, seeming to sense something beyond the walls of the room. Deliberately, the Tall Man reached into the pocket of his jacket and retrieved the reptilian Gift and the chain from which it hung. He paused just one more moment and then flung it to the ground, mere feet from where Kyle writhed spastically with the cutout.

"Take the weapon then if you're helpless without it!" King roared.

The power of the Tall Man's voice was enough to finally break Kyle free from his one-sided struggle. He saw the talisman almost instantly and dove for it with both arms outstretched.

The moment his fingers tightened against the hard surface of the obsidian creature, Kyle felt himself renewed. His lungs filled and his strength returned. His panic, however, did not disappear. It changed instead, becoming rage. Kyle was furious at King for manipulating him, at Choplin for abusing him, at Jerrod and Marion and the other Guardians for having left him alone, and most of all, at himself for becoming so piteously out of control. He cursed himself for not being strong enough to resist his captors, for being snared so easily by King's lucrative tempts, and for being so desperately afraid.

Just then, as Kyle's rage reached the critical level, the real Choplin stepped through the door. The jailor walked in casually, knowing nothing except that he'd been revived and ordered to report to King in the training room. And so there he was, right on time.

Kyle spun around at the sound of Choplin's entrance and out his free hand flew, as if by its own accord. The magic was already dangling at his fingertips, barely restrained, and then it was out, arcing across the room, tearing into a man who had no defense against it. Kyle had only wanted to feel the magic coursing through him again, but now that it finally was, he wanted only to stop it, but he couldn't. It was as if he were a bystander to his own act, an unwilling spectator.

The jailor's body shuddered as the energy streamed through him. Jagged tears ripped open across the skin of his exposed face and forearms, but no blood flowed out. The wounds were singed as if by terrible heat, sealing as soon as they opened.

Kyle looked on in horror, unable to dam up the river of power he'd unleashed. He knew that Choplin was already dead, but still the magic attacked his limp form, holding him upright when by rights, he should already have collapsed.

It was the cold laughter of Ramius King that finally pulled Kyle free. In response to the Tall Man's apparent amusement, Kyle swung around, redirecting the killing energy at his self-appointed mentor.

King, whose laughter only swelled in response, calmly extended one long-fingered hand and sent the attack ricocheting away. The streamers of loose energy raced around the room, momentarily tracing the seams where the walls met with the floor and the ceiling with brilliant flashes of blue flame.

Then, King's other hand drew forward as well, palm opened wide. At that same instant, the torrent of power that had surged out from Kyle abruptly ceased, and the black reptilian weapon reappeared in the Tall Man's hand. The talisman had zipped through the air in response to his summons, settling into his iron grip. It happened so fast, Kyle never even thought to try and stop it.

"And who said learning can't be fun?" King asked smugly.

Kyle staggered for a moment and then collapsed to his knees. He stared at the smoldering heap that was left of Mr. Choplin, his jailor. Not even the hollow pain of the talisman's absence could distract him. It was no scaly-skinned monster he'd just attacked, and it wasn't a lab rat destined for an early demise in some wicked experiment. He'd just murdered a regular guy, another average jerk like anybody you might pass on the street. He'd been made into a murderer, no better than the men who held him captive.

"I have to admit that you've surpassed my expectations once again, Mr. Adams," King said coolly in his suppressing, empowered voice. "Why do you look so miserable? You just manipulated some extremely powerful magic, used it to accomplish something that you greatly desired. Choplin was scum, the lowest sort of human being, not worthy to serve dinner to someone like you or I. I only gave him authority over you to see how you'd handle it, and you handled it exactly as I'd hoped. Taking his life was no different than taking the life of that rat yesterday, no different at all."

Kyle was still transfixed by the sight of Choplin's crumpled, smoldering form. He barely even heard the words that the Tall Man spoke.

"I want you to head back to your room and get some rest," King suggested. "I know how draining it can be to use the magic when you're not accustomed to it. I'll have someone bring your dinner in a bit, and whatever else you need. There's no rush though. Stay here and savor your triumph as long as you'd like."

With that King spun on one heel and whisked away out the door, leaving a deathly silence in his wake.

Kyle had always been something of an outsider, a loner. Loneliness had become a steady state through much of his life, an ache that could be dulled, but never defeated completely. It wasn't until right then, however, kneeling before the corpse of Choplin the jailor, that Kyle finally experienced the ultimate loneliness. What he discovered was that being the only one in the room wasn't as lonely as being the only one *alive*.

Mind Over Matter

Lying in bed that night, Kyle decided that he couldn't afford to be patient much longer. Whether he was going to try and escape or make his stand against Ramius King, he needed to do it soon, within the next few days. He couldn't allow what had happened that day to happen again, no matter what. When he made his move, they'd probably turn his collar to the highest level and let him sizzle until he foamed at the mouth and wet his pants, but he still wouldn't give in. King might even kill him, but it would be better to die than to be made to kill again.

Kyle laid there all night, repeating his vow over and over, hoping to add strength to his conviction. He stared blankly into the darkness of his room for hours, never sleeping a wink. As long as his eyes stayed open he couldn't see a thing, which was fine. He knew that if he let them fall closed, if he dared to sleep, to gaze into the world beyond the waking world, he would find the grinning face of a dead man gazing back.

It seemed to Kyle like days passed while he waited for morning to come, and when it finally did, he wished only for more time. He knew that his call would come soon, his summons from Mr. King, and when it did, his time would be up.

When the speaker in the corner of the room finally did come to life, it projected not the words of Ramius King, but those of his first general, Mason Stone. His unmistakable voice hissed through the intercom system, telling Kyle that he was to report immediately to his training room. That's all he said, and then the room fell back into silence.

Kyle recognized King's first general immediately as he entered the training room, the same room where he'd committed murder the previous day. He remembered all too clearly how the short, bald-headed man had dropped down amid the ranks of the Guardians in the basement of the firehouse. He remembered the carnage that had raged all about him. He remembered that while so many powerful looking men were brushed aside by the force of Grandma Jo's magic, the smallest among them stood fast. And there, standing before Kyle once again, was that same man, and he was apparently no worse for the wear. Not a single bruise or abrasion marked his pasty, expressionless face.

"You wanted to see me?" Kyle said, announcing his arrival.

Mason looked up at the sound of Kyle's voice, surprised that he hadn't sensed the young man's approach. He'd been lost in a daydream, thinking dangerous thoughts again about a time when he might dare to resign his position as Ramius King's second in command. The idea that he might be able to survive the response that would certainly follow that resignation still tantalized him. But for now, he pushed his musings aside so that he might attend to the task at hand.

"Mr. King has asked me to see to your morning lesson," Mason said, the words slipping out of his thin, lipless mouth. "What has he had you do the past two mornings?"

Kyle said nothing. In his extreme state of fatigue, he wasn't going to be able to come up with any convincing lies, but he certainly wasn't going to offer the truth either. He didn't want to give his substitute teacher any ideas.

"Judging by your silence, I'll assume that he tricked you into doing something atrocious. That's more or less standard for breaking the spirit of a new recruit, and judging by the look on your face, I'd say it's worked pretty well with you. If you can put your fear and anger aside for a while, I can share a secret with you this morning that will overshadow anything else you will learn about magic."

Although Mason's words were alluring, Kyle suspected strongly that they might be merely a prelude to more deception, another game that he was destined to lose regardless of how he played.

"Where is Mr. King?" Kyle asked, hoping to delay whatever lesson lay in store for him a little longer.

Mason thought for a moment and then answered, "He's interrogating a prisoner, a woman who can supposedly see the future."

"Supposedly? Do you think she can see the future?" Kyle asked.

Mason hesitated again, considering not only what he believed, but also what he was willing to divulge.

"Yes," he affirmed, "I think she can, at least pieces of it. Through her, Mr. King has seen glimpses of the future that have given him tactical advantages over his enemies. She foresaw that a threat to Mr. King's plans was hidden here in Steel City, and then I found the Guardians."

Kyle cringed at the mentioning of the Guardians. He knew exactly how it had happened that Stone managed to find them.

"Enough about that," Mason interrupted Kyle's grim thoughts. "Let's get on with your lesson. I have other matters that need tending to this morning."

With his stiff, quiet steps, Mason walked over to the long table at the far wall of the room.

Kyle turned to follow and immediately saw the black lizard. The talisman was lying atop the table, its chain folded over itself haphazardly. It might have been any ordinary trinket, left sitting wherever its owner had happened to leave it. Kyle's heart began to pound and his breath caught in his throat.

"Go on, pick it up," Mason prompted when he noticed Kyle's reaction. "I'm sure you're hooked by now and dying to hold it."

Kyle was indeed hooked, and he knew it, but being aware of the addiction didn't diminish its potency whatsoever. He rushed across the room and grabbed up the little obsidian creature as if there were ten other people racing to get it first. He clutched the Gift of Nature to his chest, breathing deep sighs of relief as its power replenished his depleted body and soul. He felt whole again, but the sensation was bitter-sweet. He hated the dependence that his relief indicated.

"Put it around your neck," Mason instructed. "You'll need both of your hands free."

Kyle did as he was told. He tried to consciously slow his breathing, to settle himself from the elation he felt at regaining the necklace and its powerful charm.

"Take this and break it in half," Mason instructed, handing Kyle a brand new stick of white chalk.

Kyle took the chalk, felt its smooth, powdery surface, and then broke it easily in half. It offered very little resistance.

"Now do the same with this," Mason said, holding out another white rod that was similar in appearance, but smoother to the touch.

"What is it?" Kyle asked as he felt the significant weight of the small object.

"It's marble," Mason answered, "and it's very strong."

Kyle pressed his thumbs into the center of the thin stone rod, but it didn't budge.

"It's tough," Kyle agreed. "I don't think I can break it." He tried again, visibly straining this time, but still it held.

"Your hands might not be able to break it, but your magic certainly can." Mason's hissing voice dropped down even softer than usual as he continued, as if he were revealing a guarded secret. "A Gift of Nature in the hands of someone like you, who has the talent, can generate power to do things much greater than break a marble rod–as long as you believe it can."

With that, Mason gestured for Kyle to step back from the table, stopping him when he was fifteen feet away.

"And your magic will break the marble rod before you leave this room," Mason added confidently.

Kyle thought back to his first lesson with King. He tried to think only of the light bulbs and not of the rat.

Mason took the marble rod from Kyle and placed it on the table.

"Try to imagine both ends pulling toward you and the middle pushing away," Mason suggested. "As soon as it breaks, the lesson's over and you're free to go."

Kyle extended his arm toward the table, felt the energy flow easily from his fingertips, reaching for a target. He saw the rod move, knew that he'd found it, and then he pulled and pushed. He thought about how hard he'd tried to break it with his hands, knowing that he'd need to generate more force with his magic than he had with his muscles. Even though it was small, the marble rod was very tough, and it wouldn't succumb easily. He concentrated so hard that he shook, but it wouldn't break.

"Hold on," Mason stopped him. "Practice once with another piece of chalk, just to get a feel for how the pressure needs to be applied."

Mason quickly made the swap and stepped back.

Once again, Kyle let the magic stretch out from his hand. He felt it float across the space that separated him from the table, guided by his will, but also having something of its own intentions. And then he felt the energy touch its target. He pulled and pushed at the chalk on the table, thinking back to how easily another just like it had broken in his hands. The thin white rod quivered once, then again, and then snapped cleanly in half, as perfectly as if it had been cleaved with a butcher's knife.

"Okay, now let me try the marble again," Kyle said, encouraged by his small success.

The thin slit that was Mason's mouth lifted at the corners just a bit. The change was so small that Kyle wasn't really even sure that he saw it.

"That was the marble," Mason whispered. "That one was exactly the same as the first one you tried with."

"But how can that be?" Kyle asked, striding to the table to inspect the broken white rod for himself, doubtful that it could truly be what his substitute instructor said it was.

"The difference between your first effort and your second was not in the material, but in your mentality. As I said before, through you the magic can do great things, but only if you believe it can. If you think that marble is too hard to break, then it is, but if you think it will break as easily as chalk, then it will."

Kyle was stunned by Mason's explanation. It sounded like rubbish, but it had to be true, at least in part. The proof was right there on the tabletop.

"That's the end of your lesson," Mason hissed. "Return to your room. I'll take the Gift."

Reluctantly, Kyle walked over to the first general. He took the chain with both hands and lifted it up over his head. Already his breathing had become raspy and his knees felt unsteady. He almost threw up when Mason took the talisman away.

With a struggle, Kyle pulled himself away then, forced himself to look in another direction, ordered himself to think about something other than the hunger.

"It's not all mind over matter though, right?" Kyle asked weakly over his shoulder as he headed for the door. "I mean, if Ramius King walked in here right now intent on knocking you into next week, you couldn't stop him, could you? Even if you really *believed* that you could?"

Mason just stared blankly, his strange, manikin-like face revealing nothing of what he thought or felt.

"I said your lesson's over," he reminded after a moment. "Go back to your room."

Kyle did just that, lurching down the hallways of the Mill, nursing a wound that couldn't be seen by those who passed him by. He needed to get back to his bed and try to get some sleep. He knew the dangers that would be lurking in his dreamscapes, but there was no way to avoid them forever. He was exhausted and the day was still young. Stone's lesson had been a short one, and there was plenty of day left. He needed to rest up and be as ready as he could be for whatever was yet to come.

DANGEROUS DOUBTS

It was one of the longest days of Michael Galladin's life, racing back and forth across the eastern half of the continental United States, desperately trying to follow a trail that was in truth not much more than a vague sense of nearness or distance. He would point the Monte Carlo west until his bond with Rosa noticeably diminished, and then he'd point the car back east, always angling to the north. The bond would grow stronger, but only slightly and only for a while. Sooner or later the connection would wane again, and he'd alter his course again. And again, and again.

He never even considered stopping to sleep. The desire to sleep had left him almost entirely from the moment he'd watched Rosa taken away at the point of a flaming knife point. In fact, he felt as alert, as full of purpose and determination, as he had in many years. They could not hide her from him, no matter where they went. They could take a slow train to Canada or a fast plane to Kashmir, and still he'd track them down, and when he did he'd make them pay for what they'd done to her, and for what they'd done to him, and for what they'd done to Sean. He wouldn't sleep again until justice had been served.

Sustenance, however, could not be denied as absolutely as sleep. The fire burning in Michael's belly consumed fuel constantly and his lean frame possessed little reserves from which to draw. Snacks and sandwiches that could be eaten from behind the wheel satisfied his needs for the most part, but eventually he needed to stop for a real meal, something substantial enough to keep him going.

Michael was already better than half way through Ohio when he finally gave in to the relentless grumbling in his stomach, deciding to pause and recover his strength with a meal. It was already afternoon, and had he known how near he was to his mysterious destination, just one more state away, he surely would have continued on even then. He'd never consulted a map during his meandering and had hardly bothered taking note of the names of the highways he traversed or the towns and states he passed through. He just kept driving and let his instincts guide him as best they could.

The place he chose to dine, or rather the place he happened along when he finally gave in to his ravenous hunger, was a small diner just off the highway that advertised breakfast served 24–7, 363 days a year. It was getting on toward two o'clock, well past the main lunch hour, and the parking lot was empty. After stretching out his stiff limbs, Michael entered the diner, jingling the bell attached to its front door, and seated himself at the counter. A blonde waitress about his age immediately appeared.

According to the waitress' nametag, her name was Florence. It was an old fashioned name for someone of their generation. She was pretty, but had a worn-out look about her that generously applied makeup couldn't quite hide, and her counterfeit smile spoke volumes about how she resented her work.

It could be worse, Florence, Michael thought to himself as she approached.

He ordered coffee, a small glass of apple juice, and two of the hearty-man's breakfast specials. To his relief, Florence didn't bother trying to make small-talk, and he was able to sit in peace and enjoy his coffee–for a while.

Just as Florence was setting down Michael's afternoon breakfast, another customer finally arrived. He was a fat, middle-aged man in a loud Hawaiian shirt that was unbuttoned halfway down to his waist. His eyelids were dark and drooping, his steps were shuffling and unsteady, and an invisible aura of sweat and alcohol preceded his approach through the diner, all indications of his state of lingering intoxication. It wouldn't have been more obvious if there'd been a sign pinned to his chest that said, "hangover."

The man chose to sit on the stool next to Michael.

"Damn, are you eating all that?" he asked upon seeing Michael's breakfasts spread out on the counter before him. "Man, you'll have to drop a serious bomb later today. Know what I mean?"

Michael didn't respond. He considered scooting down to the next stool, but there were now four plates and two glasses that would have to go with him. He decided to stay, but remained quiet, hoping the man would be offended by his silence and leave him alone.

"Hey, blondie," the man called to the waitress, "I need a coffee over here, and some sugar. And a big water!" Turning to Michael, he said, "Funny how you can drink all night and then get up the next day feeling outrageous thirsty. I feel so dried up I don't think I could sweat, spit, or piss more than a drop."

Florence arrived with the man's coffee and water.

"Sugar's already on the counter," she offered as she carelessly set the drinks down, slopping coffee over the rim of the cup.

"Oh, you must have misunderstood me," the man corrected. "You must have thought I said that I needed some sugar. What I said was that I needed some *sugar*. Know what I mean, *sugar?*"

"Don't call me that," Florence objected dispassionately.

"Come on, honey, I was just joking around."

"I guess I forgot to laugh. Probably because I was so distracted by your unique cologne." With that, she turned and left without taking the man's order.

Michael chuckled.

"Something funny, buddy?" the man sneered.

Michael continued to eat, still not bothering even to look up from his plate.

"Shit, like I care," the man said, brushing his momentary anger aside. "I must've got shot down by ten better looking than her last night, but I didn't get turned down by one not nearly as good looking as her, which suited me fine. Know what I mean?"

Michael's plan wasn't working. Clearly, the guy was too wasted or too stupid to take a hint.

"It wasn't exactly a magical night, but it was better than staying at home with the old lady?" he went on, spewing his fetid breath all over Michael and his breakfast. "I mean don't get me wrong, she's a good woman, but sometimes a guy's just not in the mood for good. Know what I mean?"

Suddenly Michael's annoyance shifted, becoming anger. He'd dealt with worse lowlifes almost constantly over the past years, and for the most part he'd just blocked them out, got whatever information he needed from them and then moved on without looking back. For some reason though, he wasn't feeling like his usual tolerant self that afternoon. He tried to convince himself that it was the effects of his hunger and sleeplessness, but deep down he knew it wasn't that simple.

"She's always on me about losing weight, paying bills, fixing this, painting that, and this, and that, and blah, blah, blah. Know what I mean?"

"No, I don't know what you mean," Michael retorted sharply, finally making eye contact. "I've never had an *old lady* to go home to, and I probably never will, and listening to you bitch about yours is really starting to agitate me. *Know what I mean?*"

The man sat there stupidly, stunned sober by what he saw in Michael's eyes and what he heard in his voice. The cup of coffee trembled in his fat fingers.

"Hey, look man, I didn't mean to …"

Michael refused to release his stare, and the words that slurred from the man's gutter drain mouth just seemed to fizzle out as he spoke them. The scent of fear now mingled into the man's hangover stench.

"Maybe you should go," Michael suggested, his voice sharp-edged and threatening. His anger continued to grow. He actually felt himself tempted to hit the man, to knock his fat butt right off his stool. He wanted to do it badly, to vent out all his frustrations through his knuckles.

It wasn't Michael though, who actually swung, but the drunk. He struck out without warning, catching Michael solidly across the cheek, snapping his head back and sparking a shower of twinkling stars before his eyes.

Michael fell off the back of his stool, but incredibly, landed on his feet. He was stunned.

The drunk didn't swing again. Instead, he turned and fled out the door without further hesitation. He practically dove into his car, started the engine, peeled out of his parking spot, and sped away from the diner with all haste.

Michael touched his cheek absently and discovered a small trickle of blood with his fingertip. He reached automatically for a napkin from the counter and held it to his face. He was speechless, shocked at what had just happened. How had it happened? How could he have let it happen? Why hadn't he just continued to ignore the man? Why hadn't his magic protected him?

His thoughts were interrupted by the whispered voice of Florence the waitress.

"I just called the cops, mister," she said timidly from the opposite end of the counter. "You should just go. You should be gone before they get here. Just go."

Michael saw that she was terrified, and not of the drunk who had hit him. She looked at Michael like he was a monster, sensing the aura of danger that surrounded him, and it made him feel sick. The look in her eyes caused him more pain than the drunken man's punch, more than any man's punch ever could.

Right at that moment, Michael found the answer to one of his questions. He knew why he'd allowed the violence to unfold.

An hour later, Michael was driving north, sticking to the right lane, staying out of everyone else's way. He replayed the scene in the diner over and over in his mind, needing to be certain that his conclusions about what had happened were correct. He was pretty sure.

The real reason that Michael's cheek was bruised, although in truth it was almost already healed by then, was jealousy. He was jealous of that drunken jerk.

He was even jealous of Florence the waitress. They were normal people, and he wanted to be like them. They weren't living fairytale lives, but he didn't want a fairytale life. Any life would be better than the no-life he'd been wandering through for the last decade and a half. He wanted a job, even if it wasn't a good job, even if it was just a drab routine that kept the bills paid. Hell, he wanted to have bills! And more than anything else, he wanted a partner, someone to quench his loneliness, to say "I love you" every night and wake him with a kiss every morning. He wanted it more than he'd ever wanted anything before, but why? Why was he suddenly so desperate for companionship after having chosen solitude for so long? The answer was obvious.

Before he'd met Rosa, Michael had never dreamed that there was any possibility whatsoever that he could ever have the things that a normal person had. She was the only woman he'd ever met who could accept the things he knew as truth, who could relate in some way to what had happened to him and understand why he'd had to make the decisions he'd made. Before her, he'd never even bothered to dream about trying to live any other way.

He felt the loneliness then like it was a real thing with weight and shape. He could feel it growing inside his chest. He felt the pressure beneath his heart and against his stomach as it crowded out everything in its way. Before meeting Rosa, he'd spent fifteen years alone, and never once during that time had he felt as desperately lonely as he felt then. She hadn't yet been gone a full twenty-four hour day, and he'd only known her for two and a half days before that.

Suddenly Michael was much less confident that he was going to be able to get her back.

Because of his feelings for Rosa, he was ready to do *anything* to rescue her, but also because of those feelings, he might be prevented from doing what was needed. Back in Miami, when Michael was being worked over by the muggers, he'd fought with all his strength to hold back the magic that would have protected him. At the diner, he'd been ready to let the magic out, to be the beater once instead of the beaten, but it hadn't answered his bidding. He'd lost his temper, lost his concentration, and at the last second before he'd been hit, when he'd willed the magic to brush the man's fist aside as it had flying bullets years earlier, it refused to respond. The magic was nowhere to be found when he finally called on it, and an intoxicated man with impaired reflexes had knocked him right off his stool. If it had been Ramius King or any of his hunters instead, Michael would have been dead.

So many years before, when Michael was a Guardian, the magic had been there as sure as his heartbeat. It rose up when he needed it, and it obeyed his commands, but that was such a long time ago. He'd spent years learning how to use the magic, practicing with it day in and day out, immersing himself in a life of discipline and training, meditation and exercise. Now, he'd spent fifteen years trying to pretend that the magic was no longer in him at all, that he'd left it behind along with his life as a Guardian. He'd known deep inside that it wasn't true, that somewhere within him the magic still endured, but he'd kept it quiet, never let it out where it could do terrible things. Now, he needed it again. He needed the magic so he could save Rosa from Ramius King, so that she in turn could save him from his own self-imposed exile. He needed it desperately, but he had no idea whether or not it would be there for him when the moment of truth arrived.

Doubting the magic terrified Michael, and he cursed himself on account of that fear, because it was that fear that could be his undoing. If he permitted himself to be distracted by fear and anger at the time of his next confrontation, as he'd done at the diner, it would be the last mistake he ever made. It would be a mistake he'd pay for with his life, and worse, it would be a mistake that Rosa would be made to pay for as well.

He tried hard to push his anxiety aside and focus on the road, but he might as well have tried to halt his breathing or the beating of his heart. His only comfort was in the fact that he knew there were no more decisions to be made. The path to his destiny stretched forth before the car he drove, and although he didn't know the way, he knew that he couldn't avoid finding it, even if he'd wanted to.

An Impossible Choice

It was afternoon when the intercom in Kyle's room came to life again. He'd managed a couple hours of fitful sleep after his morning lesson with Mason Stone, but still felt horribly worn down. After his nap, he'd sat on his bed for a while contemplating how quickly he'd forgotten his intent to make a move when the Gift of Nature was back in his hands. That morning, while under the supervision of King's first general instead of King himself, a good opportunity to try something might have come and gone, and he'd never even been tempted to act. As soon as he'd touched the Gift and felt its seductive power, he'd forgotten everything else. For the sake of everyone at the Mill who was as expendable as Choplin had been, he needed to be stronger.

It was Mason's voice once again that hissed softly down from the speaker, interrupting Kyle's quiet thoughts. King's first general said to get ready, and that was it.

One of the white-coated assistants from the lab knocked at the door a few minutes later and led Kyle away toward the main lab.

"Where are we headed?" Kyle asked the twenty-something young man. "I said, do you know where we're going?" he repeated after a moment when his guide remained silent.

"We're not supposed to talk unless they talk to us first," the lab assistant finally answered, his voice hushed and full of apprehension. "I know you're new here, but you need to wise up to how things work, and fast. They're always watching and their punishments are severe. People get killed in this place. Seriously." With that, he turned and continued on down the hallway in silence, glancing once to a video camera that followed along with their progress.

Kyle knew the lab tech was serious. He knew that people got killed in the Mill.

The chair in which Rosa was seated was so tall that her feet couldn't reach the ground and the seat didn't have any cushion at all. Even if her hands hadn't been tied to its arms and her feet to its legs, it still wouldn't have been comfortable. Being that they were, it was not merely uncomfortable, it was unbearable.

Ramius King had left her there, bound to that uncomfortable chair, for so long that she'd lost track of time. It seemed to her like it had been days, but it couldn't really have been that long, she knew. It had only been a matter of hours, but they'd been some of the longest, most agonizing hours of her life, and considering what she'd endured in her life already, that was saying something.

After spending the morning trying unsuccessfully to pry secrets from his captive fortune teller, the Tall Man had apparently thrown in the towel for the time being. Whether that was a good thing for Rosa or bad was debatable. She wasn't sure she could endure much more of the torture that came every time he forced himself into her mind, but she also had no illusions about what her fate would be when he finally gave up and deemed her useless again. He'd thought himself without further need of her talent once already, and if Michael hadn't intervened, she'd have been killed. When the order came down this time, Michael wouldn't be there to protect her. This time, when King was finished with her, she was finished.

Never in Rosa's life had she felt so exhausted. Since her abduction the previous night, she'd been forced to stay awake. It was a quiet form of torture, and an effective one. Despite her continued attempts to sound defiant in the face of her captors, her defenses were near to failing.

During most of the times between King's interrogations, Rosa thought about Michael. He'd told her that on the first night they met, when he'd saved a tourist from being mugged, that he'd fought as hard as he could fight. Even though she'd seen him get pummeled, seemingly without offering resistance, he claimed to have called upon the deepest depths of his resolve. The fight he'd been talking about had taken place inside, Rosa now realized, not out, a straining of willpower rather than muscle. After spending the night and the morning with Ramius King, she understood just how taxing that sort of internal battle could be.

Hopefully, all of Rosa's straining had not been in vain. Hopefully, she'd managed to protect Michael in the one way she could. As the Tall Man had broken into her mind over and over again, he'd managed to pry nearly all of her secrets out of hiding, and in the process, he'd also forced her to glimpse the vile memories and sinister intentions that made up his psyche. His cognitive assault was so relentless, so overpowering, that in the end he knew almost everything she knew. Her only holdout, the only thing that she managed to keep from him, was what she didn't know, but could.

With his immensely powerful magic, King enhanced Rosa's gift of foresight in a way that she'd never been able to achieve on her own. Through her talent, King was able to peer ahead in time. He'd done it before, used her vision to build his plans, avoid pitfalls, and hunt down his enemies. This time had been different though. King had been searching the future for Michael, but Rosa had obstructed his view. It had taken all her strength, but she'd stymied his every attempt to seek out the lost Guardian.

Guided by King's magic and his thought, her internal gaze into the future had tracked down Michael repeatedly, finding him right there in Steel City, and soon. It was no surprise to Rosa, who already knew that Michael would be trying to find her, but King might not guess as much. He didn't know the nature of the bond between them. And so, every time Rosa's foresight found Michael, she had to pull it in close, tuck it down into a place so deep within herself that not even the Tall Man's probing could find it. She'd exerted her will so intensely in the effort, spent herself so completely, that she suspected it might nearly have killed her, but it was a cause worth dying for. It seemed that in all likelihood, her life was nearing its end anyhow, and besides, she had no doubt whatsoever that Michael would do the same for her.

When the Tall Man had become intolerably frustrated with failing in his last efforts to extract the desired vision from Rosa, he'd stormed from the room, leaving her slumped over limply in her uncomfortable chair. A young man in a white lab coat was left with her, charged as he'd been through the day and the previous night with keeping Rosa from falling asleep while King was out of the room. Despite the fact that the young man had shouted at her, shook her, slapped her, and even shocked her with the electric collar that had been secured around her neck, Rosa felt pity for him. Not only did it not look like he enjoyed his charge, it truly looked like torturing her was torture for him as well. He only did it because he was too terrified not to. This last time, however, when the Tall Man departed, the young man failed for the first time in his duties. Instead of forcing Rosa to stay awake, he himself slumped to the floor, leaned back against the hard, concrete block wall, and drifted off. He'd been forced to do without sleep for as long as Rosa had, and exhaustion, it seemed, had finally overpowered his tenacity.

Rosa didn't even realize what had happened. She was asleep faster than the guard. She'd entered almost immediately into a vision, or at least that's what she took if for upon waking some forty minutes later. She couldn't be absolutely certain though. If it had been a premonition, then it had been a very different one from any she'd seen before. Where her forecasts were usually of dreadful events, of violence and calamity, this one had been utterly mundane. She'd seen a building, large and brick. There'd been an expanse of mowed lawn surrounding the building and a pond along one side. Floating at the edge of the pond had been … something. Well, she assumed that there had been something. It seemed like the vision had been leading her to something, but she'd awakened too soon to find out what that something was. She didn't know what to make of what she'd seen, but it probably wouldn't matter. She probably wouldn't ever see daylight again, let alone a big, grassy yard with a pond.

When the Tall Man returned, he'd probably be coming to kill her. Either that, or else he'd try again to extract Michael's whereabouts from her, which might well end up with the same result. She'd never give him what he wanted, but she didn't think she could fight on much longer. Whatever the vision had meant, if it had truly been a vision, and if it had truly meant anything, it was probably a moot point anyway.

Kyle and the lab tech were just passing by the entrance to the main lab when the whispered hiss of Mason Stone's voice spoke from behind them, bringing them to an abrupt halt. A second man followed several steps behind Mason, but his eyes were to his feet, his chin to his chest, and Kyle couldn't see his face.

"I'll take Mr. Adams from here," said the first general, dismissing the white-coated assistant who scurried away anxiously into the lab, pulling the door closed behind him.

Kyle scrutinized the man standing behind Mason, still unable to see his face clearly, but increasingly certain that there was something familiar about him.

"Don't worry about this gentleman," Mason hissed, "he's not your concern yet."

Not yet? Kyle shuddered at the words of the slate-faced man, and at what they might imply.

Very slowly, as if it required great effort, the man behind Mason lifted his head, revealing the plastic collar around his neck, and with his tired, watery eyes, he looked at Kyle and said, "They got you, too, young fella?"

Kyle gasped. It was Charlie, the old man he'd met at the Country Kitchen.

"Didn't I say it?" Charlie asked, flashing his oversized white dentures as he spoke. "I said somethin' shady was goin' on out here, and wasn't I right? Sons of bitches grabbed me as I was walkin' out my own front door, jammed me into the back of one of their fancy black cars, and now there's no tellin' what they'll do with me. Poor old Black Dog's got nobody to feed him tonight. He can't get it himself. My dog's going hungry tonight because of these sons of bitches."

"Quiet!" Mason hissed. "I don't know how you two know each other, but it hardly matters. Mr. King won't care, and if you can both manage to keep quiet until I turn you over to him, I won't care either."

Kyle looked at Charlie piteously. Despite his spouting, it was clear that the old man was terrified. The color had all drained from his face, and his eyes seemed to be blinking about three times as often as they should have been.

Kyle followed Charlie and Ramius King's first general down the hallway without saying a word. When Mason opened the door to the next room past the main lab, he motioned for Kyle and Charlie to go inside, and they did.

Kyle spotted Rosa immediately as he entered the room, still bound to the chair in which she sat by her ankles and wrists, and he froze. What purpose she and Charlie were meant to serve, he couldn't guess. Nor did he want to. All of the likely possibilities were awful.

Mason dismissed the young man who'd been set to watch over Rosa and then sat Charlie down in a chair just like hers, binding him in similar fashion. Then, pushing the intercom button beside the door, he said, "Everything is ready for you in the west room, Mr. King."

"What's this all about?" Kyle asked tentatively. "What did these people do to deserve being held like this?"

"That's a pretty good question," Rosa spouted, her voice hoarse and thin, but still laced with venom. "I don't know about this old timer, but I didn't do jack shit to deserve this."

Fixing his lifeless stare onto Rosa, Mason whispered, "Be quiet."

Rosa fell silent. Her snappy words were obviously meant to sound brave, but the way she refused to meet Mason's gaze gave away how frightened she really was. She looked terrified of him, and rightly so, he was a man capable of terrible things.

Kyle's attention was suddenly drawn to his left, to a closed doorway in the room's side wall. Other than the door, that side of the room was utterly barren, featureless. There hadn't been any noise from that direction, no flash of light or flicker of movement that might have been responsible for drawing his attention, but there was something.

Just then, the door opened and in stepped Ramius King, looming dark and daunting with the Plume of Shu mounted like a diadem atop his high, pale forehead.

Behind the Tall Man, Kyle could see one end of the Main Lab. Dr. Simpson was there, looking as timid as ever, and several of the white-coated assistants were scattered about, engaged at various workstations. One of the men that Kyle had seen sedated during his tour of the facility stood in the center of the lab, his eyes now wide and alert. The man was holding something out before him, and whatever it was, it shook in his grip as if it were alive and struggling to get free. Kyle strained to make out what the object was, but couldn't quite.

"Mason, I'd like you to keep an eye on things in there for a while," King directed his first general. "If anything even begins to get out of hand, I want to know about it immediately. I'll be just on the other side of this door."

Mason didn't respond. He turned, and with the same ever-present expression of stoicism written on his chalky face, he headed into the lab, pulling the door shut behind him.

Ramius King looked to Rosa, ignoring Kyle completely. He tipped his head back, and with sharply squinted eyes, he stared at her down the jagged bridge of his long nose. He was making a decision it seemed, or perhaps rethinking one.

"This is your last chance, Miss Sanchez," he warned, his deep voice fortified with the power of the ancient talisman he wore. "Give me what I want, or else I'll have to consider you of no further use."

"Kiss my ass!" Rosa spouted boldy in response, emphasizing her disgust with a glob of spit that she launched in King's direction. "I wouldn't give you anything but a nose job, and that's only because it would make it easier for me to look at your ugly ..."

One of the Tall Man's long-fingered hands casually lifted, and instantly, Rosa's head was flung to the side and pinned harshly back over her shoulder. It looked like an invisible wind was battering her face, but the room was silent, and so was she.

"Mr. Adams, I'd like to introduce Rosalind Sanchez," the Tall Man said, acknowledging Kyle as last. "She is my former fortune teller."

Smiling thinly, the Tall Man released Rosa and pointed one long finger across the room to where several more empty chairs lined the wall. One of the chairs slid across the floor as if pulled forward by an invisible line and came to rest again beside King, who sat rigidly, taking a moment to smooth his pant legs and straighten the headdress over his ears.

"I wish I did know where Michael was," Rosa lied, just regaining her ability to speak. "I'd tell you if I knew, because if you found him, he'd kill you for what you've done."

"No, I don't think that your boyfriend would kill me," King disagreed, smiling wickedly. "He might have had great potential once upon a time, but he's been out of the game far too long to try and become a contender now. The title is mine, and he hasn't the slightest chance of taking it from me."

"Bullshit!" she argued desperately, perhaps trying to convince herself that what he said wasn't so. "If you didn't think he was any danger to you, then why'd you send the runt and his fat partner to fetch me? You were all set to kill me before you knew about Michael. You brought me here because you know he's a threat. You really want to know about the visions I kept from you all night and all morning? I saw Michael using that feather to pick his teeth after he got done kicking your ass."

Kyle was stunned by Rosa's defiance. He wondered who Michael was, and if he was really someone who might be able to stand against King. It seemed more likely that the fortune teller was just blowing smoke because she knew that her time was running short.

King sneered, showing his teeth threateningly, and said, "Think what you will, little girl. Spend these last moments of your life lost in the grandest daydream you can conjure."

Then, reaching into the pocket of his fine, black suit coat, King produced the reptilian Gift of Nature that Kyle had wielded three times before.

"I don't want that," Kyle said weakly, hearing the lie in his own voice. He'd already guessed at the nature of his next "lesson." "I'll never be one of your murderer servants. Kill me if you want to, but I won't hurt her."

Even as he spoke, as he bravely voiced his intentions, Kyle couldn't take his eyes from the talisman. The burning in his belly was agony. His hunger to feel the rush of the magic was intense.

"Poor boy," said the Tall Man, his voice full of counterfeit sympathy, "you still think that your will is free, but it's not true. You've belonged to me from the first moment you wrapped your anxious fingers around *my* Gift of Nature. You are an addict to power that only I can give to you, and from that addiction you can never be free."

"That's not true," Kyle blurted in protest, still unable to look away from the object of his desire. "I *don't* need it. I *don't* want it!"

"Why torture yourself needlessly?" King questioned. "I'm offering you an opportunity to become more than you ever thought you could be, a chance to posses the exact thing that you want most, but you resist. Why?"

"I know I can't save that girl," Kyle admitted in defeat. "I can't stop you from doing what you will, but I can stop myself from giving you what you want."

"I disagree," the Tall Man said flatly. "You will kill that girl. You will take this talisman and loose its power on her until she's dead. I know you will, because if you don't, then I will kill both of them."

"You're a real sicko, King," Rosa interjected, "and you're a coward. Only a coward would hold an old man hostage and force a teenage boy to do his dirty work for him."

"The old man's just a bystander to all this," King continued, ignoring Rosa's interruption, and keeping his crushing stare fixed heavily upon Kyle. "Mason picked him up for me in town this morning. I suspected that I might need some extra leverage to help persuade you into completing your assignment today, and he *will* serve as that leverage. Wield the magic that I'm offering you and kill the girl as I've asked, and I'll let this man go free. If you refuse, I will kill them both myself."

Kyle's knees were suddenly so weak that they could barely support his weight. The room spun before his eyes, and a single tear trickled down his cheek. He felt like he might pass out and fought to make himself breathe. If he fainted, it would be the death of Charlie. But he couldn't save Charlie anyway, not unless he killed the girl, and he could never do that. He wouldn't.

"Don't sweat it, kid," Rosa whispered sadly, "he's not letting either of us go. It doesn't matter what you do."

Kyle didn't even hear her words. The buzzing in his head was nearly deafening, and the fire in his stomach burned so intensely that he could hardly stand up straight. He needed to hold the Gift so badly! But no, if he took it, it would take him. He had to maintain control. But if he didn't act, then he'd be sentencing Charlie to death.

"Why do you let this choice upset you so?" King asked, sounding genuinely curious. "This woman is breathing her last breaths. I've already decided her fate, and it's certain. She's not your responsibility. It makes no difference whose hand she dies by, she still dies. Do it before I do and you save the old man's life. His life is yours to give or take, and so it should be. Whatever you choose, it's nothing to fret over. Look at him, frail and decrepit, uneducated and most likely uncivilized. He's nothing like you or I. To you he's an insect, and to him you're a god.

So kill her and save him, or watch me kill them both. To step on an ant or to step over it, that's all it matters."

Kyle looked at the two people whose lives were at stake, both bound to the chairs in which they sat. Somehow, Rosa still looked defiant, even then. Charlie looked terribly pale, and beads of sweat were running freely down his face, tracing the lines of his wrinkles. He had the look of a man standing at death's door.

"I told you before, Mr. Adams," King continued, sounding impatient, "that I am not a man who's accustomed to being kept waiting. Make your choice!" The force of the Tall Man's magic filled his voice, giving it the impact of a solid wave crashing across the room. He stood then and stepped toward his captives.

The room fell into a precarious silence. King hesitated one last moment before striking, Kyle stood immobilized by his fear and indecision, Charlie struggled to breathe, and Rosa cringed in anticipation of what seemed to be her imminent death.

Then, from the direction of the main lab came a loud crash and a man's voice shouting. All turned toward the sound save Charlie, who seemed now to be oblivious to everything.

"Do you hear that, Mr. Adams?" King asked. "My test subjects, the first generation of my engineered magicians, are getting their first tastes of the power that comes with holding a Gift of Nature. It is a critical stage in my agenda, perhaps the telling point in their development, and here I am. I'm allowing my first general to oversee things in there at this vital moment because I deem your lessons to be so important. You should be immensely honored that I should allot so much of my precious time to you, but you clearly are not. Instead of thanking me, you just stand there, sniveling like a child, afraid to accept the power that I'm offering you."

Wham! Another, even louder crash, sounded from the direction of the lab. Behind the seated captives, the room's sole window, painted black like all the windows at the Mill, creaked in response to the concussion.

"Damn it," King swore beneath his breath. Jamming the reptilian talisman back into the pocket of his coat, he turned and started toward the adjoining door. "Don't move a muscle until I'm back," he warned over his shoulder, pointing to Kyle "or else I'll line you up right beside the old man and the fortune teller."

A third crash sounded, immensely more powerful than the previous two, like a dozen sticks of dynamite exploding simultaneously. The door to the lab exploded right off its hinges and shot through the air at Ramius King with the force of a car at highway speed. The door struck a barrier of magic mere inches in front of the Tall Man's face and fell harmlessly aside.

Through the doorway, Kyle could see white-coated lab assistants scattering in all directions. Dr. Simpson was nowhere to be seen, and Mason Stone was struggling to force his way through a wall of fire that appeared to be erupting from the outstretched hands of one of King's test subjects. A Gift of Nature rested against the man's chest, hanging from a thin metal chain. His eyes were wide with madness, and his voice wailed like a snared animal.

King rushed through the doorway, a bluish aura glowing all about him.

"This is our chance!" Rosa called to Kyle over the chaotic din from the next room. "Get over here and untie me!"

Her words didn't register with Kyle at first. His will to resist was so depleted that she might as well have been asking him to spread out his arms and fly. It would have seemed just as reasonable as trying to escape.

"They're still watching through the cameras," Kyle answered feebly after a moment. "They're always watching."

"Bullshit!" Rosa yelled, her voice rising another notch, forcing Kyle to give her his full attention. "Whoever's at the screens is watching whatever's going on in there, not us."

"All they have to do it hit the button and we're done," Kyle argued. "Even if I untie you, you have a collar on just like me. We wouldn't make it ..."

"That's bullshit, too!" Rosa cut him short. "If you've got magic, then you can just rip that thing off whenever you want. So do it!"

Kyle didn't do anything. He just stood there, his thoughts drawn toward the continuing pandemonium in the lab. King was over there, and he had the Gift with him. Even then, he struggled to think of anything other than how it would feel to hold the talisman again. He craved its power more desperately even than his freedom.

"Don't you want to get away?" Rosa pleaded, jerking harshly at the cords that held her hands and feet. "Don't you have a family you'd like to see again?"

He didn't.

"Don't you have friends that you miss?"

He didn't.

"Don't you have a girlfriend who's lonely without you?"

He didn't really, but ...

Lily's face appeared in Kyle's mind. It had been days since he'd seen her last, days since he'd even thought of her, but her image formed in his mind with crystal clarity. Her long corn silk hair fell over her slender shoulders, and soft light shone against her bronze skin. Her chicory blue eyes were wide and bright, and just above her narrow chin spread that shy, secret smile that he cherished.

The burning in Kyle's stomach waned for just a moment, and then it intensified again, building until it spread into his chest and across his shoulders. It was different though, than it had been. It wasn't the talisman that he yearned for, but Lily. He wanted to be near her again, wanted it even more than he wanted the talisman. He needed her, and he was ready to do anything, to risk everything, to reach her.

Kyle reached up and grabbed the plastic collar at each side of his neck. Although his mind was already made up, he hesitated, unable to stop himself from wondering if his magic would be enough without the enhancement of the Gift. He thought back to his lesson that morning with Mason. He had to believe!

Snap! The plastic strap sounded like a whip-crack when it broke free.

Kyle stared down at the torture device in his hands, feeling the flow of magic pulsing through his fingers. Then, just as the device buzzed to life, releasing a heavy current of electricity, he dropped it to the floor. The humming of the activated energy was audible even over the melee.

Without any more hesitation, Kyle rushed over to Rosa, and before she could even brace herself, he ripped the collar from her neck, tossing it away as it activated. The ties at her wrists were next, and then he moved on to Charlie while Rosa bent over to release her own feet.

The old man barely even moved as Kyle removed his collar and restraints. His eyes were open, but glassed over, and as soon as his first hand came free, it darted to his chest, grabbing up a handful of his shirt in a fist. Cold sweat coated his face, and his skin was the gray-white color of newspaper.

"Charlie, can you hear me?" Kyle whispered in the old man's ear. Then, turning to Rosa, he said, "He's pretty out of it."

"Well slap him or something," she suggested urgently as she stood up from her chair, massaging the deep red rings around her wrists. "We can't wait."

Instead of slapping him, Kyle grabbed Charlie around the shoulders and shook him. His eyes came back into focus.

"Young fella," he wheezed.

"Charlie, we have to get out of here right now," Kyle pressed, preparing to pull the larger man up out of his chair.

Charlie smiled thinly, his eyes already glassing over again.

"I got bad pain in my chest," he managed between panting breaths. "I'm not goin' to be makin' any run for it. There's no time to think about it. I don't have much left that they can take anyway, not even time, so you two get goin'."

"He's right," Rosa agreed. "If we don't go for it right now, then our chance will be gone."

Kyle knew in his head that it was true, but his heart wrenched in his chest at the thought of leaving Charlie behind. The old man was completely innocent. It was because of Kyle that he'd been brought to the Mill, and that made him Kyle's responsibility.

"Clear that window out, now!" Rosa shouted in Kyle's ear.

Her command was so forceful, so compelling, that Kyle was moving to the window even before he could consider doing anything else.

"I'm sorry," Rosa whispered, bending to Charlie's ear as the painted glass pane shattered behind her. She took the old man's hand and gave it a squeeze, and to her surprise he squeezed back, holding her fast.

"I live right down the street from the Country Kitchen Restaurant," Charlie rasped. "My Black Dog is there, fenced in behind the house. He's my best friend. Promise me you'll take care of him."

Then, before she could respond, Charlie's expression went blank and his hand went limp in her grasp.

"Go in peace," Rosa whispered, laying Charlie's cool hand gently into his lap. "You're beyond the reach of these evil men now."

After one quick glance through the doorway into the smoke-filled lab, Rosa raced to the shattered window. With a boost from Kyle, she pulled herself up and through the empty frame, cutting both her hands in the process, but barely noticing. Then, she pulled Kyle up after her. They were out.

It was the first sunshine Kyle had seen in days, and its brightness stunned him.

The grounds around the Mill were extensive, mowed lawn stretching away in every direction. Surely there would be guards posted, Kyle thought, and just like that, as if his suspicion had been the trigger, the alarm sounded.

All Kyle could think to do was pick a direction and run. And run he did, although he didn't pick the direction.

Rosa sprinted away across the manicured yard without pause, seeming to know right where she was headed. Kyle certainly didn't have any better ideas, so he followed.

The sound of the alarm was shrill and oppressive, and shouting voices soon mingled with its wail. A memory flickered in Kyle's mind, a movie he'd seen once where an attempted jail break was ended by a tower-guard's rifle. He expected that same fate to become his own at any moment. He didn't dare look back.

Kyle caught up with Rosa at the crest of a low hill, and for the first time he could see what they were headed for.

"We'll be trapped at the edge of the pond," Kyle stuttered as he ran. "We have to go a different way."

Rosa didn't change direction though. She just kept on running right toward the rapidly approaching water.

The shouting voices from behind were becoming louder, a sure sign that their pursuers were closing. A loud, but distant crash sounded over the wail of the alarm as well, another explosion in the lab.

By the time they reached the water's edge, Kyle's chest was heaving and his legs felt like they weighted a hundred pounds a piece. The bank of the pond lifted about six feet over the water's edge, and to Kyle's relief, Rosa pulled up short at its rim. He'd been afraid that she might actually dive right in and start swimming.

Rosa, hoping with all her strength that she wasn't chasing after a phantom of her imagination, fell to her hands and knees and leaned down over the edge of the bank. There, right below her, right at the spot where she'd been summoned in the vision, was an old Native American man and a young girl, and they were in a boat.

Kyle knelt beside Rosa, and when his eyes found a familiar face staring back, he nearly fainted.

"Lily!" he practically screamed. "How?"

"Come on," Lily prompted from her father's fishing boat. "We have to hurry."

Quickly, but carefully, Rosa and Kyle dropped down into the boat. The Chief already had the outboard running, and they were halfway across the Mill Pond before the first of King's men appeared over the bank. None of the boat's occupants saw them anyway, save one. While everyone else was looking ahead to where they were going, Lily was looking back– to whom they'd left behind.

An Unsettling
Possibility

The incense that smoldered atop Ramius King's oak desk was expensive, its cinnamon overtone blended exquisitely with more subtle hints of vanilla and tart cherry. The bouquet of odors was a special order that he'd paid handsomely for, but it was going to waste. A sulfur spring could have boiled up from the ground beneath his office and still the Tall Man wouldn't have noticed. Similarly, the enchanting rhythms of Tchaikovsky's Swan Lake floated across the room from two pairs of extremely high-end speakers, only to fall on deaf ears.

Frustration had settled down into King's stomach like a swallow of sour milk. The leather office chair creaked as the Tall Man crossed his legs in one direction and then the other. He leaned forward, resting his elbows on the surface of the oak desk, and then leaned back, pressing his weight into the soft animal hide of the chair. No position was comfortable.

King wondered at the day's blunders. How he'd allowed it to happen was unfathomable. His new recruit and the fortune teller had somehow escaped from his grasp, right out from the confines of his own facility. It was maddening, almost beyond belief. He couldn't figure out how either Rosa or Kyle could have communicated with anyone outside the Mill to arrange for the boat that had whisked them away.

Could there be a traitor among his ranks? It was a terrifying possibility, but such a remote one that he'd always considered it of negligible concern. His hold over every person who worked in the Mill was immensely strong. Besides, the only ones who could ever have stood a chance of infiltrating his organization were the Guardians, and now they were gone. Surely, if they had snuck a spy in among his people, that person would have done something to sabotage his sneak attack at the firehouse.

Another, perhaps even more unsettling possibility presented itself. What if the fortune teller's talent had allowed her to send out a message somehow? Her magic was strange, like none he'd encountered before, which was exactly why he'd decided to do away with her once his primary threats had been eliminated. The truth was, he didn't know the limits of her capabilities. Was it possible that she could somehow communicate with someone at a distance via her dreams, or their dreams, or whatever? And if that was possible, wasn't it also possible that she might manage other feats he'd not anticipated. *What if she got her hands on a Gift of Nature?* There was no way to even hazard a guess at how her talents might be amplified.

Such possibilities were certainly slim since the Guardians had been wiped out and their Gifts confiscated. But again, something had gone astray with that plan as well. The resurfacing of Michael Galladin after so many years was untimely at best, and possibly something worse. Plans wouldn't be pushed back any further though, not on account of a suspicious coincidence. It was, however, cause for concern. Ramius King hated coincidences. So often, they turned out to be something more.

After taking a moment to prepare himself as he always did, Mason Stone knocked against the door to Ramius King's office. It opened almost immediately, although there was no one on the immediate other side. King was seated behind his desk as usual, one long finger pointed at the door. The look on the Tall Man's face showed that his mood was dark, as Mason knew it would be. He also knew that it was apt to get even darker in a moment. He had only bad news to deliver.

"We didn't find them," Mason hissed. "The boat was abandoned about a half mile downriver, near a two-track that cut through the woods and emptied out onto Riverside Road. We followed fresh tire tracks out to the road, but there's no telling where they went from there." Mason noticed the Plume of Shu resting in its place on the shelves along the side of the room. It hardly even looked noteworthy amidst King's collection of idols, papyrus scrolls, and other precious artifacts.

"Tell me, Mason," King said, sounding thoughtful, "what do you make of all this? What would you do if you were the one in charge?"

A trap! Mason detected the underlying purpose of King's question immediately. He was testing Mason once again, looking for clues that his first general had at least considered the possibility that he might one day be the one in charge. He was fishing for mutinous thoughts.

"I think that there is another person in this equation that we don't know about," Mason answered evenly, fairly sure that nothing dangerous had been revealed in his face or voice. "I think that whoever aided in today's escape might well be the same person who helped Lily Goodshepherd evade Fat Man and Little Boy. I think it might be wise to push our schedule back until we know who that someone is."

"I see," said King, clearly scrutinizing Mason himself as much as his answer. "Do you think that this other person might turn out to be the lost Guardian, Michael Galladin?"

Mason had considered this possibility already, and his answer, as so often was the case, had been scripted in advance.

"No, I don't think so," hissed the first general. "There wouldn't have been enough time for him to travel back and forth between here and Florida. Besides, Little Boy said that when he retrieved the fortune teller, he could feel Michael's presence from quite a distance. If it had been Michael who'd helped Lily Good-shepherd escape, they would have sensed him then as well. As you know, it's not easy for one wielder of powerful magic to conceal himself from another."

"Very true," King agreed. "I'm a wielder of powerful magic. Do you sense my presence right now?"

This was not a question that Mason had anticipated, and before he could think better of it, he answered, "Only faintly, but that's because your Gift is on the shelf instead of on your head." It was a rare misstep by the careful first general.

"You noticed that, did you?" King asked pointedly. "What if this lost Guardian has not lost himself to the power as most of my hunters have? Perhaps he is strong enough to lay his Gift aside from time to time like myself, thus hiding his presence? I wonder if you would ever lay your Gift aside, Mason, were you able to do so?"

Mason didn't respond. He stood there like a clay mannequin, silent and expressionless, a blank slate from which nothing could be interpreted.

King leaned forward over his desk, locking his stare on the gray eyes of his finest soldier. But Mason just stared back, inscrutable. He didn't flinch. He didn't even blink.

"It's probably all irrelevant anyway," the Tall Man suggested, breaking eye contact. "I won't have my plans pushed back any further. With the exception of this afternoon's incident, the test subjects are developing on schedule. I've waited long enough, and I won't be made to wait longer, especially on account of two kids, a fortune teller, and some prodigal son of my conquered enemies. What I'd like you to do, Mason, is make sure Dr. Simpson has everything he needs to put the lab back in order. Continue on with the preparations for the demonstration, and if any of the troublemakers are foolish enough to show themselves in the mean time, then we'll deal with them now. If they run and hide, as will most likely be the case, then we'll deal with them later. That's all, Mason."

Without any sort of acknowledgement, the shortish man with the smooth, gray skin turned and walked out.

King sat in silence for a few moments, breathing in deep lungfuls of the room's spiced air as he thought. Then, reaching to the intercom button, he called for Fat Man and Little Boy. He would send them out to continue hunting for his escaped captives and the lost Guardian. It might just turn out that they weren't a hundred miles away already like they could, and should, have been. Of course Mason would have stood the best chance of finding them if they were still nearby, but the Tall Man hesitated to send his first general out for that particular assignment. If there was even the tiniest chance that Mason was strong enough to consider challenging King's command, then the last thing he should be doing was searching for Michael Galladin. They were perhaps the only two men alive who could possibly threaten him, and it seemed safest to keep them apart. It was grand paranoia to be sure, but being cautious was exactly how the Tall Man had survived as long as he had, and exactly how he was going to gain control over every nation on earth.

A Late Night Stroll

Less than five miles from the Mill, in a small hunting cabin set back in the deep woods, a series of strange introductions had just taken place.

A wide range of emotions churned within the cabin's four occupants, and consequently, conversation was awkward for all. Even between Kyle and Lily, words came clumsily. Behind the deep sense of relief that the two young people felt at seeing each other again were other, less obvious feelings, stronger and darker ones. Neither did much of a job trying to mask their distress, but only one offered an explanation.

Lily told Kyle about her father being taken two days earlier, the same day when the Guardians had been ambushed at the firehouse. She admitted her disappointment at not being able to rescue him along with Kyle and Rosa.

Kyle, however, didn't dare to admit the cause of his discomfort. He was horrified by the thought of Lily finding out about the things he had been tricked into doing at the Mill. His dependence on the power of the Gift was also something he'd have preferred to keep to himself, but that was going to be more difficult. The shakes were already starting in his hands, and they'd soon spread, he knew. The pains of withdrawal would intensify as night approached, twisting his insides until there would be no masking his distress. Besides, Rosa had been there at the Mill. She'd seen how the sight of the talisman had affected him. He might have been able to sell some story to Lily and her grandfather, but Rosa knew the truth.

It wasn't late, just barely dark in fact, when Rosa announced that she was ready to get some sleep. She desperately needed some rest after enduring what she had at the Mill. Her exhaustion was obvious, as was Kyle's, and no one argued that an early bedtime was in order, at least for those two.

There were a pair of bunk beds at one end of the small cabin, and the girls settled there. Lily had argued that Kyle, in greater need of rest, should take a bed, but he'd assured her that he was tired enough to sleep anywhere, and she'd believed it. A double layer of sleeping bags served as his mattress, and that suited him fine. The Chief headed outside to light up his pipe as everyone else settled in. Before climbing up to the top bunk, Lily whispered to Kyle that as far as she could tell her grandfather hadn't slept at all during the time they'd spent together.

Whether it was simply a result of his extreme fatigue, or perhaps the tremendous sense of relief he felt after his unlikely escape from the Mill, Kyle drifted off to sleep almost immediately. However, it didn't last long. At half past midnight, he jerked awake. His hair stuck across his sweat-soaked forehead and his fingernails dug painfully into his palms. As usual, he sensed a memory just lost teasing the edges of his drowsy mind. He struggled for a moment, as he always did, but couldn't recall a single image from the dream. It was completely erased.

Slowly, the wave of panic induced by the dream began to fade, but as it did, another sensation became increasingly vivid. A very different sort of ache, one that had been forgotten momentarily, was once again gaining strength. A dim streak of moonlight shone in through the cabin's sole window and illuminated the area where Kyle lay. He held his hand out into the beam, watching in despair as his fingers danced with movement that was beyond his control. The shakes had spread throughout his body, and a familiar burning feeling seared into the flesh beneath his ribs. It was a pain that only one thing could ease and now that thing was out of his reach, probably forever. A part of him was thankful that was true, but another part of him was so desperate for the healing and the exhilaration that came with holding the Gift of Nature that even returning to the Mill for it seemed almost reasonable.

Kyle suddenly became aware of his heavy breathing, of how loud it sounded in the confines of the otherwise silent cabin. Try as he might, he could no more quiet his gasping breath than he could still his trembling hand. Afraid that his panting might wake the girls, he decided to head outside. A little fresh air, he thought, might be exactly what he needed to steady his nerves anyhow.

As he slipped quietly through the cabin's rickety door, Kyle looked for, but failed to locate, the Chief. The old man was nowhere to be seen. The forest air was warm and full of moisture. Summer was drawing to an end, but perhaps there was going to be one more big thunderstorm to officially close the season.

Kyle took several deep breaths of the humid air, which served to ease his hunger only slightly, but succeeded in wiping away the residual angst from his nightmare completely. His heart rate slowed and his head cleared a little, allowing the night sounds to reach his attention for the first time. One sound in particular captured his interest.

Kyle froze, quieting himself so that he could listen more carefully and straining his eyes in the dim moonshine to try and locate the source of the sound. There was only blackness in every direction though, barely broken by the dark shapes of the trees that surrounded the cabin. But somewhere, and nearby, something was there. The sound that Kyle heard was a low rumble, too soft to be called a growl, but certainly produced by something that was capable of growling.

Cautiously, Kyle took a step forward, and then another. The sound seemed to fade away for a moment, but then returned, definitely closer than it had been before. He was moving toward it. His eyes squinted down to slivers, but still no shape or movement was visible within the deep shadows. Another hesitant step. And another.

Kyle almost thought that he could feel the heat of the animal's breath. It had to be right in front of him, but he still couldn't see a thing. He was helpless, he realized suddenly, against some sort of wild animal that could surely see better in the dark than he could.

Kyle sniffed at the air and found a fetid scent riding on the night's damp breeze. It smelled like dog's breath. Whatever was there, hiding in the dark, he had to be right on top of it.

Very slowly, Kyle reached his shaking hand out into the blackness before him, probing blindly in the direction from which the animal smell seemed to be strongest. He bent at the knees, reaching lower toward the ground. Something soft and wet touched the back of his trembling fingers.

"Damn it!" Kyle swore under his breath, but then sighed deeply with relief. He could still see almost nothing of the animal's dark body, but its droopy eyes, now open, reflected the moonlight like flashlights with dying batteries. In the next moment, they disappeared again, heavy eyelids closing them down so that slumber could resume.

Completely distracted by the craving pains of his addiction and the anxiety of his nightmare, Kyle had forgotten about Black Dog completely.

Before returning to the cabin after their miraculous getaway from the Mill, Rosa had insisted that they swing into town to pick up the old hound dog. She had just escaped the clutches of the world's most dangerous man and was still being pursued by his bloodthirsty hunters, and all she could think about was making sure that Charlie's dog was okay. And even more surprising, Lily's grandfather had agreed that her priorities were correct. A dying man's last request, the Chief had said, was a sacred thing, and fulfilling it was a responsibility that took precedence over just about anything else.

Black Dog had been napping in the back yard when they'd found him, but was ready and willing to climb into the back of Lily's father's truck when they offered him a ride. There'd been a bag of chow in the back screen room of Charlie's house, which was left unlocked, and they'd taken it along. The old hound dog had spent the rest of the day at the cabin, mostly resting his gray chin in the grass, seeming completely at peace in the cool shade of the forest.

Dropping down to one knee, Kyle scratched Black Dog's wrinkled forehead just as he had that day outside the restaurant, but the old hound didn't even stir. His breathing had returned to the rhythmical rumbling of sleep just that fast, and unless somebody else happened to stumble onto him in the dark, he wouldn't be coming around again for hours to come.

"Oh boy, the look on your face," spoke a raspy voice from somewhere in the night.

Kyle was upright in a heartbeat, but his start didn't last. The voice was a familiar one.

"How can you see me at all?" Kyle asked the Chief, just able to make out the tiny glow of the old man's smoldering pipe. "I can't see a thing out here."

"That's because you're a city kid," the Chief answered honestly. "You're used to having all them lights on all the time. I've lived here in the woods my whole life, and this little corncob nightlight's all I need to see just fine. I got the eyes of the wolf. I mean they're not yellow like his of course, but for seeing in the dark they're damn near just as good. Well, not that good maybe, but pretty good. Better than yours anyhow, that's for damn sure." A series of muffled smoker's coughs heaved harshly from the Chief's throat.

Kyle winced in response, and immediately hoped that the old man couldn't see it.

"Since we're the only ones awake, maybe me and you ought to go take us a little walk," the Chief suggested.

"I told you I can't see a thing," Kyle reminded. "That doesn't make me a very good walking partner."

There was a moment of silence while the Chief apparently thought this over. He took a deep drag from his pipe, and its contents flared to life, momentarily illuminating his leathery face. The expression that showed through in the lines of his deep wrinkles was deadly serious.

"Maybe I should rephrase that," the Chief said, and then paused briefly to loose a few more hoarse coughs. "I know that for the past few days, my grand-daughter worried almost as much about you as she did her own kidnapped father. I also know that the shake in your hands and the tremble in your voice aren't from a touch of the flu. So, I know that we need to have us a walk. Let's go."

"She was worried about me?" Kyle asked, sounding almost eager. The idea of Lily spending days thinking about him was so enticing that for just a moment, it overshadowed everything else.

"Shut up, heart-throb," the old man scolded, "and start walking."

For nearly twenty minutes they walked in silence, Kyle following while the Chief led the way. The shuffling gate of the old man never once faltered over the roots and vines and other snags over which Kyle tripped and stumbled almost continuously.

At first, Kyle's thoughts raced as they progressed. He wondered what Lily was dreaming about right then. He wondered why he was being led through the pitch-black forest in the middle of the night. He wondered if the Chief truly real-ized the nature of his affliction, and if King's men were searching for them, and how his rescue from the Mill had been coordinated, and how long it would be before genetically engineered super-madmen were unleashed upon the earth, and at least a dozen other matters of seemingly equal urgency. And then, suddenly, he quit wondering about anything at all.

Suddenly, he was so intent, so completely absorbed, in the sounds and the smells of the forest that no thought could stick in his mind for more than a fleet-ing moment. The air through which he and the old man passed was so saturated with moisture that wisps of early fog were starting to form here and there in low places and over puddles of standing water. The cool vapor was infused with the subtle flavor of the mint that was being crushed beneath their feet. It was invigo-rating.

A familiar chirping sound that Kyle still suspected to be either crickets or frogs dominated the spectrum of soft night sounds, but beneath were many fainter lev-els, filled with strange voices and barely decipherable rhythms. The soft stems and leaves of the peppermint plants caving under the soles of his shoes held Kyle's attention briefly, and then, for just a moment, there was the sound of a small ani-mal scurrying away through the underbrush. There was the steady labored breathing of the old man up ahead, like wind blowing over a wheat field, and under that, softer yet, was the rustling of leaves in the highest overhead branches of the surrounding Beech and Maple trees, as gentle as a mother's voice during a bedtime story. And faintest of all, the tiniest bit of sound that his ears could detect, was the muffled cadence of distant footfalls. They were at the very threshold of perception, a steady series of muted impacts, coming at about twice the rate of his own steps.

Kyle stopped, straining to pick out the sound more clearly from the bouquet of other noises, but the footfalls, it seemed, stopped along with him. He stared wide-eyed to his right, the direction from which the patterned sounds had seemed to emanate from, but only the indistinct outline from the surrounding foliage stood out in the dim moonlight. Kyle's eyes traced along the edge of a thick-trunked tree, probably a Beech, and then a small stand of bracken fern that grew beside the tree's base, and then a twisted little red cedar sapling beside them. Finally, his steady gaze settled on a shape that couldn't be identified.

It was a section of the dark night that seemed somehow darker than the rest, a wash of perfect blackness into which no hint of light seemed capable of penetrating. The shape was perhaps four feet tall and crested with twin triangles, almost like ears atop a …

The wolf opened its eyes then, which gathered and reflected the moonlight like golden mirrors. Shockingly close, the animal stared at Kyle with neither malice nor fear, but curiosity, and Kyle just stared back. He was too scared to do anything else.

"Well don't that beat all," wheezed the Chief's voice from up ahead. "That damn wolf hardly even shows himself to me some days, and now there he sits, practically at your feet. Hell, he looks like he's ready to fetch your damn slippers."

Aside from the Discovery Channel, Kyle had never seen a wolf. The animal that sat before him did not fit well with the notion he carried of what a wolf was. This was not a wild version of a German Shepherd, not even close. The wolf's glowing eyes caught Kyle at chest-height as it sat back on it haunches. It was huge.

What struck Kyle most though, even more than the animal's tall, sleek frame, was its calm stare. There was no indication whatsoever that the wolf was threatening, but there was also no doubt that it would never allow itself to be handled like some domesticated livestock or pet. It was a wild thing that had chosen to be seen when it could very easily have remained an invisible wraith in the night.

Kyle hardly dared to breathe.

"This is your wolf?" Kyle asked, his voice a cautious whisper.

"My wolf?" asked the old man, sounding incredulous. "What the hell are you talking about, my wolf? He's nobody's wolf and he never will be. Never could be."

"But I thought you said ..."

"I don't give a damn what I said," the Chief cut Kyle off before he could finish his thought. "Nobody can own a wolf, or any other wild animal for that matter. At least, nobody should. I tell you what, city boy, I got a free lesson for you."

Kyle shuddered involuntarily at hearing the word "lesson." He was still suffering, and would continue to suffer for a long time to come, from the lessons he'd learned during the previous days.

"All the wild animals in this forest," the Chief continued, "and all the trees and ferns and flowers, and even the land itself, none of it can ever really *belong* to anybody. There may be papers in some office someplace that says different, but I'm telling you that all that's nothing but horseshit."

Kyle smiled weakly in the dark. Hearing the hunched-over old man swearing reminded him of Grandma Jo.

The wrinkles around the Chief's mouth lifted slightly in response to Kyle's smile as he continued, saying, "That black dirt that you're standing on right now, whatever man thinks he owns it is wrong. That dirt is part of the earth, and you belong to it more than it belongs to you. You can't claim to own something that's older than the longest time you can imagine. You can't buy or sell something that'll still be around ages after you yourself have crumbled to dust. Healthy land can give men what they need to live, but land can only stay healthy as long as men don't take more than they need. If they take too much, if they aren't responsible in how they use the land, then the land won't take care of them anymore."

"But people do whatever they want with land," Kyle countered, still not daring to look away from the wolf. "They buy and sell it, burn it and plow it, and it still grows their crops and holds up their houses."

"Trust me, boy, retribution is slow coming, but it is coming." The Chief sounded suddenly grave. "The lands of this earth have been abused by the people who claim to own them, people who don't understand the balance of nature, and if they keep it up, the land won't give them what they need for much longer. He's a hell of a hunter," the Chief said, nodding toward the motionless wolf as he shifted conversation. "He could chase down every rabbit, coon, opossum, and deer in this forest if he wanted, eat all day long even if he wasn't hungry, but in a year he'd be starving, because his prey would all be gone. That's how the land would repay him for spoiling the balance. That won't happen though, because he knows his place. He only takes what he needs. He does his part to maintain the land, and so the land maintains him."

"But people don't know their place, do they?" Kyle asked. "They don't realize when they're taking too much."

"Some do," the old man offered, struggling through a series of smoker's coughs. "Less than did though. Less all the time, it seems."

The Chief turned then and continued shuffling along through the darkness. Kyle watched him for a moment, and when he looked back to where the wolf had sat a moment before, he discovered it gone, melted back into the forest like a ghost.

Not wanting to be left behind in the dark with a wild wolf lingering somewhere nearby, Kyle hurried to stay on the old man's heels.

"So how did you and Lily know where to pick up Rosa and me outside the Mill?" Kyle asked once he was back in ear shot of the Chief. "Did she smuggle a message out to you somehow?"

"I found her in my dreams, saw where she was being held, and showed her where to run to if she managed to get loose."

Kyle marveled at how matter of factly the old man made his explanation sound.

"You mean you had a vision of where King was holding her?" Kyle asked, hoping for some clarification.

"I mean that Rosa and I met on the dream plane. I know I just look like a grumpy old hermit, but I'm still the Chief of my tribe, and I got a few tricks up my sleeves, talents that have been handed down through twenty generations of my ancestors. I don't just drift away when I sleep, I move away. In my dreams, I can travel to places that I can't get to when I'm awake. Since the passing of my tribe, there haven't been many receptive souls to find on the dream plane, but that girl, Rosa, she was like a beacon to me. I found her, saw what she'd seen, and showed her where to look for me. There's powerful magic guiding her dreams, and she's only just beginning to understand it."

"She says that she sees glimpses of the future when she dreams," Kyle said, tripping over another protruding root. "That's what Ramius King forced her to do for him. He tried to make me kill her before we escaped." Kyle choked on his last words, hardly able to force them up through his throat.

"I know," the old man said sympathetically. "I've seen some of what's happened through my dreams."

"He let me use a Gift of Nature, a thing that added to the power of my magic. He tricked me into doing bad things with it."

"I know."

"I didn't want to do what I did, but I couldn't stop myself." Kyle's shaking was becoming severe, further impeding his progress along the narrow path. "And now that I'm free from him, and from the thing he gave me, all I can think about is how to get it back. I feel like I might die if I never get to hold it again. I've never felt so empty."

The Chief stopped and turned slowly back, compassion showing through the deep lines of his leathery face.

"It was a cruel thing that King did to you, Kyle. He made you dependant on a power that you weren't ready to handle. I'd like to tell you that the pain you're feeling will ease with time, that you'll get used to being without a Gift, but I'm not sure it would be the truth. I might just be blowing smoke if I promised that. I don't think you'll have the chance to find out anyway."

A chill ran down Kyle's back.

"What do you mean by that," he asked, his voice unsteady. "Even if I went back to the Mill, King would kill me for having escaped. I'd never be able to sneak in and out with one of his talismans."

"Ramius King doesn't hold all the Gifts of Nature," the Chief pointed out. "He has most of them now, but not all."

Kyle's trembling vanished in an instant. His whole body froze still, and all the breath rushed out of his lungs.

"Do y-you have a G-Gift?" he barely managed to stutter.

The Chief hesitated, hearing the mixture of dread and eagerness in the young man's voice. He regretted what he had to do, but saw no way around it.

"I don't," he answered "but I know where one waits for you, and so do you if you think carefully."

Kyle's mind raced, but no answers came.

"Until you dropped down into the boat at the Mill Pond yesterday, you'd never seen me before, right?" asked the Chief. "I'd seen you before though. So had the wolf. We were both there that day when you stumbled into the clearing, when you found the tree."

The tree? At first, Kyle couldn't think of what the Chief was referring to, but then it came to him. He remembered thinking that it was the strangest thing he'd ever experienced, but that was before everything else that had happened in the mean time. He remembered it now though, and vividly.

The Chief read the recognition in Kyle's eyes. There was no turning back at that point, he knew. Even if he walked away right then, Kyle's addiction would take him the rest of the way alone.

"When an especially strong magician dies," the old man explained, "their magic doesn't go with them to the other side. The magic remains, returns to the earth until it's born again in another form. Whatever form that may be, whatever plant or animal chance chooses to start its life at that spot, it will live a normal existence for its kind until it's claimed by another magician. Then, the bound up magic in that creature is released to whoever it was that sparked the transformation. It becomes a Gift of Nature."

"And that's what the tree is?" Kyle asked, although he already felt certain of the answer.

The Chief nodded slowly in the darkness and said, "I was only a boy at the time, and I haven't been a boy in more years that you would believe. I was checking a trapline I'd set along the bank of the Brooke River, and I felt an immense presence of magic. I followed the scent of that power until I found a man in city clothes wandering through the woods. I watched him pass from a distance, and then after a minute, watched another man trailing after him. I followed them secretly, as I could anyone in my own forest, and when the second man finally caught up with the first, I watched them fight. The force of the magic that was released that day by those two men is beyond my ability to describe with words, so I won't even try. When if was over, one of them was dead."

"And the dead man's magic went back into the earth," Kyle continued for him, entranced by the story. "It grew up into the tree."

"The man who died was a Guardian," the Chief added grimly, "the leader of the Guardians in fact. He was hunted down by a powerful dark magician, and he was killed right there on the spot where the white tree grows. I don't know how the Guardian's flight brought him to Steel City, but when I look back now, it's not all that surprising. In case you hadn't noticed, Steel City ends up being the place where a lot of big shit goes down. Can't say why, but this place isn't like the thousands of other little towns that look and smell just the same. Even the normal folks who live there in town, the ones who are completely naïve to magic, seem to sense it in a way. It takes more to shake them than it does people from somewhere else."

"And you want me to claim the tree, to make it my talisman?" Kyle whispered as if discussing something sacred.

"It's not so much a matter of what I want," the old man corrected, "but of what's got to be. I've watched Ramius King for a while now, and I've talked with Rosa about what sort of man he is, and of what he might be capable of. Now that the Guardians are gone, you are a precious few who have magic with which to fight him, and you have even fewer weapons to wield. I have watched over the tree my whole life, waiting for fate to bring the right person to find it, and claim it. Now my waiting is finally over."

"But I'm only just learning," Kyle started to argue. "There must be someone else …"

"It has to be you," the Chief cut him short. "Remember, it wasn't me or Ramius King or the Guardians who brought you to the tree in the first place. It was fate. Besides, look at your shaking hands. You're so desperate to be healed by the tree's power, you couldn't leave now even if you wanted to."

Kyle clenched his teeth, hating his dependency and his transparency. He knew that the Chief was right. He couldn't possibly pass on what he was being offered. There was no choice to be made. It was as good as done already.

"Are there other Gifts of Nature that still haven't been claimed?" Kyle asked. There almost certainly weren't, he knew, at least not nearby and not that the Chief would know about. Grandma Jo had told him how incredibly rare they were, and now the old man would probably repeat the same thing. What Kyle really wanted, the real reason he'd asked the question, was to buy a little more time to think about what he needed to do.

"I think I know of one other, but I can't be certain," the Chief answered flatly, catching Kyle completely by surprise. "If the other is truly destined to become a Gift of Nature, then it's not for you to claim anyway, so it doesn't matter. All that matters right now is you following through with the destiny that you came so near to the first day you walked into this forest."

"This forest?" Kyle asked. "Are we near the clearing?"

"We're there."

As the Chief took a long pull from his pipe, its contents seemed to glow brighter than they had before, providing enough light to reveal the circle of towering black trunks that surrounded them. At the center of the clearing, looking just as unearthly as Kyle remembered, was the white tree. Its crooked trunk and tiny, fluttering leaves seemed almost to glow with their own light, making Kyle wonder how he hadn't spotted it sooner. It was so beautiful and so mysterious that it enchanted him all over again, pushing everything else from his mind. And so it was that he forgot almost immediately about the astonishing possibility that the Chief suspected the location of another unclaimed Gift of Nature.

THE RUNE TREE

Very slowly, the Chief bent down toward the ground, arching his permanently bowed spine with obvious discomfort until he could almost reach the earth in front of his feet. Turning over his favorite corncob pipe, he spilled out its smoldering contents onto the dirt, and instantly flames sparked to life, illuminating the night with flickering yellow light. The fire spread in opposite directions, tracing the perimeter of the clearing like two model train engines racing head-on around a circular track.

The dead trees that stood like sentinels around the clearing loomed overhead in the dim light, deeply shadowed and foreboding, leaning away in their permanent pose of trauma. There was the sense that the trees were still being pushed back from the center of the dead zone, but their ancient roots held them fast, frozen in place as if petrified.

Kyle took one step forward, toward the ring of fire. Then he took another step, and then another. With every deliberate stride, the weight of the moment grew heavier across his shoulders, feeding his trepidation and stealing away his courage.

Another step moved Kyle across the flickering circle of flame, and although he was too intent on the white tree to notice, the fire fell back briefly to let him pass, as if bowing in reverence.

The dim firelight made the ghostly tree appear more surreal than when Kyle had first discovered it. Its thin ivory trunk, covered in the rune-like tracks of the woodworms, shimmered almost metallically, and the tiny leaves of its delicate branches danced in rhythmic unison as if to music too soft to hear. There was, however, not a trace of a breeze in the air. Other than the crooked, little tree's fluttering leaves, everything was as still as a painting.

Five steps from the tree, Kyle realized that the sounds of the woods had all dropped away. There was no more chirping from crickets or frogs and no more scurrying rodents' feet. The humid air had become stifling, and the perfect still-ness was allowing an early layer of fog to begin to condense over the forest floor. Only the dull voice of the nearby river, slithering by like a giant black snake, broke the silence.

Two steps from the tree, a rash of pinpricks bloomed over Kyle's skin, creep-ing first down the length of his spine, and then sweeping over his arms and legs like a swarm of crawling insects. Static electricity flooded the clearing, jumping in little arcs through the moisture-saturated air in miniature bolts of lightning, giv-ing the appearance of fireflies signaling in the dark.

As his trembling hand came to within inches of the white tree's twisted trunk, an image flashed in Kyle's mind. He saw himself standing beside Lily before Ramius King and a sprawling army of dark figures from whom an aura of stagger-ing collective power seemed to emanate. The image came and went in a heart-beat, but left a strong echo of meaning in its wake. Kyle had the odd sense that what he'd seen had been both foreign and familiar at the same time. He'd been to that place before, but not on his own two feet. It was the world of dreams through which he'd traveled to get there.

The prospect of finally uncovering even a single still-frame from his recurring dream was incredibly exciting, and yet it wasn't enough to give Kyle further pause. He was so close to the thing that he needed so badly. All his being craved the healing that would come with holding a Gift of Nature again, and now that the moment was at hand, nothing could hold him back.

An old, familiar feeling of dreadful purpose filled him as his fingers closed about the crooked trunk of the tree. Things would never be the same for him, he knew. He would never be the same.

Kyle was ready to feel the elation that he'd experienced holding the reptilian Gift in the Mill. He was ready for his withdrawal pains to be instantly healed and the burning hollow in his stomach to be filled with soothing energy. He was not ready for what he got.

The entire tree erupted into a raging ball of brilliant blue flame. Searing pain lanced through Kyle's body, and the heat from the fire felt like it was eating into his flesh. Desperately, he tried to pull himself away from the source of his agony, but his grip held firm, cemented by a bond that would soon become permanent.

His head was thrown back convulsively and his jaws sprung open. He tried to scream, tried to call out in prayer, but his voice was lost to the inferno.

Tongues of blue flame licked up and down the tree, tearing away at its thin branches and delicate leaves. The fire raced up the length of Kyle's arm, engulfing him in its hot fury, threatening to consume him as well. The whole world faded behind a curtain of azure light, painfully bright, but Kyle's eyes remained agape. He willed them to close, but like his hand, they wouldn't obey.

Kyle had never suffered in such a way. Not even the paralyzing shock of the collar he'd worn at the Mill could compare. A dark thought imposed itself through the layers of Kyle's suffering. He was dying.

Then, just as Kyle was accepting the inevitability of his own ultimate transformation, the fire evaporated. The clearing fell back into near darkness. The bright blue light was gone, as was Kyle's agony and most of the white tree. What was left in Kyle's grasp was a crooked staff of jet black. Its glassy surface was covered in the fossilized tracks of woodworms, so intricate and runelike. It was as hard as a tortoise's shell, as dark as a skunk's belly, and as light as a falcon's feather.

Then, at last, the power of the Gift was set free. It coursed through Kyle's veins like medicine, satisfying his addiction as nothing else could, soothing his pain, and filling him with strength like none he'd ever known. It was as if he'd been incomplete his whole life until right then, but had never realized it.

"It's done," rasped the wheezy voice of the old man who stood looking on from the edge of the fading fire ring. "And it's about damn time. The Rune Tree is yours now, and how it gets used is up to you."

Kyle studied the deep wrinkles of the Chief's wizened face, finding a combination of relief and sadness there that he didn't entirely understand. Something else about the old man had changed as well, something more than his expression. It seemed that his stoop had deepened somewhat. His hunched back pulled forward so far that the gnarled fingers of his leathery hands hung almost to his knees. He looked almost too tired to stand.

"Are you okay?" Kyle asked, suddenly concerned. "You don't look so good. Let me ..."

Kyle's voice dropped away before his thought was complete. Something had awakened his little voice. It was whispering insistently in the back of his mind, alerting him to the presence of some other magic nearby. Someone was coming, and not just any average someone.

Kyle spun on his heels, scanning in every direction. It was difficult to see much beyond the dwindling fire that lined the clearing.

There, just beyond the ring of flame, Kyle spotted the wolf, a still shadow, blacker than the black night that surrounded it. The animal's gold eyes glowed in the dappled light of the fire. As a low grumbling sounded from its chest, the wolf's upper lip retracted menacingly, displaying the arsenal of natural weapons that lined its long jaws. The wolf wasn't growling at Kyle though.

"I think you should have waited for daylight, old man," a deep voice spoke from somewhere just outside the clearing. "That made an awful lot of light for a dark night like this one. *We* could have seen it from a mile away."

"Don't matter," the Chief called back as he sidled over a little closer to the wolf. "It's a done deal now, and I don't give two shits about what you think."

Slowly, Kyle began to move toward the Chief. It was difficult to pick out the direction that the intruder's voice had come from, and there was still no visible sign of him. Everything beyond the clearing was masked completely by the dark and the ever-thickening fog.

"I don't know who you are, old man, or how you knew about this unclaimed Gift," said the same gruff voice from the shadows, "but I know that boy with you is the property of Ramius King. He's a man you don't want to cross."

The Chief sneered and half-shouted back, "I know all about the Tall Man. I know he holds your leash, and if he was here right now I'd cram this corncob pipe right up the left nostril of his crooked honker."

Despite the knots that were twisting in his chest, Kyle smiled reflexively as the old man spit vinegar at their unseen assailants. There was absolutely no fear in his sharp, droopy-lidded eyes.

"If you're so sure that I'm nothing but an old man and he's nothing but a boy," the Chief continued to shout, fighting off a series of hoarse smoker's coughs, "then why don't you walk yourself out here in the open instead of hiding in the weeds like some kind of wounded bunny rabbit?"

And then they appeared, Fat Man and Little Boy, walking side by side as they stepped over the diminished ring of flame opposite from where the Chief and Kyle and the wolf all stood.

Kyle recognized the striking pair instantly from having passed them in the halls of the Mill. He didn't know their names or their exact position in the ranks of King's hunters, but he knew that everyone had gotten out of their way when they passed, and never the other way around.

"Howdy, Kyle," the tiny man said in his strikingly deep voice. "You happen to know where Mr. King's fortune teller is?"

"She's right behind you, and she's holding a shotgun," Kyle answered, satisfied with the steady tone of his own voice.

The little man only smiled in response. The giant beside him didn't even do that.

"You're probably feeling pretty good with that brand new Gift of Nature in your hand," Little Boy suggested, starting slowly across the clearing. "I have one of my own, and I have a great deal of experience using it. How much experience do you have? A couple days? No, make that three short lessons in a couple days, and with a different Gift, too."

Kyle knew he needed to keep his head. With great effort, he choked down the fear that was rising in his throat, and he fought back the power that was building at his finger tips. He strained to hear beyond Little Boys voice and found the steady gurgling of the river in the distance. He blocked everything else out for a moment, keying in on the faint sound of the flowing water. As long as he stayed focused enough to hear the voice of the river he could maintain control.

"Let it loose if you want," Little Boy dared. "Let the magic free. Tear me down with it just like you did that unarmed buffoon that Mr. King assigned to be your warden." A wicked smile spread across the tiny man's face as he spoke. He knew the flames he was fanning as he crept further across the space of the clearing, the giant only a step behind.

The gurgling of the river seemed terribly faint behind Little Boy's taunts, and it took tremendous effort for Kyle to keep his focus steady. The Rune Tree was growing warm in his grip, and a tingling sensation was creeping up his forearm. The magic wanted to be let loose. The whisper of his quiet inner voice was in danger of becoming something more.

"You've got about ten seconds to make your choice," Little Boy continued, still advancing as patiently as a stalking constrictor. "That old man isn't going to outrun me, so you're either going to defend him or leave him. What's it going to be?"

The tingling had advanced up the length of Kyle's arm, over his shoulders, and up his neck. When the prickling energy reached his ears, it became a buzzing that drowned out Little Boy's voice and the river as well. The magic dangled at his fingertips, and its voice in his ears was irresistibly compelling. Logic said that he couldn't prevail against a pair of veteran opponents, but logic also said that there was no good alternative to trying.

"All right then," Little Boy hissed. He was now just several steps from being literally toe to toe with Kyle, who boldly stood his ground. The tiny man drew one hand back as if readying himself to throw a punch, and from his fist a blue light began to glow.

Abruptly, Little Boy froze in his poised position. Simultaneously, he and Fat Man stepped back and began scanning around the perimeter of the clearing just as Kyle had when he'd sensed their approach.

Like a specter materializing from the mist, out stepped Michael Galladin. He was darkly clad and a black, cloth bag hung over his shoulder.

Instantly, both Little Boy and Fat Man sprung into action. Kyle was distracted momentarily by Michael's appearance, and when the giant charged him, he didn't manage to raise any sort of defense. In a bullrush, Fat Man plowed into Kyle, sending him literally flying through the air. Before the behemoth could move to act further though, two rows of sharp, white daggers dug savagely into the back of his thick leg. A reflexive kick shook the wolf's jaws free, and sent him tumbling into the center of the clearing, where he was up instantly, growling ferociously and baring all of his freshly bloodied teeth.

Kyle struggled up to his hands and knees, fighting to regain his composure after being caught off guard. Stars twinkled before his eyes, and he couldn't seem to pull any air into his lungs. It felt like he'd been hit by a truck instead of a man.

Little Boy had slipped around behind the Chief, and he now held the tip of his fiery knife at the old man's side.

"I guess there aren't any girls around," Michael noted as he helped Kyle to his feet, his eyes fixed on Little Boy, "so you've resorted to hiding behind a geriatric instead. When are you going to quit hiding, Little Boy?"

"I never dreamed you'd be stupid enough to come to Steel City, Michael," the tiny man countered. "You're number one on Mr. King's most wanted list, and you're pretty much out of allies. We killed them all, remember?"

Michael stared back coldly, showing no hint of any fear or anger.

"The only thing I can think of," Little Boy continued, "is that you must be awful sweet on Mr. King's little, curly-haired seer. She is a cutie, I admit, but what a bitch! We were actually kind of glad when she escaped. Tired of listening to her mouth."

That finally prompted a response from Michael, but not the one that Little Boy had expected. He smiled. Michael hadn't known about Rosa's escape until right then. Mistakenly, the tiny man had assumed that the lost Guardian was responsible for coordinating the escape, and therefore, up to date on current events that he in truth was not. The escape was news to Michael, and very good news at that. His smile was also, in part, a response to Little Boy's commentary on Rosa. He could only imagine the sass that King's men must have been assaulted with while holding her prisoner.

"Me and Fat Man are about to head back to the Mill," Little Boy explained calmly, although a bead of nervous sweat dangled at the tip of his short nose. "You aren't going to follow us, because if you do, you'll follow us right into hell. If you value your life at all, you'll pick a direction to run, and you won't stop running for a long time."

"Are you really that scared to stand up and fight?" Michael asked, his voice full of contempt. "How about you, Fat Man? You going to run away with him? Again?"

The skin across the giant's face pulled taut. The muscles at the corners of his wide mouth twitched involuntarily.

Kyle watched on anxiously, trying to imagine how he could help the newcomer if things turned violent again. His fingers squeezed the Rune Tree so tightly that it quivered in his grip.

"Yes, Fat Man will be leaving with me," Little Boy answered for the giant. "And no, I'm not scared to fight you, Michael. But, I'm not one to take unnecessary risks, especially at such crucial junctures. In case you haven't heard, we're about to go public. We're about to go from obscurity to celebrity. Our big moment has almost arrived, and no chance at missing it is a chance worth taking as far as I'm concerned."

As the boy-sized man spoke, his enormous counterpart slunk back to the perimeter of the clearing. Suddenly, a tremendous creaking sound split the night from his direction, drawing everyone's immediate attention.

At the exact same moment when Fat Man pushed over one of the massive dead trees that ringed the clearing, Little Boy shoved the Chief harshly to the ground. Sharp snapping sounds echoed through the still night air as the tree's ancient roots ripped free from the soil that had anchored them for so many uncounted decades. It groaned in protest as it tipped toward the center of the clearing, falling slowly, but with unstoppable momentum, like an ocean freighter easing its immense bulk into the docks, crushing anything caught in between.

The black spire was falling through the air, a fraction of a second away from crushing the Chief beneath its massive girth, when Michael stepped into its path. The concussion of the tree striking the lost Guardian's shoulder rang out like a clap of thunder. His thin frame staggered under the impact, but he held firm. His legs were driven knee-deep into the ground beneath him.

Kyle raced to the Chief, pulling him quickly out from under the precariously balanced tree.

In a display of impossible strength, Michael shrugged the leaning monolith off his shoulder, letting it crash to the ground, and pried his buried feet up from the earth. The humming of his magic was almost palpable in the misty air. He suddenly appeared much taller than he had a moment earlier. It seemed like the whole of the clearing was hardly enough room to hold him.

Fat Man and Little Boy were already out of sight, fled back into the dark night. Only the growling wolf, standing stiff-legged on point over the glowing coals of the Chief's fire ring, indicated the direction in which they'd gone.

Seeing that the old man was more or less okay, Michael started off in that direction, intent on making pursuit, but a soft, wheezing voice gave him pause.

"Now's not the time," the Chief said, struggling with his words, fighting through a long series of hoarse coughs. With Kyle's help, he managed to get back up to his feet. "There could be more of them out there. They could find Rosa and Lily."

Kyle could see the effect of the old man's words on Michael instantly.

The lost Guardian stared off in the direction of his retreating enemies for another moment, and then joined Kyle in making sure that the Chief bore no serious injuries.

"I assume you're Michael Galladin," the Chief wheezed. "I'm Chief Redtail, and this is Kyle Adams. This was a good time for you to show up."

Michael nodded, but said nothing.

Most of the flames that had ringed the clearing were gone, and the fog had become as thick as the smoke from a poorly built campfire. The wolf had disappeared into the shadowy forest once again.

Michael shifted the black, cloth bag he carried to his back and then carefully draped one of the Chief's arms over his shoulders, motioning for him to lead the way. As they started back in the direction of the cabin, it was clear that the old man's every step sapped strength from his dwindling reserves. It was as if he'd aged twenty years in ten minutes.

THE HARD TRUTH

Kyle followed the two older men in silence. All the forest's night sounds had returned, and Kyle heard every one vividly. He no longer stumbled over roots or tripped on vines. He no longer struggled to keep his feet falling along the right path. The little voice of his magic spoke to him continuously now. Its whispers were broadcasted in all directions from the Rune Tree, and when those soft words echoed back, they forewarned of each coming obstacle, of every possible pitfall, before it was reached.

Kyle's feet, it seemed, hardly even touched the ground as he went along. The power of the Gift supported him, made him almost buoyant in the humid air. Not only was his strength renewed, it was enhanced to a level he'd never known, not even in the training room at the Mill. He floated along through the sticky night air as if atop a white cloud, but one with a dark lining. Behind the cloud, masked by the warmth of the Rune Tree's magic, was a familiar face and a reminder. The face was that of Choplin the jailor, and the reminder was that the talisman possessed no conscience of its own.

Lily was waiting outside the door of the little hunting cabin when the three men returned, soothingly rubbing the base of Black Dog's flop ears as he slept. She'd awakened not long after Kyle and the Chief had departed, and upon finding them absent, she'd decided to stay up until they returned. She didn't really think that they were likely to be in any trouble, but knew that she wouldn't be able to sleep anymore until she saw them back safe and sound. In truth, she suspected that her grandfather had probably smuggled Kyle away under the cover of darkness in order to conduct a private interview. Over the past several days, she had talked an awful lot about the new boy she'd met at school who just happened to be able to do magic like her. Undoubtedly, the Chief had caught on to the fact that her interest in him was more than passive. Her grandfather, she imagined, was just checking out Kyle for himself, watching out for her as he'd always secretly done. It seemed a likely enough explanation, but as time dragged on, her concern deepened and her suspicion grew.

When Lily saw her grandfather emerge from the woods at last, helped along by Michael, her suspicion became outright fear. The lanky man with the shock of red hair at his chin made her instantly nervous. He certainly did appear to be helping her grandfather, but there was an aura of danger that radiated from him that was unmistakable even at a distance as he approached.

The Chief briefly explained what had happened and how Michael had come to his and Kyle's rescue. Kyle listened impatiently, adding little bits to the Chief's narration here and there. He was anxious to give Lily his own account of the birth of his Gift and of the strength it lent him. Michael stood by in silence, fidgeting and glancing repeatedly in the direction of the dark cabin. He seemed to be waiting for something, and indeed he was. Mercifully, he didn't have to wait long.

When Rosa stepped out from the cabin door, just awakened by the sound of conversation, she spotted Michael instantly and rushed to him. His arms were waiting for her. They embraced tightly, but separated quickly when they became conscious of the affection they were demonstrating.

Michael's brow furrowed and his mouth dangled open, but no words, it seemed, would come out.

"Hey, I'm alright, Redbeard," Rosa answered his unasked question, letting him off the hook.

Kyle, Lily, and the Chief watched the reunion curiously. It was obvious that Michael and Rosa shared strong feelings, but they seemed a very unlikely couple, if that's truly what they were.

As the Chief repacked his pipe with a fresh wad of tobacco, he suggested that everybody else should try to get some sleep while there was still the darkness and fog to conceal their little hideout. He volunteered to keep watch, insisting that old men like him were naturally inclined to start their days early and catch up on sleep with afternoon naps. It might have been legitimate reasoning if he had in fact already been sleeping beforehand, which he hadn't. His day had started right at the previous one's end.

Kyle and Lily agreed quickly, however, retreating back into the cabin where they hoped to get a few moments to themselves. Rosa gave in after some hesitation. She was anxious to tell Michael about the things she'd learned while being held captive in the Mill, but she was still dreadfully exhausted from her ordeal and truly did need sleep. Michael flat out refused. Black Dog slumbered on in blissful oblivion.

"I'm not all that tired," Michael fibbed, knowing well that Rosa would never believe him, but feeling confident that she'd understand. "I'll stay out here and be lookout with the Chief."

A protest rushed to Rosa's lips, but she held it back. She knew that the tiny cabin would be close quarters for Michael even if she were his only company. With the two kids in there as well, he'd never be able to fall asleep if he did come inside, and he'd be uncomfortable all night. There was no point in that, so she let it go, and after embracing her mysterious knight for another precious moment, she headed inside. She didn't bother asking what was in the black, cloth bag that hung over his shoulder.

"You a smoker?" the Chief asked Michael when it was just the two of them left outside the cabin.

"No," Michael answered simply.

"You drink or play cards or shoot pool or what?" the old man pressed.

"No," echoed the reply, again without elaboration.

"You're not a smoker or a drinker, and I know from what Rosa told me that you're not married. So what are you?"

Michael gritted his teeth in annoyance, wishing he were keeping watch alone, and said, "I'm a private man."

"Oh, you're a *private* man," the Chief said with a hoarse laugh that quickly developed into a fit of smoker's coughs. "I see. So, you probably don't like some old geezer like me digging around in your *private* shit, right?"

Michael looked over at Black Dog twitching in response to whatever doggy dream he was lost in, and pretended not to have heard.

"If that's so, then you're really not going to like my next question," the Chief forged ahead, heedless of Michael's apparent reluctance to converse. "Rosa also told me that you used to be a Guardian. Why'd you quit?"

"I'm not accustomed to being interrogated," Michael said with a distinct edge to his voice.

The Chief wheezed out another raspy laugh and said, "No, I'm sure you're not. Hell, I could feel you coming from twice as far off as I could King's dynamic duo back there. I'm sure you're used to people keeping their distance, but that's a comfort you'll do without tonight."

Michael started to respond, but was cut off before he could get the first word out.

"I'm three times your age, young pup," the old man boasted, "and between you and me, I'm probably not going to be getting much older. In other words, I'm not too worried about running my mouth or pressing my luck with anybody, not even a dangerous guy like you."

"I'm not a dangerous guy," Michael argued weakly. "People just treat me that way."

"Oh, I think you are dangerous," the Chief countered. "Or you could be, at least. And I also think that you're just fine with that. I think that you like the space that people grant you. Makes it easy to be a loner and keep your dark mood intact. You see, I've got a knack for reading people, and that's how I read you."

"You don't know anything about me," Michael snapped, louder than he'd meant to. "I keep away from people for their own good."

"Actually," the Chief said after a long drag on his pipe, "I know more about you than you think."

The old man's words settled down over Michael's shoulders like a lead cape.

The Chief, noting the look on Michael's face, continued more gently, saying, "I know what happened with you and your brother. I heard the story from a Guardian I knew a long time ago. Oh yes, the Guardians knew about me hiding out here. They didn't care much though. I've been a wrinkled up old man for a long time, and my magic's never been good for much more than keeping myself out of sight. They didn't need any help from me. Anyway, when Rosa told me about you, about how you left the Guardians when you were real young, and under bad circumstances, I assumed that the two stories went together."

"If you know about what happened, then you ought to understand why I keep to myself, why I need to keep the magic locked away." Michael's voice had taken on a subtle hint of pleading.

For a moment, the old man just stared back, but said nothing. The deep creases around his eyes warped into an expression of deep sympathy.

"I want to tell you a story, young man" the Chief went on reflectively, "one that I think you'll be able to relate to. I used to run a little trapline in the winter along the bank of the Brooke River, not far from the clearing where you found us tonight. I'd get a mink or two a year and maybe a few muskrats if I was lucky. One time though, maybe ten years back, a snow-white cat stepped into one of my traps by mistake. I knew the animal, had seen it lots of times when I was watching over my granddaughter. It was her friend when she was little. I hated that it died, and I hated that it was my fault, but there was nothing I could do to make it right."

"Except quit trapping," Michael interrupted the story. "It went bad one time, so you quit in order to make sure it couldn't go bad again. Isn't that what happened?"

"That is what happened, but you're missing my point. There's a difference ..."

"I don't see the difference," Michael butted in on the old man's explanation. "You made the same choice I made. The only difference is that you killed some stray cat instead of your own brother."

The Chief sighed deeply, sounding exasperated, and said, "I can't imagine the scar that your brother's death must have left on you. You're right, I quit trapping because I felt bad just how you gave up magic because you felt bad, but there is a difference. If my family was starving to death, I'd start trapping again. It wouldn't make no difference how bad I felt about it. It'd be necessary, so I'd do it. I don't have a starving family though, so I have the luxury of choosing not to trap, of avoiding the source of my guilt."

"I don't have a family at all," Michael pointed out, "starving or otherwise."

"Oh, but you do," the Chief argued, a quick smile flashing across his leather face. "When you became a Guardian, you took every defenseless person in the world as your family. That's their thing, protecting everybody from dark magic. It's an awful tall task. I wouldn't have signed up myself, but you did. There's a shitstorm on the horizon, young man, and that means your magic can't stay on the sidelines any longer. I know that's not what you want to hear, but it's the hard truth."

"I know there's no one else left to fight King," Michael retorted sharply, struggling to keep himself from becoming angry. "I came here to stop him or die trying."

"Did you? I thought you probably came here for Rosa."

Michael looked quickly away, hiding his face for fear that he wouldn't be able to hide his emotions.

"She's in greater need than any other, I think," the Chief pointed out, "but you can't just steal her away. You must know that. He'll hunt her down to the ends of the earth. He won't risk letting her potential continue to develop. She could become a threat to him."

"I know," Michael conceded, his face still turned away toward the dark forest.

"You were born with a special gift, Michael, and it's not right for you to deny that," the Chief said gravely. "You need to be ready to take action if a chance comes along where you're able to foul up King's plans. You won't be ready if you're still holding so tightly to your brother's memory. You need to put your guilt away once and for all so that you can become the man you were meant to be. You are the last Guardian of Magic, and quite possibly the last hope of all free people."

Michael continued to stare off into the foggy night. He said nothing. What could he say?

Silence settled in for several long minutes, interrupted only by the soft snores of Black Dog.

"On second thought," the Chief said, breaking the fragile quiet, "I am a little tired. If you don't mind, I think I'll find a warm corner in that cabin to wedge myself into and rest my bones for a while. I'm sure you'd prefer to do your look-out duty in *private* anyhow."

With that, the old man set his smoldering pipe on the sill of the cabin's one small window and crept inside. Pain and stiffness were blatant in his shuffling stride. He moved with the care and unsteadiness of a barefoot man walking over sharp rocks.

Michael waited a few minutes and then settled himself down cross-legged beside Black Dog. He gave the old hound dog a little pat on the side, but it didn't interrupt his steady snoring. He was just the company Michael needed.

THE DREAM REVEALED

Kyle Adams' body lay motionless atop his double layer of sleeping bags, but his mind roamed far away.

Finding himself mysteriously transported into the midst of the looming trees of the forest once again, Kyle breathed deeply, savoring the freshness of the cool, misty air. The darkness of the night was pervasive except for one dim glow, a thin aura of light against a screen of impenetrable black. As Kyle watched, the faint blush of illumination gained strength until at last its form was revealed. The light shone out from a girl.

Brighter and brighter her golden halo grew until the girl's features became plain. She wasn't plain though. Far from it. She was beautiful and ... familiar? Although he couldn't think when or where, Kyle was suddenly certain that he had seen the girl before. And then he had it–his dreams. She'd appeared in his dreams many times.

A wave of vertigo swept through Kyle as he recognized the situation for what it truly was. He was dreaming.

He scanned quickly around, suddenly filled with dread and anticipation. He'd dreamed this dream before, and although he couldn't quite manage to retrieve its memory, it was there, hidden deep down in the pit of his stomach, and its feeling was terrible.

The girl's radiance continued to intensify, shining out with such brightness that all of the surrounding forest was painted gold with her light. Only the sky-ward reaching heights of the forest's canopy branches remained hidden in shadow.

As if staring down the sun, Kyle squinted toward the girl, overwhelmed by her brilliance, but so desperate to see her that he couldn't look away. The girl's gentle features were dour, drawn tight into an expression that mirrored Kyle's own emotions. It was clear that she, too, sensed the approaching storm, just as he did.

A flicker of movement at the edge of Kyle's peripheral vision pulled his attention away. He peered intently into the depths of the black woods, but spied nothing ominous.

But then there was another twitch of motion a second later in another direction, and then another. Suddenly, it seemed as if the entire forest came alive and stirred into motion. Sapling trees sprouted up from the ground and grew into giants in the time between heartbeats. They creaked and groaned and crowded together, dark trunk against dark trunk, fighting for room to expand. Every open space was being filled, every way out barricaded. There was no escape.

Kyle spun around, his intuition crying out in warning. There, marching through the last open lane through the otherwise impenetrable wall of trees, was a formation of black-clad men. They were so deeply shadowed that the depth of their ranks could only be guessed. Left, right, left, right, they marched, each step bringing them nearer, bringing them closer to the girl.

Kyle knew instinctively that it was the girl that the dark army sought. They were creatures of blackness and she was a beacon of light that they could never tolerate.

Kyle vowed silently to protect her, but doubted his ability to do so. The power that radiated out from the approaching legion of black soldiers was unmistakable. They would not be easily turned aside.

Kyle gritted his teeth in frustration, unsure of what he alone could do to defend the girl against such a threat. He clenched his fingers into white-knuckle fists, and in one hand he found a hard resistance. Looking down, Kyle saw that he held a staff, a crooked rod of jet-black glass, decorated from one end to the other with strange, intricate grooves.

Where fear should have been springing up into Kyle's chest like a fountain, an unexpected wave of calm settled instead. He stood alone against an army of enemies, and he couldn't guess at how his only weapon was to be wielded, and yet he was suddenly, and mysteriously, bestowed with a deep reservoir of determination and confidence. He would do whatever he had to do to protect the girl.

Kyle thrust the black staff out before him, offering his challenge, and the dark soldiers froze between strides. One man in the front line of their ranks stumbled back as if physically struck.

A low hum emanated from the staff, an inhuman voice filled with menace. The talisman appeared still, but Kyle could feel it trembling in his grip, anxious to release its power. It was Kyle himself, not the shadowy army, who would prove unbeatable.

Silence flooded the forest. Not a single sound other than the dim humming of the crooked staff floated through the damp air. The shadowy legion stood as if paralyzed, clearly hesitant to test the strength of Kyle's strange weapon. Perhaps they would opt to turn back. It was a desperate hope, but it lasted only a moment.

A colossal roar of sound like a thousand screeching voices rang out through the forest, shattering the stillness utterly. The solders of the dark army looked like kites loosed into a gale force wind, so easily and crazily were they scattered by the blast.

Kyle kept the staff held high, knowing that its power was his only chance to survive, and his only chance to protect the girl. He swallowed hard against the bile that churned in his stomach and sputtered up inside his dry throat like a geyser poised to erupt. He had to be strong. He couldn't allow the girl's light to be snuffed.

The relentless assault of the shrill sound threatened to tear Kyle physically from his feet, but he held fast, determined to stand his ground no matter what the cost. As his vision began to fade, a quick glance over his shoulder assured him that the girl was safely shielded. Her light, however, seemed drastically dimmed.

At last, the furious screeching subsided. Kyle's equilibrium was left in ruins. The arm that held the staff fell to his side, his fingers barely able to maintain their grip, threatening to let the talisman fall to the ground. As he struggled to regain his balance, he looked down through the shadowy corridor where the dark legion had stood and found them leveled like wheat just visited by the combine. All but one.

Incredibly, one tall, dark figure remained standing among the broken forms of the fallen soldiers. It was not one of the group though, Kyle realized almost immediately. It was an older man than the soldiers had been, and from him emanated an air of command that none of the others had possessed. An awkwardly crooked nose ran down the middle of the man's long, pale face. A high forehead abutted silver-trimmed black hair. Sharp, cold eyes stared intensely forward, their dangerous stare aimed not at Kyle's staff, but at Kyle himself. This man would not consider retreat, not from Kyle, and not from anyone else.

What if I can't stop him?

The thought was like an injection of poison. As soon as Kyle was infected by it, its vile influence spread throughout his body, weakening not only his limbs, but his resolve as well. He had suffered a lot and endured, but no trial that he'd yet faced could prepare him for the wrath of Ramius King.

Kyle awoke feeling completely unnerved and slightly nauseous, which was how he usually felt after just resurfacing from the dream. Two things, however, were not usual. First off, Kyle did not awake alone. There, kneeling over him, holding his hand in her own, was Rosa Sanchez. Secondly, and more importantly, Kyle remembered. In his mind, its every detail fresh and vivid, the dream lingered.

The images flashed before Kyle's wide eyes, projected by his memory against the dark interior of the cabin. He saw a forest and a troop of dark soldiers. He saw a girl. No, not just a girl–Lily! And he saw Ramius King.

"I remember," Kyle whispered, more to himself than to Rosa.

"You mean you've had that dream before?" Rosa whispered back.

Kyle looked up at the silhouette of Rosa's black curls in the dark room. In the dim light, it was difficult to judge the expression she was wearing, but what Kyle thought he saw confused him. She looked more than concerned. She looked almost panicked, as if she, herself, were the one who'd just escaped a nightmare.

"You saw it, didn't you?" Kyle asked, almost certain that it was so. "You saw my dream. You're the reason why I can remember. I've had that dream my whole life, but I've never been able to remember it until now."

"I only meant to wake you," Rosa whispered, glancing over her shoulder to make sure that Lily and the Chief were still asleep. "You were moaning. You sounded terrified. I touched your hand, and the next thing I knew I was in the forest. I saw your dream, but I wasn't really in it. I was just watching. I tried to shout out to you, but I couldn't even do that. All I could do was watch."

Kyle lay back atop his sweaty sleeping bag, struggling to calm himself, and a new and terrible thought bloomed in his mind.

"It wasn't just a dream, was it?" he asked softly, afraid to hear Rosa's response. "It was like your dreams. It's going to happen."

Rosa shook her head in the darkness, letting the dark ringlets of her hair fall forward and hide her face. She said, "I don't know, Kyle," and she meant it.

TO SEE OR NOT TO SEE

Outside the cabin, Michael Galladin sat cross-legged in the dark with his back against the smooth bark of a Beech tree. It had been over an hour since the Chief had turned in, and he assumed, incorrectly, that everyone was fast asleep inside by then.

Michael had decided to settle a little ways from the cabin while he kept watch. From the edge of the forest he could keep the cabin and small clearing that surrounded it in view, but be a little less obvious himself to anyone who might happen by. With the fog settled so thickly and the night's darkness so complete, it probably wouldn't have mattered, but as usual, he was being cautious.

A lack of light had never been a hindrance to Michael's contentment. In fact, it was just the opposite. The darkness was his friend. Whereas most people felt discomfort at having their sight diminished, fearful of what dangers might be hidden out of view, Michael was comforted, assured that he, himself, was hidden from the view of others.

The steamy air that filled the murky forest had finally cooled somewhat, but not by more than four or five degrees. With both the temperature and the humidity remaining so high even into the night, it seemed inevitable that the following day would bring rain, maybe even a thunderstorm.

Despite the fresh air, the unspoiled darkness, and the deep quiet, all features of the forest night that Michael would otherwise have appreciated after living so long on the city streets, he still couldn't manage to be at peace. His conversation with the Chief had been agitating to say the least. It had been a long time since anyone had spoken to him that way, and his hackles had gone up reflexively. He had indeed come to Steel City to save Rosa. That had been his priority, but he did realize that his responsibilities extended further. He hadn't needed the old man to tell him so. But …

A seductive proposition nagged persistently at the edge of Michael's conscious thinking. No matter how many times he pushed it away, it returned over and over again. He could sneak into the cabin right now and wake Rosa. He could slip away with her under the cover of the darkness and the fog. He could take her to a safe place somewhere far away. He could have a chance at the life he'd always wanted, but always been denied. He could … Could he?

Other than a vague, nearly forgotten, sense of duty, there was no good reason that could be put into words why he couldn't run away with her right then, but there was something that made him doubt. A sickening sense of being trapped had accompanied him with every step he'd taken since arriving in Steel City. It was like a heavy pack on his back that he couldn't take off, burdening his progress, but never revealing its contents. As foolish as it sounded, it seemed to Michael like the whole town of Steel City and all of the natural land surrounding it was filled with snares. There were hidden tripwires everywhere, and no matter how carefully he moved, no matter how lightly he stepped, he'd never be able to avoid them all. He was already caught, and despite his desire to get free, he never would. He wouldn't even try. A Monte Carlo might have carried him from Florida to Michigan, but it had been fate steering the wheel. The same fate that he had for so long doubted had brought him to Steel City, and presumably not just to pick up Rosa and leave. Because of her more than anything else, because of how she looked at him and how she trusted in him, he'd stay and play out whatever role destiny had written for him to play. He'd be the gallant knight Rosa believed him to be, even if it led him to his doom.

At that same moment, as Michael sat outside thinking about Rosa, she was inside thinking about him. She wasn't, however, thinking about the possibility of his facing Ramius King. In fact, she was considering just the opposite, the possibility that he might not have to. All along since being captured by King's goons and brought to Steel City, Rosa's greatest hope was that Michael would come and rescue her, and they could ride off into the sunset to live happily ever after. That was her highest hope, but not the scenario she considered most likely to unfold. She knew that Michael had decided to seek the Tall Man out even before her kidnapping. She also knew that outside of fairy tales, happily-ever-afters were pretty rare things.

Even while she was being held captive at the Mill and fearing for her life, a part of Rosa had dreaded Michael's inevitable arrival in Steel City. It seemed difficult to imagine that he and Ramius King could be drawn so close together, but never end up meeting face to face. Steel City was so small to hold two men like them at once.

King and his men had annihilated the Guardians, the people who for all intents and purposes had been Michael's family once upon a time. Worse yet, King had not just brought about the death of Michael's own twin brother, but had tricked Michael into delivering the death blow himself. Also, not to be forgotten, there was all of her own suffering to consider, all that the Tall Man had put her through. She was not blind, after all, and realized that she meant something to Michael as well. Could the lost Guardian draw so near to the man who was responsible for all that and resist the call to vengeance? Could fate allow the two men to move apart once again after bringing them so near? Maybe.

Michael, having once been a Guardian, seemed like the only one who could hope to stand against King, but things were not always as they seemed. She looked over at Kyle then, only just fallen back into a fitful sleep. She studied his features intently, trying to judge his age, but it was difficult in the near pitch-blackness. He was certainly no more than a teenager, still not far removed from his childhood. How much strength could be hidden in such an average looking young man? As much as his dream hinted at?

A memory sparked in Rosa then. It felt like it came from a time years earlier, but in truth it had been not even a single month past. It had been evening time and she'd been sitting alone in her apartment, flipping through the pages of an old photo album, dreaming about happier times. King had arrived with two of his thugs, the tiny one and the mute giant, the same two who had brought her to Steel City. They'd taken her to the warehouse down the road, which was a familiar and dreaded place by then. The Tall Man had forced his way into her mind, imposed his will over her own, and used her talent to read yet unwritten pages of his own future. All her thoughts and fears had been revealed to him, and only her shame at aiding his horrible agenda could compare to the anguish she'd felt at being violated so completely. And yet, that night had offered her a tiny bit of hope, for among the glimpses of foresight he'd prompted from her was the possibility of his downfall.

It had been her first peek at Steel City. It was just some little rural village in the middle of nowhere to her then, but amongst the people there was someone who had the potential to defeat Ramius King. Could that person have been Kyle? It seemed more likely that it had been one of the Guardians, in which case King had already spoiled that possible future. However, if it had been Kyle she'd sensed, then perhaps that path was one he might yet walk.

He seemed so ordinary, but obviously that wasn't so. The Tall Man had wanted to groom Kyle to become one of his hunters, and no ordinary teenage boy would qualify for that. But still, how could his brief bit of training at the Mill possibly prepare him to compete against King's power?

Maybe, Rosa thought darkly, Kyle's recurring dream was not what she had at first thought it to be. Maybe she'd overestimated the degree to which it was built of prophecy, and underestimated how much was pure fantasy. It hadn't been pure foresight, she knew, not like her own. Magic had been at work in the dream's spawning though, and she felt certain that some truth had been woven into its fabric. But how much? And how literally or figuratively?

They were questions for which there were no answers to be found, but even the faintest hope that there might be someone other than Michael to stand against King was something to hold on to.

Rosa shuddered as a tiny breath of fresh air breezed across her bare arms. Glancing over her shoulder, she discovered Michael standing in the cabin's doorway. How he'd managed to open the creaky old door without her hearing, she couldn't imagine, but there he was nonetheless, materialized from the foggy night outside as if by magic.

"What are you doing?" he whispered, looking quizzically at her bent over the now sleeping Kyle.

"He had a bad dream," she explained softly. "I was just watching him until he fell back to sleep." She left it at that. She wasn't sure what to think about the dream, let alone what to say about it, so rather than risk saying the wrong thing, she said nothing.

"Can you come out with me?" Michael asked. "Please."

Instead of answering, Rosa just stood and started tiptoeing toward the door. She hoped that he only wanted to spend time with her, but it was a faint hope to say the least. She'd heard a tension in his voice that was surely the result of more than simple loneliness.

Once they were both outside, Michael eased the door closed again, sliding it slowly and silently until it caught. Rosa took a moment to rub the floppy ears of their slumbering guard dog, and then she followed Michael to the smooth-skinned Beech tree that he'd made his post.

"Sneaking me out in the middle of the night, Redbeard?" she teased. "Not very gentlemanlike."

Michael couldn't help but smile. He was once again shocked at the power she had over him. Just a few words and a brief smile had taken him from grim to damn near giddy.

"Actually," he said, refocusing, "I need you to go for a walk with me."

"What, right now? Where?"

Motioning with a nod of his head, Michael said, "To where I left the car. It's not far."

"We can't leave them behind," Rosa declared firmly, fearing that Michael meant to flee under the cover of the foggy night.

"No, I know we can't," he assured her.

Then, to Rosa's delight, Michael took her hand in his own and led her off through the dark woods. There was still almost no light, and the fog was thicker than ever, but somehow Michael seemed able to see fine. His steps were all sure, and whenever there were obstacles that needed to be avoided, he'd pause and make sure Rosa stepped carefully as well.

"What's in the bag?" Rosa asked needlessly, looking to the black, cloth bag that still hung over Michael's shoulder.

"What do you think? If I'd have come here to go fishing, I'd have brought a fishing rod, but I came here to face the world's most powerful magician, so ..."

"So you brought your favorite wizard-whacker," Rosa finished for him.

Michael smiled again. "Can you feel the power that's in this place?" he asked a minute later. His words were so soft that the silence of the sleeping forest was barely broken.

"You mean here in the woods?" Rosa wasn't sure what he was talking about, but she was pretty sure that she couldn't sense things the way he did.

"I mean everywhere, all around Steel City," he specified. "I felt it as soon as I arrived. This isn't just another little town, and we didn't all just end up here by chance."

Rosa considered his words. There certainly did seem to be a disproportionate number of the town's current inhabitants who were gifted with the incredibly rare talent for using magic.

"This is a place destined to play host to great and terrible things," Michael went on reflectively. "Whatever we do or fail to do here today, it will be just another chapter in the story of this land, and it won't be the last. An incredible store of magic was left behind with the deaths of the Guardians. Someday, that magic will be manifested in the form of an immensely powerful Gift of Nature, perhaps the most powerful ever. Someday, someone will wield that Gift, and with it their abilities will be wondrous."

Rosa found the possibility of such an extraordinary Gift being spawned from the ashes of the Guardians fascinating, but equally compelling to her was Michael's reference to what *they* would or wouldn't do. Apparently, he meant to try and do *something*.

"You're going to try and stop him, right?" Rosa asked with obvious reservation. "I don't see how you can do it alone? How can you stop him when you're the only Guardian left?"

Michael thought about this for a moment. He stopped, turned to face Rosa, and said, "I'm not a Guardian anymore, haven't been since I was Kyle's age. I will try to stop him though. You're right about that. And you're right about another thing, I can't do it alone." Michael's prematurely old eyes held Rosa with a stare that was filled with regretful determination. "I'll need your help."

Michael's declaration didn't shock Rosa as he'd suspected it might. Obviously she'd already considered the possibility that he would call on her talent to aid him.

"You want to join with me like King did, don't you?" Rosa whispered, unable to help sounding revolted. "You want to reach inside me with your magic and borrow my foresight so that you can see into the future."

"No," Michael denied immediately, "that's not what I want to do at all." He turned then and continued on through the forest, again leading Rosa into the dark. "What I want to do is give you the ability to look ahead on your own."

Rosa swallowed hard, finally realizing what it was that Michael intended.

"This Gift," Michael said, patting the black, cloth bag that hung at his side, "has a counterpart. It's gone unused for a long time, but that can't continue. Circumstances demand that a new master claim it, and it has to be you. With a Gift of Nature you might be able to control your foresight, no longer be bound to the whims of your dreams."

"I might or I might not," Rosa pointed out, sounding frightened. "You don't really know what'll happen if I take the Gift. What about the Chief? He sent me a message through my dreams. Maybe he could do it."

"He's too old."

"What about the girl?"

"She's too young."

"What about …"

"Rosa!" Michael stopped her. "There's no one else. It has to be you. Only you can see what I need to know. Like you said," he went on in a lower voice, "I can't hope to succeed by myself."

Even as they argued, they continued on through the dark trees, Michael pulling her as much as leading her behind him.

A small tear formed at the corner of Rosa's eye as she whispered weakly, "I'm scared, Michael. I'm so scared of what I'll see. I don't want the responsibility."

"Neither do I," Michael agreed, looking straight ahead, "but we'll do what we have to, both of us. I know I'm hardly the one to be offering advice like that, but I don't want you to try and hide from your fate like I did. I never believed in fate before, but all that's happened now can't have come by chance. This has to be our destiny."

Rosa squinted at Michael as he turned back to her for a moment, struggling to read his features through the gloom. He looked so old in the low light, twice as old as he was."

"I won't do it for the memory of the Guardians," she said flatly. "I won't even do it for all the people in the world who might become King's slaves. I'll only do it for you. I owe you my life. If you ask me to take the Gift, then I will."

"I must," he whispered. "You must."

Rosa's sight was so diminished by the dark and the fog that she didn't spot the car until they were practically on top of it. It was parked on a short stretch of two-track and surrounded by a dense grove of fir trees. Being black, the car was effectively invisible at night and would be fairly inconspicuous where it was even during the day.

When Michael popped the car's trunk, there was only one thing to see. It was a black, cloth bag just like the one Michael wore over his shoulder. The points of the antler lent the bag their odd shape, leaving no doubt as to what was inside, not that visual confirmation was needed anyhow. Rosa could sense the presence of the thing even before the trunk came open. It was more than simply an awareness of the Gift's proximity she felt though. It was more personal than that, more specific. It felt like the thing was calling to her.

Impulsively, Rosa reached down into the trunk and snatched the bag up. She threw its cord over her shoulder and then turned to face Michael.

"I'll take it out by morning," she promised. "I want a little time alone to get myself ready for whatever's going to happen."

An argument rose up Michael's throat, but he clenched his teeth and swallowed it back down. He'd asked Rosa to do something that she was rightly terrified of doing, and she'd agreed for his sake. If she needed a couple more hours, then she'd have them.

WEDNESDAY,
SEPTEMBER 6

The Eighteenth Green

Lily awoke late Wednesday morning, but still managed to beat both Kyle and her grandfather out of bed. While Kyle tossed and turned atop his double layer of sleeping bags, the Chief sat wedged in a far corner of the cabin, his chin against his chest, as still as a fallen log. His raspy breaths were practically growls. The lines of his leathery face looked deeper to Lily than they had before, as if he'd aged another ten years during the night.

As quietly as she could, she climbed down from the top bunk and slipped out the door. The fog was so thick that when she waved her open hand through the air, her palm became coated with clinging moisture. Unlike other foggy mornings she remembered, the ground level cloud wasn't cool, but warm and sticky.

At the very edge of her vision, Lily spotted Rosa and Michael standing together next to a large Beech tree. Their heads were leaned close as if whispering, and their hands were joined. Just then, Rosa started to move away. Michael held her hand as she retreated, pulling it to his mouth and kissing it quickly before surrendering it. In the next second she was gone, melted away into the fog.

Still without making a sound, Lily stooped over and scratched Black Dog's wrinkled forehead, his secret spot. Immediately, he lifted his head and affectionately licked her hand.

"He likes you," Michael said as he approached the cabin, causing Lily to start.

"I didn't mean to bother you," she apologized softly.

"It's no bother." Michael cocked his head slightly, studying the girl, perhaps noticing something about her that he'd missed during the dark night. "Dogs know who the good people are."

Lily just smiled, and continued to accept sloppy doggy kisses on the back of her hand.

Michael, like everyone else, was stunned by Lily's shy smile. There was such a wonderful sweetness and innocence in her. And maybe something else as well.

"Where's Rosa going?" Lily asked after a moment, growing uncomfortable under Michael's curious stare.

"Michael considered his answer for a moment, and than said simply, "She needed a little time alone. Is the Chief really your grandfather?" he asked, moving conversation in another direction.

"Yes he is," she confirmed, "but I've only known that myself for a few days. I've only known him for a few days." Lily bit her lip and stared down at her own feet. "I don't think he's well," she offered weakly.

"No, I don't think he is," Michael agreed. "I could tell last night as we were walking through the forest. Just like you, he has magic. I could sense it right away when we met. His magic is failing though. It's been maintaining him for a long time, keeping him alive when by rights his natural time's already come and gone. I don't think he can hang on much longer."

Lily shuddered at the frankness of Michael's words. Tears gathered at the corners of her clear, blue eyes.

"You should be thankful that you got to know him while there was still a little time," Michael offered, trying to sound understanding.

"I am," Lily said, her delicate voice quavering. "I just wish my father was here, too. He's still …"

"I know where he is," Michael stopped her. "Rosa told me what happened. He might still be okay." Michael gnashed his teeth together, disgusted with himself for implying what he had. "I'm sorry, I didn't mean for that to come out how it did. My social skills are rusty, not that it's any excuse."

Lily looked up and found Michael's stare, instantly dissolving his train of thought. Even through the dense gray fog, her eyes shone like blue gems.

"I know what you meant," she assured.

Just then, Black Dog rose to his feet, arched his back and stretched deeply, a low yawn slipping out from between his droopy lips. To Michael's great surprise, the tired, old hound walked directly to him and settled back down to the ground with his graying chin coming to rest right atop the toe of Michael's shoe. Reflexively, Michael stooped down and gave the dog a little scratch behind the ear. Black Dog let out a deep sigh, closed his eyes, and drifted back to sleep.

When Michael looked back up to Lily, he found her smile back in place.

"That's good enough for me," she said. "Dogs know."

"So, you think I'm a cooked turkey, eh?" spoke a wheezy voice from over Lily's shoulder. "Think I'm on the eighteenth green? Think the checkered flag's out? Think ..." A painful sounding mix of coughs and laughs interrupted the string of questions. When the Chief recovered, he said more gently, "Well, you're right."

Twin tears appeared at the inner corners of Lily's blue eyes. When they slipped free, they drew two shimmering lines to the corners of her thin, trembling lips.

"Don't feel so sad, Princess," the old man whispered as he shuffled over from the cabin door. When he reached her, he wrapped one arm around her narrow shoulders. "I'm like a candle in a dark room. When my light goes out, you won't be able to see me anymore, but that won't mean I'm gone. Understand?"

"I think so," Lily whimpered softly, swallowing hard at the lump in her throat.

The Chief leaned away, fighting off another string of deep, wheezing coughs. When he recovered enough to speak, he said, "I'm going to go, Princess. My time's real close now, just like Mr. Galladin here figured. I need to go to a place where I can close the deal the way I want to. What I want you to do is give me a big hug and then let me go. Can you do that?"

Lily's grief wouldn't let her respond with words. Instead, she threw her arms around the old man's shoulders and hugged him tightly.

Buried down beneath the heavy layers of sadness, a tinge of anger added to Lily's distress. Although she felt guilty for it, there was anger in her, and it was directed toward this strange and endearing old man who was about to go off to die on his own terms. She should have been hugging him her whole life. She could have been if only he'd let her. Her tiny family of two had needed help, but he'd stood aside. She'd needed a grandfather, but he'd kept hidden.

"I'm glad for the time we had," Lily whispered, doing her best to steady her voice.

"It'll be alright," the old man whispered in reply. "Everything'll be alright."

And with that, the Chief slipped out of Lily's embrace and started away from the cabin, shuffling out into the mist with obvious difficulty, leaning heavily on his weathered walking stick. In a moment, he was gone from sight.

With unsteady steps, Lily moved slowly in his wake, but as she neared the Beech tree, Michael reached out and restrained her from behind. His hands settled as gently over her small shoulders as if he thought her to be made of glass, and yet even his most delicate touch was uncontestable.

"Your grandfather wants you to let him go," he reminded gently, "and so you must. Come on, let's go wake Kyle. I'm sure he'll be better comfort to you than me."

Lily didn't argue with that, nor agree with it. She just closed her eyes and submitted to the heartache that filled her, willing to let Michael lead her wherever he would.

One Last Thing

Rosa had wandered through the fog-clogged trees for what seemed like a long time, but her progress was slow and she knew that she'd probably traveled less than half a mile. A soft gurgling sound had reached her ears eventually, and as she continued on it grew steadily louder. It was happenstance mostly that led her to a relatively shallow, but fast moving stretch of the Brooke River. She was far too preoccupied to be concerned about her destination. Her only concern was what would happen when she finally reached wherever it was she was going.

The woods fell away some fifty feet from the river, and over the space that separated the trees and the water, the soft, mossy soil gave way to hard, lichen-coated stone. The stone ended in an abrupt edge that hung over the racing river like a natural viewing deck built four stories high. There was no view that particular day though, for the fog was thickest over the chilly current. If not for the water's gurgling voice of warning, Rosa might have wandered right over the precipice and taken a plunge that she couldn't possibly have survived.

It was apparent that she couldn't go any further, so she stopped there, folded up her legs beneath her, and set the black, cloth bag down onto the damp stone before her. It took a half an hour for her to build up the nerve to dump out the bag's lone content. The inky black antler tumbled out unceremoniously, bouncing twice before settling into stillness.

She hardly blinked as she stared at the strange fossil. How something so innocent looking could possess such power, she couldn't imagine. What its power would do to her, what it would reveal to her, she could only guess.

Another half hour slipped by while Rosa studied the dim shimmer of the ant-ler's surface, the gentle curving of its sharp tines, and the unbidden trembling of her own hands. Finally, frustrated with her own procrastination and convinced that no matter what she did, she'd never really be ready anyhow, Rosa reached toward the Gift.

"You look like you're afraid to touch that thing," called out a wheezy voice from the edge of the forest behind her. The words were immediately followed by a series of whooping coughs that momentarily doubled the speaker over at the waist.

"You scared me, Chief," Rosa called over her shoulder, struggling to slow her breathing back down since the big moment had been temporarily delayed. "I thought I was all alone out here."

"You are all alone," he agreed, "and so am I. It's the way some people are des-tined to be."

That struck Rosa as a very strange comment, and she had no idea how to respond to it.

"Actually, I sort of need to be by myself right now," Rosa offered suggestively, anxious to follow through with her task before her courage waned.

"Well you can be by yourself in just a second," the Chief promised. "You could've gone anywhere this morning, but right here is the one place I need to be."

"You mean you didn't follow me here?" Rosa asked, genuinely surprised.

"Hell no, I didn't follow you. I came out here to die, and this just happens to be the spot where I'd prefer to do it. This just happens to be the very spot where the last ten chiefs of my tribe have come to kick the bucket."

"That's not funny, Chief," Rosa said hesitantly, straining to see the old man's face through the fog so that she might better judge his sincerity. "I don't think that your granddaughter would like to hear you talking that way."

"Lily already knows," he said dispassionately. "I told her before I left the cabin, and now I'm telling you. In just a second, I'm going to go walking right over the edge of that stone ledge. It'll be the last *walking* that I ever do. After that, no more Chief Redtail."

"I really don't think that you need to sign out just yet, Chief." Rosa could hear the fear in her own words as her voice betrayed her. "And even if it was your time, I don't think that would be the best way. You wouldn't want Lily to find you washed up somewhere downstream."

Another series of ragged coughs broke out, mingled with muffled laughter. The Chief was left clutching at his chest with one hand while gripping desperately to his walking stick with the other. He steadied himself with several short, but controlled breaths, and then said, "Where I'm going, Lily won't find me. I'll keep my eyes on her though. I'll keep my eyes on you, too. You're going to be needing help, and maybe sometime I'll be able to give it."

Slowly, almost dragging himself over the surface of the stone shelf, the Chief reached Rosa's side. The black antler lay before her, coated in morning dew.

"I don't have many regrets," he whispered, "but seeing you there with that Gift of Nature within your reach, well, I have to admit to one. I'd have liked to have stuck around long enough to see what's going to happen next. I suspect Ramius King and his thugs might be getting their parade rained on once you four get it together a little bit."

"Us four?" Rosa asked, sounding absolutely astonished. "You can't be serious. I assume the *us four* you're referring to would be Michael, who hasn't used his magic since he was a teenager, Kyle, who didn't even know he had magic until last weekend, Lily, who still won't have a Gift of Nature if I take this one, and last and also least, me, with my foresight that so far has been of greater use to Ramius King than to any of us."

"Good Lord!" the Chief exclaimed with a weak laugh. "You sure do spout when you're worked up about something. For your information, that's exactly the four I was talking about." The old man had to pause for a moment then, obviously short of the breath and energy needed to keep speaking. "Four just might be enough," he suggested thoughtfully once he'd recovered somewhat. "The right four people can make a tribe, and that's a powerful thing. King's soldiers will never be a tribe, because they're only loyal out of fear. That limits how strong they can be, no matter how many they are."

"Woohoo! I'm joining a tribe and I didn't even know it," Rosa cheered sarcastically. "Will we dance around the fire to make it legit?"

"Listen here, little girl." The old man's voice was suddenly steady and deadly serious. "The fact of the matter is that you four are going to have to do whatever you can to stop the Tall Man. There's no one else. And whatever you can do isn't going to be enough unless you work together. You're not a tribe yet. You can't be a tribe without a Chief. Or a Chieftess."

"Ya, that'll be the day," Rosa retorted incredulously. "Rosalind Sanchez, Chieftess of the Guardians of Ma ..." The final word stuck in Rosa's throat stubbornly. *Chieftess of the Guardians of Magic.* The words echoed in her mind. Why did they sound familiar? Why did they seem to fit together so easily? It felt like déjà vu, like something she'd forgotten, like something from a dream. From her dreams?

"Ah-ha, there it is," the Chief said, pointing one gnarled old finger at Rosa. He sounded gratified. "I can see it right there in those lovely brown eyes of yours. At least some little part of you already knows. I think you're on the right track. And unless I'm forgetting something, getting you on track was the very last thing I needed to do. I made the big rescue at the Mill, sold the Gift of Nature I'd been watching to just the right buyer, and now finally, recruited the next leader of the Guardians of Magic. Hot damn, I really finished with a flurry, didn't I?" A painful sounding string of coughs followed his spiel, doubling him over once again.

"You don't need to do this, Chief," Rosa suggested hopefully, trying to push everything but the old man's immediate welfare to the back of her mind. It was no small task considering the other topics of conversation. "What you need is a doctor."

"Death isn't something to be afraid of it you're ready for it," he responded, "and I'm beyond ready. I'm overdue."

In the Chief's hoarse voice, Rosa heard conviction and calm, and she knew that there would be no changing his mind. Taking a deep breath, trying to ready herself to witness the old man's passing, Rosa said gravely, "Thank you for rescuing me and Kyle, and thank you for the advice." She wasn't really all that sure that she truly was thankful for the latter, but it certainly wouldn't have been appropriate to say as much under the circumstances.

"I tell you what," the Chief wheezed as he continued dragging himself closer to the ledge, "if you really want to show your gratitude, I would make one final request of you."

"Anything."

"There's this dog, a wolf actually ..."

"Oh, you've got to be kidding me," Rosa whispered under her breath.

"What's that?" the Chief asked, thankfully not quite able to make out Rosa's words. "Anyway, he's been like my best friend, and I'd sure appreciate it if you'd talk with him and keep him company for me."

"Where is he?" Rosa asked, realizing that she'd never seen a dog, or a wolf, since she'd been around the Chief.

"Oh, he's around," the old man offered in response. "He's always around someplace. He mostly keeps to himself anyway. Even catches his own food. I'm sure he won't be any trouble for you at all." The Chief smiled strangely as he spoke, as if enjoying some secret irony that he alone recognized.

As he moved on, the Chief leaned so heavily on his weathered walking stick that it appeared to Rosa that it was supporting more weight that his own two legs. It was hard for her not to run to the man, to throw her arms around his shoulders and help him along, but she knew she couldn't. As he'd said, this was his last walk, and it was one he had to take alone.

About ten feet short of his final destination, the Chief started to chant. His hoarse, choked voice barely reached Rosa's ears at first. His low grumbling began to change almost immediately though, clearing and raising in pitch. As if by magic, the frail, old man's gruff chant became the song of a strong youth, perhaps his own voice from some time long ago. But it didn't stop changing, didn't level out. It kept rising and sharpening until it stretched beyond the range of any man, young or old. It grew, in fact, beyond the range of any person, a shrill and piercing shriek.

Once again, Rosa was struck by a sense of familiarity, but this time she knew why. Just a couple of months earlier, someone had brought an osprey into the veterinarian clinic in Miami during her shift. Its wing had been broken by a glancing blow against the windshield of a minivan. They'd patched it up pretty well before sending it on to a wildlife rehabilitation center, but it had screeched the whole time, and its voice had been unmistakably reminiscent of that which now came impossibly from the old man.

With his toes at the precipice, the Chief straightened himself with difficulty and cast his walking stick over the edge, where it disappeared instantly into the fog. The shrieking died away, returning the scene to eerie stillness.

Then, turning back to face Rosa one last time, the Chief said in a strong, youthful voice, "You're going to need faith to get through what's coming."

"Faith in what?" Rosa asked. "What are you talking about?" She was so surprised by the Chief's comment that her response came weakly, probably too low to be heard over the voice of the river, or so she thought.

"Faith in what people are always talking about when they talk about faith," he answered as if it should have been obvious. "The *big* faith. The faith that I'm counting on to catch me when I fall. You'll be needing it, too. You won't be able to make it through what's coming without faith."

Those were the Chief's last words. He threw his arms out straight as if he might soar away on them as wings, and then he leaned forward and disappeared into the mist.

Just then, the high, piercing raptor voice returned, filling the air with its shrill call. Just a brief moment after the shriek returned, a broad, dark shadow appeared through the mist, rising up from beneath the cliff face. It looked like some sort of wide-winged bird, but it was there and gone again in a second, and Rosa was left feeling unsure of her impressions. She didn't even feel altogether certain that it hadn't merely been the combined effects of her overstressed nerves and overactive imagination.

She was sure of one thing though. She was sure that she'd never heard what should have been an inevitable splash landing. Perhaps the Chief's faith had indeed caught him when he'd fallen. It was a thought that inspired hope, and not just for the Chief's sake.

THE CALL TO ARMS

Edward Charleston York stood alone in a room filled with people. The room was the cafeteria in the Mill, and the people filling the room were the hunters of Ramius King, including Mason Stone, Fat Man and Little Boy, and all the others. Amidst the company of such radically unique versions of humankind, York did indeed feel very alone.

The prim assassin stood off to the side of the room, as still and quiet as he could be, trying not to draw any attention from the magicians. Since his failure in Miami, things had become more difficult for him around the compound. Snide comments and menacing looks made him feel like the guy who'd missed the would-be game winning penalty kick. The Mill was his locker room, and those monsters were his teammates.

Except for Fat Man and a couple others who were likewise ill-suited to the low bench seats, the hunters were seated around the folding dining tables. It was striking, not to mention downright frightening, for York to see them all assembled as such. It was a rare occasion when King brought them all together in one place, particularly a place as confined as the cafeteria. In general, it made for a combustible atmosphere. There were too many individuals among them who thought too highly of themselves to give any consideration to matters such as common courtesy. A room full of men who all think themselves to be godlike to some degree was a dangerous place, and wisely, York was trying to stay out of the way.

Each and every one of those egos was checked immediately though, when the Tall Man entered the room, the Plume of Shu perched atop his high, pale forehead. His presence was announced immediately and wordlessly, a wave of power and peril that none among the hunters could ever mistake or ignore.

King was only a few steps through the door, and already York noted that nearly every conversation across the room had died to silence. Everyone looked tense, filled with anticipation. Such a rare assembly could only be explained by an announcement of rare gravity. Rumors had run rampant through the Mill recently, many involving the possibility of a lone-surviving Guardian, some lost soldier who'd been hidden away for many years, but had now resurfaced. For York, of course, it was much more than just a rumor. Absently, the assassin's hand went to his scar, scratching at an itch that had plagued him perpetually for fifteen years.

There was other talk as well, whispers about some ultimate design of the Tall Man's that was nearly ready to unfold. Some even hinted at the possibility of King breaking the code, showing himself to the world as he really was, revealing his powers in public. The ramifications of such an action were mind-numbing. People everywhere would be wrenched away from the comfort of their epidemic naiveté, and King and his minions would be finally freed from the shadows that had kept them hidden from view for so long. Although he didn't know for certain, York strongly suspected that this, too, was more than foolish gossip. The Guardians were gone and the Tall Man's pet doctor was engineering magicians. Because of these two things alone, the world was a very different place than it had been a year before. The impact hadn't been broadly felt yet, but that might well change, and soon.

As King moved into position, Mason Stone rose stiffly from the table where he'd been seated and strode in his ever deliberate manner to the front of the room to join his master, positioning himself meaningfully at the Tall Man's right.

"Silence!" King boomed over the assemblage, his voice laced with the power of his magic. It was a needless command. No one was going to be distracted from the forthcoming address, whatever it consisted of.

York felt his throat go dry as the silence in the room grew deep. There was a sense of loose energy all around him, standing the hairs of his forearms on end. He stood out from the wall and resisted the urge to shuffle his feet. Stillness, it seemed, was safest.

"My loyal soldiers," King began, his voice carrying easily across the room, "our enemies are destroyed. Their former strength has become our renewed strength. Our time of slinking in the shadows of lesser beings is over. Our time to rule has come. As of this day, the stealth and subterfuge upon which we've so heavily depended in the past will no longer be necessary."

York bit his lower lip, considering the possible implications of the Tall Man's words. Stealth and subterfuge were his fortes, the things that made him useful. He remembered all too well how King had chosen to deal with the fortune teller once he'd perceived her usefulness to be expired.

"Each of you is my servant, and so it will remain, but now each of you will become a master as well. I will place you upon thrones in every major nation on earth and you will lord over numbers beyond counting."

A ripple of subtle movement passed through the assembled hunters. York supposed that each of them was imagining themselves perched atop a golden chair, deciding the fates of their subjects at a whim. They would grant life and permit death casually to the *normal* people they ruled. People like him.

"By sunset tonight, this town will belong to us. Six months from now our domain will include the entirety of North America, and in a year every single person on the face of this planet will owe allegiance to one of my governors and in turn, to me."

Now the silence of the room was perfect. Even the undercurrents of breathing and fidgeting were gone. Everyone was utterly stunned.

"I read doubt in your eyes," King accused, "but what I say is true. The armies of this world have no weapons with which to threaten me. Only the Guardians have hindered my ascension up to now, and a lack of talented soldiers. The Guardians are gone, and talent has now become something that I can bestow upon whomever I choose. Behold, your comrades." King threw out one long arm dramatically, and a thin, cool smile spread across his face.

The door through which King had entered flew open again, and in strode Dr. Simpson's first generation of engineered magicians. They marched in perfect mechanistic unison. Their eyes were glassy, but their expressions were intense, and the power that radiated out from them was evident even to Edward Charleston York.

On and on they came until their ranks created a complete perimeter around the room, their numbers equaling seven times that of the assembled hunters. Other than the slave laborers that assisted Simpson, only the doctor himself, Mason Stone, and Ramius King had known the actual number of subjects involved in the Mill's experiments. They were the only three men in the cafeteria whose faces did not reflect shock.

"As each of you have served as soldiers to my first general," King continued, gesturing toward the statue-like Mason Stone at his side, "now these men will serve you."

York saw a wave of anxious shivers run through the assemblage of hunters. Soon, their ambitions for power would be fulfilled and their hunger for violence would be sated. York felt a chill as well, but one of a very different sort. A sickening feeling was churning in his stomach as he listened to the Tall Man's propaganda, a feeling that in these new plans, there might be no role for him to play.

"As soon as we're finished here, we'll begin gathering up the people of Steel City," King went on. "I've *borrowed* a news anchor from a major television network, and tonight he will commentate for a video that I will then distribute—globally. It will demonstrate the fate of any people who refuse to submit to my rule. It will mark the end of one era and the beginning of another. It will be the beginning of the next chapter in the history of human civilization."

King's last words were almost completely lost in a roar of cheers and growls that echoed wildly throughout the cafeteria. Edward Charleston York stood in silence with his back pressed flat against the wall, wishing that he could melt right into the concrete blocks and disappear from view. The void that separated him from the Tall Man's hunters was suddenly blatant and broad. What these men were about to do was nothing at all like what he did. There wasn't going to be any professionalism or tact involved in the hunters' slaughter of Steel City's populous, no restraint nor discrimination. They would be like foxes in a chicken coop, killing beyond the needs of their hunger, unable to stop until every prey within reach lay dead.

A strange thought occurred to York. It was strange because it was new, because he hadn't thought it before. The separation between the hunters and himself was magic, but as King had just said, that was a talent that could now be acquired. That secret power that had always been an exclusive gift of birthright was now up for grabs. There would be no limit to his deadliness if magic was added to his repertoire of assassin's skills.

Just then, Dr. Simpson's engineered magicians began filing back out of the cafeteria, a steady line passing mere feet in front of where York stood. He studied the men's faces intently, scrutinizing their eyes and their expressions. Another person standing in his place might have mistaken the blank faces of the men as stoic soldiering, but York knew better. What he was seeing wasn't concentration, but a lack of concentration. The men were drugged, walking in a stupor where all they knew was what they were told. They were out of it enough to be freed from their doubts, but they weren't too out of it to follow orders. They were powerful slaves, but slaves nonetheless. They'd been given a great gift, but they'd paid for it with their wills. That, York decided, was much too high a price for him.

THE STEEL CITY
ROUNDUP

The last person that Rosalind Sanchez thought of, just before she reached her hand toward the longest tine of the antler, was Sean Galladin, the Guardian turned Guardian Hunter, the young man who'd been made into a monster. Was it possible that the power of the Gift could turn her into a monster of sorts as well? Rosa's mental well-being had been driven to the breaking point in the past by the strain of her premonitions. What if those visions now invaded her waking mind as well? Or if they encompassed a much wider range, a state or country full of suffering people instead of a few city blocks? How could she possibly handle that sort of relentless psychological assault? What would become of her if she couldn't?

All that kept Rosa's hand moving unsteadily toward the talisman was the knowledge that she had no choice. Too much was at stake. Too many people were counting on her. Michael was counting on her. She couldn't back out.

With the tip of her index finger, Rosa touched the tip of the antler's longest tine. For a moment, nothing happened. She felt a rush of disappointment, and a tinge of relief as well, but both were short-lived. It began as washes of color against the curtain of fog that surrounded her, appearing magically before her eyes. Dim bits of green and red slowly grew toward vividness and eventually focused into rough shapes. Here and there, small hints of movement flickered. The vague hues and silhouettes were mysterious, impossible to make any sense of. She strained, peering into the earthbound cloud as if what she struggled to see were hidden merely by mist rather than by time and space. Without her willing them to do so, Rosa's fingers closed tightly about the black bone.

An explosion of light momentarily forced Rosa's eyes down to squints. A bit of green became a street sign and a bit of red became a car parked in the distance. A vague boxy shape turned into a building, a restaurant, and the subtle movements within its borders became people shuffling around behind a wide window. Or rather, being ushered around.

The perimeter of the superimposed scene expanded out in all directions. More buildings and people and cars and trees were added as if painted onto the fog by the quick hand of an invisible artist.

It seemed to Rosa that the fog persisted even in her vision, that it filled not only the forest that actually surrounded her, but also the streets that were conjured within her mind. She saw people being huddled together in a large group at the center of the intersection of those streets. They looked scared. More and more were being herded into the group by several huge, hideous figures that seemed almost caricatures of real people. All except one, that is. One of the herders was tiny, just the size of a child.

And then everything clicked. In a flash of insight, Rosa recognized exactly what she was seeing. The place being revealed in her daydream was Steel City, and that tiny person herding people together was the same man who'd delivered her to Ramius King, the one Michael had called Little Boy.

One last bit of understanding dawned on Rosa just before she grabbed up her Gift of Nature and tore back into the forest. What were the odds that she'd seen a glimpse into the future of Steel City when the fog was just as extraordinarily thick as it was right then? Not nearly as good as the odds that it wasn't the future she'd seen, but the present.

By the time Rosa reached the cabin, she was so out of breath that she could barely speak. Kyle couldn't understand a word of what she was trying to say, but he did recognize the panic in her voice, the same voice he'd heard stay cool under the gravest of circumstances. Something, he knew, must be very, very wrong.

For whatever reason, Michael was able to understand Rosa more easily, catching the gist of her explanation right away, and then hurrying everyone out the door of the cabin and leading them hastily through the forest to the Monte Carlo.

It was a quick and quiet ride into town. Michael drove and Rosa joined him in the front seat, while Kyle, Lily, and Black Dog crowded together in the back.

Awakened from his midmorning nap by Rosa's boisterous arrival back at the cabin, the tired-eyed, old hound dog seemed adamant about accompanying the group to wherever they were headed. Rosa tried twice to make him stay behind, but gave in after that, knowing that they couldn't afford to waste time. He'd struggled to keep up as they'd hurried to the car on foot, and by the time they'd driven back out to the main road he was asleep again, sprawled across Kyle's and Lily's laps in the back seat.

At Rosa's suggestion, they parked the car a little ways down a dirt side road about a quarter mile outside of town and walked through the woods from there. That way, she reasoned, they could keep hidden while they did their reconnaissance. If things really were as they had appeared to her, then they needed to be as cautious as they could be.

From the edge of the woods behind The Bar, the scene looked just as it had in her vision, except that things had obviously progressed since then. The group of people who'd been rounded up totaled something like three dozen. A ring comprised mostly of grown men, but also several women, surrounded the group, keeping the young and the elderly behind them like zebras fending off a lion. However, even the stoutest among them was sadly frail compared to a zebra, and their adversaries were far deadlier than lions.

Several of King's surviving hunters stood guard around the congregated townsfolk. They were towering beasts of men, tarnished and twisted by the magic that empowered and poisoned them. Their strength wasn't going to be tested by any of the captives no matter how desperate they became. With such imposing guards, fear alone would keep things in order.

Just then, the sound of an approaching car drew everyone's attention, including all the captives as well as their captors. The posture of the guards became rigid in an instant.

"It's him," Rosa whispered. "It's Ramius King."

The Tall Man strode down the center of Main Street in a stately manner, exuding the smug pride of nobility. He wore his usual ensemble of black on black, but a matching cape, long and trailing, had also been added for effect. Behind him and a step to his right walked Mason Stone, and a few steps ahead walked a defeated looking young man that Kyle recognized as his escort from the Mill. The lab-tech had apparently drawn a different duty for the day. He scattered ashes from a wooden box before King's feet, a grim substitute for a red carpet.

"What do you think those ashes are from?" Lily asked tentatively.

"What or who?" Rosa answered.

Kyle flinched in spite of himself. He couldn't help thinking that the car had come from the direction of the firehouse.

King proceeded to the assembly of townsfolk, and there he stopped, appearing to inspect the area. He pointed here and there, issuing commands that could be heard but not understood from where Michael, Rosa, and the kids crouched, hidden behind The Bar. He seemed to be organizing, figuring out the last minute details before ... something.

"We've got to get those people out of there," Michael whispered urgently.

"I don't see how we can now that King's here," Kyle argued, his stare never shifting from the Tall Man. "We might stand a better chance against all the others without him than against him alone. With them and him here, we don't have any chance at all."

"He's not arranging a spelling bee out there," Michael pressed. "Those people are going to die if we leave them. I won't leave them." Slowly, his hand moved to the black bag hanging at his side.

In unison, Kyle, Lily, and Rosa looked at Michael, each judging for themself the quality of his oath and fearing what might happen if the lost Guardian refused to accept the apparent inevitability of their circumstances. They all saw the same thing. As always, Michael's intention was absolute. He would do what he felt he was obligated to do, even if the odds of his succeeding were slim to none.

"Wait!" Rosa hissed, grabbing two hand fulls of Michael's shirt just as he started to move out from his hiding place. "For me, Redbeard, just wait one second. Let me think."

Rosa's mind raced with desperation. If she couldn't come up with a way to convince Michael to hold back, then this would be their last parting. If he tried to save those people right then, it would be the anticlimactic finale of his do-gooding career.

Michael pulled Rosa close against him and whispered in her ear so only she could hear, saying, "You know I can't walk away from this. I'm already carrying all the regret that I can bear. I couldn't live with the ghosts of all those people, too. You know I couldn't."

Rosa couldn't think of anything to say or do. She felt helpless. Michael started to pull away, but then froze.

"What is it?" Rosa asked under her breath.

Michael closed his eyes and tilted his head slightly, apparently straining to hear some faint sound. "Someone's coming."

The four of them all spun around together, and just in time to see a figure walking through the woods in their direction. Whoever it was, they seemed to be moving casually, without hurry or stealth. Even though the person was headed straight for them, no one made any effort to abandon their hiding place. If they tried to move out of the approaching person's path, they'd risk revealing their position to King and his hunters.

"Mr. Ulrich?" Lily said uncertainly, popping up out of her hiding place as the approaching figure drew to within thirty feet.

Immediately the man stopped, and his face showed surprise and then delight.

"Lily? My God, is that really you?" The man hurried forward, throwing his arms around Lily like a serviceman seeing his daughter for the first time after a long overseas tour. "We've been so worried. I've been out walking the woods every day since you've been missing. Everybody has. Where have you been? Is your Dad okay? What about Charlie? Have you seen Charlie Wright and his dog? Who are these people? Are they ..."

Michael grabbed Aaron Ulrich, the owner of the Country Kitchen Restaurant, by his shoulders and thrust him down beneath the cover of the tall weeds. Lily ducked back down as well, remembering the precariousness of their circumstances.

"We need to keep quiet, Mr. Ulrich," Lily whispered.

Ulrich followed the others' gazes in toward the center of town. The first person he saw was Fat Man. The behemoth was carrying a woman out through the entrance of the Country Kitchen. He held her tucked under one of his enormous arms as another person might carry a bunch of laundry or a duffel bag.

"Laura!" he gasped, fighting uselessly against Michael's iron grip, which had caught him quickly about the upper arms. His voice was suddenly less hushed. "You have to let me go," he pleaded, sounding frantic. "That's my wife!"

Michael struggled to restrain Ulrich, Ulrich struggled to get free, and Lily and Kyle struggled just to keep their cool under the mounting tension of the situation. Rosa, however, was still struggling with the same problem she'd been struggling with before the restaurant owner had arrived. How could she stop Michael from marching into battle against Ramius King and all his hunters, a battle that couldn't possibly be won? And then, in a flash of inspiration, it came to her.

"Be quiet and listen to me," Rosa ordered. Although she still spoke softly, her tone was changed, full of new authority, and she won the immediate attention of both Michael and Ulrich. "I know what to do. Look, Redbeard, we can't keep this man from his wife, even if going to her puts him in danger. Forcing him to stay here only threatens to give away our position and endanger us all."

Rosa hesitated for a moment, allowing doubt to threaten the integrity of the idea that had struck her as perfect a moment earlier. All of a sudden, it seemed like a shaky plan at best.

"Come on, Mr. Ulrich," she urged the restaurant owner forward slightly, moving them several feet ahead of the others. "I'm going to let you go to your wife, but the truth is that you aren't going to be able to protect her from those men. Truthfully, that man behind us is probably the only one who can, but he'll need help to do it–your help."

Ulrich looked uncertain, but said, "If it keeps my wife safe, then I'll do it. Anything."

While Michael, Kyle, and Lily looked on in confusion, Rosa leaned in close to Ulrich, whispering in his ear so that her words would stay private. After a moment, the restaurant owner nodded, a gesture of understanding, and then moved out into the open. He hesitated once about half way to his destination, perhaps catching his first clear glimpse of the disfigured creatures who were standing guard around the assembled captives.

"I have a message for Ramius King," Ulrich shouted from where he stood at the edge of Main Street, "from the last of the Guardians of Magic."

One of King's hunters rushed out to Ulrich, and then drug him back to the center of the intersection where the Tall Man stood waiting.

"What the hell was that all about?" Michael asked, his voice full of accusation. "You sent a message to King? From me?"

"No, not from you," Rosa corrected, unable to meet Michael's stare as she spoke. "I sent him a message from a last remaining group of Guardians, a few who were away when the firehouse was attacked. I gave Mr. Ulrich directions to the old hunting cabin and told him to tell King that the last Guardians would be waiting for him there, and that they were ready to discuss terms of surrender. I made it up hoping that we might be able to lure King away. If he left, then you might have a real chance of helping those people."

At first, Michael couldn't even respond. He just stared at Rosa in disbelief, trying to decide if he'd heard her correctly, if she was being serious.

"King will never believe that, Rosa. The odds of him being taken in by that sort of deception are one in a million, and even if he did buy it, he'd never go himself to deal with it. He'd probably send Fat Man and Little Boy. I can't believe you did that without even discussing it with me first. Who put you in charge?"

"I put myself in charge, Redbeard," Rosa snapped back, sounding defensive. "You keep insisting that you're not a Guardian anymore. I assumed you didn't want to be in charge, but somebody needs to be. I don't need you to approve my ideas." Rosa paused, took a deep breath, and lowered her voice back down to a safer level. "Mr. Ulrich was going to go anyway, so it didn't hurt anything to try."

"It didn't gain anything either," Michael added, "because King would never fall for …"

"Look," Kyle interrupted, "he's leaving."

Astonishingly, Kyle was right. Ramius King had been standing face to face with Aaron Ulrich just a moment before, but now he was moving hastily away, barking orders to his hunters and urging the lab-tech to keep pace ahead of him with the ashes. A few seconds later, a black Lincoln sped past along Riverside Road.

"I don't believe it," Michael whispered, sounding genuinely astonished.

Rosa smiled broadly, clearly pleased with herself and anxious to let it show. She said, "See, Redbeard, I know what I'm doing. Now give me the car keys."

"Where are you going?" Michael asked, digging the keys for the Monte Carlo out of his pocket.

"I'm taking these kids somewhere safe," she answered as if it should have been obvious. "You don't want them here when the shit hits the fan, do you?"

"Of course not," Michael agreed quickly. His voice sounded uncertain though, and his eyes were full of suspicion.

"As soon as I get them somewhere safe, I'll come right back," Rosa assured. "Don't do anything while I'm gone unless you absolutely have to."

And with that, Rosa turned and led the kids quietly back into the forest.

"I can't believer we're just going to leave him there all by himself," Lily said once they were well into the woods and safely out of view.

"We're not," corrected Kyle, looking not to Lily, but to Rosa. "At least I don't think we are. At least not for the reason you think."

Rosa smiled, glad that Michael wasn't as shrewd as Kyle.

A Necessary Deception

Aaron Ulrich was no more than thirty feet from the group of captives when his wife spotted him. He gave her a hard look that said to stay quiet, and immediately there were tears streaming down her face. He looked away quickly, fully aware that his own composure was near to failing.

Ulrich's brutish escort led him to a tall, black-clad man, clearly the one in charge.

"I am Ramius King," the Tall Man said in a voice so powerful that it crushed Ulrich's courage. "You have a message for me?"

For a moment, the restaurant owner couldn't remember what it was he was supposed to say. All he could think about was King's voice. It wasn't just strong, it was electric, powered by something more than breath and vocal chords.

"I have a message from Michael Galladin," Ulrich managed.

"And that message is?" King prompted, his grim face showing disgust in response to Ulrich's cowering.

"He says ..." Ulrich swallowed hard, suddenly suspicious that the Tall Man might not believe in *don't shoot the messenger*. "He says that if you're truly worthy to rule, then you'll meet him man to man and prove it. I have directions to where he's waiting."

King said nothing at first, showed no reaction whatsoever for several long seconds. Then, very slowly, his top lip pulled up into a dangerous sneer.

"I could take care of Michael," suggested a shortish, gray-skinned man who stood several steps behind King. "I would embrace the challenge."

"No, Mason, that wouldn't do at all. I'll not begin my reign by refusing a challenge from my last able enemy. I will go and take care of the Guardians' prodigal son myself."

"Shall we delay the demonstration?" asked the smaller man through a lipless mouth that barely moved as he spoke.

"No. I'll not be delayed any longer. Not another day. Not an hour. Carry out the demonstration while the sun's high and there's at least some visibility through this accursed fog. If I'm not back in time, do it without me, but make sure the camera is running. I want the tape duplicated and ready for distribution by morning."

"Yes, sir," Mason acknowledged as his master spun around and strode away. "It'll be done."

After Aaron Ulrich relayed the directions that Rosa had given him, he was added to the group of captives where he quickly found his wife. She was shaking with fear. He tried to reassure her, but his voice failed in the effort.

"So King thinks that he's headed off to a showdown with Michael?" Lily asked. "And what you told Michael was a lie?"

"Yep, that's pretty much it," Rosa agreed. "I bought some time, I hope. How much time will depend on you two."

Both Lily and Kyle swallowed hard, suddenly afraid of what part of the plan they were meant to play.

Kyle gritted his teeth, grabbed Lily's hand, and asked, "What do you need us to do?"

Rosa bit her lip, hesitating before answering. Doubt was washing over her again. Was she really going to send these kids on such an incredibly dangerous chore? It was appalling to do so, but she had to think of the big picture, the greater good.

"If King shows up at the hunting cabin and nobody's home, he'll be back in Steel City within a half an hour," Rosa began, hating the fear that she read in Kyle's and Lily's eyes. She hoped that her own eyes looked more confident than theirs, or at least more confident than she felt. "If he shows up and senses the presence of someone with magic nearby, then he probably won't leave right away. If you guys were just in the area, not close enough for him to see you, but close enough for him to sense you ..."

"Then he'd think Michael was there somewhere," Kyle finished the thought for her, "and he'd take time to look around. We'd be bait to keep him occupied for a while."

Kyle's choice of words made Rosa shiver, made her accept fully the hard truth of what she was asking them to do. She bit her lip again, and said, "That's right. The longer King is away from town, the better the odds are that Michael will find a way to free those people."

"Then we'll do it," Lily said boldly, squeezing Kyle's hand hard.

Kyle nodded in agreement.

"We need to get going," Rosa added, continuing on in the direction of the car. Lily and Kyle followed at her heels. "It'll take King a while to find the cabin by the directions I sent him. We'll be able to beat him there, but I don't know by how long. Once we get there, you two will need to find a good hiding place a safe distance away from the cabin, and you'll need to know where you're going to retreat to if he starts moving in your direction. I don't want you taking any chances. Keep plenty of distance between yourselves and him. Kyle, I don't have to tell you what would happen if you got caught."

Lily looked over to Kyle and saw reflected in his eyes the shadow of what he'd endured at the Mill. Had her father suffered likewise? She pushed the thought away quickly, knowing that she couldn't allow her fear for him to take hold of her again. She needed to be strong.

Black Dog was waiting for them in the car, his wet nose smearing streaks across the back window. He seemed as alert as his droopy features were capable of seeming.

"Don't worry, boy," Lily said, scratching the old hound dog behind the ear as she and Kyle climbed into the back seat, "Rosa will keep you safe."

Rosa cringed at Lily's words as she started up the car, unsure that she was deserving of such confidence.

As soon as Rosa and the kids were out of sight, Michael moved to a patch of soft-looking green moss sparkling with dew drops and settled into a meditation pose. The seat of his pants was damp almost immediately, but he didn't mind. He hardly even noticed.

From his place of concealment, Michael watched as a man stepped out from the group of captives at the intersection. He was pretty tall, but the features beneath his scraggly blonde beard were those of a young man. Probably just a high school kid, Michael thought. Probably skipping school, and that's why he was in town when King's hunters started rounding people up. Bad choice on his part, or at least bad timing.

Michael could hear the young man's voice rise, full of panic, but couldn't quite make out his words. His head swung back and forth, his eyes searching, looking for a direction to run. He never got the chance to try.

From a distance of some twenty feet, one of King's hunters who'd been assigned to guard duty lunged forward. He was on the young man so quickly that the motion was nearly blurred from vision. He wrapped one oversized hand around the young man's throat and hoisted him into the air as if he weighed next to nothing.

Even in sight of such violence, Michael didn't so much as twitch. He had slipped into the mode of perfect calm that was his preparation for dangerous tasks. Right then wasn't the time to move, and so he wouldn't. Not yet. He wouldn't allow an emotional response to prompt him into an ill-advised course of action. He'd only get one chance to help those people, and if he moved too soon or hesitated too long, then he'd be sealing their fate. He had to stay ready, but be patient.

He closed his eyes, but only saw a new set of dangers projected against the back of his eyelids. He supposed that he was glad that Rosa had volunteered to remove the kids to a safe distance, but something about it felt odd. He would be better off not having to worry about them once things got ugly, he supposed, but in truth they might have been able to help. Or if not both of them, then maybe just Kyle. Lily was the one who'd known about her magic the longest, but the fact that Kyle held a Gift of Nature and that he'd endured his time as Ramius King's captive made him the more likely of the two to be of use in a tight spot. It was surprising that Rosa hadn't thought the same.

Or had she?

Michael's eyes snapped back open. He'd thought it impossible that King would fall for the story that Rosa had offered, and it probably was. Whatever message she'd really sent, it surely wasn't the one he'd heard.

Aaron Ulrich had said that his message was from the last of the Guardians. Rosa had told Michael that it had been a reference to a fictitious group of survivors from Grandma Jo's ranks, but maybe his first thought had indeed been the right one. Rosa had probably sent a message from him, probably a challenge. That was just about the only thing that could have tempted the Tall Man away.

Michael cursed under his breath, doubly angered for being lied to and for having a challenge issued in his name, one that he couldn't keep. And of course, that's exactly why Rosa had lied to him. She'd known that he would never abandon the townsfolk, and she'd guessed, apparently correctly, that a duel with his last worthy challenger was the one thing that might draw King away. She'd done precisely what she'd needed to do to get the Tall Man to leave, but keep Michael where he was.

Michael smiled thinly, pushing his initial anger quickly aside. What a clever girl she was.

THREE STAGES SET

Rosa watched the kids hurrying away from the car hand in hand. Brave wasn't a strong enough word to describe them, she decided. She'd asked them to play hide-and-seek with the most dangerous man on the planet, and they'd agreed because they'd believed it was the right thing to do. It was a display of poise and principle that couldn't have been expected from most distinguished elders. Finding it in a pair of adolescents was a marvel.

After she started the car, purely out of habit, Rosa pulled down the visor and checked her reflection in the mirror. She looked like she hadn't had a shower in a while. *Imagine that.* She was completely without makeup, her hair was a mess, and the bags under her eyes looked like they belonged on the face of an eighty-year-old drug addict with insomnia. She looked dirty and tired and … tough.

The corners of Rosa's mouth pulled up into a sly half-smile. There was a part of her that liked what she saw in the mirror. She'd spent such a long time being afraid, waiting for her next visit from the Tall Man. Even when her talent allowed her to make a difference for people in need, she was always at the sidelines, making a call and then watching someone else do the real work. The woman staring back from the mirror didn't look like the type to pass the buck. She looked tough enough to kick some ass on her own. Whether it was true or not, she'd soon find out.

Knowing that there wasn't any time to waste, Rosa threw the visor back up into place and shifted the car into drive. Next stop: the Mill.

As soon as Lily and Kyle caught sight of the cabin, they started looking for the right spot to make their hiding place. The directions that King was following would undoubtedly delay him somewhat, but if he arrived earlier than they expected and found them wandering around, they'd be out of the plane without a chute. Knowing that time might be short, they settled into the first suitable place they found. It wasn't perfect, but it was pretty good, and it was certainly better than being caught out in the open when the Tall Man arrived.

The spot they picked was underneath the sagging branches of a Weeping Willow. The tree's dangling tendrils would hide them, but not so completely that they couldn't see out a little. The area directly between the tree and the cabin was also on the marshy side, half covered with ankle deep water and waist-high reeds. If King did manage to spot them somehow, or guess the direction in which they were hidden, then it would take significant time for him to traverse the little wetland.

Hopefully, Kyle thought, they wouldn't have to test that very big *if.* Hopefully they were close enough to the cabin for the Tall Man to sense their proximity, but not so close that he could get a bead on their location. All they wanted to do, after all, was give him cause for delay. Rosa had been adamant that the object of this ploy was just to buy a little time, nothing more.

Lily shivered as she shifted her seat on the hard ground, searching for a position that would be comfortable enough to keep still in. Indeed, Kyle realized, noticing her reaction, the air temperature had started to fall. He perceived the change, but was hardly bothered by it. He felt like he'd have been alright even if he'd been sitting in a tub of ice water–just as long as he had the Rune Tree in hand.

Kyle gently slid his open palm along the smooth surface of his newly claimed Gift of Nature, gratified by the energy he felt slipping back and forth between the talisman and himself. He thought about setting the staff aside for a moment. He hadn't since he'd awakened it the previous night. He should know, he decided, what to expect when he finally did let it go. However, when he ordered his hand away, it didn't respond.

A cool chill ran down Kyle's back as a series of painful memories flashed through his mind. Could something like what happened in the Mill ever happen again? Was the Rune Tree inherently different from the reptilian talisman King had provided him with? If not, then could he really expect to control it any better? Or might it control him? Might it already be controlling him?

Again, Kyle willed his hand away from the Gift, and again it refused.

"You look scared," Lily said softly, distracting Kyle from his fretting.

"But you don't," he replied, surprised to see a whisper of a smile on her face. "How come?"

"I was just thinking about the first time I saw you. You were toe-to-toe with Brent Dickers, ready to duke it out in defense of someone you barely even knew."

Kyle smiled as well, remembering the incident in the hallway of Steel City High School. He could count the days that had passed since then on his fingers, and yet it seemed like a long time ago.

"I bet Brent wouldn't be so anxious to tangle with you now," Lily suggested.

Kyle wasn't quite sure what she meant by that, and he asked, "Because of what happened to him?"

"No, I mean because of what's happened to you. Before the Mill, someone could have taken you for just any average guy, but not now. Something's changed in you. I can see little signs of it in how you stand and how you talk. Sometimes when someone is forced to endure something terrible, they're never quite the same person again that they were before."

Kyle thought about that for a moment. Of course he was different since his imprisonment at the Mill and his *lessons* with Ramius King. That was obvious to him, but he hadn't really stopped to consider the possibility that those differences weren't only internal.

"And then again when you came back to the cabin with that staff," Lily continued, "there was a feeling around you sort of like how it is with Michael. Not exactly like that, but sort of. I don't think anyone could miss it, including Brent Dickers. I doubt he could even look you steady in the eyes now."

It sounded like a compliment, the girl of his dreams telling him he'd become a bona-fide tough guy, and yet Kyle didn't feel all that good about it. What he felt was that old, familiar sense of purpose, of a destiny either great or terrible that couldn't be escaped. Correction, hadn't been escaped. Every instinct told him that was the case. The critical fate he'd always sensed up around the bend, the moment he'd been waiting for all his life, had finally arrived.

"*Please* shut up," Rosa urged, poking her head back into the car for the third time. She'd parked down another of the two-track lanes that cut periodically into the woods just as Michael had earlier. She was only a little ways down from the Mill, maybe a few hundred yards. She intended on walking the rest of the way through the cover of the trees and trying to find a way to sneak in unnoticed. Even though King's hunters were all miles away in town, the place wouldn't be completely abandoned, she knew, and it wouldn't take a superhuman magician to stop her. Any average jerk standing guard might be enough.

But she couldn't fail. She couldn't! She'd left Michael and the kids in terribly dangerous positions, but truth be told, the task she'd assigned to herself might prove the most crucial. The man she was after possessed the potential to loose unprecedented evil upon humankind. Ramius King was the one who wanted to rule the world, but the secret to his plans depended heavily on someone else. Fortunately, that someone else just happened to be the one whom Rosa was uniquely prepared to confront.

"Why can't you pipe down? Not a single peep since you were willed to me, and now, when I need you to be quiet, you finally find your voice."

Black Dog continued to bark, apparently not understanding or not concerned with his new master's pleas.

Rosa threw her head back in frustration. The fog was starting to thin, but still hindered sight enough to keep the car hidden unless someone happened by pretty close, but that wasn't going to matter if the hound dog in the back seat was barking his head off. Anyone within earshot would be able to follow the sound straight to the Monte Carlo.

"Fine," Rosa gave in at last, moving aside and letting the dog out, "you can come with me if you're going to be so bullheaded about it. I warned you that it was a bad idea though. Remember that."

Black Dog calmly licked the finger that Rosa had pointed at him, not looking worried in the least.

A new and disturbing question formed in Michael's mind as he continued his silent vigil from the wooded outskirts of Steel City. If Rosa had tricked King into leaving and himself into staying, then where had she gone with the kids? Surely, she wasn't tucking them away somewhere safe as she'd claimed. She wouldn't try to confront King herself, he was certain of that. She of all people knew better. So where had she gone?

Something about the group of captives caught Michael's attention just then, distracting him from his contemplation. A majority of the group had clumped together into small, tight clusters. At first, Michael thought that it was fear that prompted them to huddle together, but as he watched more closely he realized that wasn't the case.

One of King's hunters who'd taken a walk down Riverside Road just a few minutes earlier was returning with two additional prisoners squirming in his grip. He added the pair, an elderly couple, into the group, and then turned and headed back in the direction from which he'd come, presumably to continue on with his collecting. As the man shuffled down the center of the street, he rubbed the back of his muscular forearms, first one and then the other. Michael took a long, deep breath, and when he let it out, it turned into steam as soon as it passed between his lips.

Lost in his meditation, Michael hadn't even noticed until right then, but as the fog had finally begun to thin, the temperature had plummeted, perhaps by as much as twenty degrees in as many minutes. Looking up, he saw ominous dark clouds pushing in high from the west. As if on cue, the wind picked up just then, sending the leaves and branches of the trees that surrounded him into motion.

The noon hour was barely gone, and yet the air had the feel of evening already, prematurely dark and cool. Foul weather was almost certainly on the way. It was a fitting backdrop, Michael supposed, for what was to come.

A sickening feeling of inevitability washed over him as he began to tug at the shock of red hair that hung from his chin. There wasn't going to be a right moment to try and rescue the captives. There wasn't going to be any opportunity to sneak them away in secret. There wasn't going to be any reasoning with their captors, and there wasn't going to be any help on the way. There was going to be a fight, the fight of his life.

As Lily pulled her arms inside her shirt, Kyle wrapped his own arms around her narrow shoulders. It was a clumsy motion on account of the fact that Kyle still seemed incapable of setting aside the staff, even for a little while. The temperature was dropping fast, and although the fog had finally dissipated for the most part, the sky was darkening and a breeze was picking up. Aside from the swishing of the willow's swaying tendrils, all was quiet.

"I haven't seen a single animal or bird since we got here," Kyle commented, brushing away a few loose strands of Lily's corn silk hair that had blown across his face.

"I remember my father telling me that animals can tell when a bad storm's coming," Lily commented. "He said they know when it's the right time to hide. It must be the right time."

Kyle nodded, thinking to himself that Lily was probably right about the approaching storm. The animals, he thought, were probably right, too. Considering who was on the way, under cover was certainly the place to be.

"I bet that my grandfather could have taught me all sorts of stuff about nature if we could have …"

Lily's voice trailed off, leaving her thought unfinished. Something had distracted her, a sense of alarm that couldn't be mistaken for anything but what it was. She looked fearfully back toward the cabin.

"Here we go," Kyle whispered in her ear.

The same young man who'd preceded King in town stepped into view near the front of the cabin, spreading a fresh carpet of ashes as he shuffled along. The Tall Man was just several steps behind.

Kyle and Lily looked at one another with expressions of extreme apprehension. King looked like a black-clad giant standing in front of the tiny cabin, and his presence was oppressive even at that distance. Their plan, having appeared reasonable enough only moments before, suddenly seemed foolish.

The Tall Man stood as still as one of the towering trees that surrounded him, not bothering to knock at the cabin door or peek inside. He threw his head back after a moment, pointing his long, crooked nose to the sky like a predator searching for the scent of his next meal.

"Who is that out there?" King called loudly, scanning the forest around him. "Surely not Michael Galladin. If you thought I might confuse you, whoever you are, for the long, lost Guardian, then you were gravely mistaken. If you think that you're hiding at a safe distance from me now, then you're mistaken again."

Kyle and Lily shuddered simultaneously. They had underestimated Ramius King. To call it a dangerous error in judgment would be a colossal understatement, and they both knew it.

"Come out, come out, wherever you are," the Tall Man taunted as he started away from the cabin in their direction.

Rosa looked down at Black Dog and found him staring up at her. Somehow, she imagined that his expression was one of expectancy.

"Quit looking at me like that," she snapped. "We'll go in just a second. This is nothing to rush into." Rosa cringed in response to her own excuse. Actually, this was exactly the time for rushing ahead, she knew. They needed to hurry.

Despite her efforts to convince Black Dog to stay at the car, and despite the fact that he wasn't much of a protector, Rosa found herself reluctantly glad for the company. The old hound's eyes couldn't see much beyond thirty feet, and his stiff legs couldn't move fast enough to chase down anything faster than a lame turtle, but he was there, and when it came right down to it that was all he needed to be. She wasn't alone.

They stood near the edge of the grounds that surrounded the Mill, still hidden within the first layer of the forest. Several acres of mowed lawn surrounded the facility, and as far as Rosa could see there was no way to avoid crossing over it, and thus, revealing herself plainly for anyone who might happen to be keeping watch.

Black Dog nudged Rosa's leg with his wet nose, whimpering softly, urging her ahead.

"All right, boy," she agreed finally, "let's go for it."

They moved out of the woods together into the open, walking as fast as Black Dog could manage and as slow as Rosa could stand. There was a door straight ahead of them with large windows to either side. Michael probably would have just smashed the door off its hinges, but that wasn't an option for her. Maybe it would be unlocked, but probably not. If it was locked, then she supposed she'd have to break a window. Or knock. Neither option was very sneaky.

It was a decision that Rosa never had to make, because just as she was nearing the door, it opened, and out stepped Edward Charleston York.

A KILLER MEAL

Judging from the look that spread across Edward Charleston York's smooth, aristocratic features, he was at least as surprised to see Rosa as she was to see him, if not more so. After all, she was the one trying to sneak into his lair, not the other way around. However, while her own surprise was mixed heavily with dread, the assassin's was clearly tinged with delight.

York scanned back to the edge of the forest, momentarily ignoring Rosa and the growling hound dog that stood rigidly beside her.

"You surely didn't come here alone?" he asked, sounding hopeful. "It would seem a terribly foolish thing to have done."

Black Dog, sensing Rosa's fear, stepped forward protectively. His gray jowls shook as he growled, but the overall effect came up a little short of intimidating.

York's thin lips pulled up at the corners, forming a sinister smile. Both his hands disappeared momentarily into the pockets of his finely tailored jacket, and when they reappeared one held a fresh cigar and the other his favorite killing knife. Rosa recognized it immediately.

"This had been such a dreary day for me," York offered, sounding casual, "right up to this point, but what a turnaround this will be. You are a rare blemish on my nearly flawless professional record, and coincidently, you are also the sweetheart of the man who nearly killed me. Slipping this blade between your ribs will be …"

"Not as easy as you think," Rosa blurted, failing to sound confident. "It just so happens that Michael is coming right behind …" Seeing the disbelieving grin on York's face, Rosa decided not to bother finishing her lie.

"I was going to say the icing and the cake," the assassin offered, the eagerness in his voice building audibly. "I must say that I've never found much satisfaction in doing away with geriatrics, even of the canine sort, but I do believe that I'll deal with this decrepit mutt first. I'd like you to have the displeasure of watching."

Instead of cowering away or whimpering as Rosa might have expected, and certainly would have understood, Black Dog only increased the fervor of his growling.

Rosa was genuinely touched by the old dog's grand display of bravado, but it wasn't going to do him or her any good. She turned her head back for a moment, looking in the direction from which they'd come. She pictured herself sprinting back across the yard. She'd have to leave Black Dog behind if she made a run for it, and after York finished with him, he'd probably run her down before she could reach the forest anyway. Fleeing didn't seem like a very good option. Besides, turning back meant failing, and she couldn't fail this time, no matter what.

Edward Charleston York took a first measured step forward, tumbling the slender cigarillo rhythmically across his fingers and brandishing his silver blade.

"Indeed," York said, apparently thinking aloud, "this will be just the pick-me-up I need."

A hawk swooped overhead just then, flying so low to the ground that its swoosh could be heard by both Rosa and York.

The assassin paused for a moment, staring up into the sky, straining to see where in the thinning fog the bird had disappeared to. "Right on time my, friend. I'll supply you with fine dining tonight." Then, looking back to Rosa, he added, "Do you suppose he's ever sampled fortune teller before? It seems unlikely."

The bird appeared a second time, a silent shadow that skimmed through the heavy air so low that the assassin ducked reflexively.

"It's a Red-tailed Hawk, I believe," York commented in his maddeningly placid tone. "They're common around here, but I've never seen one demonstrate such aggression."

Rosa's brown eyes widened in wonder. *Redtail?*

As the bird began to circle overhead, keeping concealed in the lowest layer of clouds, its voice came to life, shrieking as if enraged.

"I don't recall ever hearing one cry out like that either," York reflected. "How strange."

The hawk screeched incessantly, hardly pausing long enough to retrieve fresh breath.

"He does seem awfully insistent. I wonder if he might be trying to call for help. Perhaps he's not here in pursuit of carrion after all, but to try and assist you in your debacle. Tell me, Miss Sanchez, are you acquainted with any of the local raptors?"

Rosa didn't respond. She stared up into the sky, captivated by the bird's calling, ignoring York's rambling completely.

"I say, if he's trying to rally the troops, he's going to find it a difficult task." Facing back up to the sky, York hollered, "We're all alone out here! There's no one to hear you!"

Suddenly, the bird fell silent. In the absence of its shrill, persistent voice, the grounds fell into a fragile stillness. Even Black Dog, Rosa noted, had finally stopped growling. The lids over his tired eyes sagged heavily, and his long, pink tongue hung lazily out from the side of his mouth. He looked completely, and inexplicably, calm.

When Rosa looked back at Edward Charleston York, she saw that his expression, too, had changed. All the expectation and amusement had vanished from his face. He stared at her with eyes that seemed almost … terrified. On second thought, she decided, he wasn't actually staring at her at all, not quite.

Spinning around so quickly that she nearly lost her balance, Rosa found herself face to face with an enormous black wolf. It had drawn to within ten feet without making even a whisper of sound.

"Easy, boy," she whispered needlessly, reaching down to Black Dog. The old hound dog didn't need to be restrained, or eased, or anything else. His lazy eyes shifted from Rosa to the wolf and then back to Rosa. He appeared to be just about as "at ease" as he could possibly be.

The wolf, however, did not. The jet-black animal stood with its long legs stiffly locked and its feet spread wide. Its upper lip curled back, baring a set of long, white teeth that locked together like a closed vise, and the skin over its snout compressed into tight wrinkles. Its hypnotic, yellow eyes shone as if they actually emitted a light of their own. The potential savagery that was promised in the wolf's stare surpassed anything that even the cruelest man could ever be capable of, even Edward Charleston York.

Rosa's initial terror at finding herself so near to the imposing beast waned somewhat when she realized that it wasn't her that its yellow eyes were fixed upon.

Edward Charleston York, a true professional among professional killers, had made very few mistakes in his career. That night, outside the Mill, he made his last. What he should have done was stand his ground and meet the wolf's stare. If he had, if he'd found the courage to, then it might have just stared back. Instead he ran. He showed his retreating hind quarters, a sight that no predator could resist.

The wolf remained still for a moment, its long head swinging to the side as it tracked the progress of its fleeing prey, and then it sprang into pursuit. It only took a few seconds and maybe twice as many long strides and the distance between them was closed.

Rosa continued on toward the door, aware that she still had work to do and that precious time had been lost. As she moved, she kept her face forward, her eyes ahead. She resisted the urge to look back. However, there was no blocking out the screams of Edward Charleston York.

Hiding in Plain Sight

Sitting cross-legged in the weeds behind The Bar, watching Ramius King's minions herding together the people of Steel City, Michael Galladin came as close as he ever would to understanding what it was like to have Rosa's gift. As clearly as he ever would, he glimpsed into the untold future. He envisioned himself standing in the middle of the intersection where the townsfolk were assembled. He saw himself surrounded by the Tall Man's hunters, fighting to the death, struggling to stay alive long enough to give the captives a chance to escape. He saw himself embracing the talent that he'd tried so long and so stubbornly to deny.

Michael wondered about the magic that was buried within him, the anxious river that he'd kept damned up for so long. *And when the levee breaks?* He could only guess at how the magic had changed during its years of neglect, how it had faded or grown or evolved.

It was odd, he knew, that he should suddenly feel so confident that the magic would be there at all. Until a short count of days past, he'd held his talent completely in check for a decade and a half. He'd tried to forget it completely, to wipe it away from his life, and he'd succeeded—for a while. Ever since stepping foot into Steel City though, the magic had been right there at the surface, impossible to ignore, poised to break free at the slightest provocation. And provocation would be coming soon, Michael knew, and it wouldn't be slight.

One of King's hunters passed through The Bar's parking lot just then, coming dangerously near to where Michael sat concealed. The man had been patrolling the perimeter of the town ever since Michael and the others had arrived, and he seemed none too enthusiastic about his assignment. Every so often the man would turn his head toward the center of the intersection and the group of huddling townsfolk. Although he wore a loose, brown robe that mostly hooded his face and kept his expression hidden, Michael imagined that it was hunger, not concern, that kept drawing his attention. There was a reason, after all, that Ramius King called his men hunters instead of soldiers or guards. They were vicious, bloodthirsty killers, twisted to the brink of becoming whatever lay beyond the limits of humanity, and none among them would ever be satisfied keeping watch or patrolling the perimeter, especially with the promise of bloodshed ringing in their ears.

The sentry was just about to leave the parking lot and move out onto Riverside Road when Michael had an idea. He'd been studying the hunter's long robe, estimating the man's height and the width of his shoulders, shaping a plan that might give the captives a chance.

With as small and subtle movements as were possible, Michael slid free the black, cloth bag that hung over his shoulder and set it on the ground before him. He loosened the bag's neck and spilled its sole content out onto the earth. The antler landed softly, soundlessly. In the dim light of the prematurely darkening evening, it looked like a rather plain thing. There was no gleam to its surface, no sharpness to its edges. If someone else had stumbled across it while walking through the woods, they might have thought it to be made of plastic, just a worthless trinket.

Carefully, Michael set the black bag aside. It settled into a small puddle where it immediately began to soak up water and mud, but Michael paid it no mind. He wouldn't be needing to hide his talisman again—ever.

After taking a deep breath to center himself, Michael reached out and grasped the Gift. Its power erupted through his body so quickly and easily that he couldn't help but gasp in response.

At the same moment, the cloaked hunter at the edge of the parking lot halted as abruptly as if he'd heard a gunshot. He inclined his head back and tilted it to one side as if straining to hear a faint sound. Then, very slowly, the man turned and started toward Michael's hiding place.

The other hunters that Michael could see appeared oblivious. With so many wielders of magic congregated around the town, Michael's taking up the Gift was only distinguishable to the man nearest by, the only man he'd wanted to notice.

As the suspicious hunter crept cautiously forward, Michael silently slid the antler into place. Each tine of the forked bone slid through a loop of leather attached to a glove that was one of Michael's few keepsakes from his life as a Guardian, and the knobby base fastened at his wrist. The arc of the main beam cradled over the back of his open hand, and the dagger-like points angled forward beyond the tips of his fingers like oversized claws.

Michael could feel the magic right there at his fingertips, so hot that it burned, so anxious that only with fierce concentration could he hold it in. He needed to maintain control, he knew. If he let the magic run free, then the game would be up, and his one chance to save the captives would be blown.

Michael's view of the hunter's approach was blocked almost completely by a low-growing cedar tree. He could hear the man's soft steps though, and would be ready to act the instant he stepped into range. He could only hope that his target would be a tick slower, a tiny fraction of a second too late to react with adequate defense.

An unbidden thought intruded upon Michael's concentration, one that threatened to ruin his focus completely. He might never see Rosa again. How strange, he reflected, that from a lifetime full of regrets, that would be his greatest, to never get another chance to lose himself in the fortune teller's soft, brown eyes, to laugh at one of her tirades, or to be mesmerized by the dancing of the that rogue curl that was always falling across her face.

Just as Michael gritted his teeth and swallowed those dangerous thoughts away, the robed hunter stepped out into the clear. In the next moment, the antler strapped to his hand tore through the air, and through the middle of the loose, brown robe. The bone claws flashed blue at impact, but dulled again immediately.

King's hunter crumpled as if his legs had disappeared from beneath him. He landed in a heap and never moved again. The hood fell back from his face, revealing features that were more Hollywood movie monster than human being. The magic that had consumed his soul had also twisted his body, leaving him a hideous distortion of whatever man he used to be.

Seconds later, clad in a concealing brown robe, Michael Galladin strode overtly into the street.

Neither Lily nor Kyle dared even to breath as they watched in horror as Ramius King stepped away from the cabin and into the first layer of the surrounding forest. It seemed at first that the Tall Man was going to head straight for them with no hesitation, as if he could see through the branches and leaves that concealed them as easily as through thin air. After just ten long strides though, King paused, appeared to consider something for a moment, and then continued on, but in a slightly different direction.

Over the course of the next several minutes, the kids watched the same mysterious pause and shift repeated over and over. Sometimes a direction change would bring the Tall Man slightly closer, but then the next one would send him off course again. However, it soon became apparent that all in all he was drawing gradually nearer, and would surely discover them eventually.

Although none of them could have known it, the back and forth wandering of Ramius King bore a close resemblance to the interstate travels of Michael Galladin just the previous day. The setting and the circumstances were vastly different, and the scale of the motion was miniaturized to a tremendous degree, but the look of it, and the logic behind it, was the same.

The closer that King drew, the tighter Kyle squeezed his arms around Lily's thin shoulders, until it neared the point of becoming painful to her. She didn't object though. He was trying to protect her, she knew. Whether he could or not was another matter entirely, and one about which she felt much less confident.

Michael made it to the group of captives without drawing any unwanted attention, but once there he encountered a difficulty that he'd not anticipated. The point of his disguise was that it hid his face and the Gift of Nature that he carried. It kept his identity a secret and enabled him to pass by the hunters and reach the townsfolk. To that purpose, the disguise had worked fine, but it was the destination rather than the journey where Michael had failed to consider things closely enough. Even with a series of long, jagged slashes through the mid-section, the brown robe had been enough to fool not only King's men, but their captives as well.

Michael moved casually around to the far side of the prisoners, trying move with patience as well as purpose. At the moment, King's hunters were least concentrated on that side of the group, guarded by only one man who was dividing his attention between the captives and the dark clouds that were rolling in overhead. Not until he was about to step in among the people did Michael finally realize his oversight. None of the townsfolk had stirred in response to his initial approach, but as he turned to face the group and then proceeded to step forward toward one of the men at the group's perimeter, things became suddenly complicated.

"I won't let you hurt them!" the man said boldly, puffing out his chest and baring his teeth. "You'll have to kill me first!"

Michael stood dumbly, recognizing how foolish he'd been to imagine the captives accepting him without fear. As far as they knew, he was one of the Tall Man's killers, one of their captors.

Fortunately for Michael, there was one man among the townsfolk who saw the situation for what it really was, and he was alert enough to act without hesitation.

"Get him in here," Aaron Ulrich hissed as he grabbed two handfuls of the brown robe and tugged Michael forward.

"What seems to be the problem?" hissed the icy voice of Mason Stone a moment later as he walked around from the other side of the intersection. "Who's shouting?"

"There's no problem," answered Ulrich in as calm a voice as he could muster. "Some people get quiet when they're scared, and some get loud. We'll keep him quiet." He looked up into Stone's lifeless, gray eyes, but then looked quickly away, unable to meet his unblinking stare for more than a moment.

"Keep him quiet," Mason whispered dispassionately, "or let him scream until his voice fails. It hardly matters."

BAD MEDICINE

To Rosa's great relief, the first hallway that she stepped into was completely deserted. In fact, aside from the forced air from the vents above, not a single sound reached her ears. What if the Mill really was empty? What if the doctor and his test subjects had left along with King and his hunters? No, she tried to reassure herself, they had to be there, because ... well, because if they weren't then she was screwed.

Halfway to the end of that hallway, Rosa spotted an ancient looking fire extinguisher hanging on the wall that was familiar. They'd drug her past that very spot on the way to her interrogation room. It was a chilling memory to relive, but it was also a good sign. The main laboratory was just ahead.

Before moving on, Rosa threw one last look back at the door through which she'd entered. There, flopped over on his side with his four feet together in the roped-calf position, was Black Dog. Apparently the ordeal with York and the wolf had been all he could take for the moment, as he'd collapsed immediately once inside and fallen into a deep, fluttery-eyed sleep. Rosa wasn't sure that leaving him there alone was safe, but she imagined that accompanying her wasn't likely to prove any better an alternative. If things went badly for her, maybe he could slip back outside somehow and be gone before anyone found him. It was frail optimism.

Rosa reached the main lab moments later. She flattened herself against the wall just outside the open door that led inside, and the faint mumbling of a single voice reached her ears.

"Next," the voice spoke more clearly, but then returned to low, unintelligible muttering. "Next," he repeated clearly a few moments later.

Rosa listened to the steady pattern for a full minute before finally remembering her limited timeframe and forcing herself to peek around the edge of the doorframe. The lab was filled with men, dozens of them. All but one were toe to heel in a long winding line, but it was the one odd man out who she'd been looking for.

"Next," Dr. Simpson called again when he was ready for another test subject. The next man in line stepped forward and with a sigh of gratification accepted a shot in the arm. Simpson continued to mumble beneath his breath as he administered the shot. Rosa still couldn't make out any of his words, but his voice sounded edgy, rising and dropping in pitch erratically like a hyper child or a madman.

"Dr. Simpson," Rosa spoke timidly as she took one cautious step through the door, "I need to talk with you."

The doctor looked to her with a look that was part confusion and part disbelief, almost as if he suspected she might just be a figment of his imagination. He looked past her then for a moment, searching for an escort that wasn't there. None of the men in line even glanced in her direction. If they'd noticed her arrival, they didn't show it.

"My name is Rosa Sanchez," she introduced herself. She was relieved that no one was attacking her, but was suddenly unsure about how to continue.

"I, ah, know who you are," Dr. Simpson said, his brow knitting in thought. "You're Mr. King's, um, fortune teller, the one who escaped. Why are you here?"

Rosa took several more cautious steps into the room and said, "I'm here because I need to talk to you about …"

"Next," the doctor interrupted, motioning for the next man in line to move forward so that he could receive his shot.

Rosa stood in silence for a moment, struck by the strangeness of the scene. Large amounts of debris were piled here and there throughout the cavernous space of the room, leftovers from the disaster that had enabled her escape.

Cautiously, she moved forward again, drawing to within arm's length of the doctor and asked, "Think you could spare me a minute of your time?"

"Not really," he answered honestly. "I have, ah, a lot of work to do. Would you, um, be willing to give out some shots while you talk?"

The question struck Rosa as so odd that she didn't even bother answering. "I came here to convince you to release your hold over these men."

The doctor paused again and looked to Rosa with such profound disbelief spread across his face that he almost appeared amused.

"Does that strike you as funny?" Rosa inquired, not finding the tiniest scrap of humor in the situation herself. "That man," she said, pointing to the next test subject in line, "is a slave because of the drugs that you're feeding him."

The doctor's half smile became complete, and a look of manic anxiety filled his bloodshot eyes.

"A slave? Yes, ah, that's true, but they're much more than that. I've turned them into supermen. They've given up their wills, but they've been rewarded with a talent for magic, and they've more rewards in store. Soon, these men will be lords over countless thousands."

"But you are lord over them, aren't you?" Rosa asked hesitantly, unsure of what to expect next after the doctor's strange reactions. "That's why you drug them, right, so you can control them?"

"That's, ah, part of it, but not the most important part," he went on conversationally. "The main reason for the mind-numbers is so that they, ah, are free to believe deeply in the magic. These men lived their whole lives trusting that such was the stuff of fairy tales alone. In order for them to use the abilities that I've brought to life in their genome, they must forget all those deeply rooted beliefs. That's where the, ah, drugs come in. Next."

"These men didn't ask to be upgraded," Rosa pointed out. "I'm sure they wouldn't have accepted the trade-offs you've forced upon them. You've stolen the most precious …"

"I've done what I've had to do!" Dr. Simpson raged suddenly, spinning around to stand nose to nose with Rosa. "Don't try to appeal to my conscience, little girl, because I don't have one anymore. You wouldn't be able to sleep tonight if I told you about the things I've done to these men. I've stripped away their every desire and passion, and I've turned them into monsters, and in the process of doing so I, too, have become a monster, only I'm a worse kind of monster, because *they* are the products of *my* evil!"

"You're not the evil one, Dr. Simpson," Rosa whispered, trying to resist the urge to back away. "I know about the hold that King has over you. I know you never would have done any of this if not for your …"

"You don't know anything!" he screamed. "You don't know what it's like trying to walk around carrying this much guilt. I feel like it's crushing me. I feel like I'm rotting inside, like I'm already dead. And this place is my hell."

Rosa scanned across the room. The men in line still stared blankly ahead. None reacted in any way whatsoever to Simpson's raving.

"Next!"

As Dr. Simpson took the arm of the next man in line, Rosa reached out toward him. She had tried the subtle approach and failed, and now it was time to try something more direct.

"Restrain her," the doctor ordered as he backed out of her reach just in time to avoid contact.

Immediately, the nearest of the zombie-like test subjects reached forward and grabbed a handful of the back of her shirt. Then, with unnatural strength, the man hoisted her into the air, instantly cutting off the circulation to her arms and head.

"You, ah, see now what I meant about being the worse sort of monster," Dr. Simpson commented. "Even after all that I've done to these poor fellows, they're still only as nasty as I, um, order them to be. It is his strength that restrains you, but it is my will. Do you see that?"

Rosa's mouth gaped, but her voice couldn't push past the neckhole of her shirt, which was cutting painfully into her throat. Her arms flailed for a few seconds, but then they fell limp, hanging awkwardly in a half-raised position like a scarecrow's. A deep crimson blush bloomed in her cheeks and tears formed at the corners of her eyes.

"Did you really come here to reason with me?" the doctor asked, stepping closer. "Did you think that you might be able to show me the, ah, error of my ways, the potential repercussions from empowering these men as I have? I understand exactly what I've done, and I loathe myself for it in ways that you cannot begin to imagine. What you don't understand is that I don't, um, have a choice. I never have."

With her last reserve of strength at her last moment of consciousness, Rosa threw her head back, a final spastic thrash to try and break free before the lights went out. She was so near to unconsciousness, she didn't even hear the crunch when the back of her head connected squarely with the nose of the man holding her.

The doctor cringed at the sound of cartilage being crushed, but he didn't move.

Rosa dropped to the ground in a heap as the man released his grip, and at first all she could do was gasp for air and wait for her vision to clear. When she looked up at the man she'd struck, there was blood gushing from both his nostrils, but his eyes remained glassy and subdued. Experimentally, the man touched the blood with a fingertip, seemingly unsure about what to make of it. Rosa probed at an aching point at the back of her own head, wondering dismally if she might have taken about as much of the blow as she'd delivered.

"You, ah, do have spirit, little girl, I'll give you that," the doctor observed, sounding calmer. "I can see why Mr. King has had such difficulty, um, manipulating you." Simpson tilted his head once again, scrutinizing Rosa's face as she picked herself unsteadily up from the floor, and suddenly his eyes were filled with pain. "I am sorry for what I've done, you mush believe that, but ..."

"Do I remind you of her, Doctor?" Rosa asked, guessing at his thoughts. "She was short like me, and she had the curly hair, too."

Dr. Simpson turned his head away, staring at some random point on the wall. Rosa could see the muscles of his jaw clench as he gritted his teeth.

"I know what your wife looked like," Rosa continued more softly, "because I saw her through Ramius King's memories. When he was trying to extract things from my mind, he inadvertently leached things out. I doubt he was even aware of it. I saw how his father abused him when he was little, and I saw how he murdered his father when he was still not much more than a child and claimed the Plume of Shu as his own. I saw how he killed and conspired to get to where he is now. I saw how he fought and eventually destroyed the Guardians. And I saw how he stole you away from your life, from your family." Her voice faded as she spoke that last word, letting it linger for a moment in the antiseptic air of the laboratory.

"You, ah, saw where he's, um, keeping them?" Simpson asked, his voice now trembling.

As Rosa studied the man's face, she could see that at least part of him already suspected the truth. She said as delicately as she could, "He never kept them anywhere. He's controlled you all this time by threatening to hurt your family. He told you that if you didn't produce the results he wanted, or if you tried to run away or call for help, or if you tried to take your own life, then he'd punish your wife and your son. Those were empty threats. He couldn't possibly have followed through with them."

The doctor began to shake all over, and his eyes squinted closed.

Rosa glanced behind her quickly, assuring herself that the man she'd head-butted wasn't finding any enthusiasm. To her relief, he remained as passive as ever, stupidly awaiting his next order as the blood continued to trickle from his broken nose.

"You're lying," Dr. Simpson hissed, finally recovering enough to find his voice. "You're making it up. You're trying to trick me into abandoning my work for Mr. King, but I won't, because he'd hurt them if I did. I'll do every terrible thing he asks me to do for the rest of my life, but I won't do anything that might endanger my family." He was starting to blubber, his words becoming sloppy like a drunk's.

Rosa felt cold and empty inside as she listened to the doctor's pitiful self-delusion. He wanted them to be okay so badly that he was convincing himself it was so. He couldn't tolerate the thought that they might already be dead, nor the realization that he'd done everything he'd done in that laboratory for nothing.

"You obviously don't have, um, a spouse or a child, do you, little girl?" Simpson asked, his tone shifting suddenly from sorrowful to angry. "If you had any idea what it's like to have a family who, um, depends on you, then maybe you could understand why I've done, um, what I've done. As it is, you, ah, don't, so you can't!" The doctor pointed a finger into Rosa's face. It shook so hard that it looked like he was being electrocuted. "That's, um, why I'm not inclined to stand here and listen to you judge me when, ah, you don't have the least understanding about, um ..."

Rosa's impatience finally overcame her sympathy. She rushed forward, catching the doctor completely by surprise, and tackled him to the ground. He was on his back before he could bark out another order to his engineered magicians, and Rosa was straddling his chest, one hand held tightly over his mouth and the other pressed firmly against his forehead.

Simpson thrashed for a moment and then went suddenly still. His eyes flew open wide, but Rosa knew that he wasn't seeing through them anymore.

One Chance for
Redemption

The dark clouds that had swept in toward Steel City seemed at first to slow and then to settle into place directly over the town, almost as if it had been their intended destination. For the moment, Kyle and Lily were only damp, sheltered beneath the canopy of the willow, but beyond its drooping branches the ground was already soaked and the rain was falling straight and hard, fat drops that splattered apart at impact. Inexplicably, Ramius King appeared to be keeping desert-dry as he continued to snoop around through the woods, drawing ever nearer to his hidden quarry. To the kids, it seemed that he must be somehow immune to the weather's assault.

From the dark underbelly of the willow, Kyle and Lily sat in silence, keeping their eyes locked on the Tall Man except for occasional looks to one another. Hold tight or run? Each glance they shared repeated the question in silence, but neither had an answer.

They should have made a break for it already, Kyle suspected. Eventually, King would ferret out their hiding place, and when he did, they'd be out of options entirely. Logic said that taking flight was the thing to do, and yet they hesitated, too scared to think logically. An old man chasing two teenagers on foot should have been like a tortoise chasing wild cats, but Ramius King wasn't just any old man. He had more than muscles to propel him.

Even as King drew parallel with their position, just forty feet from the willow's outermost dangling locks, they waited. Even as he continued past, making them nearer to the cabin than he, they kept still. But when out of the corner of his eye, Kyle saw the Tall Man come to a sudden halt, stand up straight as a telephone pole, and swing his cruel eyes and crooked nose around in their direction, he knew it was time to go.

"Come on, Lily," Kyle urged, tugging her up to her feet.

With their hearts beating in their throats, the kids dashed ahead, back toward the cabin. Fresh mud and standing water made the uneven footing extra difficult, but with their hands still locked together, every misstep was righted before either of them went down completely and precious seconds were lost.

Kyle thought that maybe they could reach the cabin before King caught up with them. Maybe they could rush past the Tall Man's driver and reach the car, and maybe the keys would still be in the ignition. And if all those maybes worked out, then maybe, just maybe, they'd have a chance. It was reckless hope at best.

Halfway to the cabin, Kyle stepped onto the slick trunk of a fallen birch tree, and his foot slid out from under him. Rather than risk pulling Lily down along with him, he jammed his staff into the soft earth, desperately struggling to regain his balance, which he did–barely.

In the heat of the chase, neither of the kids noticed the wet ground sizzle at the touch of the black tree, nor had they noticed the faint blue glow that had come to life all along its twisting length.

Two steps later, Kyle swung the staff at a low hanging branch, intending only to sweep it aside as they passed. Instead, the limb was severed as cleanly as if he'd swung a machete instead. They were gone before it hit the ground.

Suddenly, Ramius King's presence became oppressive behind Kyle, like an actual snag tugging at the back of his shirt. The urge to look back was terrible. Kyle knew that doing so would be a mistake though, and under the circumstances any mistake could prove to be a fatal one. A glimpse of Lily's face revealed that she, too, sensed the Tall Man closing in. Apparently, the temptation to look back was too much for her to resist.

At the moment when Lily's head turned, a brilliant flash flooded the forest in bright, blue light, setting the heavy raindrops into an instant of frozen relief like stars in the sky of a clearer night. The flash was there and gone again in a heartbeat, and in its absence the dark of the evening seemed deeper than before.

Kyle's arm was tugged sharply to the side as Lily went limp and fell. Without a second's hesitation, he scooped her up and continued on. She felt impossibly light in his arms. Finally, the increasingly bright glow of the Rune Tree became impossible for Kyle not to notice. Even as he saw it though, he had no spare moment to wonder at its meaning.

"It's time for your next lesson, Mr. Adams," King's voice shouted practically in Kyle's ears.

A terrible pain bloomed in Kyle's stomach, an acidy burning that he hadn't felt since claiming the Rune Tree. His inner voice was pleading for action, and not quietly. The magic wanted out.

Although Lily felt feather-light in his arms, Kyle knew that trying to carry her through the forest at speed would be like trying to swim with his hands bound together. There was no point in trying to run any further, he knew. He couldn't possibly outdistance the Tall Man carrying Lily, and by trying to do so, he'd only tire himself before the inevitable confrontation. There was no sign of the car or its driver, which meant there were no options left. So, as he reached the small clearing in front of the cabin, Kyle stopped, laid Lily gently down onto the muddy ground, and then turned around to face the most dangerous man in the world.

When it was over, Dr. Simpson fell to his knees at Rosa's feet, his head buried in his hands. He shook like he'd just been hauled up from arctic waters, but Rosa didn't see any tears. She suspected that he might have run dry. He'd certainly had plenty of reason to spend them.

The memories had poured into the doctor more easily than Rosa had hoped. It had taken only seconds, but judging from Simpson's reaction, he'd seen everything clearly enough and believed it to be truth.

"He killed my wife and my ..." The doctor's voice failed. A moment later when he regained some trace of composure, he whispered, "Why did you do this to me?"

Rosa turned away, fighting back the revulsion she suddenly felt toward herself. She, as much as anyone in the world, knew what it was like to have someone force their way into your mind. She looked down at the quaking form of the doctor, disgusted about what she'd done, yet still confident that it had been necessary.

"You would never have believed me without seeing it for yourself," Rosa answered softly. "I'm sorry, but the only real proof I could offer you were the images from King's own memory."

Rosa glanced over her shoulder at the long line of blank-faced men still waiting for their injections. They remained completely oblivious to the drama.

"All this time I thought I was protecting them, but they were already gone," Simpson murmured into the sleeves of his shirt. "Everything I've done to these men, I've done for nothing."

"I understand how painful this is for you," Rosa said, taking Simpson by the shoulders and hauling him up to his feet, "but I need you to focus and listen to me. You've done terrible things, and there's no taking them back, but there's still time to stop these men from compounding your sins. You know what they'll be capable of when they're set loose, and they'll have Ramius King's will guiding them, not their own. Because of what you've done to them, they don't have any will left."

Dr. Simpson seemed to stare right through Rosa as she spoke, appearing unaffected by her words.

Growing frustrated and impatient, Rosa gave the doctor a hard shake and shouted, "I don't have time to spend convincing you! Someone I care a great deal about is out there risking his life trying to save people he doesn't even know and owes nothing to. You, however, owe quite a bit. I know what King did to you, but now his control over you is gone. You made these monsters, and now you're going to unmake them! I don't know how, but you're going to find a way! You damn well better or we're all screwed—you, me, and everybody else in the whole damn world."

"What if I can't?" the doctor asked, his voice steadying slightly. "What if it's too late?"

"This is your one chance for redemption, Dr. Simpson, and you will find a way to undo what you've done." She paused for a moment, waiting for his eyes to find hers. "I know you won't fail, because you know that your son is watching."

As Rosa strode back down the hallway in the direction from which she'd come, she listened carefully behind her, but heard nothing. She couldn't know if she'd done the right thing, if she'd done enough, but she'd done what she could. The rest was up to the doctor. As long as he had a hold over the engineered magicians, she couldn't force him to do anything, but she'd set his feet upon a path that he hopefully wanted to walk. She was asking for a lot from him, but he could risk a lot. He had nothing left to lose.

About half way back to the door through which she'd entered the Mill, Rosa found Black Dog. The old hound was reared up on his back legs, scratching intently against the metal surface of an anonymous looking door. He stopped when he noticed her approaching, and with his sad eyes full of expectation, he looked up at her and barked one clear bark. Somehow, it sounded like a request.

A barrel-bolt lock had been installed outside the windowless door. Rosa tried knocking, but when no response came she slid over the bolt, threw open the door, and poked her head inside.

"You're not so scary looking," commented a man from inside the dark room, shielding his eyes against the fluorescent light that streamed in from the hallway.

"And you're not so slick with the compliments, if that's what that was supposed to be."

The man looked nervous and confused. His eyes dropped down to Black Dog for a moment. He said, "You're not one of them, are you? You don't belong here either?"

"Hell no I don't belong here," Rosa laughed. "In fact, I was just leaving. Care to join?"

"Absolutely," he agreed, stepping out into the hallway and accepting a sloppy doggy kiss on the back of his hand. "I was kidnapped and brought here against my will," he explained needlessly. "I have a daughter, Lily, who might be in danger as well. It's all my fault. I couldn't protect her."

"Your daughter *is* in terrible danger," Rosa confirmed, "but it's nobody's fault but mine."

As Kyle turned, an explosion of blue fire erupted through the air from the far side of the clearing. He caught a brief glimpse of the Tall Man standing there with one long-fingered hand extended and the Plume of Shu shining brilliantly atop his brow, and then the flames burst forth, engulfing everything.

With impossible speed, the Rune Tree rose in defense. It seemed to Kyle that the talisman had reacted before he could, carrying his arm along with it instead of the other way around.

All around Kyle the flames whipped and thrashed wildly, but they didn't touch him. Nor did they touch Lily, who'd awakened and was cowering behind him, hiding underneath the protection of his Gift.

Kyle dared a quick glance over his shoulder to make certain that Lily was safe. Remembered images from the dream flashed in his mind, pictures that paralleled the real scene playing out before him much too closely to be explained away as coincidence. At least part of the dream had clearly been premonition, and the moment it prophesized had arrived.

Too bad, Kyle thought, that he'd awakened before the dream's resolution. He'd know how it ended soon enough though.

Despite the fact that the captives were crowded tightly together, Michael moved through the group easily, choosing a spot near their center to sit and resume his meditation. A ring of space formed instantly around him. Even Aaron Ulrich, who stood quietly with his arms wrapped around his wife, kept his distance. The townsfolk were willing to let Michael in among them because of Ulrich's reassurance that he wasn't a threat, but they weren't about to go rubbing shoulders with him. Even with so many of King's hunters about, the last Guardian's presence was practically palpable at such close proximity.

Michael took a deep breath and closed his eyes. Rain was falling steadily, and although the hood of the robe he wore kept the drops out of his eyes, he was already soaked through and through. With some difficulty, he blocked out the panicky whispers of the captives surrounding him and the smell of their fear. He ignored the protests from his half-frozen fingers and toes and shunned his own voice of logic, which was making grim predictions about his odds of success, and of survival. He swallowed his emotions down to the deepest pit of his stomach, hoping that he could keep them there until it was over, knowing what might happen if he couldn't.

No obvious trace of the wolf or Edward Charleston York caught Rosa's attention as she, Lily's father, and Black Dog hurried back across the yard outside the Mill. There was bound to be some evidence left behind from the assassin's gory demise, but she was hardly inclined to look for it. A hard rain was falling, and presumably the wolf had drug its meal away to some sheltered place where it could dine at its leisure. It was a terribly grim thought, but in it Rosa found grim satisfaction. *Justice.*

"Good boy," she hollered over the growing noise of the wind and rain. "The Chief would be proud." She hoped that the wolf was still close enough to hear her.

Lily's father looked cautiously around the grounds, wondering who Rosa was speaking to. He didn't see anyone. Honestly, he didn't care who she was talking to, or even if she was crazy and talking to herself. All he cared about was finding his daughter and making sure she was safe.

Maneuvering through the woods was more difficult than it had been before the arrival of the storm. The ground was muddy and slick, and the lowest tree branches flailed in the wind as if they were angry, flicking their sharp fingertips painfully across the trio's exposed skin. Despite the encumbrance of the foul weather though, they pushed ahead with the utmost haste. That is, until they reached the car.

It was at that moment, when Rosa pulled open the driver's side door of the Monte Carlo, that she realized how far ahead of herself she'd gotten. She was in a big hurry to get somewhere, and rightly so, but the truth of the matter was that she didn't actually know where it was she was rushing to go. There were only two options, but choosing between them seemed suddenly impossible.

On one hand, there was Michael. She'd left him alone, and by now he might well be taking on all of Ramius King's hunters by himself. He was the man who'd saved her life, the man who'd given her his solemn pledge of devotion, and she'd abandoned him. She'd done it for all the right reasons, but she'd done it nonetheless. She had to get back to him.

On the other hand, there were the kids. She'd left them to play cat and mouse with Ramius King himself, the most dangerous man alive. Regardless of how they'd already been tested and what they'd already endured, they were still just teenagers. They'd agreed to do what they could only because they'd understood that there was no one else to do it. She had to get back to them.

Once Lily's father and Black Dog were in the car, Rosa sat down on the ground beside the driver's door, ignoring the mud and the rain, and lifted the strap of the black cloth bag over her head. She hadn't even opened the bag to look in upon the Gift since her revelation by the river earlier. The ability that it enabled her with wasn't what she'd needed to deal with Edward Charleston York or Dr. Simpson, but a remote view was exactly what she needed right then.

After closing her eyes and recalling a picture of Michael in her mind, Rosa reached into the bag. With ease and speed beyond what she could possibly have hoped for, the magic sprang to life. An image of the main intersection in Steel City bloomed in her mind. The townsfolk were huddled together in twos and threes, covering their heads in defense against the pelting rain, and there at the center of the group, looking utterly oblivious to the raging storm, sat Michael Galladin.

Rosa inhaled a deep lungful of air as she released her grip from the antler, suddenly realizing that she'd been holding her breath. A second gasp was for Michael, a sigh of relief. He was poised for action, but the critical moment hadn't arrived yet.

A tapping sound pulled Rosa's attention away. When she turned, Lily's father was staring down at her through the car window, a look of concern on his face. She showed him her index finger, asking for a second.

Closing her eyes again, Rosa reached deeper into the bag, sliding her fingertips along the smooth surface of fossilized bone. She thought about Kyle and Lily, pictured their faces in her mind. An instant later she saw them, and then she saw Ramius King.

"No!"

Seconds later, the Monte Carlo was tearing down the little dirt lane through the forest, skidding dangerously on the soft mud. The rain was falling in sheets so thick that Rosa could barely see the trees flying past both sides of the car, but she wasn't about to slow down. She knew that if it wasn't too late already, it would be soon.

OUT OF OPTIONS

It took all of Kyle's strength to hold back the relentless flood of blue fire. More than just heat and light, the flames weighed down against Kyle's shield of magic as if they were tons of surging fluid, like a tidal wave of mud or molten lava.

When the inferno finally died, it didn't dwindle down gradually, but disappeared utterly in a single moment. In the wake of the fire stood the Tall Man, his head tilted to the side and a look of curiosity spread over his face.

"You're not dead," he observed casually. "I've never been one to appreciate surprises, and the fact that you're not dead surprises me a great deal."

"I'm happy to disappoint you," Kyle barely managed as he gasped for air.

King's head tilted a little further, and he said, "There's the explanation behind your survival, a new toy. So, Mr. Adams, you really did find a brand new Gift of Nature, just as Little Boy told me. Remarkable." The Tall Man's hungry stare moved up and down the length of the Rune Tree for a moment, but then shifted to Lily, who was picking herself up from the ground behind Kyle. "Is that lovely young lady behind you Lily Goodshepherd by chance?"

Kyle glanced over his shoulder. Lily looked scared, but not panicked. Somewhere behind her, still out of sight, was the car that King had arrived in, but where it was exactly Kyle could only guess. Not that it made any difference anyway. Even if he did know the car's precise location, he and Lily would never be able to reach it now that the Tall Man had reached them. They were in his grasp.

"I must say," King continued, "I'm fairly annoyed at being drawn away from a very important event under false pretenses like this, but I suppose acquiring the girl will serve as some consolation. I can always use a new recruit, after all." King smiled wickedly in response to the horror he saw in Kyle's eyes. "If you think you can stop me from taking her, Mr. Adams, then go ahead. Show me what you can do with your fancy, new stick."

Kyle didn't respond.

"I've been spending some time with your father, Lily," King said, his eyes never leaving Kyle's. "I think I've been enjoying it more than he has."

Kyle felt Lily's hands clamp onto his upper arms from behind. She was shaking.

"Of course now that I have you," the Tall Man continued, "his usefulness has probably expired. Keeping him around would only make your transition more difficult." The wicked grin broadened beneath King's long, crooked nose.

It was getting hard for Kyle to hear. The buzzing in his ears had become a screech over which little else could be understood. The Rune Tree, although it appeared still, felt alive in his grip, pulsing with energy. Its light, having faded after King's assault, was growing intense once more.

"I can sense how desperately you want to feel the rush of magic surging through you, Mr. Adams," King tempted. "Why do you hold back? You know what I'll do to her if she goes with me. The only way to protect her from the same suffering you endured is to fight me. You don't have to defeat me, only keep me occupied long enough to give her a chance to escape. Are you too scared even to try to save her life?"

A bright flash of lightning revealed the scene in a moment of harsh, white light. Every tooth in the Tall Man's smile gleamed.

Kyle tried to slow his breathing, tried to ignore the buzzing in his ears and the twisting ache in his stomach. It was so hard to resist, especially when he wasn't sure that resisting was the best thing to do anyway. It might be that what King was saying was true. It was so hard to think over the sound of the Tall Man's voice and the hum of his own anxious magic and the constant drum-roll of the rain, which was falling in sheets, but somehow still avoiding Ramius King.

Kyle let his eyes fall closed and focused on the cadence of the falling drops. Incredibly subtle differences, indistinguishable before, suddenly became as obvious as if they were different notes in a musical chord. The drops that struck the muddy ground echoed with a slightly more muted timbre than those that landed in puddles. There were sharp, staccato impacts of drops that struck leaves of the nearby trees and dull, muffled pats of others that fell against the soft surface of his hair and shirt. In total, the countless tiny touches of sound added up to something incredible, something musical.

In order to bring the gentle background noise of the raindrops to the forefront of his attention, Kyle was forced to push away the other, bolder sounds, including the buzzing voice of his own magic. As long as he could hold on to the music of the raindrops, he could maintain control. If he could keep his mind that quiet, then it would be his own will, and not the magic's, that chose his actions.

"I'm surprised again at the self-control you're demonstrating, Mr. Adams," King said, sounding genuine. "You certainly didn't learn that from me. I suppose that's Grandma Jo's influence shining through." The Tall Man paused for a moment in thought, and then inclining his head to the side, he said, "I'm pretty sure that she was thinking of you when I killed her."

Kyle's concentration slipped as the words struck him, but he reeled himself back in quickly, knowing that if he leaned too far, he was bound to fall.

"You were the only one left for her to protect," King continued. "I imagine she was feeling very sad for you as I skewered her to the wall in that basement. She must have known what I was going to do to you, and what I was going to make you do for me. What you will still do for me."

"You're wrong," Kyle argued, pleased to hear his own voice cutting easily through the wind and the rain. "The magic won't control me, and neither will you." Lily's hands tightened around his arms, lending him strength. "And you won't be taking Lily anywhere. I swear it."

Another steak of lightning split the sky almost directly overhead.

"Then you plan on stopping me, I take it?" King asked, his wicked grin, which had faded momentarily, stretching wide once again. "If the young lady is to be leaving, then send her away now. Once we begin, you won't want her nearby. Without a Gift, she'll be a defenseless bystander. When I collect her later, I want her to be undamaged."

Kyle turned back to Lily, but before he could speak, she said, "I won't leave, Kyle. You wouldn't leave me, and I won't leave you."

"Maybe you could reach help," Kyle suggested weakly, knowing that she'd never fall for his lie. "Maybe ..."

Another flash of light prompted Kyle to spin back around, forgetting his argument. It wasn't just lightning this time, he knew. The light was blue, and it was persistent. It was the light of the Tall Man's magic.

"That was your last chance, Mr. Adams, and you missed it."

As Kyle turned back to face his enemy, he felt Lily's hands go limp and fall from his arms. Obviously, she was seeing what he was seeing, and the shock of it had loosened her grip. Kyle doubted that King was right, that they'd ever really had a chance, but if they had, then he was certainly right about the second part—they'd missed it.

The Story of a Lifetime

Through a small gap between the huddling townsfolk that surrounded him, Michael could see Mason Stone. Ramius King's first general stood in the perfect stillness that was his natural state, staring up into the sky. A torrent of raindrops battered the smooth surface of his face, but he seemed unbothered. His gray eyes never even blinked.

After a moment, Stone dropped his cold stare back down to ground level and made a beckoning motion with one hand. A familiar figure immediately approached.

"We can't afford to wait any longer, Little Boy," Mason whispered once the tiny man was within earshot. "Soon it'll be too dark for a proper recording, and Mr. King said that he won't tolerate any more delays. The demonstration has to take place tonight, and for it to be tonight it has to be now."

Little Boy acknowledged with a slight bow, which also served to hide the hungry smile that he suddenly seemed unable to force away.

"Make sure the camera crew is ready," the first general commanded softly, "and round up the other hunters. It's time."

"Yes, sir," replied the undersized man eagerly, and then he was off.

Mason took note of Little Boy's anxiousness, reading it easily in the tone of his voice and the bounce of his stride. He, like the other hunters, lusted for the violence and was ready to lose himself in the magic he possessed and gorge himself on the defenseless lives gathered at the intersection. To acquiesce to such primitive desires was pitiful to the first general. Not that he felt sympathy for the townsfolk, but the fact that they posed no threat made them ungratifying prey. He'd be more than content to leave the demonstration to his bloodthirsty underlings and save his own efforts for a more worthy opponent, if any still existed. There was at least one man left for him to fear, of course, but it wasn't time for that, not when that man was about to make him second in command of the world.

Michael also noticed the renewed vigor in Little Boy's stride as he hurried away after his brief conversation with Mason Stone. Guessing at the nature of that conversation, and the cause for the tiny man's new enthusiasm, wasn't difficult. Time was almost up.

Although the Plume of Shu still glowed brilliantly at its perch atop the Tall Man's brow, it was no longer the primary source of the blue light that haloed his dark silhouette. Extended forward proudly in his long-fingered hands, hands that had been empty just moments before, was a spear built of blue fire. The ephemeral weapon was as long as King was tall, and it ended in three wide prongs. From its dancing flames came a low, grinding sound like a heavy truck driving slowly across loose gravel.

The word *skewered* echoed painfully in Kyle's mind. Surely, he thought, this was the weapon that had ended Grandma Jo's life.

"You can't protect her from me, Mr. Adams," King said, grinning evilly. "You may have great potential, but right now you're only a novice and I am the master of masters. You can't possibly stand against me."

"I'll try anyway," Kyle promised solemnly, calling upon his every reserve of courage just to keep his voice steady.

The Tall Man's smile broadened in response, and he said, "Such nobility. I didn't teach you that either."

"Because you don't know anything about it," Lily chimed in over Kyle's shoulder, her delicate voice barely penetrating the din of the storm.

Without any salute or ceremony, King attacked, and the speed of his motion was unnaturally fast not only for a man of his age, but for any man of any age.

Again, the Rune Tree responded seemingly of its own accord, flying forward to intercept the Tall Man's flaming trident a foot short of Kyle's face. Although he'd managed to maintain discipline enough to keep the magic from controlling him, the Gift he wielded still seemed to be responding to something like a will or instinct of its own. Whatever it was, Kyle was grateful for it. It had saved his life and Lily's in turn, at least for the moment.

However, although King's weapon had been kept from finding its mark, the momentum of the strike couldn't be negated by Kyle's counterblow. The force of the impact sent Kyle crashing back into Lily, and then they both toppled to the ground in a heap. Thanks to the heavy rain, their fall was cushioned by fresh mud. A small, hard object dug painfully into the small of Kyle's back though, about the kidney. Reflexively, he reached for the object. Surprisingly, his fingers found not the rough, uneven edges of a stone, but the smooth surfaces and square corners of a tiny metal box.

At first Kyle didn't recognize the thing for what it was. Not only was it coated with mud, its polished silver surface had also been charred by fire, staining it gray and black. A quick wipe against the soaked, but still relatively clean front of his shirt revealed partially obscured, but legible writing. It said, *The Doors*.

"A little dramatic, I know," spoke the almost elated sounding voice of the Tall Man. Clearly he was enjoying the rush of excitement that the violence prompted within him. "I simply couldn't help myself. Besides, who's going to accuse me of having poor taste once I've laid claim over the whole world? *I enter upon the ashes of my enemies.* It sounds epic, and so it should. Mine will be an epic conquest."

Kyle squeezed the Zippo lighter so hard that his fingers turned white and his fist shook. An image of Jerrod Thomas' face materialized before his closed eyes, and try as he might, he couldn't push it away. Jerrod's voice spoke in his ears, offering a smoke and then the use of his car, teasing him about the girl from the restaurant. Kyle struggled to quiet the replaying conversation, but failed, unable to make himself forget. Relief came only when the buzz of the magic within him grew so loud that it drowned out everything else.

Sensing that he was once again nearing the threshold of the magic's domination, Kyle strained to focus on the sound of the falling rain, but it was like trying to hold a tufted dandelion seed on the open palm of his hand. The tiniest breath of air and it was lost again. His control was slipping.

The stage was set, the characters were in place, and the camera was rolling. Ramius King's hunters were arranged in a large ring surrounding their captives, and they all looked like men just walked out of the desert spotting a tall glass of cold water. The massacre that was about to occur wasn't just something they craved, but something they needed, an act to give meaning to the talents that were their defining traits.

The storm raged on furiously. The flashing streetlight that hung over the center of the intersection was held out almost sideways by the strength of the wind, and the lightning had become practically continuous. The temperature had plummeted and the rain mixed with sleet and then tiny balls of hail that left stinging welts where they struck bare skin. A few of the townsfolk tried to shield their faces from the bombardment of frozen projectiles, but most didn't bother. Whatever pain and discomfort they were suffering as a result of the storm was dulled greatly by the overwhelming terror they felt at seeing King's hunters closing in.

Standing in front of the Country Kitchen, just a step outside the circle of hunters, was Mason Stone. The falling ice pellets pinged against the first general's marble features like bee bees striking a concrete wall. Patiently as always, Mason scanned across the intersection to be certain that everything was set. Things had to go right the first time, he knew. The captives wouldn't be up for a second take.

"I will leave the order up to you, Little Boy," Mason whispered into the ear of the diminutive hunter standing directly in front of him. "Just remember to keep it one at a time. If everyone goes charging in at once, the camera's view will be obscured."

"Yes, sir," the tiny man responded dutifully. "The world will never be the same after this night. I know just who to send in first."

Nearby, a graying, middle-aged man in a rain-soaked suit and tie prepared to deliver the story of a lifetime. Although racked by fear and freezing cold, the man's voice stayed even, which would have made him proud under other circumstances. His whole body was shaking violently, and there didn't seem to be anything he could do to stop that, but he sounded steady.

"I'd like to remind everyone who might eventually see this tape that I have been brought to this place against my will. The same is true for my cameraman. Neither of us have had any opportunity since our abduction to contact the police or anyone else who might have been able to intervene in what I am increasingly certain is going to be an unthinkable act of violence here in the small town of Steel City, Michigan."

The man paused for a moment, struggling to wipe his eyes with a handkerchief retrieved from the inside pocket of his jacket. The shaking of his hand was so pronounced that it appeared seizure-like, but still his voice remained unbroken.

"Our captors, who have formed the large ring behind me, are not normal men. What I at first took to be elaborate disguises and prosthetics, I now believe to be actual … *abnormalities*. Some among them are drastically oversized, larger by far than any professional athlete or bodybuilder that I have encountered. Others appear to have extensive malformations in their skeletal structures, facial features, skin, teeth, eyes ... They're like monsters, like real, living monsters."

The sound of some commotion behind the man distracted him momentarily. When he turned back to the camera his face was stricken.

"One of the *men* has just broken out of the ring formation and is moving toward the captives. He is immense, one of the very largest. There appears to be something in his hand. It might be a club or bat of some kind, and it's glowing with blue light. Actually, I think that it's on fire. Yes, I can clearly see blue flames on the surface of the club, but I can't see what's fueling them, and I don't know how the fire isn't extinguished by this downpour. It's a very bizarre sight. It's almost like the thing is burning by magic."

A volley of muffled shouts rose from the intersection.

"The giant man is raising the flaming club over his head. The people are trying to move away but they're surrounded, and there's nowhere to go. They can't ... There's nowhere ... God help them! God help us all!"

The Ultimate Sacrifice

As Kyle and Lily lay sprawled in the mud, the Tall Man towered above, his dark clothes as neat and dry as if he'd just put them on. The features of King's long face were set into deep contrast by the eerie blue light that radiated from the fiery weapon he held, making him appear almost skeletal.

Kyle managed to pull himself back to his feet just in time to receive the Tall Man's second attack. Instead of trying to block the blow completely as he had before, Kyle deflected the flaming trident just enough to avoid its path, sending the triple points into the muddy ground beside him where they flash-boiled the pooling rainwater, raising a cloud of steam.

King tore his trident free effortlessly and proceeded to swing again and again. Each attack was turned away by the Rune Tree by a smaller margin than the previous one. Kyle backpedaled furiously, trying desperately to maintain his footing. He knew all too well that if he went down again it would be over.

As King beat Kyle back further and further, the duel moved away from the only unarmed person present, Lily. Kyle was doing all he could just to stay on his feet and keep the Tall Man's weapon from reaching him, and he certainly couldn't hope to maneuver the battle in one direction or another. However, he could see that Lily had room to run if she would, and it gave him a little hope. If she took off right then, and if he could keep King occupied for a few more precious seconds, then she might still have a chance to get away.

Out of the corner of his eye, Kyle saw Lily climb back to her feet and spring into motion. Then King was on him again and all his attention was once again required to parry, which is why he didn't take note of the direction in which Lily ran. It wasn't what he'd been hoping for.

Instead of fleeing, Lily charged toward the combatants, too afraid for Kyle's safety to consider the unlikelihood that she could be of any help.

Despite his intentness on battering through Kyle's defenses, Ramius King still had peripheral perception enough to sense Lily's approach. Before she came within ten feet of the Tall Man, he threw out one long-fingered hand in her direction, palm flat forward. Instantly, Lily was knocked from her feet by the force of his magic and thrown back down into the mud as if she'd been snared in a net of invisible mesh.

Already brought to the brink of blind rage after the discovery of Jerrod's lighter among the ashes, Kyle lunged forward in response to seeing Lily brushed so casually aside. He hurled himself against the Tall Man with all his strength and anger. The sound of the rain was now impossible to hear through the whistling of the wind in his ears and the roaring of the two burning weapons. Knowing that his control was lost, Kyle gave himself over completely to the power of his magic and the will of the Rune Tree.

Ramius King was caught off guard by the renewed intensity of his much younger adversary, but even as he was forced to retreat several steps, his face continued to beam delightfully. He hardly looked like a man afraid for his life. Almost passively, he brushed aside several long, arcing sweeps of the Rune Tree with his fiery spear, as easily as if he were waving a butterfly net at a fluttering Swallowtail.

Caught up in the rush of his fury, Kyle failed to notice the ease with which King turned away his blows. He swung over and over again at the Tall Man, and each time the flaming trident was there to intercept, until one time it wasn't.

After blocking and backing away from Kyle's attacks perhaps a dozen times, King changed tactics. He sidestepped an overhead slash of the Rune Tree completely, his speed so blinding that no deflection with his own weapon was necessary. Kyle's Gift sailed past harmlessly and struck the muddy ground like a sledge hammer—mere inches from Lily's head.

Kyle looked down in horror as steam rose from the ground he'd singed. Half a foot over and he'd have killed her.

Lily's eyes drifted slowly open, momentarily peaceful as her memories shifted back into order. She'd been unconscious since King had knocked her down.

In an instant all the rage evaporated from Kyle. The tormenting screech of the magic within him died to a whisper in a heartbeat, and the blue light that shone from the Rune Tree dimmed to a pale glow. He tried to ask Lily if she was okay, but his voice wouldn't come. The realization of what his anger had nearly cost him was devastating.

"Kyle, look out!" Lily screamed, her words lost in a concussive boom of thunder from the black clouds overhead.

Kyle threw the Rune Tree up in defense a tiny fraction of a second too late. The glowing Gift of Nature met the Tall Man's flaming trident in time, but the power to stop the blow wasn't gathered yet.

As the crooked, little tree flew out of his grip, Kyle twisted instinctively, trying to dodge the deadly points of the Tall Man's fiery pitch fork. He mostly did. The outside tine of the spear just grazed his upper arm as the weapon slammed into the earth beside him. So slight was the contact that if the weapon had been forged of steel instead of magic he'd have escaped with only a scratch. Instead, an ugly, black gash was seared into Kyle's arm below the shoulder, a burn that couldn't have been inflicted so quickly with an acetylene torch.

Kyle and Lily cried out simultaneously, and the Tall Man laughed in response, savoring the pain he saw in their faces and heard in their voices. He jerked the tips of his weapon free from the steaming mud and raised the spear over his head.

"Here's a lesson that I myself have never learned, but still can teach to you, Mr. Adams," King hissed through his beaming smile, "how to lose."

The agony of the wound to Kyle's arms was so excruciating that he never even heard the Tall Man's words, but he hardly needed to. Petrified by fear and pain, Kyle watched on as the death blow started to fall, never even considering trying to dodge away or reach for his lost weapon. Time seemed to drag as the blazing points of the trident drew nearer, the blue flames dancing in slow motion. King looked ecstatic. Only two feet to go …

And then Lily dove into the weapon's path.

The Last Guardian of Magic

The townsfolk who'd been squatted down on the ground, cowering in little groups of two and three, returned to their feet as Fat Man neared. The brute's flaming club was held high over his head, poised to strike. The captives who were closest to the approaching giant pushed back into the rest of the group. Some skittered away, but not far. They were trapped. They moved as a group to the far side of the circle, opposite Fat Man's approach, careful to keep out of the reach of the men who made up that side of the ring. All except one, that is. One among them remained where he was, sitting cross-legged with his face hidden behind a dark hood and his hands tucked into the sleeves of his long, brown robe.

As Fat Man came to within several steps of the straggler, he paused and cocked his head to the side, showing curiosity. He might have been wondering if the man had died already as a result of fear or exposure to the elements. Then the hood lifted ever so slightly, not enough to reveal the face beneath, but enough to prove that whoever it was, they were still alive. Wind and sleet tore viciously against the seated figure, but he didn't flinch or sway.

Fat Man, appearing relieved that the cloaked figure was still alive to be killed, stepped forward, his toothless smile rising at its corners. He reached down with his free hand, grabbed the seated man's cloak behind the hood, and hauled him up effortlessly to a standing position. With his ephemeral weapon cocked behind his head, he drew in a deep breath, gritted his teeth, and ...

"Fat Man!" Little Boy's deep voice called out in warning, barely cutting through the din of the storm. The smallest of King's hunters had just recognized the cloak.

Fat Man looked over his shoulder in response to hearing his partner's voice, but whatever else Little Boy was saying was lost in a roar of thunder. When he turned back to his would-be victim the hood had fallen away from his face.

An explosion of blue light flared at the center of the intersection, causing all the cowering townsfolk and King's hunters alike to shy away reflexively. When the flash died, Fat Man lay on his back, the fiery club vanished from his hand. A deep, black slash had been opened across the giant's wide chest, stretching from one armpit to the other. He was still as a stone, as was the man standing above him with his hands held out wide. In one of those hands the man held a glowing claw of black bone and in the other a flaming blue sword. The song of the sword rang out like the climax note of a diva's aria.

"I told you what would happen the next time you touched me," Michael reminded, well aware that Fat Man couldn't hear him. He'd been dead before he hit the mud. Then, turning in a slow circle so that every one of King's hunters would be sure to see his face as well as the weapons he held, Michael called out in a strong, clear voice, "I am Michael Galladin, and I am a Guardian of Magic. These people are under my protection. Release them, or else test your strength against my own.

No one moved at first. The brutal mix of rain and sleet and hail pummeled everyone relentlessly, but no one seemed to be paying it much attention at the moment. Then King's hunters rushed in to answer Michael's challenge. All but one.

A Mother's Gift

The Tall Man's flaming trident was spearing through the air, just inches from Lily's chest, and it became to Kyle as if time froze. There was a cruel and unnatural pause in which he was able to consider the scene stilled before him. He saw murder in the smile of the man from his nightmares and death in the eyes of the girl of his dreams.

Then, the most incredible thing happened. Or rather, the most terrible thing, the thing that seemed so certain, did not happen. Lily didn't die.

At the exact instant when King's weapon made contact, Lily Goodshepherd's slender form burst into a whirl of blue fire.

Kyle's hands and feet dug madly into the slick mud beneath him, sending him squirming back from the devastating heat of the flames. His eyes though, never turned away.

Ramius King's spear dissipated in a heartbeat, blown out like the wispy flame of a birthday cake candle. He, too, reeled back from the inferno engulfing Lily. The look on his face was part awe and part terror.

Never once, even as the torturous flames licked over every square inch of Lily's body, did she think that she was dying. By some instinct that had lain dormant until right then, she understood exactly what was happening. Though the touch of the fire was agony beyond description, the energy that it brought to life within her was incredible.

It was the magic of her ancestors, passed on through the countless generations of her grandfather's people, gathered in ever greater concentration as their numbers dwindled until at last Lily's mother alone held their collective strength. And when she, the only member of the last pure-blooded generation of the tribe, passed on, the magic was freed to the whims of nature once again. There, in the antiseptic environment of the delivery room, the magic sought out a new life to inhabit, a life that could one day be transformed into a Gift of Nature. Naturally, it found the brand new life that was as near as another life could ever be. So it was that as Lily Goodshepherd was born into the world, and the light of her mother's life was simultaneously snuffed out, an exceptional magic was bequeathed in an extraordinary fashion.

A Raging Storm

Michael moved through the street like a miniature tornado, devastating and impossible to touch. The fiery sword he held slashed long arcs through the rain and hail and anything else that was caught in its path. The obsidian antler raked through the air, hissing with lightning speed, blocking attacks from all sides and tearing down enemies like a machete through dry grass. King's hunters charged in fearlessly, the sight of their fast falling comrades fueling rather than deterring their aggression. For their stubbornness, Michael rewarded them with quick death.

The magic, the power that Michael had denied for so many years, held no bitterness for its long banishment. It came easily at his bidding, hungry to be freed, glad for a purpose to serve.

The intensity of the storm seemed to respond to the fury of the battle, rising to an angry gale the likes of which had rarely been witnessed before in that part of the world. The pellets of hail grew to the size of marbles, sending the townsfolk scurrying to the shelter of the Country Kitchen. Even the reporter and his cameraman abandoned their epic footage and fled to safety. Their faces crowded together in the restaurant's windows, transfixed by the fantastic battle being waged outside.

As Rosa turned the car onto Riverside Road, she was struck with a strange thought. When she'd glimpsed the scene at the cabin with Ramius King and the kids, she'd broken away instantly, panicked by what she'd seen and desperate to reach them as quickly as possible. She hadn't even taken one second to scrutinize the image, but now, strapped into the driver's seat of the Monte Carlo, she did. Something about what she'd seen had been oddly familiar, something beyond the people and the place, something ...

The memory of a vision rose to the surface of her mind, one that had been prompted from her not by the wandering of dream-thought, but by the prodding of a cruel and powerful magician. It was the vision that had ultimately led everyone to the tiny town of Steel City, Michigan. She'd seen a flickering light in that vision, one that could conceivably have been flashing lightning. She'd seen a dark night and the Tall Man, and most importantly she'd seen the shadowed outline of someone whom her senses told her possessed the potential to do something that perhaps no other could, kill Ramius King. Could one of the kids turn out to be that person? It was hard to believe, but certainly not impossible. *Impossible* was a word that Rosa was done saying.

As she ground the gas pedal into the floormat, Rosa squinted her eyes down to slits, straining to see through the melee of the storm and keep the car in the center of the road. Beside her, Lily's father braced his arms against the dashboard, and in the back, Black Dog slumbered on, miraculously undisturbed.

Charred and twisted forms lay scattered haphazardly about the intersection of Main Street and Riverside Road. Inhuman faces stared wide-eyed into the falling sleet and hail, their gruesome features frozen by death and the cold. The expressions captured in those features showed the anguish and rage of their last living moments. Someone just arriving upon the scene might easily have believed them to be Halloween masks.

At the center of the intersection stood Michael Galladin. He wore the tattered remains of the long, brown robe he'd stolen, its torn edges singed black. Steam curled out from his nostrils into the chill evening air like dragon's breath as he struggled to ease the burning in his lungs. The dark circles around his eyes looked like depthless caverns in the blue, neon glow of his blazing sword. The shock of red hair that hung from his angular chin was coated with sleet, giving the impression of ice on fire. He looked like a man at the brink of death, or perhaps just returned from beyond.

"I appreciate you giving me a chance to catch my breath like this," Michael said to the only other man left standing. "That was pretty strenuous." Severe pain infected his body in a half dozen different places where his defenses had been breached, and it took a monumental effort to keep his voice steady.

Mason Stone didn't respond. He just stood there like part of the landscape, motionless and seemingly emotionless.

"If you surrender now, I'll let you go," Michael bluffed boldly. He could feel that his injuries went deeper than skin and muscle, and he knew that his magic could maintain him for only so long.

No reaction showed through Mason's marble features. He remained statue-like for another long count of silent seconds.

"I remember your brother," Mason hissed as he started cautiously forward at last. It was the first clue he'd offered since the fighting began that he was indeed alive and not frozen to death at the streetside. "I wasn't Mr. King's right hand then, but I was well on my way and anxious to reach the apex of the ranks. At the time your brother was King's favorite. I was jealous enough of Sean that I considered killing him. I wasn't certain that I could, but I was tempted to try. I suppose things would have been easier for you if I had. I wonder if you wish that I'd done him in then and saved you from that awful tragedy?"

It was Michael's turn to keep quiet. He wasn't about to be goaded into doing something foolish because his temper slipped or his guilt flared. He didn't have the energy for it.

As Ramius King's first general came to a halt ten feet from Michael, his strange, gray eyes scanned once over his opponent, judging his remaining strength and searching for points of vulnerability.

"We both know that you're not about to walk away from this," Michael said, his voice barely cutting through the storm, "because we both know that King would kill you for retreating. So what are you waiting for?"

"I'm letting your wounds bleed out a little longer," Mason answered evenly as a particularly large ball of hail struck his bald scalp with a crack. "I don't have the impression that you'll be recharging your batteries while we delay. I'm waiting for your pain to take hold and your magic to wither."

Michael was dumbfounded momentarily by the blatant honesty of the response. "You speak bravely for an unarmed man," he threatened as he held forward his flaming sword, pointing its tip directly at Stone's chest. The weapon's eerie song continued to ring out, although its light seemed to be faltering.

"If you think me defenseless, then take your best shot right now," Mason dared, offering his square chin like an overconfident prizefighter.

Michael, knowing that his remaining strength would only continue to ebb, was happy to oblige.

ONE MISTAKE

When the flames around Lily died, disappearing in a heartbeat, so did the sense of awe that had at first struck Ramius King at seeing them. The fear that had been mixed with that awe, however, did not disappear. To the contrary, the Tall Man's trepidation escalated tremendously. The extraordinary scene playing out before his eyes was hauntingly familiar. It was the prophecy of Rosalind Sanchez coming to life. The dark night and the flashing lightning–it couldn't be coincidence. The fortune teller had foreseen his doom and now, for the first time since the destruction of the Guardians, it seemed a real possibility, especially considering the fact that he'd just witnessed the birth of a human Gift of Nature, something that had never happened before.

King lunged forward through the aura of light that surrounded Lily like a star's corona, intent on killing her before she had a chance to discover what powers the transformation might have bestowed. Even as he moved, the flaming spear reformed in his grip.

Lily, dazed and confused from the shock and the physical trauma of her transformation, never even flinched when the attack came. She made no attempt whatsoever to defend herself from a blow that could have slain a bull rhinoceros, and yet she was unhurt. As King's slashing weapon reached the halo of light that surrounded her, its fire dimmed and its momentum died. The magic of her grandfather's tribe, the heritage of power that had only just been awakened from its long latency, repelled the Tall Man's assault.

King stumbled backwards several steps, stunned at the utter impotence of his attack. A subtle shaking became apparent in his limbs, and suddenly the color of his dark suit deepened and ruffled at the touch of wind and precipitation. The flames of his trident and the glow that surrounded the Plume of Shu perched atop his brow deepened as well, their previously bright blue light intensifying to indigo and then violet. A screech of arcing energy sounded from the weapon. He was focusing all his strength into it, intent on breaching Lily's protective aura before she had a chance to gather herself.

When he lunged again, the Tall Man no longer seemed to float above the ground as he had before, and the whistling wind threw ice and rain harshly into his unprotected face. The three-pronged spear appeared to carry unstoppable weight though, as he lifted it high over his rain-soaked head.

Lily, her head clearing at last, looked up just in time to see King posing over her like a lumberjack. She dropped back flat against the muddy ground, but had no time to try and back away as another devastatingly powerful blow came crashing down. Once again, the magic protected her, but by a much smaller margin than before, failing to turn King's weapon aside until it was so close to her face that she could feel the heat of its flames. The light around her dimmed drastically, like a candle flame at the end of its wick.

Ramius King, caught up completely in the frenzy of his aggression, hefted his weapon over and over. His face was a mask of manic rage. He would spend every last iota of his energy in order to eliminate this newly perceived threat. It was his sole purpose, the only thought that occupied his mind, which is why he was so completely shocked to see the blunt end of the Rune Tree come protruding out through the center of his chest, its odd, meandering grooves glowing like sunlit sapphires. The obvious consequences of the sight escaped him at first. The fiery trident evaporated from his hands.

It was a blow that not even Ramius King could possibly survive, a heart-breaker.

Very slowly, Kyle retracted the fossilized tree, feeling the vibrancy of its energy diminish as it slid free from the gruesome sheath of flesh and bone.

Just as slowly, Ramius King turned. The deep creases of his long face were smoothed somewhat, and his eyes were glassy and flooded with rainwater.

"It was you," he whispered bitterly, a gurgling sound mixing with his voice. "You were the one in the fortune teller's vision. I suspected you from the first time I saw you outside the school, but I let you live. How could I have been so careless? How could my plans be toppled by a single misjudgment, by one mistake? How could …"

Then the Tall Man froze, his jaw fell open and his eyes fell closed. The last glimmer of blue light faded from the Plume of Shu just as it slid free from his high forehead and fell quietly to the muddy ground. The wind eased, the rain and hail died away, and a single flake of snow fluttered down from above and settled gently upon the tip of King's long, crooked nose. As if the little crystal of ice weighed a hundred pounds, he crumpled beneath it. The dark tunnel that had been burrowed through the center of his torso smoldered for another moment, and then his stillness became complete. The most dangerous man on earth was dead.

A Brand New Girl

The wipers beat back and forth over the windshield of the Monte Carlo at their fastest rate, but they couldn't keep pace with the storm. Rosa struggled to keep sight of the double yellow line that split the lanes of Riverside Road and keep the car centered over it. By driving in the middle of the road, she figured that she had a few feet of buffer zone in either direction if she started to slide. The young man driving the black Lincoln from the opposite direction was thinking the same thing and driving the same way.

Before they finally became visible to one another, Rosa and the young man in the Lincoln were only seventy feet apart and headed toward one another at about five miles per hour over the speed limit, which was about three times what could have been considered reasonably safe under the conditions. Both drivers jerked their steering wheels to the right, swerving back into their own lanes. For a stomach-turning moment, both car's wheels lost their fragile grip on the half frozen road before grabbing hold again just in time to keep on the concrete. A sparrow couldn't have flown between them as they passed.

"Man!" gasped Lily's father beside Rosa, his eyes as big as ping pong balls. "Where's that guy running to so fast?"

"Where's he running from?" Rosa corrected. "That's the real question." She was thinking about the black luxury car that had ferried her up from Florida. She couldn't be sure that the one they'd passed was exactly like it, but knowing what she knew, and suspecting what she suspected, it probably was.

After speeding past the lane that led back to the cabin and having to backtrack to find it, Rosa aimed the car into the forest once again. She drove down the dirt two-track more cautiously as the wind eased and the hail turned into gently fall-ing snow. Driving conditions were actually improved somewhat, but in Rosa's stomach, she felt suddenly certain that there was no longer any need for haste. Her instincts told her that whatever fate awaited the kids and Ramius King, it had played out already to its conclusion. They hadn't made it to the cabin in time to intervene or interfere. As it turned out, they never made it to the cabin at all.

Kyle and Lily materialized in the beams of the Monte Carlo's headlights about halfway back to the cabin. They walked hand in hand and their shoulders were dusted with fresh snow. The pure white flakes contrasted starkly with the jet-black of Lily's long hair, which billowed out behind her in the fading wind like an ebony flag.

Apparently a side effect of her transformation, the corn silk blonde hair that she'd worn her whole life had been stained to a depthless black that shimmered like polished obsidian. It matched the crooked staff that Kyle held as well as the fossilized vulture feather that was tucked into his back pocket.

The physical evidence of Lily's change wasn't limited to her hair color. A very faint aura of light, a remnant of the brilliant glow that had haloed her earlier, could still be seen from the corner of the eye. It was too slight to detect looking straight on, but in a quick glance, or at the barely noticed edge of peripheral vision, it could still be perceived.

Before the car had quite come to a halt, Lily's father sprung from the passen-ger's side door and rushed to his daughter. She vaulted forward as well when she saw him, and they embraced in the street like they'd been separated for months. Their desperate joy at being reunited was proof of the deep fear that they'd both felt for the other's wellbeing. It had only been a few days since they'd seen each other last, but there had been the real chance that they might never see each other again.

"What's happened, Pumpkin?" Lily's father whispered into her ear as he ran his fingers through her raven hair.

"I'm a brand new girl," Lily answered between quiet sobs of relief. "It was mom's magic. There was so much more of it in me than I knew." Then, pulling herself free from her father's arms, she said, "Daddy, this is Kyle. He's my boy-friend."

Kyle stepped forward at the mention of his name, but before he could offer his hand to Lily's father, he paused.

"Your what?" he asked stupidly, immediately wishing he could take the words back.

"You are going to be my boyfriend, aren't you?" Lily asked softly, her eyes falling shyly to the ground and her mouth curling into a secret smile.

"Sure," Kyle replied enthusiastically, disgusted with himself again for failing to come up with something more appropriate. "I thought I already was," he amended with a smile of his own.

"Boyfriend?" Lily's father was eyeing Kyle up and down, noting the strange staff he held as well as the dripping mud that more or less covered him from head to toe. As he drew himself up to full height and puffed his chest, he said, "I'm not sure that I'm comfortable with my daughter dating someone that I don't know anything about."

"Daddy, please," Lily groaned. "I don't think you're going to be able to intimidate Kyle. He just killed the most powerful man in the world."

"You killed someone?" Lily's father gasped. "My daughter will not have a boyfriend who's killed someone!"

"But, Daddy, he did it to save my life. In fact, if he hadn't done it, that man was going to enslave the whole world."

"Oh, well," Lily's father mumbled, apparently reconsidering, "I suppose those are compelling circumstances …"

"This has to be the most ridiculous sounding conversation that I've ever heard," Rosa cut in, silencing the others. "I just need to make sure that I'm understanding one thing correctly. Ramius King is dead?"

In response, Kyle reached slowly to his back pocket, and from it he produced the Plume of Shu. Each falling snowflake that found its way to the feather's slick surface melted instantly as if it were a ready branding iron.

Rosa sighed deeply with relief. All the terrible memories associated with the oldest Gift of Nature and the man who had wielded it flashed in her mind. The rest of the world wouldn't have to suffer the Tall Man's evil as she had. Then the moment of elation passed. Finding Kyle and Lily safe and sound was a miracle, but on that particular night one miracle wasn't enough. She needed to get to Steel City as quickly as possible, but as she thought about the time that had passed since they'd left Michael, and about the snow-covered roads, she knew that it was going to take another miracle to get her there in time.

"Get in the car, everybody!" she ordered, sounding very much in charge. "We have to hurry."

Improving the Odds

The first brave souls were just emerging from the shelter of the restaurant as the Monte Carlo approached "downtown" Steel City. The storm had died, and so had almost all of the dangerous men who had fought amidst its fury. The snow fell slowly, the flakes wide and soft, and the thin blanket of white they laid over the ground effectively camouflaged the gore that was scattered about. The ruined carcasses of Ramius King's fallen hunters were rendered faceless and formless and could almost have been mistaken for boulders or tree stumps or any other similarly innocuous lumps beneath the snow.

The flashing light that hung over the center of the intersection hadn't flashed for about twenty-five minutes, since the power had failed all over town. Directly beneath the darkened streetlight was one of the snowy humps, a taller one than the others. Thin wisps of mist slipped periodically from near its top, but it was as still and quiet as a stone.

Everyone in the car stiffened as the nearly deserted intersection came into view, but only Rosa spoke.

"Shit."

She parked the car in the middle of the road and rushed forward over the fresh snow to the kneeling figure at the middle of the intersection. She couldn't help but notice that the white-coated shapes she passed were not boulders or tree stumps. She paused briefly beside one mangled corpse that had lost an arm and the lower half of one leg. The arm lie frozen nearby, but the foot and ankle were nowhere to be seen. A shiver ran through her that had nothing to do with the cold.

"Michael?" she whispered hesitantly toward the robed figure that knelt some fifteen feet away. His face was hidden within the robe's deep hood.

"It's me," he answered back.

Rosa rushed forward at hearing Michael's voice, but stopped just short of throwing her arms around him. Something in his tone gave her pause.

"I can't believe that you saved all those people," Rosa gasped, a thought that spilled out as words without her consent. "You beat all of King's hunters by yourself."

"I saved the people," he agreed, his voice as fragile as one of the falling snow flakes, "but I didn't beat all of King's hunters. Not quite."

Rosa's head snapped up and her eyes scanned around the intersection and the surrounding buildings, but there was no one to see except the kids, Lily's father, and a small group of townsfolk who huddled together near the entrance of the Country Kitchen.

"Are you looking for me," hissed a voice from somewhere nearby. The exact source couldn't be judged.

"It's Mason Stone," Michael whispered just loud enough for Rosa to hear. "He's hurt bad, but probably not as bad as me."

Rosa's eyes returned to where her knight crouched beneath the snow-covered folds of the long robe. It sounded like his voice would barely come out. She didn't want to think about what his words might imply.

"I take it you found your magic okay?" Rosa whispered to Michael.

Though no one could see it, Michael smiled slightly beneath his concealing hood. He answered, "It was like riding a bike downhill with the wind at my back. But I'm spent. It's taking all the strength I have left just to do what I'm doing right now."

"I'm not sure why you're not running away, fortune teller?" hissed Mason's slithery voice from the shadows. "As soon as I catch my breath, I'm going to come out there and finish off the last Guardian of Magic. If you're still standing beside him, you'll share his fate." Something about the first General's voice also sounded slightly off.

Kyle and Lily walked cautiously into the intersection, taking up positions on either side of Rosa.

"I don't think so," Kyle offered as he planted the butt of the Rune Tree into the snow.

Slowly, Mason Stone emerged from a deep shadow at the front of the Post Office. His clothes were torn and scorched all over so that much of his gray, concrete-like skin was exposed. Black burn marks crisscrossed over his body as well, and in several places it appeared that small chunks of his "flesh" had actually been torn away. He held one arm tightly against his abdomen as if he was holding in his own bowels, but that wasn't the case. What he was protecting was just as vital though.

"I was only your substitute teacher, Mr. Adams," Mason hissed as he shuffled forward, "and I hardly feel that we bonded during that one lesson. Expect no quarter if you get in my way."

As Stone stepped into the cluttered space of the intersection, Michael rose awkwardly to his feet. All of his former gracefulness was absent. As he turned, squaring his slumped shoulders to his adversary, the hood fell back, giving Rosa and the others a quick glimpse of his face and a deep gash that nearly connected his right temple with the fiery goatee.

Rosa rushed forward, stepping in front of Michael. Facing Mason, she said, "If you leave now, we'll let you go."

Mason stopped, pausing for a moment in silence, which Rosa took as a good sign. Perhaps he was actually considering it.

"If I left, I wouldn't go far," he hissed finally. "Mr. King will be back at any moment, and I'd hate to miss seeing what he'll do to you. To *all* of you."

"Mr. King won't be joining us," Kyle said, retrieving the Plume of Shu from his pocket and holding it out in plain view.

Although his expression remained blank, Mason's lifeless eyes fell to the talisman of his master and didn't leave it for several long seconds.

"Go, Mason," Michael encouraged, his voice still sounding terribly frail. "You're hurt, and now you're outnumbered as well. You might not be able to beat us all."

"I already beat *you*," Mason responded.

Rosa struggled not to look over at Michael. She needed to keep herself together.

For several long, silent moments, Stone stood frozen like a statue. Kyle tightened his grip around the shaft of the Rune Tree, feeling its warmth rise in reaction to his building anticipation.

"I'll go," Mason answered at last, his voice a bitter hiss, full of venom and frustration. "But know that we'll meet again, fortune teller." Without another word, the shortish man with the bald head and the cold, gray eyes turned and started to move away. He shuffled slowly down the center of Main Street, never so much as looking back over his shoulder. Within seconds, he was out of sight, lost in the steadily falling snow.

"Are you sure we should let him go?" Kyle asked quietly into Rosa's ear.

"We're not ready for him yet," she answered matter-of-factly. "We might be someday, but not yet."

"But once he's gone …," Kyle began to argue.

"I can find him wherever he goes," Rosa promised, patting the black, cloth bag that hung at her side. "He can't hide from me."

She started to say something more, but just then Michael collapsed to the ground.

SAYING GOODBYE

"Michael!" Rosa half-screamed, dropping to her knees and taking his head in her hands. "Come on," she called to Kyle and Lily, "we need to get him inside."

"Wait," a familiar voice called from a short distance off. It was Aaron Ulrich rushing over from the direction of the Country Kitchen. A dozen more of those who had emerged from the restaurant in the wake of the storm, including a prominent news anchor, were at his heels. "We'll carry him," Ulrich offered. "He saved our lives."

Rosa kept Michael's head cradled in her hands as Ulrich and five others stepped forward and carefully locked hands beneath their savior's battered body, forming a gurney with their arms. As gently as possible, they hoisted him up from the ground and carried him into the restaurant. An elderly woman held the door as they moved inside, and one of Ulrich's waitresses ushered them back to the breakroom where there was a soft sofa on which Michael could lie.

"Everybody out," ordered a gray-haired man who had pushed his way to the front of the tightly packed group of onlookers. "He needs space and I need quiet."

"Dr. Daniels is a retired family physician," Ulrich whispered into Rosa's ear. "I'm going to go get some clean towels and water. The phone lines are down and cell phones never work way out here, but I'm going to send someone ..."

"Don't bother," said the old doctor as he bent over Michael. "There's nothing anybody could do, no matter how quickly they got here."

"What are you saying?" Rosa asked, sounding panicked. "Of course we're sending for help. If he's still alive, then that means ..."

- 432 -

The ex-physician had cut Michael's shirt down the middle with a pair of kitchen shears, and as he laid the two sides apart, Rosa saw clearly what had been done to the man, *her* man.

"Whatever power this man has," the old doctor continued, "whatever it is that allowed him to do what he did out there, it must be what's keeping him alive now, but I can't believe that it'll last. There's no recovering from injuries like these. I'm sorry." He laid the shirt back in place.

Rosa desperately wanted to argue, to order someone to do something, but she couldn't think of what. Surely there had to be some way to save him. If his magic was keeping him alive, then there had to be magic that could heal his wounds. There had to be something she could do.

"We need a minute alone, guys," spoke Michael's voice so softly that his words were barely audible even in such close quarters.

Ulrich and the doctor looked to one another, nodded in silent agreement, and then silently stepped out into the dining room with the others, leaving Michael and Rosa to themselves.

"Pretty amazing, isn't it?" Michael whispered, his lips barely parting as the words slipped out.

"What you did was more than amazing," Rosa agreed, taking his limp hand in hers and pulling it to her chest. She shuddered when she felt how cold he was. She tried to summon a reassuring smile to her face, but couldn't quite manage it.

The tiniest hint of a grin flashed at the corner of Michael's mouth, and he said, "I meant the snow. This is your first snow, right?"

Twin tears streamed down Rosa's cheeks. She couldn't find her voice to tell him that he was right. Of course he was. She could count the number of days they'd known each other on her fingers, and yet, incredibly, he knew her better than anyone else ever had.

"I meant to buy you a new clarinet, but ..." Michael left the thought unfinished, perhaps realizing that he had energy left for only so many more words.

As pale and stiff as a corpse's, Michael's hand pulled slowly free from Rosa's grip and rose toward her face. A single, stubborn curl of dark hair fell across his frozen fingers, and again the flicker of a smile appeared.

"So beautiful."

The words came out so airy, so ethereal, that Rosa couldn't be sure if she'd actually heard them or just read them in the tiny motion of his lips. She knew instinctively that they would be his last.

She took his icy hand and pressed it to her face, willing her warmth to reach him. She clenched her teeth, closed her eyes, and fought to keep her tears from becoming sobs. Then a bright light flashed in her mind, a light that gradually took shape. An image materialized, a teenage boy standing in front of a large cluttered desk. Behind the desk sat an old lady who sipped from a mug of steaming liquid. It took a moment before Rosa realized that the image was coming from Michael. It took another moment for her to recognize that the boy was him and the old lady was the one from her visions, the one they'd called Grandma Jo.

Over the next several minutes, Michael showed Rosa the whole of his training as a Guardian. He also showed her where she could find the Guardian's written histories and a stash of their sacred artifacts. Even as the order's past was being revealed to her, Rosa could begin to imagine its future, its new leader as well as her first two recruits.

Eventually, the images faded from Rosa's mind, leaving her alone. Michael was gone. She never got to tell him how deeply she truly cared for him, but that was nothing to fret over, she knew. He'd seen it inside her for himself, and thus known it as surely as another person ever could.

A deep, pervasive bubble of cold swelled inside Rosa's chest, compressing her lungs and making it hard for her to draw breath. The final words of another dying man rose from her memory, and with them came insight and understanding. It was then, at that very moment, that Rosa needed the faith that the Chief had spoke of before making his departure from the land of the living. Only faith could reassure her that Michael wasn't gone, but moved on, and without that faith, she couldn't have gone on herself.

"Wherever you are, Michael, all my love goes with you."

Thursday,
September 7

The End and the Beginning

The snow melted during the night, not even lasting to daybreak, and by eleven o'clock the next morning the sun was high and bright, the sky was clear and blue, and the temperature had climbed to nearly seventy. All evidence of the previous night's freakish, wintry weather was gone, and only the many downed branches and the lingering power outage proved that there had been a storm at all.

A few strong-stomached volunteers had the gruesome leftovers of Ramius King's hunters cleaned up by midday. They also gathered together the strange black talismans that the men had carried, many of which had to be pried up from the drying mud where they'd been trampled underfoot. The entire collection fit neatly into the trunk of the Monte Carlo.

At the Mill, dozens of men were waking up from the worst nightmares of their lives. They found themselves in a strange place with long gaps in their memories. They were frightened and disoriented, but they would find their way back to their homes soon enough. All but one, that is. For one, every terrible memory of what had transpired at the Mill remained cruelly intact. The doctor had, however, seized his one chance for redemption.

On a clover-covered hillside near the Brooke River, not far from the little hunting cabin, Michael Galladin's body was laid in its final resting place. All the townsfolk whose lives had been saved by Michael's valor were present, along with many of their family and friends, including Officer Bart Packard, whose girlfriend had been among the captives. The kidnapped news anchor and his cameraman were also in attendance. They watched as their defender was returned into the earth, and then one by one they departed, masking the fresh turned soil over his grave with a blanket of wildflowers. Surprisingly, none of them seemed anxious to speak with one another about what had happened, let alone to go tell anyone else.

Rosa, Lily's father, and the kids stayed long after the others had gone, but eventually they, too, knew that it was time to move on. Only Kyle spoke, the few words he could recall from the ceremony he'd witnessed in the basement of the firehouse.

In the distance a wolf's howls could be heard, and overhead a circling hawk shrieked incessantly. Closer by, an old, black hound dog rested his graying chin on his forepaws. His eyes drooped, but he managed to stay awake for the duration of the informal service.

"He lived his life and gave his life for the ideals of the Guardians," Kyle spoke solemnly, "for honor and freedom."

Rosa nodded approvingly, then turned and started away. "Come on," she urged, "this tribe has work to do."

978-0-595-47345-8
0-595-47345-8

Printed in the United States
112112LV00003B/4-21/P